PRAISE FOR
KEN GODDARD

PREY

"*Wildfire* is an afterburner of a thriller, an incandescent torch that burns up the pages in a flurry of action and speed."
—Tampa *Tribune*

"Terrific!"
—*Publishers Weekly*

"Two-fisted . . . Authentic . . . Relentlessly violent. Not for the fainthearted."
—*Kirkus Reviews*

BALEFIRE

"Taut, well-written . . . Shocks the reader into experiencing the deadly ruthlessness of terrorist violence. From page one, *Balefire* pulls the reader into the explosive climax."
—Mary Higgins Clark, author of *Where Are the Children*

"A one-of-a-kind novel of suspense like *Day of the Jackal*. A tale of stunning realism."
—Steven Shagan, author of *The Circle*

"Contains elements that are reminiscent of . . . Eric Ambler's love of intrigue, Joseph Wambaugh's feeling for cops and Ian Fleming's passion for technically sophisticated gadgets."
—New York *Newsday*

"*Balefire* comes at you like a firestorm. . . . The action starts fast then accelerates straight through to the last page."
—John Saul, author of *The God Project*

**By Ken Goddard from
Tom Doherty Associates**

*Prey
Wildfire*

WILDFIRE

♦

KEN GODDARD

A TOM DOHERTY ASSOCIATES BOOK
NEW YORK

This is a work of fiction. All the characters and events portrayed in this book are fictitious, and any resemblance to real people or events is purely coincidental.

WILDFIRE

Copyright © 1994 by Ken Goddard

A Forge Book
Published by Tom Doherty Associates, Inc.
175 Fifth Avenue
New York, N.Y. 10010

Forge® is a registered trademark of Tom Doherty Associates, Inc.

ISBN: 0-812-52302-4
Library of Congress Card Catalog Number: 94-32704

First edition: November 1994
First mass market edition: October 1995

Printed in the United States of America

0 9 8 7 6 5 4 3 2 1

This book is dedicated to George and Jane.

WILDFIRE

◆

ACKNOWLEDGMENTS

I owe a debt of gratitude to Bob and Linda Crites, whose ever-dependable commentary is always right on the mark, and to all my special agent, police, and wildlife officer buddies, whose dedicated efforts and cheerful comradery continue to provide the inspiration.

"You know, some days, I really think both sides go too far."

—Anonymous Special Agent
Division of Law Enforcement
U.S. Fish and Wildlife Service

Excerpts from the Field Notebook of FBI Supervisory Special Agent Al Grynard

U.S. DEPARTMENT OF INTERIOR:

Fish and Wildlife Service:

<u>Division of Law Enforcement, Special Operations Branch:</u>

David Halahan	Chief, Special Operations Branch
Freddy Moore	Deputy Chief, Special Ops Branch
Larry Paxton	Acting Team Leader, Bravo Team
Henry Lightstone	Special Agent, Bravo Team
Dwight Stoner	Special Agent, Bravo Team
Mike Takahara	Technical Agent, Bravo Team
Thomas Woeshack	Special Agent/Pilot, Bravo Team
Paul McNulty	SAC, Bravo Team, killed by ICER
Carl Scoby	ASAC, Bravo Team, killed by ICER
Len Ruebottom	Special Agent/ Pilot, killed by ICER

<u>National Fish and Wildlife Forensics Lab:</u>
Roger Dingeman	Forensic Scientist

National Biological Survey:

Dr. Kimberly Wildman   Survey Group Leader,
Yellowstone

U.S. DEPARTMENT OF JUSTICE:

Federal Bureau of Investigation *(Supervisory Special Agents):*

Al Grynard   ASAC, Wildlife Special Task
Force

Reggie Blackburn   Electronics Specialist

Hal Owens   SAC, Bahamas Special Task
Force

Jim Whittman   Commander, Hostage
Recovery Team

U.S. Attorney's Office:

Theresa Fletcher   Deputy U.S. Attorney

THE ICER COMMITTEE:

Harold Tisbury   CEO, ICER
Chairman, Cyanosphere VIII

Sam Tisbury   CEO, Cyanosphere VIII

Alfred Bloom   CEO, ABM Industries

Sergio Paz-Rios   Chairman, Amazon Global

Nicholas Von Hagberg   President, European Oil & Gas
Association

Wilbur Lee Edgarton   CEO, Moss Mariner Mining
Group

Jonathan Chilmark   President, NW Timber
Alliance

OPERATION COUNTER WRENCH (SURVIVING SUSPECTS):

Gerd Maas	Assault Group Leader, ICER
Roy Parker	Assault Group, ICER
Alex Chareaux	Cajun poacher

LEGAL FIRM OF LITTLE, WARREN, NOBLES & KOLE:

Jason Bascomb III	Senior Attorney
Walter Crane	Senior Investigator
Calvin Green	Attorney
Williston Fordham	Attorney

CITY OF BOSTON:

Rico Testano	Boston Police Homicide Sergeant
Sal Boracatto	Illicit seafood dealer
Tony Boracatto	Illicit seafood dealer

CREW OF THE *LONE GRANGER:*

Bobby LaGrange	Owner, retired SDPD Cop Ex-partner of Henry Lightstone
Justin LaGrange	Son of Bobby LaGrange
Mo-Jo	Bahamian native

SUSPECTS & VICTIMS—RELATED HOMICIDE INVESTIGATIONS:

George Hoffsteadler	Illicit gun dealer
''Fred''	Free-lance surveillance expert
''Carlos''	Free-lance surveillance expert

| "Valerie" | Bodyguard a.k.a "Anne-Marie"—sailor |
| "Riser" | Hired Assassin, Wildfire Conspiracy |

WILDFIRE CONSPIRACY:

Leonard Harris
"Ember"
"Eric"
William Devonshire Crowley

Prologue

The supervisory ranger at the Sequoia National Park stood in front of the all-too-familiar sign and shook his head in frustration.

It was exactly where the woman had said it would be. Just off the main hiking path through one of the most spectacular stands of great redwoods in the entire park. The supervisory ranger figured that a minimum of a thousand tourists had probably seen and read the sign before one of them decided to go to the effort to report it.

Like the first three signs, the letters on this one appeared to have been machine-carved out of what looked like an aluminum alloy blank that was precisely thirty inches long, eighteen inches high, and three quarters of an inch thick. Prior to the machine carving of the letters, the blank metal sign appeared to have been chemically coated with a dark green/brown camouflage pattern. As a result, the machined letters seemed almost to glow in the shaded light of the old growth forest.

If it hadn't been for those letters, the supervisory ranger realized, the highly effective camouflage-patterned coating would have made the sign almost completely invisible. Which didn't make any sense at all.

Unable to help himself, he read the deeply imprinted words once again.

AND
ONE DAY SOON
WHEN THE EMBER FALLS,
AND THE SKY IS FILLED WITH FIRE
HE SHALL RISE UP
FROM OUT OF THE DARKNESS
AND NONE SHALL STAND BEFORE HIM.

For reasons that he couldn't quite explain, the supervisory ranger found the words chilling. He shook his head again, and then examined the bolts . . . confirming the worst, which was exactly what he had expected.

The heads of the two lag bolts used to fasten the sign to the seventy-two-foot redwood were about three inches across, completely rounded, and cast with a new three-dimensional notch design in the center that would require a special matching tool for removal. In addition, the bolt had been countersunk into the sign to a depth of approximately an eighth of an inch, which meant that there wouldn't be any way to get a grip on the rounded head with a pair of pliers or channel locks.

And if the lag bolts were like those on the other three signs the park rangers had found so far, they would be about three-quarters of an inch in diameter and eighteen inches long and cast out of hardened steel. Which also meant that the only way to remove the sign, without causing extensive internal damage to the tree, would be to drill a series of holes through the aluminum around the bolt head.

The last such removal had taken five hours because the power needed to cut through the tough aluminum alloy had rapidly drained the batteries on their portable drill. And all that, of course, had attracted a lot more attention among the hiking tourists.

Which was probably exactly what the idiots who put it there had in mind, the ranger thought morosely.

He decided that he'd better call the local hardware store

and order more batteries and charging units for their drill. It could turn out to be a long season.

"Goddamned religious nuts," he muttered, still feeling uneasy, because in spite of what he and his fellow rangers had been telling the public, none of them were completely convinced that religion was the issue.

There was another possibility that he didn't want to think about at all.

It was eight-thirty in the evening when the Learjet touched down at the Mahlon Sweet Municipal Airport in Eugene, Oregon, and then taxied over to a small butler building at the far end of the tarmac.

To the aircraft mechanic who would spend the next four hours making a routine service check of the Learjet's two powerful engines and related electronics, the man who stood up from the controls and then exited the plane through the drop ramp with a nylon kit bag in his hand looked a lot more like a defensive end for a professional football team than a skilled private pilot.

The mechanic watched the man walk through the chain-link gate and get into a small dark-gray minivan, then shrugged indifferently as he began to lay out his tools. Regardless of who the man was or what he did for a living, he was paying twice the normal rate for a nonroutine service check on what appeared to be a very well-maintained aircraft. As far as the aircraft mechanic was concerned, that was all he needed to know about his client.

At nine-thirty that evening, the extremely tall and muscular driver of the dark gray minivan turned off a main road about twenty miles south of Eugene, Oregon. He continued on for about a quarter of a mile on a narrow, winding dirt road surrounded by a dense growth of scrub oaks and firs. Finally he came to a stop at a wrought-iron gate.

Reaching out the driver's side window, he pushed the call button and then waited.

"Yes?" the electronic voice rasped.

"I'm here to pick up my merchandise," the tall man said, speaking slowly and carefully in the direction of the post-mounted microphone.

"Your name?"

The man hesitated for a brief moment, and then said: "Riser."

"The number of primary items in your order?"

"Eight."

"You're early," the electronic voice said accusingly. "Your appointment is for tomorrow afternoon."

"My schedule has been changed," Riser responded.

"Can you come back tomorrow morning?"

"No, I need the items today."

As Riser started to turn away from the microphone, a movement in one of the nearby trees caught his attention. His eyes followed the leap of the gray squirrel from a bare-limbed oak to the protective foliage of a tall evergreen. That was when he spotted the reflection off the glass.

There hadn't been a camera lens in that tree six months ago, when he had last come by to pick up the disposable tools of his trade. Or maybe there had been, but he simply hadn't noticed it, Riser reminded himself. Even now that his attention was focused, it took him a good thirty seconds to locate the entire system.

There were two separate video surveillance units, each mounted in a sealed and weatherproofed box about twenty feet off the ground on opposite sides of the road. Each of the boxes had been carefully painted in an irregular camouflage pattern to match the surrounding vegetation. Even the barely visible segments of electrical conduit that wrapped around to the backs of the trees and then—presumably—extended down into the ground and out to the main house, had been carefully colored to blend in with the supportive tree bark.

This was a new and unexpected development, and one that Riser didn't like at all.

"We will have to reschedule the other appointments," the electronic voice finally responded. "That will require a ten-percent penalty charge for the inconvenience.''

"Fine.''

There was another, shorter pause.

''Do you have all the money with you today, including the penalty charge?''

"Yes.''

''Okay, drive in through the gate, take a left at the *Y* intersection, and drive up to the door marked *C* as in Charlie. When the roll-up door opens, drive inside, stop the car, and shut off the engine. Stay in the car until someone contacts you. Can you remember all that?''

"Yes.''

Riser waited patiently for the wrought-iron gate to open. When it did so, he drove in, took the left-hand turn at the *Y*, and stopped in front of the warehouse door marked *C* as in Charlie. After a few moments the large roll-up door started to rise. He drove inside the sheet-metal warehouse, parked in the middle of the three parking spaces facing the darkened indoor range, turned off the engine, and set the keys on the floor just under the driver's seat. Then he sat there and waited for the warehouse door to close.

They had directed him to the largest of Hoffsteadler's three test firing ranges, the man realized. He remembered from previous visits that this one had eight firing positions with staged target sites at three, seven, fifteen, twenty-five, and fifty meters.

For a brief moment he wondered if their selection of the larger range was significant. Then a muscular young woman with intriguing but clearly understated facial features, deep blue eyes, French-braided light-brown hair, loose-fitting overalls, and canvas deck shoes appeared out of the shadows and walked over to the driver's side of his car.

Had she made the effort, he decided, she would have been extremely attractive, perhaps even seductive. He wondered why she chose not to do so.

"Mr. Riser?''

"Yes.''

"Mr. Hoffsteadler is ready for you now."

"Where?"

"Up the ramp and to the left. You enter the range through the second door . . . after I check you for weapons," she added in a calm and controlled voice.

He noticed, as he stepped out of the van and stood to his full height of six feet ten inches, that she hesitated for only a moment before she stepped forward, shaking her head and smiling briefly at the realization that the top of her head barely reached the center of his sternum. Deliberately leaving herself open to any number of possible strike or control moves, she brought both of her hands inside his jacket, up to his armpits, and then around his thickly muscled back in a slow and careful manner.

As her practiced hands slid behind the waistband of his jeans, he wondered if she realized that she was the designated sacrificial lamb—the one that Hoffsteadler had set up to die first, in the event that anything went wrong.

Yes, she knows, he decided after a moment. *She just doesn't care.*

He smiled as he considered that last part.

Submitting himself to the thorough pat-down search with complete indifference, he observed that she was wearing a police-model Kevlar vest under the overalls, and that the restraining strap on her hip-holstered double-action, 9mm Beretta 92FS semiautomatic pistol was secured. The weapon was designed to hold fifteen rounds in a staggered magazine, and one in the chamber, and was rigged for a right-hand forward draw from a protected holster. An extra magazine pouch was mounted horizontally on the left front side of her webbed belt, with the snaps opening toward the belt buckle, combat-speed-loading style.

He also observed, as he led the way up the ramp and in through the narrow doorway, that she maintained a constant distance of about eight feet between them, with the outer edge of her left shoulder lined up with the inner edge of his right arm. In doing so, she was keeping her left hand in a position to deflect easily a grab or lunge, and her right hand clear for a smooth draw.

That's good, he nodded approvingly. *At least give yourself a chance.*

He judged her to be approximately five ten, twenty-five to twenty-eight years of age, professionally alert, sexually attractive in a hard and uninterested sort of way. And probably absolutely deadly if given the necessary stimulus, he decided.

The only thing that bothered him was her sense of indifference, or overconfidence, whichever it was.

There were some interesting possibilities, but he reminded himself that it would all depend on how things went with the confirmation and the payment.

They entered the staging area, and he immediately lost interest in his female escort. The first things he noticed were the fifty-five-gallon drums that had been placed in the middle of the range, just beyond the twenty-five-meter mark.

In firing lane five, six of the barrels had been lined up, one behind the other, on a two-foot-high wooden platform.

In firing lane six, four more barrels were double-stacked side by side, with two on the top and two on the bottom.

Riser paused for a moment, more out of curiosity than anything else, to examine the unusual arrangement of targets, if that in fact was what they were. Then he turned his attention to the far side of the range.

There he observed five men—all of whom were visibly armed—a portable workbench, and two display tables, all arranged side by side to the left of the firing positions. The workbench was on the far left. The two display tables were covered with black velvet. The one on the far right held what looked like a wooden case that measured about twelve inches on a side by three feet long.

George Hoffsteadler was waiting for him in front of the middle table.

"Good to see you again, Riser," Hoffsteadler said in a

neutral voice as he stepped forward and took the man's hand in a firm grip.

George Hoffsteadler was well aware that "Riser" was not the name that his huge and intimidating client had used on his previous visits, but that didn't concern him in the least. Especially since *he* hadn't bothered to use his own given name in over forty-five years. In point of fact, Hoffsteadler actually found it preferable that his customers used varying pseudonyms in making their highly illegal and therefore extremely lucrative purchases. If nothing else, it greatly simplified his already minimal record-keeping system.

George Hoffsteadler was an extremely tall and slender man with elongated fingers, limbs, and facial features of an individual who appeared to have been born on a basketball court. In fact, most people would have been astounded to learn that Hoffsteadler, as far back as he could remember, had never held a basketball in his life. Born and raised deep in the West Virginia mountains, where pieces of flat ground were at a premium, George Hoffsteadler and his brothers had quickly discovered more profitable interests to pursue than mere sports.

Completely self-confident by nature, and paranoid only out of professional habit, Hoffsteadler was one of a very small number of people who were not immediately intimidated by the arrival of the man who now called himself "Riser."

One, because at six feet and eleven inches, George Hoffsteadler was able to stare eye-to-eye at his huge and menacing client without having to look up.

And two, because he was certifiably crazy.

George Hoffsteadler had been an illicit gun dealer for nearly fifty-one of his sixty-five years. And in that time, aside from a general description or two, he had never once showed up in an FBI or ATF report, nor had he ever been convicted of a state or local weapons violation. Mostly because the few people who might otherwise have been willing to testify against Hoffsteadler and his gun-manufacturing brothers were absolutely convinced that they would disappear within twenty-four hours if they ever chose to do so. Three local men had already suffered that fate.

Hoffsteadler considered his lack of a police record to be one of the major personal accomplishments of his life, and one that he fully intended to maintain for the remainder of his illicit career. Which was why he continued to pay top dollar to employ four of the most lethal combat shooters he could find in the area as personal bodyguards and "general keepers of the rules," as he put it.

One of the bodyguards was standing behind the main display table. A second was sitting in an enclosed target-control console directly behind the firing positions. A third was positioned in a homemade M-60 machine gun turret, constructed out of welded steel plates and bulletproof glass, that overlooked the entire range. The fourth was standing eight feet behind Riser with the outer edge of her left shoulder lined up with the inner edge of his right arm.

Hoffsteadler's two younger brothers, both highly skilled gunsmiths, sat at the small portable workbench, dressed alike in white jeans and denim aprons and supporting nearly identical handlebar mustaches. In front of them, on the oil-stained wooden surface, was a wide array of precision tools, cleaning rods, gun oil, and cloth patches. They were prepared to make a wide range of adjustments to their hand-crafted weapons on the spot. Or, if necessary, to take them back into their fully equipped machine shop for a complete retooling. Like their older brother, both men wore Beretta semiautomatics in matching hand-tooled leather shoulder holsters.

"You got lucky," the gun dealer said. "We finished the last piece on your order yesterday evening, and one of the other buyers can't make it today anyway, so what I'm going to do is cancel out that penalty. I think you'll like what the boys did on this batch. Take a look for yourself."

He gestured with his hand at the display table, the entire surface of which was covered with a long piece of black velvet. Six pistols and two submachine guns, each finished in a nonglare black matte, were arranged in the center of the table, along with stacks of clearly marked magazines and several boxes of ammunition for each weapon. There were two replacement barrels for each of the pistols.

All six pistols appeared to have been designed around the standard 92FS Large Frame Beretta semiautomatic pistols that Hoffsteadler and all his staff carried, except that these particular handcrafted weapons were approximately twenty percent larger in the grip. They were also fitted with precision-machined silencers of varying lengths and thickness, each in a matching nonglare, matte black finish.

The submachine guns appeared to have been modeled after the Heckler & Koch Model HK54 submachine gun. They, too, were fitted with precision-machined silencers that accounted for almost two thirds of the total barrel length.

"As requested, one of the pistols is chambered for the .22 long rifle, one in 9mm Parabellum, and the remainder for the 10mm FBI standard round. Both submachine guns are chambered for 10mm also, which turns out to be a real nice matchup. As you might expect, the silencers are most effective with the .22 long rifle and the 9mm, although I think you'll like what we did with the 10mm stuff," the elderly gun dealer added with undisguised pride.

Wordlessly, Riser stepped forward and examined the 10mm ammunition boxes, noting that each one of the white cardboard packages was marked with the warning: RESTRICTED. FOR LAW ENFORCEMENT USE ONLY. Opening up one of the boxes, he randomly selected and examined three of the lethal cartridges and nodded in apparent satisfaction.

Then he picked up one of the pistols chambered for the 10mm FBI cartridge. After evaluating the enlarged grip, weight, and balance of the weapon, and confirming the silk-smooth action that was characteristic of firearms manufactured by the Hoffsteadler brothers, Riser looked over at the bodyguard and held up four fingers.

The bodyguard nodded, selected four rounds of 10mm

ammunition from an open box, fed them into a magazine, and handed it to Riser, along with a pair of ear protectors. He tossed the ear protectors aside and examined the magazine. Then he stepped forward to the leftmost firing position, loaded and armed the pistol, held it at his side in his left hand, and growled the word, "Fifteen."

The bodyguard at the console thumbed a button, and a man-sized target popped up fifteen meters away in the first firing lane.

In one smooth motion Riser brought the pistol up to shoulder level and fired twice. The heavy bullets punched through the target dead center, head and chest.

"Twenty-five," Riser said as he switched the pistol to his right hand.

The first target dropped away as a second target popped up at the twenty-five-meters distance. Again, two holes appeared dead center, head and chest. The baffling in the precision-machined silencer had effectively reduced the velocity of the 10mm round to subsonic levels, producing a gunshot that sounded more like the *thunk* of a small ball peen hammer striking a four-by-four post.

Riser nodded in satisfaction, walked back to the display table, set the smoking semiautomatic pistol down on the black velvet, and picked up the one chambered for the .22 long rifle.

In seven more sequences, a total of twenty-eight more rounds struck dead center, head and chest, the last group with the select switch of the submachine gun on single fire. The woman bodyguard was watching intently now, intrigued by this huge man who had such a gentle and deadly touch with firearms, but still vaguely frightened by the cold and deadly expression in his eyes. She understood now why George Hoffsteadler had placed all four of his bodyguards on duty for this sale.

"Are you satisfied?" Hoffsteadler asked as Riser set the submachine gun back down on the display table.

"Yes." Riser nodded curtly. "What's that over there?"

He gestured with his head in the direction of the second display table.

"Oh, yeah, I thought you might like to see one of our new products, the first of a new line." George Hoffsteadler smiled as he walked around behind the second table. Reaching forward with what appeared to be loving care, he opened the ornate wooden case.

Inside the case was a weapon unlike anything Riser had ever seen before.

At first glance it looked like a short and extremely heavy double-barreled shotgun. But when Riser walked over to the end of the table and saw the deep rifling grooves in the two cavernous stainless-steel barrels, he knew better. *No,* he smiled to himself, *definitely not a shotgun.*

"May I?" he asked, and then, when Hoffsteadler nodded, reached forward and gently picked up the weapon in both hands.

"Something special we made for one of our hunting friends," the elderly gun dealer said. "A classic four-bore, double-barreled, break-open rifle. Machined out of a solid block of weapons-grade stainless steel. Stock and grip are solid American walnut. The barrels are one inch in diameter and twenty-four inches long. Puts out a nineteen-hundred grain slug at seventeen-hundred-and-fifty feet per second."

Riser stopped examining the weapon long enough to blink in surprise and then stare at Hoffsteadler.

"Why?" he asked.

"Guaranteed to go in one end of a bull elephant and out the other without stopping for lunch." Hoffsteadler grinned.

Riser shrugged indifferently, then went back to examining the weapon.

"Twenty-five pounds, total weight, and enough of a kick to put even somebody your size right on their ass if they're not careful," the gun dealer went on. Then he paused for a tantalizing moment. "You want to give her a try?"

Riser looked up at Hoffsteadler, paused, and then nodded.

The gun dealer gestured to the bodyguard at the middle

display table, who reached down and brought up a wooden ammunition box with a hinged top. Hoffsteadler opened the top, selected two of the gleaming four-inch-long brass cartridges, and handed them over to his huge client. "One's a solid slug, the other's double-ought buckshot," he said. "You're talking a hundred bucks a shot here, so try not to miss."

Then Hoffsteadler reached down for the discarded ear protectors. "I think you're going to want ears on, this time," he added as he adjusted the headset over the man's ears.

Riser walked over to the number-five firing position, instinctively aware that Hoffsteadler and all four of his bodyguards had gone on alert. Ignoring them, he broke open the breech of the weapon, fed the two heavy cartridges into the side-by-side chambers—buckshot on the left and slug on the right—shut the breech, released the thumb safety, and then stared at the target.

From his position, the six fifty-five gallon barrels were lined up directly behind each other. All he could see was the front of the first barrel and the tops of all six. He started to raise the gun, but then hesitated and turned his head to look back at the display table area.

"Clear?"

Hoffsteadler nodded and waved him the go-ahead signal.

Returning his attention to the line of barrels, Riser placed his left foot forward, braced his back foot, and raised the double-barreled rifle to his shoulder. He took time to adjust the butt of the weapon tight against his thick, muscular shoulder. Then he slid his finger over the right forward trigger, aimed down the short barrel, and squeezed.

Even with the ear protectors on, the concussive effects of the explosion within the contained firing range were stunning.

The recoil slammed Riser's massive upper body backward, but he kept his eyes open as he absorbed the shock, wanting to see the effect of the impact. It was every bit as spectacular as he had expected.

The immediate impression was that all six drums had somehow managed to explode in sequence, each detonation occurring a microsecond after the previous one. The transfer of energy from the massive slug to the inert masses of water blew all six lids and about two hundred and fifty gallons of water skyward. The rest of the water seemed to disappear in an explosive cloud around the six violently ruptured metal barrels.

Nodding to himself, he walked over to firing lane number six, paused, brought the massive weapon up to hip level, centering his aim at the middle point where the edges of all four drums came together, and then squeezed the rearmost left-side trigger.

This time the four barrels seemed to disintegrate into a pyrotechnic display of metal shards and vaporized water.

Riser saw motion out of the corner of his eye. It was the guard in the M-60 machine-gun turret, holding his right hand in a thumbs-up position and grinning.

Smiling to himself for the first time that day, Riser walked over to Hoffsteadler. Being careful, because the breech and barrels of the stainless steel weapon were now extremely hot to the touch, he placed the burned powder-smeared rifle in the gun dealer's waiting hands.

"How much?"

"Seventy thousand," Hoffsteadler replied. "Hundred bucks a round, slug or buckshot, but I'll give you a twenty-percent break in case lots of fifty."

"I'll take it. And two hundred rounds, half and half," he added in a deep, dispassionate voice.

"I thought you might like it, but you understand we're talking a minimum of six months for delivery?"

"No, I want this one," Riser said simply.

"Sorry, but the customer who ordered this one has a hot date with an African bull elephant all lined up and ready to go." Hoffsteadler smiled. "He asked first, so he gets number one. Number two is all yours."

"Fair enough." Riser shrugged. "I have to get going. Can

you pack up my merchandise?''

"Sure. Valerie, you want to help me . . .''

In turning to respond to Hoffsteadler's instructions, the woman bodyguard momentarily lost track of her position relative to the right arm of her huge and fearsome charge.

In that instant Riser turned and drove his fist into her exposed solar plexus, driving the air out of her lungs. As he did so, he spun her around, snapped open the restraining strap, yanked the 9mm Beretta semiautomatic out of her unsecured hip holster, and then sent her stumbling headfirst into the display table, where the second bodyguard was already reaching for his pistol.

The first jacketed 9mm Parabellum slug caught the distracted bodyguard square in the forehead just as the muzzle of his pistol was starting to clear his holster. The second and third rounds dropped Hoffsteadler's two gunsmith brothers out of their workbench chairs like a pair of pop-up targets.

George Hoffsteadler had something less than a second to absorb the fact that his brothers were dead and that he was still holding his cherished four-bore rifle in both hands—rather than reaching for his holstered pistol as he should have been doing—when the fourth high-velocity 9mm bullet shattered the bridge of his nose and buried itself into the soft tissue of his brain. He was dead by the time his knees started to buckle.

Which left two.

Riser was already diving for the ground, wrenching the four-bore rifle out of George Hoffsteadler's dead hands, when the man in the turret—who had been caught off-guard by the spectacular effects of the exploding fifty-five-gallon drums and the suddenness of Riser's actions—sent a stream of 7.65mm machine-gun rounds ripping right to left through the display tables and the entire left-side wall of the staging area.

The vengeance-seeking bodyguard managed to shred both display tables and the workbench, along with a considerable portion of the surrounding landscape, with his initial sustained burst from the lethal M-60. He was starting to transverse back, left to right, sending out a second lethal stream of copper-jacketed projectiles at the rate of ten per second when suddenly, over to the far right, he saw the huge man with the fearsome expression in his eyes come up to his knees with the four-bore rifle in his hands.

Working out of desperation, the bodyguard tried to swing the barrel of the heavy machine gun around in time. But before he was halfway there, the four-bore roared again. The nineteen-hundred-grain lead slug exploded through the turret's armored glass and tore the bodyguard's spine in half before exiting through the back wall.

At the onset of the shooting, the fourth bodyguard had initially chosen to barricade himself behind the relative security of the two-by-six boards that made up the front wall of the console booth. But the sight of the thick piece of armored glass in the M-60 turret exploding apart in all directions caused him to change his mind. He came up fast, triggering three 9mm pistol rounds in the general direction of Riser's last observed position. Then he turned around and lunged for the back door, just as a second nineteen-hundred-grain slug ripped apart the four-by-four corner post and sent splintered chunks of two-by-six boards ricocheting into the bodyguard's exposed back.

Finding himself face down in the debris, groaning in pain and still partially stunned, the bodyguard cautiously tried to move his limbs. He was amazed to discover that all his arms and legs were still attached and that he didn't seem to be losing any significant amount of blood.

Driven forward by his screaming survival instincts, he was starting toward the back door again, which was now dangling open on one hinge, when he heard the all-too-distinctive sound of the four-bore's breech being snapped closed.

Realizing that he was trapped, and that there was no time or chance to do anything else, the bodyguard twisted around to face his adversary. He was starting to come up in a desperate crouch, with the 9mm Beretta extended out and firing as fast as he could pull the trigger, when the four-bore roared once more and forty-six double-ought buck pellets sliced through the splintered interior of the console booth in a tight pattern. Nine of the 33-caliber pellets struck the bodyguard from head to groin. He too was dead before his head hit the ground.

In the intervening moments it took for the female bodyguard to recover from the stunning impact of Riser's fist being driven into her vest-protected stomach, all the firing had stopped.

Reacting to her carefully honed survival instincts, she immediately reached for her pistol. It was only as her fingers brushed across the empty holster that she remembered: it was her mistake that had set the disastrous firefight into motion.

Furious with herself, she looked around frantically. The first thing she saw was the blood-splattered body of her fellow bodyguard lying under the shattered remains of the display table. Then she saw his unfired 9mm Beretta lying within two feet of his limp and outstretched hand.

She was starting to come up onto her hands and knees, getting ready to dive for the pistol, when she saw Riser out of the corner of her eye.

He was standing to her right, less than twenty feet away. He held the four-bore rifle firmly against his hip, the double barrels aimed directly at her upper body. The front view of the two cavernous rifle barrels was frightening, but it was the absolutely terrifying expression in the huge man's deadly cold eyes that seemed to turn her muscles into jelly.

For a brief moment she wondered if George Hoffsteadler's horribly lethal new weapon was now loaded with slugs or buckshot. Not that it would matter in the least, one way or the other, she reminded herself. Dead was dead.

Then, having no idea what else to do, and still furious with herself for having lost her concentration at the crucial moment, she came up unsteadily to her feet and just stood there, staring into the face of death with her deep blue eyes. To her utter amazement, she realized that she was no longer afraid.

Tensed against the anticipated moment when the explosive discharge from the four-bore would rip into her body and end her life, it took her a moment to realize that he was saying something to her.

"What?" she rasped.

"Take off your shirt *and* your vest," he repeated.

She hesitated, wondering why he was even remotely concerned about the vest. If he intended to kill her, too, all he had to do was pull the trigger. She knew with absolute certainty that her Kevlar vest would offer far less protection against Hoffsteadler's terrifying four-bore than the armored glass on the obliterated M-60 emplacement.

And besides, she thought morbidly, *even if it's loaded with buckshot, instead of slugs, all he has to do is aim for my head.*

For a brief moment, as she started to unbutton her shirt, it occurred to her to wonder if his instructions could possibly have anything to do with sex, and to think about how much of her pride she might be willing to sacrifice in an attempt to save her life. But then—as she slowly removed the shirt and the thick vest, exposing the mirrored pair of scarlet Macaws tattooed on the smooth inner curves of her full bare breasts, and observed the clinical expression in his dark, foreboding eyes—she realized with a sinking heart that he had no personal interest in her at all. Or at least none that she could detect.

"Put your shirt back on," he said with cold indifference.

She was starting to rebutton the front of her shirt, her chest muscles tight with fear as she tried not to think about what was coming next, when he asked in a deep, resonate voice: "Do you know how to sail a boat?"

She started to say "What?" again, because it didn't make any sense. But then she quickly forced herself to concentrate because there might be a chance after all. She already knew in her heart that nothing else mattered—whatever the trade was, whatever it was he wanted her to do, would be fine with her.

She would do anything to survive. Anything at all.

"Yes, I can sail a boat. Why?"

"I need someone who is capable of taking a large sailboat out into the ocean. You seem to be unemployed at the moment," Riser added without the slightest trace of irony or amusement in his cold and foreboding voice.

The woman blinked.

She started to say: "How large a sailboat?" but it immediately occurred to her that that might be the wrong question to ask.

"How . . . how do you know you can trust me?" she finally asked instead.

"Do you blame yourself for Hoffsteadler's death?" he asked, completely ignoring her question.

The woman hesitated again, wondering if there was a right or wrong answer or if it even mattered.

"Yes, of course I do," she finally replied. "It was my fault."

"Do you feel grief? A sense of personal loss?"

She looked down at the sprawled, bloody body of George Hoffsteadler, the man who had paid her exorbitant salary without hesitation, but who had also teased her mercilessly in front of her fellow guards. The man who had "accidentally" brushed against her breasts or patted her butt dozens of times, and then laughed when she had turned away, embarrassed and enraged, but refusing to respond. The man who was now dead because, in the span of one second, she had failed.

"No," she said, realizing as she spoke the words that it was a truthful answer. Hoffsteadler's death didn't matter to her at all.

"Good." Riser nodded. "I expect the same degree of loyalty. Nothing more, nothing less. Success will be rewarded. Failure will result in immediate punishment. Disloyalty will result in death. Do you understand and agree to the terms?"

"Yes," the woman said calmly, wondering what it was she was doing, other than—for the moment—saving her life.

"Good. Do you know where Hoffsteadler maintains the video recorders and the tapes for his surveillance system?"

"Yes."

"Show me," he ordered. "And then go back to doing what you were told to do."

"What's that?" she asked, confused.

"Pack my merchandise. It's time for us to go to work."

Chapter One

Special Agent Henry Lightstone dug his lethal hands deep into his jacket pockets as he walked slowly along the narrow asphalt pathway that curved through the historic Boston Common.

Alert and ready now, but having no idea as to whom or what or why, he was waiting with growing impatience for the converging pair to make their move.

The problem was, as Lightstone reminded himself for the third or fourth time that evening, it didn't make any sense. The team hadn't made any controlled buys yet. And it was much too early in the game for any organized opposition to be sending out tags. So it had to be some kind of amateur situation. A couple of local muggers, or hopeful car-jackers, or a mistaken identity on a blown drug deal. Something like that.

But there were at least two of them, and they hadn't been acting like amateurs at all so far. So Lightstone had been forced to keep moving in the opposite direction from the team's safe house. Thinking, as he did so, that it would have been nice to have had a little advance warning. That way he could have been wearing something more substantial than a long down jacket and a knit watch cap to ward off the increasingly cold winds and rapidly falling snow.

At least a set of woolen long johns and warm gloves to go along with his jeans and flannel shirt, he thought wishfully, starting to feel the effects of the bone-chilling wind through the light denim pants. And ideally, the pair of insulated winter boots in his duffel bag in place of his comfortable, low-cut desert hiking shoes that were already starting to get cold and damp from walking through the accumulating slush.

He hadn't bothered to dress any warmer because he had only intended to walk down to the local grocery store for a newspaper and a pound of coffee. It had never occurred to him that an hour later, at five-thirty in the evening, he might still be wandering around the city of Boston in a growing snowstorm.

And even if such a possibility *had* occurred to him, the weatherman had been reporting a steady barometric reading all day, with no expected change in the storm patterns over the next twenty-four hours.

But all that had changed in a matter of a few seconds when the barometer and the air temperature had suddenly started to drop rapidly—and when he decided, mostly on a whim, to cross the street through a break in traffic rather than at the light.

They obviously hadn't been expecting that.

So now, instead of walking directly back to their concealed safe house with an evening newspaper and a can of coffee under his arm, Henry Lightstone was searching for a place that was suitably remote. Preferably a small clearing surrounded and concealed by bare-limbed trees. Or perhaps the shadow side of an isolated building. Or even, if it became absolutely necessary, the far end of a darkened alleyway. It didn't really matter, just as long as it was someplace that a streetwise Bostonian or an equally wary tourist would instinctively avoid at all costs.

Which was to say, a place where a sudden moment of opportunity might become overwhelmingly tempting, if and when they chose to take it.

He had been walking in an elliptical pattern for almost forty-five minutes, deliberately leaving himself open to an approach because he wanted the answers right now, *before* he and his fellow wildlife agents set their new covert operation into motion, rather than later, when the entire team would be exposed.

Who they were.

What they wanted.

And why.

He had first sensed their presence, and then caught their movements at the corner of his peripheral vision, when he had suddenly crossed over to the other side of the street, and then—at the last moment and more out of habit than anything else—turned right instead of left, retracing his route in the opposite direction down the busy sidewalk.

Thinking back, Henry Lightstone realized that it had been the timing of their reactions that had caught his attention. They hadn't been ready for his sudden change of direction, and their attempts to recover had created brief but discernible breaks in the pedestrian flow of traffic on the crowded and slippery sidewalks. Not enough of a break to pinpoint the trackers themselves or to confirm any kind of intended action. But more than enough to suggest that some kind of focused activity—focused, that is, upon his physical movements—might be going on in his immediate vicinity.

In other words, a surveillance.

There were at least two of them out there, he figured. Two and possibly a third, because even after he had managed to jar them out of their pattern a second time (which gave him a better sense of their distance and relative positioning), he still had an uneasy sense of some other presence lurking out there in the growing darkness. Something dark and sinister and hidden, and therefore, at least in Lightstone's suspicious mind, something infinitely more dangerous.

But what?

Henry Lightstone was very much aware that only six months ago he and the surviving members of his covert team had accidentally tripped across an illicit conspiracy—codenamed Operation Counter Wrench—between government and big business to destroy the environmental movement, using as their primary weapon a lethal band of twelve international counterterrorist experts. The fact that he and his fellow agents had survived and persevered, in the face of overwhelming odds, Lightstone knew, had far more to do with luck, happenstance, and comradery than anything else.

But the Counter Wrench gang had been taken out, Lightstone reminded himself. Gerd Maas, Alex Chareaux, and Roy Parker were in custody. Buddy and Sonny Chareaux were dead. And so were the bureaucratic ringleaders, Reston Wolfe and Lisa Abercombie.

A clean sweep.

And now the team was working a brand-new covert operation, in a completely different part of the country, so there shouldn't have been anyone hanging around that they needed to worry about.

Or at least nobody that we know anything about, Lightstone corrected, remembering that there were still some loose ends regarding Abercombie and Wolfe's foiled conspiracy plans to ransack Greenpeace and Earth First!—not to mention several of the other major environmental activist groups—that he and his fellow agents hadn't managed to unravel yet. Such as the source of the millions of dollars that the two had used to fund their illicit operation. And the possibility that there were other conspirators still out there, waiting for a chance to renew their assault on the environmental movement or to take their revenge upon a small team of conspiracy-foiling agents.

But even taking all those issues into account, the fact that he was being followed while walking through the middle of Boston Common, in the state of Massachusetts, at the onset of a new covert investigation, was still extremely disturbing to Special Agent Henry Lightstone.

The reason being that as far as he and his fellow agents of Bravo Team were concerned, they had managed to pull off a classically clean penetration. After two months of preparatory groundwork, and five weeks of hands-on construction to link up the warehouse and safe house, not a single person had displayed anything more than a casual interest in their activities.

Or at least not until now, Lightstone reminded himself as he continued to stroll slowly along the narrow asphalt pathway that wove through the historic Boston Common.

He could have stopped at one of the public phone booths and called for backup, but he didn't want to do that. Not until he got some answers.

He had already tried to expose the tag on the main streets in downtown Boston. But within minutes the streets had suddenly been filled with hundreds of people leaving work early, hurrying to their car or bus or train before the unexpected storm tied everything up. Everyone was walking fast, and hunching forward, and using hoods and scarves and umbrellas to protect themselves from the ice-cold gusts of wind and flurries of wet, sticky snowflakes, which meant he wouldn't be able to see their faces.

Lightstone quickly realized that his chances of exposing and identifying the pair on the basis of a spontaneous reaction to another one of his unexpected moves were minimal at best. They were alert now, and they wouldn't make that same mistake again. Not if they were as professional as they appeared so far.

So instead Henry Lightstone had begun working his way in the direction of the historic Boston Common, where there would be fewer innocent people around and better opportunities for both sides, if that was how it was going to go down.

Out in the open now and away from the protective buildings, Lightstone found himself exposed to the full force of the intensifying storm. Like the rapidly fleeing city work force, he too was forced to hunch forward and use the hood of his jacket in order to protect his head and face from the freezing wind and numbing cold. Which, in turn, made it difficult to keep an eye out for any precipitous movements by his supposed adversaries.

He was coming up on the statue that had been constructed

in memory of the Boston soldiers and sailors who had died during the Civil War when he was suddenly aware that he was being stared at by a solitary figure, who had been standing in front of the statue, with his back to the asphalt pathway, before he suddenly turned around. A young man who, from all outward appearances, hadn't expected to encounter a raging snowstorm either when he decided to stand around in a light jacket, on an exposed hilltop, out in the middle of Boston Common.

Henry Lightstone watched the solitary figure carefully as he maintained his steady pace. And, in doing so, he noticed that the expression in the youthful face suddenly changed from hopeful expectation to visible and almost stricken disappointment.

Not the one you were expecting, am I? Lightstone thought as he continued on past the now desolate figure, noting the youth's fair features, the ice-covered granny glasses, the black portable computer case clutched in one hand, and his thoroughly soaked tennis shoes. *Poor bastard, hope whoever it is you're looking for shows up pretty damn soon.*

But then Lightstone immediately forgot about all that because he was coming up on the Park subway station, and he suddenly decided that a quick phone call might not be such a bad idea after all.

Larry Paxton, newly appointed assistant special agent in charge of the U.S. Fish and Wildlife Service's reinstituted Bravo Team, a covert entity of the service's two-hundred-and-twenty-agent Division of Law Enforcement, had been growing increasingly worried by the minute. When the phone rang, he was pacing the bare wooden floor of the second-story loft that he and his fellow agents had converted into temporary living quarters pending their move to the newly created safe house.

Paxton whirled around and started toward the phone, but Mike Takahara was closer to the couch and beat him to it.

"Yeah?" Takahara paused and then smiled. "Henry?

Where are you? . . . Oh, yeah? Well, it's about time you checked in. Larry's been wearing a path in the carpet for the last half hour, and he's about ready to drive us . . . what? Yeah, sure, hold on just a second."

"Where the hell is he, and what the hell's he doing?" Paxton demanded as he and Dwight Stoner and Thomas Woeshack stood around the couch, listening intently to the one-sided conversation. But the Japanese-American technical agent waved them off as he grabbed for a pen and paper.

"Okay, go ahead. Tremont to Avery to what? . . . Okay, yeah, I know where that is. Where do you want us?" He paused again. "You sure? How many are there?" Takahara paused again. "Okay, just watch yourself. We're on our way."

Paxton and Stoner were already reaching for their jackets and shoulder-holstered pistols when Mike Takahara, slightly overweight but still visibly muscular under his dark blue golf shirt, stood up from the couch.

"What's going on?" Thomas Woeshack, an Aleut Eskimo agent, and the youngest and least experienced member of the covert team, asked, having failed to recognize the critical words in Takahara's side of the phone conversation.

"Hopefully, nothing too serious," Takahara said as he and Woeshack quickly strapped on their own shoulder-holstered weapons. "Just Henry doing what he seems to do best."

"Yeah, what's that?"

"Acting like a human magnet for every little piece of trouble that happens to cross his path," the tech agent replied.

The alley that Henry Lightstone selected had a number of useful advantages.

First of all, it was entirely surrounded by two-story brick warehouses, most of which looked as if they'd been built in the early fifties. Secondly, about halfway in, the alley made a sharp ninety-degree angle to the left, so that the back half couldn't be seen from the street. And finally, the electrical wiring in the few remaining light fixtures over the few locked doorways had apparently either shorted out or simply rotted away long ago. As a result, the only light available in the rearmost and hidden section of the alley came from the diffuse cloud reflections overhead.

It was, by its very nature, a cold, dark, and foreboding place. And given its immediate proximity to the city of Boston's infamous Combat Zone, it was exactly the kind of place that streetwise residents and innocent tourists alike would have instinctively avoided like the plague.

But being neither a resident of Boston nor a tourist, Henry Lightstone continued walking until he was within fifty feet of the dead end. Then he stopped, turned around, stood in the middle of the alleyway, and waited.

It didn't take them long. And thanks to the echoing effects of the high brick walls, not to mention the decade-long accumulation of dirt, rocks, trash, and other miscellaneous debris scattered about on the cobblestone roadway, Lightstone heard them coming long before they appeared.

To Henry Lightstone's amazement, both men actually seemed to be startled by his sudden appearance, as though it hadn't occurred to either of them that they might actually be confronted in a dark alleyway by the object of their hunt.

Or more likely, their surveillance, he thought, deciding that in spite of their scroungy and menacing appearance, neither of these men looked much like a member of an opportunistic mugger team.

So what did you expect, that I was going to run blind into a dark alley and cower in a corner? Or that I was going to lead you right into the back door of the safe house? Christ, what the hell did they tell you guys about this deal? Or more to the point, what didn't they tell you?

But in spite of their visible surprise, both men recovered quickly.

"Well, well, well, *look* what we have here," the Hispanic-featured man said.

One of them was tall, black, heavyset, dark bearded, and dressed in heavy boots, blue jeans, a military surplus overcoat, and a dark watch cap. The other was of Hispanic origin, Puerto Rican, Lightstone guessed. Shorter by about six inches, lighter by a hundred pounds or so, and dressed almost exactly like his scowling companion, except that his jeans were tight and made from some kind of fake-aged gray-black denim. Both men were wearing tight black gloves, and the taller of the two was now holding what appeared at first to be a heavy bicycle chain in his right hand, except that Lightstone could see small bladelike protrusions poking out along the outer edge of the chain at about two-inch intervals.

For a brief moment it occurred to Henry Lightstone to wonder where a mugger in the city of Boston would have found a chain-saw chain.

The two men had positioned themselves in an angled line across the alley so as to block any escape. And since the taller one had deliberately placed himself in the background, Lightstone decided that the smaller Hispanic was probably going to turn out to be the designated talker.

"Hi," the covert agent responded.

"So wha'cha doin' here, man? You lost or something?"

"Must be." Lightstone shrugged. "I was looking for the subway. Guess I took the wrong turn," he added, staring calmly at the two men.

The Hispanic hesitated, appearing to be confused and uncertain as to what he was supposed to do next.

It was now absolutely clear to Henry Lightstone that these men hadn't been expecting this kind of response from their intended target at all.

So what do you do now, follow instructions or wing it? Lightstone thought, suddenly finding himself intrigued by some of the more interesting possibilities.

"Maybe you need some directions, huh?" the Hispanic said.

"Maybe."

The smaller man glanced over at his companion, apparently seeking and receiving some kind of reassurance. Then he continued. "You know what I think, man? I think you need directions real bad."

"You're probably right," Lightstone conceded. "Maybe you guys can help."

The smaller man grinned widely, exposing a significant gap between his front teeth. "Okay, that's more like it. So how much you willing to pay?"

"Oh, I don't know." Lightstone shrugged. "What's the going rate for directions around here? A quarter?"

"A *quarter*?" The Hispanic blinked and turned back to his companion, apparently unable to believe his ears. "You believe that, man? This guy gets himself lost in the Zone, like a friggin' dummy. And we offer to help, like a couple o' nice guys. And all he wants to fork out for all our trouble is two bits. Two lousy bits!"

The smaller man suddenly whipped his head around to face Lightstone again, only this time he held a wide-bladed knife out in his extended hand. Lightstone recognized it as a K-bar fighting knife of the type that had been issued to U.S. Marines in World War II: a well-made, multifunctional, double-edged fighting weapon. And in the hands of a trained killer, absolutely deadly and frightening tool.

"You see this, man?" the Hispanic tracker snarled, stepping up closer to his seemingly unimpressed victim.

"Looks sharp." Lightstone nodded, watching the other man a little more closely now. "You want to be careful you don't cut yourself."

"What?"

"Go home to your girlfriends, guys," Henry Lightstone said softly, "before you get hurt."

The Hispanic's eyes seemed to bulge outward in a mixture of disbelief and rage. Uttering a savage growl, he lunged forward and slashed at Lightstone's face. Then he gasped in surprise when the federal agent almost casually deflected his attack with a sweeping forearm and locked his wrist into a tight double-handed grip.

Henry Lightstone was still watching the second member of the surveillance team when he twisted his assailant's wrist sharply, causing the Hispanic tracker to scream in agony as the knife clattered on the cobblestone driveway.

Maintaining the hold, Lightstone waited until the taller black man made his move, stepping in fast and whipping the chain-saw chain around in a rapid blur over his head. Then, using the leverage of the wristlock, the agent sent his cursing Hispanic assailant staggering backward and right into the downwardly sweeping arc of the lethal chain.

Realizing too late what was happening, the shorter man made a futile effort to protect himself with his broken wrist. But he was much too slow, and his partner's effort to pull back on his swing only made things worse. The chain-saw chain whipped across his face—tearing deep bloody gouges out of his cheek and hand—and he screamed again, dropping to his knees and rolling over on his side in agony.

"Gawd damn!" the black man cursed as he saw the dark blood dribbling through his partner's clenched fingers. Flinging the chain-saw chain aside, he started to reach for the 9mm semiautomatic secured to his belt behind his back. But then he froze when he found himself staring into the barrel of a 10mm Model 1076 Smith & Wesson double-action pistol aimed right between his eyes.

"You don't want to do that," Henry Lightstone said calmly.

The black man brought his hands back up slowly and nodded, indicating that he understood.

"Put your hands behind your head, interlocking your fingers, and then spread your feet," Lightstone continued, and then waited for the man—who was now completely cooperative—to follow his instructions. "All right, good. Stay that way. Now what's your friend's name?"

"What?"

"Pay attention. I said, *what's your friend's name?*" Lightstone repeated.

"Listen, man, Ah don't know. . . ."

"Shut up and listen to me," Lightstone ordered in a cold voice, keeping the Smith & Wesson semiautomatic dead-centered on the man's broad nose. "If you fail to respond to my instructions, or if your friend tries to stand up or does anything stupid with his hands, then I'm going to put a hollow point between your eyes, and then one between his, and then walk back out to the street and call the cops. You understand what I'm saying?"

The black man nodded.

"Now what's his name?"

"Carlos."

"And your name is?"

"Fred," the black man muttered unhappily.

"Carlos, did you hear what I just said to your buddy Fred about you getting up or trying to do something stupid with your hands?" Lightstone asked.

The stricken Hispanic tracker responded with a burst of abusive Spanish through his bleeding fingers, but he stayed down.

"Care to translate that?" Lightstone asked.

"He understands," the man who might or might not have been named Fred responded.

"Good. Does he carry a piece too?"

The black man hesitated.

"Never mind." Lightstone shook his head impatiently. "Okay, Fred, what I want you to do is bring your feet back together, right, just like that. Now turn around slowly to face the wall to your left—right there, that's it—and spread your legs again. A little farther this time. Good."

Stepping around and behind the tall, spread-eagled assailant, and keeping an eye on his temporarily disabled partner, Lightstone reached under the black man's jacket and removed the 9mm semiautomatic. After releasing the magazine and jacking the live round out of the chamber, he quickly disassembled the weapon and tossed the slide, receiver, barrel, and mainspring into a nearby trash can.

A quick one-handed search from the man's head to his ankles—conducted while Lightstone kept his own pistol tight against his side to discourage any thoughts of a desperate grab or spin move—confirmed that the taller and presumably more dangerous of the two trackers was now completely disarmed.

Stepping back, Lightstone quickly moved around and knelt down by the still prone Carlos. A second quick search turned up another identical 9mm semiautomatic—the parts of which also went into the nearby trash can—and a small switchblade. Lightstone tossed both knives back into the darkness of the alleyway, and then gestured with the Smith & Wesson at the black man.

"Okay, Fred, help him up."

Silently the black man obeyed.

Henry Lightstone waited until both men were standing up, the man supposedly named Carlos still muttering threatening curses and clutching a bloody hand to his severely torn cheek. As he did so, the federal agent held the 10mm pistol down at his side.

"I suppose it'd be a waste of time to ask if either of you happen to remember the name of the person who hired you?"

Silence.

"Yeah, that's what I figured." Lightstone nodded. "And I don't suppose it would matter much, one way or the other, if I decided to take you guys over to the local police station and let them ask the same question, right?"

More silence.

Shaking his head and sighing to himself, Lightstone slid the Model 1076 Smith & Wesson back into his concealed jacket pocket holster, then reached into the front pocket of his jeans and pulled out a quarter. "Now, about those directions . . ."

"Say what?" the black man growled, his forehead furrowed in confusion.

Lightstone tossed the coin to the taller of the two trackers, who caught it out of reflex.

"I'm still lost." Lightstone shrugged, staring straight into the man's furious eyes.

"Gawd damn it all!" the black man swore as he flung the coin aside. Then, before Lightstone could do or say anything else, the two men glanced at each other, then turned and ran.

Within a matter of seconds they were out of the alley and running down the street toward the southern edge of Boston Common at a frantic pace.

About thirty seconds later Henry Lightstone came out of the alley. He paused for a moment, looked around, and then walked over to a dark sedan parked along the curb and got in on the passenger side.

"You okay?" Dwight Stoner, the huge, six-feet-eight, three-hundred-pound member of the covert agent team inquired.

"Yeah, sure." Lightstone nodded. "Where is everybody?"

"I dropped Mike off at the far corner of the park, and put Larry and Thomas out on the wings," Stoner said as he started up the car. "Larry figured that he and Thomas could probably run a little faster than Mike and I if they had to."

"They will. Those guys are rabbits," Lightstone said as he reached for the pack-set radio on the seat.

"Bravo Two, anybody out there?" he spoke into the radio mike.

"Bravo Five, I'm in the middle of the park, heading, uh, due west," Special Agent/Pilot Thomas Woeshack's distinctive voice echoed within the rented sedan.

"Bravo One, I lost them. Last I saw, they were heading northwest, toward that old graveyard," Larry Paxton responded, sounding as if he were almost out of breath. "Watch for them coming your way, Snoopy!"

Lightstone nodded at Stoner, and the huge agent sent the sedan roaring out into the snow- and slush-filled street.

"Snoopy"—Lightstone spoke into the radio mike—"if you spot them, give them some distance and keep your eyes open. I took away their toys, but they may have a buddy out there somewhere.''

"Bravo Three, copy," Mike Takahara acknowledged. "Haven't seen anybody yet. What am I looking for?"

"Salt-and-pepper team," Lightstone said. "The tall one's black with a full beard. The short one's Hispanic, handlebar mustache. Both wearing boots and dark green military fatigue jackets, Vietnam era.''

"Nobody like that's been by here so far," Mike Takahara responded.

"Okay, we're on our way," Lightstone said. "Meet you all at the corner of Charles and Boylston."

Five minutes later the five covert agents were standing together at the intersection of Charles and Boyston streets, Paxton and Woeshack still trying to catch their breath.

"You know, a couple years ago Ah'd have kept up with them mothers, no problem," Larry Paxton grumbled as he leaned against a light post.

"That's the problem with getting to be the acting boss." Lightstone grinned as he and Stoner and Takahara continued to search the darkness. "A guy starts sitting in those fancy chairs, feet up on the desk, secretary bringing him coffee and doughnuts, he's bound to go soft."

"Ah ain't got no fancy chair, and Ah ain't got no fancy desk or secretary neither," Paxton growled. "All I got is you idiots, which ain't much right about now, let me tell you."

"Good thing you don't," Mike Takahara chuckled, slapping Paxton on the back. "Otherwise we'd probably have to talk Stoner into carrying you back to the house over his shoulder. Be downright embarrassing."

"Somebody's got to do some work around here," the huge agent agreed.

"Speaking of which, do we still have an operation?" Lightstone asked, turning to Paxton.

"I don't know." Paxton shook his head, still looking disgusted with himself. "Let's go back to the apartment, check in with Halahan. See what he thinks."

"He's gonna be pissed at us if we've blown this one," Mike Takahara predicted.

"Yeah, so what else is new." Paxton nodded gloomily.

"You mean we might have to start over again somewhere else?" Thomas Woeshack asked, looking dismayed.

"That's the beauty of undercover work," Lightstone said as the agents started walking back toward the car. "Just when you think you know what you're doing, the bad guys get into the act and start confusing the shit out of everything."

"Does it happen this way very often?" Woeshack asked.

"As far as I know," Lightstone said with a sigh, "every damn time."

The two chastened surveillance specialists, who were in fact named Fred and Carlos, were nearly a half mile away from the intersection of Charles and Boylston streets when Carlos—weakened by the loss of blood and the sharp pains in his broken wrist—finally had to stop to catch his breath.

"You see them?" he gasped, bracing and concealing himself against a nearby inset wall, and holding a blood-stained handkerchief to his face with his one good hand, while his better-conditioned partner maintained a lookout.

"No, I think we lost them back at the graveyard."

"God, I hope so."

Carlos was starting to wheeze now, sounding asthmatic, although his Marine recon-trained partner correctly guessed that it was more likely the result of delayed shock. "Gotta get—hospital, face and arm fixed. Then—gonna hunt that bastard down."

"Got news for you, man, we ain't gonna be going to no hospital." The man named Fred shook his head.

"What do you mean?"

"Ah *mean* we ain't going to no hospital," the black man repeated. "We're gonna be in enough shit as it is. Ain't no need to make things any worse."

"Hey, it wasn't our fault. . . ." Carlos started to protest, but his partner shook him off.

"Listen, man, we blew a tail. Simple as that," the black man said solemnly. "Our orders were to tag the people coming out of that apartment and ID their contacts, period. The man didn't say nothin' 'bout us getting ourselves made, and then facing up the guy in some alley."

"I'm telling you, the guy was going for the safe house." Carlos shook his head. "You could tell, the way he was making those moves. And you know what, I'll bet you a hundred bucks the entrance was in that alley too. If he hadn't heard us coming, we'd have had it nailed."

"Maybe." The black man shrugged, sounding unconvinced.

He had been maintaining a careful vigilance of the route that they had just taken, but in doing so, he had failed to notice the dark van that had pulled up to the curve about a half block up the street.

"Maybe, my ass." Carlos shook his head, his breath still coming in ragged gasps. "I'm telling you, we had the bastard, whoever the hell he is."

"He ain't no goddamned fish dealer, Ah'll tell you that much right now."

"You think he's a cop?"

"Maybe. Kinda acted like it. But that don't make no sense either."

"Why not?"

" 'Cause a cop wouldn't have—" Fred stopped, his eyes widening in fear.

Seeing the expression in his partner's eyes, Carlos whirled around and found himself looking up in shocked disbelief at a huge, dark, and absolutely terrifying form.

Then he whispered: "Oh, God."

It was the last sound he ever uttered.

Chapter Two

Somehow, William Devonshire Crowley managed to control his trembling upper torso long enough to look at his watch.

It was 4:45 P.M.

His heart sank.

It wasn't supposed to be happening like this. The weather service had been predicting no change in the storm patterns and a low of 36 degrees all morning. Which was why he had decided to wear a light down jacket to his three-thirty meeting at Soldiers and Sailors Civil War Monument in the middle of Boston Common.

But the snow had started to fall at three-fifteen, just as he stepped out of the Park Street subway exit. Within minutes it had begun to accumulate—heavy, wet, and slippery—on the surrounding paths and trees and park benches. Hardy tourists, determined to walk the Freedom Trail no matter what, buttoned up their jackets and hoods, and lowered their heads into the wind.

And all that time, while the temperature continued its steady drop into the twenties, his contact never showed.

"Christ's sake, where the hell are you?" he rasped.

More of a prayer than a curse, because William Devonshire Crowley was becoming desperately afraid.

He had spent the entire hour and a half trampling a slushy circular path around the tall concrete monument, searching for some sign of the man he was supposed to meet and feeling the icy wind cutting deeper and deeper through his light down jacket. And for the last forty-five minutes, at the end of every completed revolution, turning his head away to avoid seeing again those first two ominous lines on the monument's inscription.

Crowley's shoes were soaked, his ears were frozen, his hands numb and weary, and his entire body was trembling now. But his uncontrollable shivering had very little to do with the cold.

He was so scared now, so overwhelmed by a growing sense of utter hopelessness, that he thought he might drop to his knees and start to cry at any moment.

He turned away from the long, narrow asphalt path that he'd been monitoring with such feverish intensity, to stare once again at the distant subway station. He desperately wanted to run to that station and scramble down the long stairway and jump onto the first train going out of the city of Boston. Anywhere, was fine, it didn't matter. Just as long as it was far enough away where he wouldn't ever have to face that huge, hulking, and absolutely terrifying man again.

Then he turned back and froze when his eyes went immediately to the hunched-over figure approaching in the distance.

Oh, my God, he's here.

Crowley felt his arms and hands and mind and backbone, and every other part of him that he could imagine, go numb.

Somewhere in the depths of his sanity, a voice was screaming at him to run. To go as far and as fast as he could, right now, before it was too late. But much in the manner of a small rodent that suddenly finds itself face to face with a slowly approaching serpent, Crowley quickly discovered that he couldn't run. Couldn't even move, for that matter. All he could do was stand there, with a growing sense of apprehension and dread, and watch the hooded figure with the wide shoulders and easy stride continue his approach, knowing that when he reached the statue, he would . . .

Then, still fifty feet away, the hunched-over figure suddenly straightened up, and Crowley's eyes widened in shock.

No, wait, it's not him! It can't be!

William Devonshire Crowley didn't know whether to scream out his frustration or simply break down and cry out of pure relief. So rather than do either, he just continued to stand there and stare at the hooded figure of Henry Lightstone as the mildly curious covert federal agent glanced his way and then continued walking on past the statue.

Crowley watched Lightstone disappear in the growing darkness, and then turned back to his increasingly desperate search for the man he had to find. Absolutely *had* to.

"Goddamnit, where the hell *are* you?" he rasped again as he continued to search among the crossed pathways and bare trees surrounding the low hilltop through his ice-streaked glasses.

He realized now that he really had no choice. He had to find the huge, hulking, and fearsome dark-coated figure and talk with him again. That was the only way that everything could be all right again. The only possible way.

"Come on. Please. Be here," he whispered to himself as he transferred the increasingly heavy laptop computer to his less-fatigued hand. "Please!"

Although, during the last hour and a half, it had certainly occurred to Crowley many times that he might be better off if he never saw this incredibly frightening man again.

In fact, the more he thought about it, *far* better off.

He understood now, much too late, that he had been unbelievably stupid from the very beginning. What had seemed like a lark, an adventure, when he'd first been offered the job—*When was that? Only three days ago?* he thought incredulously—had long since become a living, walking, hulking nightmare.

And even worse, a nightmare with unforgettable and absolutely terrifying eyes.

No matter what he did, no matter how hard he tried, William Devonshire Crowley simply could not erase the chilling memory of the man's eyes. How they had narrowed and then turned cold and hard when Crowley told him that the deal would have to be renegotiated. And how they had lost all expression when Crowley had added that the most his employers would be able to pay was four hundred thousand dollars apiece, rather than the initially offered five hundred thousand.

Think about it, Crowley had suggested in a shaky voice, realizing only at that moment that he had almost certainly gone too far. *We'll meet here again at three-thirty this afternoon. Right here, in front of the Soldiers and Sailors Civil War Monument. Work out all the details. Win-win situation all the way around. I guarantee it.*

And how the man had stared at him that one last time before he turned away. Stared at him with an expression that was so cold and malevolent and threatening that Crowley had nearly wet his pants right there in the park.

We want you to try to bargain him down. Get us a deal if you can. You're good at that sort of thing, Crowley. That's why we hired you.

That's what they had told him at the airport.

Christ, didn't they realize what this man was like? Didn't they understand?

"Goddamnit, it's not my fault! I only did what they told me to do!"

Crowley tried to scream the words out in a roar of iron-willed defiance. But his voice broke on the word *fault*, and the rest of it disintegrated into a whimpering sob that was completely inaudible beyond a dozen feet in the growing storm. Not that it mattered, because there was no one on the low exposed hilltop to hear him anyway. Or at least no one that he could see.

His body was trembling so hard now and his hands hurt so bad that he could barely hold onto the handle of the computer case. But he didn't dare set it down. He understood now that the little laptop computer was his primary lifeline back to his accustomed world of privilege, luxury, and warmth. Not to mention sanctuary from huge, hulking men with terrifying eyes, he reminded himself prayerfully. He couldn't even bear to think about the computer being stolen, so he kept switching it back and forth between his numbed and aching hands as he continued to scan the bare-treed landscape.

Distracted for a brief moment, Crowley allowed his gaze to travel up the base of the monument, back to those first two lines of the dedication that had been inscribed in the high concrete surface many years ago:

TO THE MEN OF BOSTON
WHO DIED FOR THEIR COUNTRY

It was the sight of those chilling words, and the memory of the terrifying expression in the man's eyes, and the sudden overwhelming realization that he really *had* gone too far, that sent William Devonshire Crowley scrambling down the slippery asphalt pathway in a frantic dash toward the distant Park Street subway entrance. Running as if he were being pursued by ghosts. Or demons.

Or him, he thought, too panicked now to even look back, as he ran even harder past the empty and desolate Frog Pond, for fear of what he might see.

Can't wait any longer, he told himself as he nearly knocked three elderly women to the ground in his haste to get through the green sheltering doors of the subway entrance and down the slush-splattered stairs and into the relative security of the underground train station.

Have to get back to the hotel. Have to let them know. Get them to call it all off before . . .

He looked back over his shoulder as he fumbled with the small token. At the top of the stairs a huge dark figure was standing in the doorway. Driven by mindless fear, Crowley plunged through the turnstile and ran for the green commuter train that was just getting ready to depart the station.

It was only when he was on board, clutching onto the overhead rail and trying to catch his breath, that he became aware of the eerie shadows and shapes in the surrounding darkness of the underground tunnel. The steel support and cross beams standing out like angular black scarecrows in the dim glow of the dangling bare light bulbs. The criss-crossing lengths of black cable snaking out of the darkness in all directions. And the hidden corners and side tunnels that could easily conceal a hundred evil and terrifying men.

The images that had been lurking in the shadows of Crowley's consciousness while he was desperately circling the monument began to take shape in his mind again. Images that had warned him to stay out in the open, where people could see him.

And to avoid dark and isolated places—like subway tunnels—where he could be trapped.

Oh, God.

William Devonshire Crowley swung his head around frantically, staring wide-eyed at the handful of passengers who swayed with the rocking motions of the double-car commuter train as it slowly braked to a screeching stop at the Boylston exit. He couldn't see him, but that didn't necessarily mean anything.

As the doors slid open and people began to move in and out of the car, Crowley watched it all happen with a paralyzing sense of impending doom. The man wasn't here, in this car, but he could be in the next car. Or in the tunnel. Or at the exit by his hotel. Waiting for him.

The doors had just started to close again when William Devonshire Crowley suddenly came up on his shaky legs and lunged through the opening. In doing so, he caught his shoulder and slammed the computer case against the closing door as he staggered out onto the narrow walkway of the underground station.

The immediate sensation that nearly overwhelmed Crowley was that of being enclosed in a black wire cage. It took him a moment to understand that the thickly coated metal screens weren't there to close him in, but rather to guide him to the exit. Then he looked to his right and saw the wide gaping mouth of the dark tunnel he had just left.

He knew that was still two stops away from his destination, but that didn't matter. Nor did it matter if he froze to death running the remaining four blocks to his hotel. What *did* matter was the fact that he had to get back out into the open.

Right now!

This time, in his haste to escape, he caught the computer in the turnstile and nearly ripped the handle off the case. He almost started screaming in an uncontrolled frenzy before he finally managed to wrench the case loose and scramble up the thirty-four steps and out the doors into the freezing wind and blowing snow.

Then his heart nearly stopped again when he realized that this exit came out at the southeastern end of the Commons, and that he hadn't escaped at all.

Frantically clutching the handle of the laptop computer case that had grown so incredibly heavy over the past half hour, he began running on a diagonal course across the dead grass toward the street that would take him to his hotel.

Fifteen minutes later William Devonshire Crowley staggered into the middle of Copley Park, a completely open and public space that sat diagonally across from the Westin Hotel. He was gasping for breath and shaking uncontrollably as he set the computer case down between his legs. He looked first across the street at the Westin's modern glass entryway. And then back at the phones. And then finally over at the huge wood and iron doors of the eighteenth-century Trinity Church.

One or the other, and he had to choose quickly.

The greatest temptation was to run for the church, with its ancient brownstone walls and high steeples and life-sized replicas of the saints, and beg whoever was inside for sanctuary. That was what he desperately wanted to do. But Crowley didn't know anything at all about the Episcopalian religion and therefore had no idea if sanctuary was even a viable option.

What if they made him leave, and the man was out there, waiting for him?

The phones were about thirty feet away, mounted within a

six-pack-like array of tall black painted cylinders. He was sorely tempted to call for help, but he couldn't call his employers because he didn't know their phone number. Security reasons, they had explained. Didn't want him to call in on an open line. That was why they had provided him with the computer.

He couldn't call his employers, and he couldn't call the police either, because he didn't have the slightest idea what he could possibly tell a cop that would make any sense.

What? That I'm scared and that I need help because a man gave me a scary look?

A man that I'm trying to hire for four hundred thousand a pop to kill people I don't even know?

And for people I don't know either?

Yeah, right.

So instead of seeking help or sanctuary or almost certain arrest for conspiracy to commit *something*, William Devonshire Crowley simply prayed that he wasn't heading straight into a trap, and started across the street to his hotel.

Chapter Three

They had no corporate name or insignia to identify themselves. No embossed business cards. No heavy bond stationery. No listing in the World Wildlife Fund's annual Conservation Directory. Only the bottom two floors of a four-story brownstone building in Reston, Virginia. And a street address in eighteen-inch-high numerals of black anodized aluminum.

And an all-consuming mission:

To seek out and destroy seven greedy and powerful men, the creators and manipulators of ICER, in a manner that would shock and disrupt the entire industrial world.

And then to ignite that world into a roaring inferno of destruction and rebirth.

All that joined together by a single word, spoken in quiet recognition or whispered with fevered emotion between fellow conspirators:

Wildfire.

To the inner core, the chosen ones, this word brought forth images of valleys and forests and cities and towns all crumbling, one after the other, beneath the roaring path of a driven and unstoppable and insatiable flame.

And to the larger—and still growing—assemblage of true believers, this word offered the only hope for a planet overrun by disease and famine, and pollution and war and all the other excesses of a species that was running out of control as fast as it was running out of resources: the chance to start over. To be cleansed, and then reborn once again out of the devastation of smoldering ruins.

And thus this word described perfectly a small but increasingly fanatical group of environmental extremists who were better known—to the extent that they *were* known—for their fiery rhetoric and their rabid newsletters and their extremist beliefs than for any pretense of environmental ethics—much less any concern for other members of their species.

It was for this reason that they wisely chose to remain hidden, sending out their fiery rhetoric via anonymous mailings and carefully isolated Internet bulletin boards, while they made ready for their day of righteous glory.

Two of the large, corner basement offices of the small and innocuous brownstone building that housed Wildfire were connected—by two pairs of small isolated metal doors and two long and narrow concrete tunnels—to a huge eight-story, twenty-four-hundred-slot parking garage. These hidden access and escape routes offered the clandestine group an easy means of entering and leaving their concealed headquarters building without being observed or identified.

In one of those offices Leonard Harris, a sixty-three-year-old, short, baldish, and overweight man with a predilection for rolled-up sleeves, loosened bow ties, and computerized fantasy games, looked up as the small metal escape and access door to his dimly lit office opened.

A tall, slender woman, dressed in skintight black leggings and a loose black-and-purple sweatshirt that came down to her hips, and carrying a rifle case, entered the darkened room. Setting the rifle case against the wall, she shut the door, set the locks, and then walked over to the cluttered computer workstation.

"Did you have fun?" he asked.

"I like it," she nodded, kissing him gently next to his ear. He could smell the burned gunpowder in her hair.

It had been her birthday present: a Remington Model 7400 autoloading rifle, chambered for the 30-06 Springfield round, and capable of holding four in the magazine and one in the chamber. He had originally planned to order it in the smaller .222 round, to reduce the recoil and to save wear and tear on her spare frame, but she had insisted on the more powerful cartridge.

"Not too much for you?" He smiled as his hands moved across the keyboard reflexively, saving his most recent corrections to the program.

"It was perfect, just perfect. There's just one problem."

"Oh, really, what's that?"

"Shooting it makes me horny," she whispered in a rough, feminine voice, stroking her right hand gently along the grizzled jowls of her mentor, lover, and fellow inner core conspirator. "I want to see the Wildfire."

"You're the ember. Light it," he whispered back, turning around in his chair as he brought his hands up and over her hips, and under her sweatshirt, to cup her small, firm breasts in his soft hands.

"Now?"

"No, later," he rasped as he picked her up and carried her over to the made-up daybed in the far corner of his cavelike office, a daybed that also served, on occasion, as an alternate desktop and bookshelf, as well as a place to wait and sleep when the projects were set into motion.

It was her wish to be known only as "Ember." Because of the imagery, certainly, but also because the leader of a clandestine and fanatical group such as Wildfire *had* to remain anonymous if she wished to maintain her position . . . and her freedom.

Of the twelve members of the inner core, only Harris and one other knew her real name. But Leonard Harris, a.k.a. Eagle, had long since instituted the use of the code names. Especially since, according to the group's cherished and often repeated parables that Harris himself had created, it would be the eagle who carried the ember to the chosen place of ignition, where the wildfire would begin.

It was a role that Harris—an inveterate loner, escapist, and dreamer—had longed for all his life; and one that he had sworn to carry out, no matter what the cost.

They made love in the manner they did everything else: loudly and passionately and hurriedly. Aware, as always, that while their emotional energy might be limitless, their resources were not. And because their self-imposed mission was so vast and so overwhelming, there was little time for this sort of diversion. But the heated and twisted emotions that drove both of them forward with such furious intensity also—and inevitably—drove them to each other, like fuel and flame.

Finally they lay next to each other in the darkness, naked and sweating and gasping for breath.

"You could set the whole thing into motion, torch it off, just like that," he whispered in a hoarse voice.

"It would be beautiful." She smiled. "Find us a way."

"Don't I always?"

She turned to face him, her long, slender frame stretched out past his shorter, stockier, sixty-three-year-old body. It was when they lay together like this that they realized how different they were from each other, so completely different.

It was only in their fevered eyes and emotions that they were the same.

"Yes," she whispered, "you do. You always do."

"Tell me where you want to be. I'll get you there," he promised.

"I can see us soaring high above that place, circling, waiting for the moment," she said in a raspy whisper. "And then, finally, you release me . . . and I'm falling."

"I can see you falling," he said. "A glowing ember in the darkness, dropping away, becoming smaller and smaller—and then everything below—the entire world—erupts into a billowing flame that roars outward in all directions."

"Driven by the wind."

"Yes, darling, that's right." He nodded solemnly.

"You will be the wind," she whispered into his neck, "and I will be the fire."

And their passion rose once again.

Later, much later, when they were dressed again and sitting on the remade bed, leaning against each other, her chest against his back, she spoke softly into his ear.

"Eric wants to see you."

"I know." Harris nodded, balancing his chin on his hands and his elbows on his knees as he stared off into the dimly lit darkness of his large, isolated office.

"He says he's sorry."

"He should be. It was a stupid mistake."

"To use Crowley?"

"No, to send him in the first place."

She sighed. "It wasn't all his fault. I encouraged him."

"I know," he said softly.

"But it's so much money," she said after a while.

"Pieces of paper and bits of data, all meaningless." He shrugged.

"Meaningless after, but essential before," she offered, not aggressively this time, because the argument was long past. And it was never a question of the end, only the means.

"Yes, you're right." He nodded. "It's just the timing, and the fact that this Riser can be so volatile and so dangerous."

"But you can handle him, can't you?"

"Yes, I can handle him," Harris said, confident, because he was one of the acknowledged game masters of his era, but uneasy nonetheless, because this time the game was real. He'd already decided upon a strategy and had set it into motion, and he wondered if this was the time to tell her. He decided it was.

"But to do so," he went on smoothly, "we're going to have to make some changes in the game plan."

He could feel her stiffen behind his back.

"What kind of changes?" she whispered softly, but he could sense the edge to her voice.

"Turn Riser against the agents too."

"You mean directly?"

"Yes."

As the seconds went by, he felt her torso muscles start to relax as she considered the possibilities.

"It would keep him focused, wouldn't it?"

"And busy." Harris nodded. "Much less time to focus on us."

"What about the cost factor?"

"The entire scenario becomes much simpler for him this way. There's no reason why he should want more money. If anything, we should get a discount."

"It makes sense." She finally nodded. "When can you set it into motion?"

He remained silent, staring out across the darkened room.

"You already did it, didn't you?"

He nodded slowly.

"You knew I wouldn't object," she said. It wasn't a question.

"I knew you wouldn't *care*, one way or the other," Harris said matter-of-factly. "And you don't, do you?"

"No," she whispered softly into the back of his shoulder. "Should I?"

"The agents are just pieces on the board." Harris shrugged. "Which means they're expendable, just like everyone else."

She paused, and then said: "But what about Eric?"

"What about him?"

"He thinks they're the white hats, 'the heros'—the ones who defeated Maas and Wolfe and Abercombie."

"Through the eyes of a child." Harris smiled.

"But you'll explain it to him, make him understand the . . . necessity?" she said insistently.

Harris nodded.

"Please don't be angry with him . . . about Crowley," she whispered.

"I'm not angry. Just disappointed."

"Don't forget, we need him. I wish we didn't. I wish we could do it ourselves, just you and I, without all the others. But we can't. I can't," she added, with only the slightest discernible trace of bitterness.

"I know." Leonard Harris nodded, all too aware of her personal demons. And then: "When will he be here?"

She looked down at the luminous glow of her watch.

"In a half hour or so, maybe less."

"Then you'd better get going," he said reluctantly.

"I'll be back soon."

"When?"

"Soon," she said, pressing herself tightly against his bowed back as she bit gently at his ear. "Very soon."

Twenty minutes later Leonard Harris was back at work, monitoring one of the three computer systems on his extended workstation, when he heard a hesitant knock on the small metal door at his back.

After looking up and checking the small monitor overhead, Harris reached under the workstation table to his right and released the lock mechanism. Of the twelve inner-core members of Wildfire, only Eagle and Ember had keys to that particular door.

"Hello, Eric," he said when the young man closed the door behind him and walked over to stand next to Harris's desk.

"Hi."

"Have a seat."

"Thanks."

By contrast to Harris, he was a tall, slender, dark-haired, and well-groomed young man in his early twenties. He sat there looking uncertain, as if not quite knowing how to start the serious part of the conversation.

Then he finally said: "Heard anything from Crowley?"

"No, nothing yet." Harris shrugged as he gestured with an open hand at the blank computer screen at his far left.

The youthful newcomer looked at his watch. "What time were they scheduled to meet?"

"Three-thirty, at the Commons."

"It's ten after five. Crowley should have checked in by now."

"*If* the meeting was successful, he should have reported in by four-thirty at the latest," Leonard Harris agreed. "Since he hasn't, I think we have to assume that the meeting was a failure."

The young man blinked. "What?"

"A failure," Harris repeated. "It's not all that surprising, really. In fact, if anything, it was almost predictable."

"Why do you say that?"

There was a dangerous edge to the young man's voice. An edge that hadn't been there earlier when they had first discussed the issue. Harris was pleased. Perhaps it wouldn't be so bad, after all.

"Because we negotiated a deal with an extremely dangerous individual, and then we sent Crowley out to break it." The heavyset man shrugged.

The use of the word *we* rather than the more accurate and appropriate *you* immediately caught Eric's attention. "Yes, so?'' he said after a moment.

Harris thought he could detect a little bit of the more customary arrogance in the young man's voice.

"People like our Mr. Riser may not be accustomed to having their contracts renegotiated," he said quietly, watching the young man's face.

Come on, kid, stay on your feet, the baldish executive and acknowledged game master thought to himself. *Don't disappoint me. This is where it starts to get interesting.*

"But he's a businessman, just like anybody else, right?"

"Yes, I suppose, at some level, he is just a businessman." Harris shrugged.

"Then all this is bullshit," the youth said insistently. "Because when you get right down to it, this is nothing more than a business deal, and business deals get renegotiated all the time when circumstances change. That's the way things work. This Riser character ought to understand that, for Christ's sake! And after all, five hundred thousand for each phase is a hell of a lot of money for what we're asking him to do. I mean, we could have hired a guy off the street for a hundred times less."

"And we would have gotten exactly what we paid for," Harris responded calmly. "Don't forget, we've asked him to perform an extremely complex and dangerous mission. And as much as anything else, we're paying for his technical expertise, which we will *not* find on the street, no matter how hard we look."

"I still think we're being robbed, but I understand your point," the young man grumbled. And then, after a moment: "So what do you think happened to Crowley?"

Harris shrugged. "My guess would be that Riser took offense at his proposal."

The new look that suddenly appeared on Eric's face caused Leonard Harris to worry for a brief moment. If facial expressions were any basis for judgment, his youthful assistant seemed to be considering this fairly obvious possibility for the first time. And if that was the case, Harris told himself, then Wildfire could be in serious trouble.

"Do you really think Crowley might have blown the deal?"

Harris chewed at his lower lip. His fingers tapped absent-mindedly against the edge of the keyboard as he stared again at the dark, blank screen.

"Given Riser's rather fearsome reputation, and Crowley's youthful inexperience, I would say that's a very real possibility." He finally nodded.

"So what does that mean for us?"

"Among other things," Harris said, "it may very well mean that we have to start over again."

"Christ, Leo, we can't screw this whole deal up now! We need Riser. How the hell are we going to do it without him?"

Leonard Harris sighed, more out of fatigue than irritation. He had spent the last three hours monitoring the computer terminal in this small, isolated basement room himself, because a task like this couldn't be assigned to an underling. Especially an underling like Eric.

He was tempted to snap back at his young assistant, to remind him that it was he—Eric—who had sent Crowley out on what might still turn out to be an absolutely disastrous mission. But Harris didn't do that, because there wasn't any point in it. Eric was one of the essential members of the inner core of Wildfire. One of those cold and ruthless business executive types who had been trained to use their inherited wealth, parental influence, and predatory skills to move up fast in a large and prestigious organization. He wouldn't listen.

From outward appearances, the young man looked like little more than a preppy wimp in his horn-rimmed glasses, school tie, button-down Oxford shirt, and casual deck shoes. But Harris knew better. He'd spent the last eighteen months functioning as Eric's mentor. Training him how to fit in. To rise up and swim with the big sharks. And how to make his early moves without being discovered and destroyed in the process.

Aggressive, arrogant, manipulative, suspicious, and very much accustomed to doing things his own way, Harris thought with a smile. Not an easy subject, by any means, but he thought he'd done a good job with Eric. Or at least he hoped he had.

"Yes, of course we need Riser," Harris agreed. "Or someone like him. That goes without saying."

"So what are we going to do if Crowley *doesn't* check in?"

Instead of answering, Harris continued to tap his short, stubby fingers against the keyboard.

"The first thing to do would be to send someone up to Boston and find out what happened," he said after a moment.

"Are you sure that's wise?" the young man asked, more cautious now that he had begun to comprehend the nature of the risks involved.

"We'll have to know what happened in any case." Harris shrugged. "We can't leave a loose end like Crowley running around the neighborhood. Especially not now."

"Yes, I suppose you're right," the younger man conceded. "Who do you think we should send?"

That's right, in a situation like this, seek out advice immediately. You need to find someone to share the risk, just in case the situation calls for a fall guy, Harris thought approvingly. That was a fundamental principle of life in the cutthroat world of businesses and bureaucracies throughout the world. He wasn't the least bit concerned by the fact that the student had already begun to turn on his teacher. That, too, was an integral part of the game. Besides, there was an elegant solution to that temporary problem.

"Actually, I would think that the logical person to send would be you," Harris said thoughtfully.

"Me?"

"Why not?" The older man shrugged. "After all, you're

one of the very few people around here who knows what Crowley looks like, which might turn out to be an essential bit of knowledge if it became necessary to identify a body.''

''But—but I—''

''And you *were* the one who sent Crowley back out to try to renegotiate with Riser, on your own authority,'' Harris reminded gently. ''So there's always the issue of leadership to be considered, not to mention the fact that Crowley would respond to you.''

''But if Riser—'' The suddenly pale-faced youth started to whisper when Harris interrupted.

''Of course, if you should happen to make contact with Riser in the process of trying to locate Crowley, accidentally or otherwise, then we would have an additional problem, because Riser would almost surely want to interrogate you.''

''Interrogate me?'' Eric could barely force the words past his larynx.

''Interrogate. Torture. No doubt all the same thing, as far as our Mr. Riser is concerned,'' Leonard Harris said. ''And we certainly can't allow you to be interrogated or tortured, because you know too much. Names, places, things like that.''

''That's right,'' the youth said quickly. ''I do know too much. And besides,'' he added in a deeply humbled voice, ''I have my own jobs to do.''

''Exactly.'' Harris nodded. ''So we'll send a couple of new people from our legal team to check things out from a safe distance, perhaps posing as representatives of Mr. Crowley's family, while you continue to monitor, among other things, the trial of Mr. Maas and Mr. Chareaux.''

''Do you think that they'll be—uh—okay, if Riser's still out there?'' the youth asked hesitantly.

''Oh, I think they'll be just fine,'' Harris said confidently. ''After all, the ones I'm thinking of are young and energetic and—thanks to Harvard Law School and the United States Marine Corps—extremely well trained. And, most importantly, Riser has never seen either of them.''

"I was just thinking about his reputation."

"Of course. But don't forget, we still have the primary advantage. We know a great deal about him, and he knows little or nothing about us."

"Assuming that Crowley hasn't told him anything."

"Which was exactly why you elected to use Crowley in the first place," Harris reminded pointedly. "In spite of his family contacts, he really doesn't *know* much of anything about us. Or at least nothing useful, isn't that right?"

"Oh, yeah, sure." Eric nodded, his face relaxing into its more characteristic, predatory expression. "How long do you think we should wait before we send them in?"

"Let's give Crowley another half hour. If we don't hear from him by"—Harris glanced at his watch again—"let's say six o'clock, then we'll turn our associates loose to see what they can find."

"That sounds good."

"Yes, I agree." Harris nodded. "And while we're waiting, I think we would be wise to consider how we might make better use of those wildlife agents to keep our Mr. Riser fully occupied."

At the end, having reached his sanctuary unscathed, William Devonshire Crowley discovered that the door was the worst part of all.

He stood there in the hallway in front of his tenth-floor hotel room for a good thirty seconds before he was finally able to summon up the nerve to put the key in the lock. But even then it took the distant sound of an elevator door coming open to jar him into action.

Whimpering with fear, he wrenched the key to the right, shoved the door open, lunged forward into the room, slammed the door shut, threw the dead bolt, turned on the light, and then whirled around wide-eyed, with his back against the door, to face the interior of his room.

No dark figure.

No movement.

Nothing.

Almost crying with relief, Crowley quickly looked into the bathroom, the closet, and under the beds—which turned out to have solid box supports for the springs. Working frantically now, because he *had* to be sure, he pulled up both sets of mattresses and springs and looked underneath. Then he checked to verify that the two wooden cabinets did, in fact, contain a small refrigerator and a TV set instead of a patiently waiting killer.

Only then, when he was absolutely *sure* that he was alone, did William Devonshire Crowley unzip the black computer case and put the laptop computer on the desk.

His hands were shaking so badly that it was all he could do to plug in the power adapter and make the connections between the built-in modem and the hotel room telephone.

His employers had programmed the miniature computer to load automatically all the necessary communications software and hand-shaking commands during the booting-up process, so all Crowley had to do was turn on the power switch and wait.

Finally, after a considerable amount of electronic humming, sixteen words appeared on the screen.

HELLO WILLIAM. ENTER YOUR MESSAGE NOW (HIT SHIFT AND F10 KEYS TO SEND, ESC TO QUIT):

Closing his eyes in heartfelt relief, Crowley began to type furiously with his still shaky hands.

I HAVE MADE CONTACT WITH RISER AS DIRECTED. ADVISED HIM WE HAD TO RENEGOTIATE CONTRACT. HE SEEMED VERY UNHAPPY. WE AGREED TO MEET AGAIN AT BOSTON COMMONS, SOLDIERS AND SAILORS MONUMENT, AT 3:30 P.M. I WAITED UNTIL 4:45 P.M., BUT HE

DIDN'T SHOW. STRONGLY, REPEAT STRONGLY,
ADVISE THAT YOU

Crowley froze when he heard a noise. It sounded as if it
had come from the bathroom. He immediately got up and
moved away from the computer and the door.

"Oh, no, that can't be," he whispered faintly to himself
as he backed up against the curtained window, staring at the
short hallway leading to the locked hallway door.

The bathroom was to the left, the front door straight
ahead, and the closet door to the right. From where he was
standing, he could see that the chain latch was in place and
the deadbolt was turned to a horizontal position.

He knew it was impossible for someone to have come in
through the door, but he rechecked the bathroom and the
closet anyway, just to be sure. Reassured, he returned to the
computer. There were two messages waiting on the screen:

CROWLEY, WHAT'S THE MATTER?

And:

CROWLEY, ARE YOU THERE? IF SO, ANSWER
IMMEDIATELY.

Sounds like they're worried, Crowley thought. *Good.
Serves them goddamned right, what I had to go through.*

YES, I'M HERE. SORRY, THOUGHT I HEARD
SOMEONE OUTSIDE THE DOOR.
  IS RISER THERE WITH YOU?

Good God, no, Crowley thought, stunned and shaken by
the idea. *Didn't they understand what was happening up
here? No, of course not. Why should they?*

NO.
  WHERE IS HE?

I DON'T KNOW. I TOLD YOU, HE NEVER
SHOWED UP AT THE MONUMENT THE SECOND
TIME. WHY DIDN'T YOU TELL ME THAT?

He heard the noise again, only this time it was louder and
more distinct. Like a soft *thunk*.

Feeling his heart start to pound, Crowley slowly got up
from the chair and moved toward the locked and bolted front
door. Walking as silently as he could on the thick carpet, he
inched himself forward until he could peer through the peephole in the door.

Nothing.

Releasing a pent-up breath, William Devonshire Crowley
stepped away from the door with a smile, glanced into the
empty bathroom once more, and then opened the door to
check the closet.

That was when he began to scream.

Leonard Harris and his youthful apprentice were waiting
anxiously at their computer terminal when the black screen
suddenly came alive.

THIS IS RISER.

Even though they were several hundred miles away from
the Westin Hotel, and completely isolated by a carefully
crafted electronic message-switching system, both men felt
their chest muscles tighten around their hearts.

Finally Harris reached for the keyboard.

YES, RISER. GO AHEAD.
I UNDERSTAND YOU WISH TO RENEGOTIATE.
FINE. THE PRICE IS NOW SIX HUNDRED THOU-
SAND EACH. YES OR NO. DECIDE NOW. THERE
WILL BE NO FURTHER NEGOTIATIONS.

The two men—student and teacher—looked at each other
for a long moment before Harris cocked his head and then

waited. The implication was clear. The time had come for Eric to accept responsibility for his actions and thereby take his place among the adult sharks. Either that or sink back down into safe obscurity while his mentor made the yes-or-no decision.

Finally, albeit hesitantly, the young man nodded in agreement.

Leonard Harris's short, stubby fingers moved quickly across the keyboard.

WE AGREE.
  GOOD.

Harris paused thoughtfully, and then began typing again.

WHAT ABOUT CROWLEY?

The was another long pause while the computer screen remained blank, then:

THERE WILL BE NO CHARGE FOR CROWLEY.

Chapter Four

"No, that's not true at all, Jonathan." Samuel Ericson Tisbury spoke calmly into the phone. "I *do* understand your concerns. It's your risk assessment that I'm questioning."

Tisbury paused to listen.

"No, Jonathan, it's not that. I just find it incredibly difficult to believe that after all this time we could still be the subject of a legal inquiry."

Harold Ericson Tisbury II walked into the corner penthouse office just in time to hear the last sentence spoken by his one and only son: the fifty-eight-year-old chief executive officer of his far-flung mining, extracting, milling, and plating enterprises. He tilted his head questioningly, his bushy white eyebrows furrowing with sudden concern.

Sam Tisbury covered the mouthpiece of the phone with his hand. "It's Jonathan."

Harold Tisbury nodded in silent understanding. Selecting the familiar overstuffed chair to the right of his son's expansive desk, the seventy-nine-year-old board chairman and family patriarch sat down and crossed his thin legs. Then he reached across the desk for the ebony-framed photograph of the Tisbury family.

After staring at the familiar photograph for a long moment, Harold Tisbury put the expensive frame back on the desk. Then he sat back, folded his thin, wrinkled hands across his sparse lap, and closed his eyes with a tired sigh.

"No, Jonathan," Sam Tisbury went on smoothly, "I can assure you that Harold feels exactly the same way I do. It's been what, six months since we lost Counter Wrench? And since that time there hasn't been a single shred of evidence to suggest that these damnable federal wildlife agents—much less the FBI—are even aware that we exist, much less investigating us."

Sam Tisbury drummed his fingers silently on the tabletop as he listened patiently.

"Yes, of course, Jonathan. That's absolutely true. Any attempt to bring the committee together again, even now, is bound to involve some degree of risk. But Harold and I have discussed this at great length. Basically, we feel we're going to be taking a chance anyway, no matter what we decide to do. At least this way, if something *does* go wrong, God forbid, we'll be in a position to defend ourselves in a unified manner, rather than as seven disorganized and possibly panicked individuals."

He paused again to allow the man on the other end of the line to finish his troubled discourse.

"No, Jonathan, we've been watching for exactly that sort of thing very carefully. As far as I'm aware, no member of the committee has come under any type of law enforcement surveillance during the last six months. Why? Have you heard anything different?''

Sam Tisbury's face registered his surprise. "Oh, really? That's odd, I was just in contact with Alfred a few hours ago, and he didn't mention anything of the sort.''

Alerted by the sudden shift in his son's voice, Harold Tisbury's eyes came open.

"Well, yes, I suppose that's true. It *would* be difficult to follow someone in a sailboat without being discovered,'' Sam Tisbury chuckled, and then turned serious again.

"But in any case, Jonathan, Harold and I want you to know that we do share your concerns. And I agree, it's very tempting to just stay low for a few more months, keep our heads down and hope that nothing goes wrong. But given the current political situation and the nature of some of our current projects, we're just not certain that we can afford to maintain that strategy much longer.''

Harold Tisbury suddenly realized that his son was staring at him. Meeting his son's questioning gaze, the elder Tisbury nodded slowly.

"We've always known that our window of opportunity with respect to the environmental groups was going to be very narrow,'' Sam Tisbury went on. "But even so, we've suffered a very serious setback with Counter Wrench. And if they should *ever* sense that they have us on the run . . .'' He left the rest unspoken.

"What? Yes, of course, Jonathan. Either way, Harold and I will understand completely. Take your time. We'll wait for your call.''

After leaning forward to hang up the phone, Sam Tisbury made a small, precise checkmark next to the fifth name on his list. Then he turned to face the man with whom he had worked and played and conspired for the past forty-two years.

Since the day he had turned sixteen—Sam Tisbury smiled, remembering his ceremonial transformation from a child into a businessman. A ceremony that had long ago become a mandatory rite for every male born into the Tisbury family, carried forth as a family tradition for nearly six generations.

And with any luck, perhaps even for a dozen more generations, the CEO of Cyanosphere VIII thought to himself as he addressed his father.

"Well, that's the last of them."

Harold Ericson Tisbury II, wealthy industrialist, Chairman of the Board of Cyanosphere VIII, father, grandfather, and the current Chief Executive Officer of ICER, nodded in apparent satisfaction. "I take it Jonathan is being his normal, paranoid self?"

"I think the idea of having to use the telephone at his club in order to communicate with us has made him terribly nervous," Sam Tisbury said.

"It's just a precaution until we have the scrambled satellite phones," the elder Tisbury reminded.

"Yes, he's aware of that, but you know Jonathan. The man's a compulsive worrier. God knows how he ever managed to make it to the position of CEO without having a nervous breakdown."

"Anything specific this time?"

"Apparently, one of his technical people heard a rumor that the FBI has developed a computer program capable of breaking the matrix codes used in scrambled cellular telephones."

"What?" Harold Tisbury blinked. "That's absurd." Then he seemed to reconsider the possibility. "Is there any chance he might be right?"

"The complexity of the codes times the number of possible variations times the number of phone calls in one year." Sam Tisbury smiled. "We're talking about a pretty big number to crunch, Pop."

"Yes, but is there any such thing as a 'big' number anymore?"

"You may have a point there," the younger Tisbury

conceded. "But even so, and even if they could—which I still doubt—I can't imagine that the FBI would be willing to risk the public outrage that would ensue."

"No, I suppose not."

The old man seemed to lose himself in his thoughts for a long moment. Sam Tisbury waited patiently, solemnly aware that these periods of introspection, if that was what they were, had become more and more frequent over the past couple of years.

Thinking back, he realized that there had been a half dozen times in the past few months when he'd stopped by his father's office and had found the old man in a daze, staring vacantly at the identical family picture they both kept on their desks.

Tisbury tried to convince himself that it was simply the inevitable result of his father's growing old. He wanted to believe that. But he knew in his heart that there was more to it than just the simple passage of time; the Tisbury males traditionally enjoyed robust good health well into their nineties.

But none of them ever had to face the things we've had to face, Sam Tisbury reminded himself, and then wondered if that really was true.

"And speaking of public outrage . . ." Harold Tisbury said hesitantly, blinking as if suddenly becoming aware of his surroundings again.

It had become the central topic of both their lives over the past couple of years, Sam Tisbury thought. That and ICER. The two things that they really had in common, ever since the traumatic events that had led to his emotional divorce and his mother's tragic death.

"You mean Crucible?"

"Yes, how is it going?"

"We expect to have all the first two thousand beta units completed by Friday," Sam Tisbury said in a carefully neutral voice.

"Really? That soon? That means we can begin scheduling

the first tests by the end of this month.'' Harold Tisbury smiled.

Thank God, Sam Tisbury thought, realizing with a sense of relief that it was going to be a technical discussion. It was better that way, for both of them.

''Yes, I would certainly think so.''

''Wonderful. And what about the—uh—fuel situation? Have we experienced any subsequent problems in that area yet?''

''No, not yet. And as a matter of fact, I really don't think we will,'' Sam Tisbury said. ''Once the security concerns were addressed, all three parties viewed it as a win-win situation. We were fortunate, of course, to get all the permits for the research worked out with the previous administration. But even so, I'm not sure that anyone could have possibly predicted that the collapse of the Soviet Union would occur so quickly. Or with such a wonderfully ironic side benefit.''

''How many deliveries have we received so far?''

''Three.''

''How far will that get us?''

''Enough for the first series of tests. After that, if all goes as we expect, we'll either expand the program ourselves or license the technology to the Russians, however they wish to handle it. And it doesn't matter what they decide, because either way, both sides will win.''

''And in the process, the Tisburys will revolutionize the mining industry once again.'' Harold Tisbury smiled. ''And not just that. If those new thermostat units prove viable, the shale oil industry will become a completely new ball game. And that's just the start.''

''If the environmentalists don't drag us down into a tar pit of legal actions first.''

''They won't,'' Harold Tisbury said confidently. ''We just have to get organized again. And speaking of that, did you ever get a chance to explain the technical details to Jonathan?''

''I sent him the basic information last week. He's interested, certainly, but I think he's also looking for an excuse to hold back for a while. He understands our need to keep both Crucible and ICER moving forward. But all things considered, I think he'd much prefer that we all dig the foxholes deeper and then backfill with concrete. At least for another six months."

"But did he agree to consider the idea of a meeting?"

"Yes."

"Good. Now what was this business about Alfred?"

"Another one of Jonathan's rumors. This one had a pair of FBI agents snooping around Alfred's corporate headquarters."

Harold Tisbury froze in place.

"Did Jonathan follow up?" he asked carefully.

"He contacted Alfred by letter, using a bonded courier. Apparently Alfred didn't know anything about it. Claimed he hadn't even heard the rumor. But he sent a message back saying he'd check into it."

"When was that?"

"About two weeks ago."

"Did Alfred mention anything in his fax about the FBI contacting him? Anything at all?"

"No."

Harold Tisbury walked over to the fifteenth-floor penthouse window. He remained there, staring out at the panoramic view for almost a minute, until his son finally broke the silence.

"We keep coming back to the same question. Are we really doing the right thing by trying to get together again this soon?"

Harold Tisbury hesitated for another long moment before turning back to face his trusted business partner.

"Sam, the elections were an absolute disaster. We can't depend on what few connections we have in the new administration to keep things under control. If we continue to hide, stay down in our foxholes as Jonathan would put it, the tree huggers will simply move in with their shovels and bury us.

Besides, with Crucible about to come on line, what other choice do we have?''

"Disband the committee," Sam Tisbury replied evenly. "Destroy all the records. Everyone go their separate ways."

"And let them win?"

By "them," Harold Tisbury meant Greenpeace and Earth First! and all the other activist environmental groups that were determined to hold the major industrial groups accountable for all the environmental damage they had caused—and would continue to cause—in the name of progress and profit. The tree huggers. The people that Harold and Sam Tisbury and all their fellow industrialists feared more than anything else in the world.

"Better they should win an occasional battle than we should lose the war." ·

"I agree, but it shouldn't come to that."

Sam Tisbury was quiet for a long moment.

"Do you really think we can hold them all together?" he finally asked.

By "them," Sam Tisbury was now referring to five very wealthy and powerful industrialists who—because they viewed the activist "Green" groups as environmental terrorists—had joined together with Harold and Sam Tisbury three years earlier in a conspiracy to create the International Commission for Environmental Restoration.

Otherwise known as ICER.

Under the leadership of Harold and Sam Tisbury, and using the fiery emotional leadership of a beautiful young woman named Lisa Abercombie and a U.S. Department of Interior patsy named Reston Wolfe, the ICER group had assembled a lethal counterterrorist team. Twelve highly trained men and women—Germans, Japanese, and Americans—led by a fearless and maniacal killer named Gerd Maas—who possessed all the necessary combat, technical, and intelligence-gathering skills necessary to tear apart the environmental movement from within.

The committee had named their first mission Operation

Counter Wrench, as a fitting counterpoint to the environmental cult novel *The Monkey Wrench Gang*.

They had committed millions of their corporate dollars to the creation of an ultra-modern underground training center beneath Whitehorse Cabin in Yellowstone National Park, and used their political connections to staff the facility with the finest trainers the U.S. Military had to offer.

They had picked their targets with care.

And turned their fearsome team loose.

And they had lost.

In retrospect, all because of a single, thoughtless act of greed and arrogance on the part of their Department of Interior patsy. That and the incredible, unyielding dedication of six covert special agents from the U.S. Fish and Wildlife Service, who refused to be backed off from their investigation.

"Fucking Federal Government employees, for God's sake," one member of the committee had raged helplessly as the underlying cause of the Whitehorse Cabin disaster became known.

Harold Tisbury seemed to be mulling over his son's question in his mind.

"Yes," he finally said, "I do."

"I'm glad you feel that way, because from my perspective, it's going to take a miracle," Sam Tisbury said flatly.

"You know, Sam, in spite of our many differences, all of us on the committee are very much alike," Harold Tisbury said as he continued to stare out of the huge picture window. "We're aggressive, arrogant, manipulative, and suspicious. And accustomed to doing things our own way. It's no wonder we find it so difficult to work together."

"Much less to trust each other," Sam Tisbury added.

"Yes, there's that too."

"Which is exactly what I'm worried about."

"What, that one of the members will decide to strike out on his own? Go to the FBI?"

Sam Tisbury nodded solemnly. "Given the nature of the

potential charges involved, I think it's entirely possible, if not inevitable.''

Harold Tisbury sighed. "I'd like to believe that you're mistaken about that, Sam. I really would.''

"So would I, but what about Alfred?''

Harold Tisbury paused another long moment as he continued to stare out at the city lights in the distance, and the surrounding darkness.

"What about him?''

"Lisa's death affected him terribly. You know that.''

Harold Tisbury nodded, remembering the feverish sense of commitment in the dark, smoldering eyes of Lisa Abercombie. The woman who had provided the emotional leadership for Operation Counter Wrench. And the one who had willingly, almost eagerly, accepted the greatest risk of all. Oh, yes, he could understand Alfred Bloom's anguish all too well.

"But Alfred was the one who gave the order.''

"Only because we told him to,'' Sam Tisbury reminded.

"Yes, that's right,'' Harold Tisbury whispered almost to himself. "We did, didn't we?''

The elderly industrialist remembered the last meeting of the ICER Committee all too well. The impassive report presented by investigator Walter Crane that described, in chilling legalistic detail, the enormity of the committee's failure. And then, after Crane had departed with all his carefully organized files and slides, the emotional discussion that followed. The arguments. The accusations.

And then the unforgettable expression on Alfred Bloom's face when the vote was finally taken.

They had voted six to zero, with Bloom understandably abstaining, to cut all possible connections between the International Commission for Environmental Restoration and Operation Counter Wrench.

Cut them irrevocably, they told him, and do it now.

Alfred Bloom had stared down at the table as the verbal votes were cast. Then, without another word to anyone, he had picked up a phone and done exactly that.

"How is he holding up?"

Harold Tisbury asked the question for appearance's sake only, because he already knew exactly how Alfred Bloom was coping with the death of Lisa Abercombie.

Not well at all.

And then too, Harold Tisbury reminded himself, it wouldn't do to let his only son know that he'd gone out and hired his own personal team of private investigators to monitor the activities of his fellow conspirators, Sam Tisbury included. Especially when Harold Tisbury had every reason to suspect that his relatively youthful and aggressive offspring had done exactly the same thing. A thought that made the old man smile.

"He's drinking again." Sam Tisbury shrugged.

"Heavily?"

"Police have been called on at least three occasions in the past month."

"Has he said anything?"

Has he said anything important that might have been recorded in a police report? was what Harold Tisbury was asking, even though he already knew. Or at least he thought he did.

He had hired the best investigative agency available to tell him what his fellow conspirators were doing on an hourly basis, and he had hired a second group to analyze their reports. But Harold Tisbury had not risen to his exalted position in the industrial world by limiting his sources of information or taking them for granted. There was always something to be gained from listening to another point of view.

"No, not that we know of."

"We have copies of the reports?"

"Yes, of course."

Harold Tisbury closed his eyes and sighed.

"What about the others?" he finally asked.

Sam Tisbury clasped his hands behind his back as he considered his answer. "Nicholas wants to extract Maas, put together another team, and go forward immediately.''

"*Extract* Maas?"

"Those were his exact words."

"Incredible. Absolutely incredible."

"Don't forget," Sam Tisbury reminded, "Nicholas was the one who helped Wolfe recruit Maas in the first place. He probably feels a certain sense of responsibility."

"Or concern."

"Yes, that too."

"Take a man accused of murder, a man with a reputation like Maas, out of federal custody? How in the world does he propose to do that?" Harold Tisbury asked, a faint smile appearing on his aged face.

"I don't know. I didn't ask."

"Do you think he's serious?"

"I think Nicholas is very possibly the most serious man I've ever met in my entire life," Sam Tisbury replied evenly.

"But he's also unfailingly practical," Harold Tisbury reminded. "He can't help himself. It's his Teutonic upbringing."

"I know, and that's what concerns me the most." The younger Tisbury nodded. "If Nicholas is ready to discuss the idea at our meeting, then he probably has the whole thing worked out on a flow chart."

"God help us," the elder Tisbury rasped, shaking his head slowly.

"Wilbur continues to believe that we have gone too far," Sam Tisbury went on. "I would expect him to vote to disband the committee and then regroup at a much later date."

"Do you think he's afraid?"

"Wilbur afraid? About as much as a crusty old rattlesnake that's been backed into a corner," Sam Tisbury chuckled. "Wilbur's a poker player, Pop. He believes in cutting his losses, so he can come back and play another day."

"What about Jonathan?"

"Ultimately, I think Jonathan will support Nicholas, but only so far. He's just as cautious as Wilbur, but he has no illusions about the future of his enterprises, especially now that the tree huggers have a sympathetic ear in the White House. If anything, I would expect him to vote for some kind of distraction."

"Such as extracting Maas from federal custody?"

"Or arranging for an appropriate accident." Sam Tisbury shrugged.

"Against *Maas*?"

Sam Tisbury couldn't tell if his father was simply startled, intrigued, or—more likely—absolutely shaken by the idea.

"Of the three in custody, Maas is the only one who can link any of the committee members to Operation Counter Wrench," the younger Tisbury reminded.

"But he won't talk, will he?"

"As far as we're aware, Maas didn't speak two words to the authorities while he was in custody."

"But Nicholas wants to get him out anyway, just to make sure?"

"Nicholas would be the first one impacted if Maas *did* choose to talk. You can see his point."

"What about Sergio?"

"Difficult to say." Sam Tisbury shrugged.

"Your best guess?"

"If the vote is open, I would expect Sergio to pound his fist on the table and declare his support for Nicholas to the death. If we choose to vote in secret"—Sam Tisbury paused—"I think he will go with Wilbur."

Harold Tisbury nodded in a thoughtful manner and then hesitated for a moment before turning to face his youthful business partner and adviser. He had been trusting his son with the secrets and strategies of his rapidly expanding industrial empire for more than forty-two years. But Harold Tisbury had also learned long ago that survival was ultimately a very personal and very solitary affair.

Even a beloved son had to be watched occasionally.

"And what about you?" Harold Tisbury asked in a deliberately casual voice.

"You mean how will I vote?"

Harold Tisbury nodded, blinking his watery eyes. He was tired. It had been a long day and an even longer evening, and he wanted to go home. But he had to resolve this issue first. One way or the other.

"I've faced up to my demons a long time ago, Pop," Sam Tisbury said calmly. "God knows I don't necessarily agree with everything we've done. But as I've told you before, when it comes right down to it, I'll vote with you . . . to stay alive, to stay out of jail, and to win."

"By whatever means it takes?"

The expression in Sam Tisbury's eyes had turned cold and hard. "Of course. What other way is there?"

Harold Tisbury smiled. *That's my boy,* he thought. *Trained you well, didn't I?*

"Then we have nothing to worry about."

"Except for failure and fate and the courage of our friends."

"Yes, of course." Harold Tisbury sighed heavily, feeling his aged body giving way to the fatigue in spite of his determination. "Those must always be our primary concerns."

"Not to mention those four surviving wildlife agents, who could still cause us trouble if they continue to probe into the deaths of their friends," the younger Tisbury added. "Especially now that we're right on the brink of putting the Crucible project into the first phases."

"Yes, that's right, we never did come to an appropriate decision on those wildlife agents, did we?" the elder Tisbury mused.

"No, we didn't."

"Especially that one bastard." Harold Tisbury nodded, his eyes suddenly lighting up in spite of his fatigue. "What was his name?"

"You mean Lightstone?"

"Yes, that's the one." Harold Tisbury nodded, his deeply lined face darkening with barely suppressed rage. "Lightstone. Henry Lightstone. We can't forget him, can we?"

"No, we can't." Sam Tisbury shook his head slowly, his words taking on a hard edge as his eyes turned deadly cold. "There's a balance due on Special Agent Lightstone. And one way or another, it will be paid."

At that moment the phone on Sam Tisbury's desk rang. He listened briefly, hung up the phone, and then looked up at his father.

"That was Jonathan," he said. "He's in."

Chapter Five

They had been coming together more frequently now, although neither of them would have admitted that it had anything to do with a growing sense of their own mortality.

"Simply a pleasant way to pass the time," Ember growled deep in her throat, and her "Eagle" had been all too willing to agree.

Drifting pleasantly in the aftermath of his own orgasmic bliss, Leonard Harris found it easy to maintain a firm presence inside her as he continued to gently caress her muscular shoulders and her small firm breasts. Satiated and content, he waited for her shuddering to stop, gently running his fingers around the visible bruises on her right shoulder caused by the heavy recoil of the high-powered 30-06 rifle, as her breathing returned to normal.

She started to roll off of him, but he shook his head and held her tight, so she simply relaxed all the way, and then snuggled her mouth and chin in close against his hairy neck.

"Uhmm," she murmured. "That was nice."

Even though they'd made love like this hundreds of times, Harris was still amazed to discover that he could feel every one of her firmly toned leg, hip, abdominal, and chest muscles against his much softer body. He told himself that he truly loved the fiery activist for her devious mind, but he also knew that he was absolutely addicted to her sensuously lean and heated body. It was as if she had a fire burning within her that could not be extinguished, he thought, knowing that—in a way—it was absolutely true.

He waited a little while longer, until he too was completely relaxed, and then said:

"Crowley's dead."

He felt her stiffen.

"How?" she whispered.

"Riser killed him."

He could feel her swallow hard before she spoke again. "Are you sure?"

"Yes."

"Do you know why?" she asked quietly, keeping her head tucked firmly against his neck. Not wanting to know, but as the leader of Wildfire, unable to say so. Even to someone as trusted as Leonard Harris.

Harris sighed. "Riser killed Crowley because Eric sent him in to renegotiate the contract."

"Are you sure it was the contract?"

Harris nodded slowly. "Eric told Crowley to try to renegotiate the price down to four hundred thousand for each phase. Riser refused, and instead raised his price to six hundred."

"A hundred thousand *more*?"

"That's right."

"But that's over a—" she started to say, but he interrupted.

"Riser also said that there would be no more negotiations. Killing Crowley was his way of making that point."

She was silent for a long moment, and Harris simply remained still, feeling her heartbeat and her breathing grow steady again as she lay there on his chest.

"So what are we going to do about it?" she finally asked.

"Nothing."

"Nothing?" She brought her head up and stared into his eyes. "Why not?"

"Because there's nothing we *can* do," Harris said as he gently rolled her over to the bed. "If you hire a man like Riser to do a job, and he does it, then you pay him. You don't question his methods or his ethics. You just pay."

"And if we don't?" Her voice was cold and hard now. She couldn't stand to be told no. He knew that. But he also knew that he had to be firm. There was no other way.

"Then he'll hunt us down and destroy us. And in doing so, he will also destroy Wildfire."

It was that last part that jarred her.

"But how could he possibly know—" she started to demand, but Harris silenced her by placing two of his fingers gently against her swollen lips.

"For starters, he could have easily tortured Crowley before he killed him."

"But even if he did, what could Crowley tell him about us, or about Wildfire?" she protested. "He didn't *know* anything. That was the whole idea of using him for that purpose."

"Crowley could have given him Eric," Harris said. "And once he has Eric, he can get to us. It would just be a matter of time."

"So we're going to pay him? Six hundred thousand each?" Her voice was filled with disbelief.

"Yes, we have to."

But then she seemed to consider something.

"What if we delayed payment?"

"The contract stipulates, very clearly, that the money transfer is to occur within twenty-four hours of verification. There are no provisions for any delays."

"But that's something we *could* renegotiate if we—" she started to say, but Harris shook his head.

"Don't even *think* about it," he whispered.

"But six hundred thousand apiece. How can we *possibly* pay him within that time frame?"

"We have the funds," he said quietly.

She blinked and then realized what he was saying.

"All of it?"

Harris nodded.

"But that means . . ."

"Wildfire would have to be delayed." Harris nodded.

Ember looked stricken.

"For how long?" she whispered.

"Long enough for our fund-raising to replenish the accounts. At the rate we've been going, a few weeks at the most," he said softly. "We can live with that." He immediately regretted the words as soon as he spoke them, but she didn't seem to notice.

"But once we have control, the money issue would be completely irrelevant. We could even pay him a bonus."

"Eric is well positioned for what we need him to do, but fiscal control is something else entirely," Harris said. "You have to remember that federal investigators and auditors will be sifting through every file cabinet, every spreadsheet, every computer file, searching for clues and motives. And the media jackals will be doing their own sniffing and scratching—you can count on that too."

He paused and then said: "In the very best of circumstances, it will take months before all the legal questions are resolved . . . and we don't have *that* much time."

Ember was silent for another long moment. And then:

"There may be another way to avoid paying Riser," she whispered.

"You mean sacrifice Eric?"

She nodded, stone-faced, but he saw the flicker in her eyes.

"Riser would find us eventually," he said. "It might take him a little longer, but he would find us."

"Are you sure?"

"Yes, without question. He'd have to. That's how he maintains his reputation and his price. Besides," he reminded, "we still need Eric, both now and in the future if Wildfire is to continue. It would be nice if it . . . hadn't turned out that way, but it did, and we have to go forward from that point.''

She nodded, her eyes filled with a fermenting mixture of anger and frustration and sadness.

"Have you talked with him recently?'' he inquired, knowing that this too was a sensitive issue.

She nodded.

"How was he?''

"Not very happy,'' she said quietly.

"Do you think he's aware of our . . . relationship?''

"I think so,'' she whispered, staring down at the rumpled sheets.

Harris sighed. Jealousy was one more complication that they didn't need right now.

"He's immature,'' the baldish executive said. "He needs to understand that the two of you have—what?—grown apart.''

"I think he's just feeling lost, and probably lonely too,'' she said quietly.

"I thought he had started seeing someone.''

"He certainly tries to give that impression, but I don't think there's anything to it,'' she said. "Sometimes I think I should try to find someone for him.''

"How do you think he'd respond to something like that?''

"Not very well,'' she admitted.

"If nothing else, we know one thing for sure,'' Harris said with a slight smile. "He won't be lonely much longer.''

"No, I don't suppose he will. Not with all that money.''

"And speaking of money,'' Harris said, "I just spent some more on another present for you.''

"Oh, really? What did you get me?''

"Nothing much. Just a couple hundred rounds of .30-06 armor-piercing.''

"You found it?'' Her eyes lit up with anticipatory pleasure. "Where?''

"A friend.'' He shrugged.

"Is it here? Can I see it?''

"It's out in the car."

"I promised Eric that I'd take him out to the range today, let him fire the rifle," she whispered. "Do you think I could try some of it out, see how it kicks?"

"I think that would be a wonderful idea." Harris smiled. "Just make sure you have a decent backstop." And then: "I'm glad you're doing things with Eric. I think it helps to keep him busy."

Ember nodded in agreement. "He really seems proud of the fact that all the signs are finally up."

"Pride in ownership. And you have to admit, the sign idea was brilliant, even though having to do all the installations at night, with the heavier sound-deadening drills, has made the whole operation a lot more expensive than we figured, both in time and money."

"That's okay, it's going to be worth it," she said, her eyes suddenly gleaming again, childlike. "There's something else he told me."

"What's that?"

"The Crucible production is way ahead of schedule. He said they'll have two thousand units tested and ready to use by this Friday. Can you believe that?" she said in a raspy whisper. "Two thousand."

"Really?" Harris could see that she was starting to breathe more rapidly now, and it didn't take much imagination on his part to figure out what images she was seeing in her fevered mind.

The drop . . . and the wind . . . and the rapidly blossoming fire.

She started to run her hand down his chest.

"I don't want to wait," she whispered again.

"We have to."

"But we could do it ourselves," she said, "with the Cessna."

"What, *all* of them?" he chuckled.

"We rigged the drop racks to hold a hundred, so we could do the entire Yellowstone part in one trip, remember? A hundred at a time is only twenty trips.''

"But a trip is a thousand miles, with rest and refueling in between,'' he reminded.

"It would take us awhile, but we could do it and still be able to pay Riser . . . if they'll let you pick them up.''

"They will,'' he said confidently. "That's all been arranged. But what about you? Do you have the strength?''

"I have all the strength I need if I *want* to do something. You, of all people, should know that.''

"Yes, but—''

"I want to do it,'' she said insistently. "I *have* to do it. I can't wait much longer.''

"Yes, I know,'' he said, feeling a combination of sadness and elation as her hands became more active, "but what about Eric?''

He was trying to concentrate on the problem, because he knew it was important, but he knew he was lost because he had already allowed his right hand to drift across to the warmth of her silky thigh.

"Uhmm, that feels nice. Do we need to involve him?''

"For access to the storage units, yes, we would have to.'' Then, after a moment: "Do you have any idea if he'll be in town this weekend?''

"He said something about going fishing with his father down in the Bahamas,'' she said indifferently as she snuggled herself in closer. He could feel the heat that was starting to radiate from her entire body now.

"Oh, really?'' He was having to force himself to concentrate. "When?''

"I don't know,'' she murmured as she bit tentatively at his ear. "Sometime this weekend, Saturday, I think, or maybe it was Sunday. I can't . . .'' Then she paused in her handiwork to blink in sudden realization. "Wait a minute, do you think . . .''

"It's possible,'' Harris said,

"How possible?'' she demanded, her eyes widened.

"We know they've got to get together again sometime.

Why not this weekend?"

"It's starting to happen, right now, isn't it," she whispered against his ear.

Her dark eyes seemed to be glowing in the darkened room. He groaned as her teeth sank deep into his earlobe.

"Yes, I think so."

"Then we *have* to do it now. We *can't* wait."

"I need to get hold of Eric then, immediately," he said, even though he knew it was hopeless now. Both of them were too far gone.

"Later," she whispered in his tingling ear. "Can you take me up again, now?"

"Another falling ember in my talons?" he said as he brought his hands up under her breasts. Her nipples felt like two hot coals in his palms.

"Yesss, take me up and drop me," she hissed. "Make me see them. Make me see the flames."

Chapter Six

Dr. Kimberly Wildman found the first one by accident.

A field group leader for the Department of Interior's National Biological Survey, Wildman had been assigned the job of documenting the entire ecology and biodiversity of the northwest quadrant of the State of Wyoming. Her assigned survey area included the Shoshone and Bridger–Teton National Forests, the Wind River Indian Reservation, and the crown jewel of the Park Service: Yellowstone National Park.

It was an absolutely monumental task that was expected to take a minimum of eight to ten years.

For a staff, Wildman had a deputy group leader; twelve site teams, each comprised of one biologist and one field technician; one secretary, three clerks, two computer programmers, and a statistician under her command. Based upon supervisory duties alone, she could have easily spent the vast majority of her work hours in her spacious and comfortable Yellowstone Park headquarters office, churning out reams of data from this crucial first-phase survey site to keep dozens of Washington office statisticians and bureaucrats happy for years to come.

But Dr. Kimberly Wildman had been aggressively fighting the sexist attitude that "women can't pee in the woods" for the better part of her professional career. So when one of her biologists called in sick at eight o'clock that Tuesday morning, she didn't even hesitate.

Reaching under her desk, she pulled out the field kit that she kept packed for exactly this sort of opportunity, notified the deputy team leader that she could be reached by radio, if absolutely necessary, and then walked outside where the stranded field technician and the truck were waiting.

They were checking live traps, and searching for trap WYNWLT-1332 that had been torn loose from its mooring, when Dr. Wildman's metal-tipped hiking stick struck metal.

It took the two of them almost five minutes to clear away the brush, and there it was: a green camouflaged metal plate, attached to the base of a huge Douglas fir with a pair of large steel bolts.

"What is it?" the field technician asked.

"I have no idea," Dr. Kimberly Wildman replied.

"Think it's one of ours?"

"No, I can't imagine that it would be." Wildman shook her head as she ran her gloved hand across the smooth camouflaged surface, searching in vain for some kind of identification markings. Then she examined the oddly notched bolt heads. "But I can tell you one thing, whoever mounted it here certainly didn't want some hiker taking it away as a souvenir."

"The Park Service?"

"I suppose." The survey group leader nodded. "At least I can't think of anyone else in this area who would go to this much effort to attach a blank metal plate to a tree.''

Although Dr. Kimberly Wildman had no way of knowing it—because in spite of being sister agencies within the Department of Interior, communications between the National Park Service and the National Biological Survey were not *that* comprehensive or efficient—the metal looked very much like the etched metal signs that park rangers had been finding bolted to big redwood trees all over Sequoia National Park. But there were two significant differences:

Instead of being prominently displayed, like the ones in Sequoia, this metal plate was hidden. It was obvious that someone had gone to a lot of work to conceal it. And instead of bearing a deeply engraved message of questionable religious impact, this one—aside from its chemically etched green camouflage surface—was absolutely blank and smooth.

"Wait a minute," Dr. Kimberly Wildman said, looking skyward, "I think I see what's going on here."

"What's that?"

"There's an eagle nest in this tree."

"Really, where?"

"Step back over here and you can see it—a snag up at the top," the team leader said.

"Okay, got it," the field technician said. "So this must be some kind of Fish and Wildlife Service marker then."

"Looks like it."

"Too bad it doesn't have some kind of location identifier," he commented. "It would make a great reference point."

"Oh, I think it still can," Dr. Kimberly Wildman said as she reached into her pack and pulled out her portable computer. After calling up the appropriate program, she began to type:

METAL PLATE, BLANK, GREEN CAMOUFLAGE COATING,

She looked up at her assistant. "What do you have for dimensions?"

The field technician quickly moved in with a measuring tape. "Uh, make it eighteen by thirty by—uh—three-quarters."

Dr. Wildman went back to her typing:

METAL PLATE, BLANK, GREEN CAMOUFLAGE COATING, 18"×30"×3/4", ATTACHED TO DOUG FIR WITH TWO STEEL BOLTS WITH SECURITY CONFIGURED HEADS. IDENTIFIES BALD EAGLE NESTING TREE.

She looked down at the miniaturized global positioning satellite receiver hanging from her vest, typed the coordinates into the database, and then closed up the computer.

"Okay, we'll keep an eye on this tree. See if we can spot a nesting pair," she said. "Now let's get back to finding that cage."

Chapter Seven

Henry Lightstone's mind was clearly elsewhere, so Mike Takahara waited until the two of them were alone in their rented car and heading out of the Boston Police parking lot before he said, "So what's Rico going to do when he finds out you lied to him?" The tech agent referred to Detective Sergeant Rico Testano of the Boston Police Department, an old friend of Henry Lightstone's who had shown up just in time a few hours back in the warehouse Bravo Team was using for its storefront sting operation dealing illegal wholesale seafood here in Boston. Already, Bravo Team was on the verge of nailing Tony and Sal Boracatto and their wise-guy operation tracking in contraband seafood. On the verge, that is, if the Boracattos hadn't gotten word about the operation maybe being compromised.

"What, you mean those two guys in the alley?"

"Uh, yeah," the tech agent said hesitantly, realizing that he must have missed something.

"Built-in hazard of the job." Lightstone shrugged as he carefully maneuvered the rented automobile along the snow- and slush-covered road, all the while keeping his eye on the rear- and side-view mirrors. "In homicide people lie to you all the time. Suspects, victims, witnesses, it doesn't matter. You get used to it after a while."

"Fellow cops too?"

Lightstone smiled briefly.

"It's not exactly that we lie to each other," he said, concentrating his attention now on the side mirror. "What happens is that every now and then we hold back something. Especially if the information seems a little vague or contradictory or if it might mess up something we're working on ourselves. Things are usually confused enough in a homicide investigation as it is. No point in adding more complications to somebody else's job if you don't have to."

"Which doesn't exactly answer my question."

"No, I guess it doesn't," Lightstone agreed. "The answer is that Rico knows I'm holding something back on those two, and he more or less trusts me to tell him if there turns out to be a clear link to his case. Knowing Rico, I think he'll probably be pissed when he finds out all the details, no matter what. But he's a big boy. He'll get over it."

The traffic lights in the intersection up ahead were still green, and Lightstone let his foot up off the accelerator a bit. He didn't necessarily want to beat the light on this one.

Mike Takahara remained quiet for a moment, working his way back through the conversations of the past couple of hours. Rico had shown up at the warehouse when the Boston police responded to a distress signal from one of their own. The cop who sent the "officer needs help" call, along with his partner, had attempted to play the muscle while a Boston building inspector shook down Henry Lightstone and his team for alleged license violations. Things had turned nasty after one of the cops broke Thomas Woeshack's arm in two places with a chop from a nightstick. This triggered Dwight Stoner and Henry Lightstone into action. The building inspector and the two rogue cops ended up on their asses in need of medical attention, but not before the one cop managed to send the beeper signal that called in the cavalry. If Henry Lightstone hadn't known Testano from a homicide investigator's convention years ago when Henry was a detective for the San Diego PD, Bravo Team's covert operation, code-named Operation Fish Net, would have been blown.

Then, after Rico Testano called off the Boston Police, he took Henry and Mike to the Westin Hotel on Huntington Avenue just off the Commons to eyeball firsthand a bizarre triple murder scene. A young couple, yuppie lawyers, had been killed in their room. Then the killer had cut through the closet wall of their room into the closet of the adjoining room where a young man in his twenties had been shot to death at close range. The only clues in the young man's room were the height of the man-sized hole in the closet, and a ripped-out connector cord from a computer modem. Then, to top it all off, Rico had mentioned the brutal bludgeoning deaths of two apparent muggers—one of whom looked like he had been slashed first by the multiple blades of a chainsaw chain—right nearby in an alley just off the Common.

Now, in sudden realization, Takahara said, "It was the kid, wasn't it? You held something back on him too."

Lightstone nodded slowly, and then smiled in satisfaction as the lights up ahead switched to yellow. "Rico was right, you've got a real sharp analytical mind. Probably make one hell of a homicide investigator, if all the shit that goes with it didn't drive you crazy first."

"My dad was an FBI agent," Mike Takahara said conversationally. "Retired a couple years back. When I was a kid and he'd come home late, he and I would stay up late working those brain-teaser puzzles he'd picked up on his trips. Used to drive my mom crazy.'' The tech agent smiled. "He'd tell me about some of the things he and his partners did at the scenes. Tried to get me interested in forensics and the crime scene work, but I never thought I'd be able to handle the bodies and blood and all that stuff. Thing is, I didn't even like cutting up those frogs in biology class. Too damned messy.''

"As I recall, that sort of thing didn't seem to bother you much when we were going thorough your house counting bodies a few months back,'' Lightstone commented, letting his foot up off the gas a little more as he silently counted off the seconds.

Then, just as the light turned red, he powered the small vehicle into a controlled right-hand turn.

"Hey, when somebody smacks you across the head, hangs you on a pipe, and then starts cutting people up right in front of you, it's real easy to develop a whole new perspective on blood and bodies,'' the tech agent replied. "Far as I'm concerned right now, as long as neither one of them are mine, they don't bother me at all. But I didn't have that perspective back then, so I went into computers instead. Figured I . . . hey, wait a minute, this isn't . . .'' Takahara started to say.

But then he caught himself, shook his head in embarrassment, and began watching his own side mirror as Lightstone continued to accelerate the sedan up the slush-covered road.

A dark gray van was signaling for a right-hand turn at the intersection they had just left. But then the driver seemed to hesitate before coming to a complete stop. When the light changed, the van went straight on through the intersection.

"What do you think?'' Lightstone asked, slowing down as the two agents watched the van disappear from their side mirrors.

"Looked like a good possible to me. Where was it?''

"Parked across the street from the police station. Driver made a quick U-turn after we turned right out of the parking lot, then stayed back in the left-hand lane. Local plates. You get anything on it?''

"Late model Dodge minivan. Dark color. Tinted side windows. Nobody in the passenger seat.''

"What about the driver?''

"Nothing useful,'' the tech agent said. "He might have been looking our way when he went through the intersection. Couldn't tell.''

"Are you sure it was a he?''

"No, not really. Fact is, I don't think I could say either way. Why, is it important?''

"No, probably not. Just getting jumpy in my old age,'' Lightstone said as he continued on up the road in a direction away from their safe house residence.

"Or maybe just a little paranoid?'' The tech agent grinned.

"Same thing. You feel like taking the long way home?''

"Yeah, sure. Nice night for a drive,'' Takahara said, staring out at the slush-filled roadway as the windshield wipers swept slowly back and forth, trying to keep up with the rapidly falling snow.

They drove in silence, both men watching their side mirrors and the intersections ahead, before Takahara finally said, "So what was the deal on the kid?''

"I saw him out in the park earlier this evening, hanging around that Soldiers and Sailors statue, when I was trying to isolate that tag team,'' Lightstone said. "Acted like he was waiting for somebody. Standing out there in the wind and snow, freezing to death, and looking like he was half scared out of his mind.''

"With good reason, as it turned out.''

"Yeah, apparently.'' Lightstone nodded. "Funny thing is, though, when I first saw him, I was kind of bent over, trying to stay out of the wind. At first, he acted like he thought I was the person he was looking for. Or at least until I straightened up a little bit. Then he knew I wasn't.''

"Was he close enough to see your face?''

Lightstone thought for a moment, replaying the scene in his mind. "When he first reacted? No, not really. Besides, it was getting dark and I had a watch cap on and the hood up on my jacket."

"Maybe he figured it out when he realized you weren't tall enough," the tech agent suggested, referring to the height of the closet cut-out.

"Yeah, that's what I was thinking too."

Both agents were silent for a few moments.

"So what about those two guys who were tagging you?" Mike Takahara asked.

"What about them?"

"The way you described the whole deal, they had to be focused on you from the start. No reason in the world a couple of muggers would focus in on a healthy male when they had all those women and kids and old folks hurrying around, trying to get home, to choose from."

"Sounds reasonable." Lightstone nodded agreeably. "What else?"

"Well, from the sound of it, these guys were a couple of experienced trackers who, somehow, managed to screw up three times in a row. First of all, by letting you spot their tail, which was probably bad luck on their part as much as anything else."

"Agreed," Lightstone said.

"Secondly, by letting you lead them into that blind alley, and then turning it around, which I gather was their fault all the way, because two experienced guys with guns should have had you. And finally, by running back out of the alley and right into our reverse tag."

"Okay, so?"

"So maybe somebody monitoring the whole deal didn't like what he saw and got pissed. Somebody big enough or strong enough to break the necks of two muscle guys without making any noise in the process. Maybe a guy about seven feet tall who likes to scare the shit out of people, and go through walls to kill them, but doesn't know much about computers?''

"There's one little problem in your logic," Lightstone said as he continued to drive slowly and carefully through falling snow.

Mike Takahara remained quiet and thoughtful for almost two minutes.

"The only problem I can think of," he finally said, "is that it all adds up to a hell of a lot of coincidences for one evening, unless . . .''

"Yeah?" Lightstone glanced over at his tech agent partner.

"Unless the big guy, or somebody running him, is focused on us?''

"That's the problem." Henry Lightstone nodded.

"Yeah, but what the hell kind of sense does that make?'' Mike Takahara demanded. "I mean, what possible connection do we have with a pair of yuppie lawyers on vacation, a kid with a computer who hangs around statues pissing in his pants, and a couple of idiots who can't even get a mugging right?''

"I don't know. None of it makes much sense when you get right down to it," Lightstone admitted.

Mike Takahara suddenly realized that they were back in the general area of their covert warehouse operation.

"We going back to work?''

Lightstone shook his head. "No, just thought I'd cruise through the neighborhood once more before we head home. See if we pick up any more interest.''

They drove down the street in front of the warehouse. Lightstone was concentrating on the mirrors and the poorly illuminated street and the intersecting alleys that were even darker. So it was Takahara who first noticed that the light over the entrance of the warehouse had been broken.

"Looks like those damn kids have been at it again with the rocks," he commented. "Remind me to go pick up a couple more bulbs tomorrow morning.''

Then, as they came closer to the warehouse, the tech agent spotted a brief flicker of light reflected off the inside of the small window mounted in the entry door.

"Looks like Paxton and Stoner are still here. Halahan must not have made the flight after all."

Lightstone looked over at the darkened alley and the warehouse doorway, then back down the street. "You sure they're in there? Looks awful dark to me. Besides, I don't see the car anywhere around here."

"Yeah, pretty sure. I saw a little flash of light through the window. Figure they're probably in the back office finishing up the reports and wondering where we are."

Lightstone glanced down at his wristwatch. "You know, it's getting kinda late to be working. And if we go in there, Larry's going to want our reports. Why don't you give them a call on the radio, see if they want to go get something to eat. It's been a long time since lunch."

"Yeah, no kidding," the tech agent said. He reached under the seat for the concealed radio mike.

"Bravo Four to Bravo One or Three."

There was a delay of approximately five or six seconds before the raspy response came back over the speaker that Takahara had concealed in the dashboard of the rental car.

"Bravo One, go."

"Hey, Larry, Henry and I are getting hungry. You guys ready to take a break?"

"Sounds good to me. Where do you want to go?"

"Probably not much open this time of night," Mike Takahara said. "How about Denny's?"

"Sure. Where are you at?"

"Right outside the warehouse."

"Ten-four, we're en route from the airport. Be there in five."

In the second or two that it took Technical Agent Mike Takahara to process Paxton's comment through his mental computers and get back on the radio, Henry Lightstone had already taken his foot off the accelerator and was reaching forward to shut off the car headlights.

"Bravo One, Bravo Four, who'd you leave in the warehouse?"

The engine of the mid-sized sedan was running on idle now, but the car's forward momentum kept it rolling down the darkened street. In the relative silence Mike Takahara could hear the crunch of the freshly fallen snow being compressed by the wide tires.

"Nobody," Paxton replied. "Woeshack's still at the hospital. Stoner and I are enroute with Halahan."

"Did you guys remember to set the alarms before you left?"

"What? Yeah, I'm sure we did because I was the one who set them. What's going on out there?"

Ignoring Paxton's question, Takahara set the radio mike aside, quickly reached down under the seat, and pulled out a small receiver. The top row of lights were all showing a steady bright green. The tech agent muttered an obscenity.

"What's the matter?" Lightstone demanded.

"Somebody shut off the alarms to the warehouse, and it wasn't any of us," Takahara replied as he slipped the receiver back under the seat and picked up the radio mike again. "And I think whoever did it is still in there."

The expression on Henry Lightstone's face turned deadly cold.

Before Takahara could say anything, Lightstone swerved the sedan over to the curb, braked to a stop, and set the transmission into park. Then he was out of the car and running toward the front of the warehouse.

"Bravo Four, Bravo One, what's going on out there?" Larry Paxton repeated.

"We may have somebody in the warehouse," Mike Takahara said. "I saw a flash of light about thirty seconds ago when we were driving by. The receiver's showing all the alarms are off, and no indication that they were tripped first."

"How the hell did that happen?" Paxton demanded.

"I don't know. Whoever's in there either has the codes or—"

"Where's Henry?" Paxton interrupted.

Takahara looked out through the driver's side window. In the almost total darkness in front of the warehouse, he could just barely make out the familiar crouched figure. "He's at the door."

"Tell him to hold back until we get there," Paxton ordered.

"Ten-four. I'll . . . uh—oh, too late, he's already in," Takahara said, watching helplessly as the covert team's mercurial wild-card agent disappeared through the small entrance door.

Larry Paxton cursed over the air waves, causing the tech agent to be grateful that the team now had scrambled radios and would thus be spared another bureaucratic reprimand from the FCC.

"What's your ETA?" Mike Takahara asked, his eyes scanning the streets, watching for any sign that the intruder had some kind of support or backup waiting outside. He couldn't see anybody, but that didn't necessarily mean anything.

"At least five."

"Okay," the tech agent said. "Try to make it less if you can. I'm going in there to back him up."

For a long moment Mike Takahara thought that Paxton was going to order him to stay back. But then he finally heard the double-click acknowledgment over the radio. Sighing to himself, Takahara pulled the 10mm Smith & Wesson semiautomatic out of his shoulder holster, stepped out of the car, gently shut the door, and then started across the street.

Henry Lightstone had quietly slid his key into the oiled door lock and turned it slowly counterclockwise until it came to a solid stop. After hesitating a brief moment to listen for the sound of footsteps, he crouched down, shoved the door open, dove in to the concrete floor, and rolled to his left.

He waited there on the floor with the 10mm double-action pistol outstretched in both hands until the door closed silently on its carefully oiled hinges, returning the interior of the warehouse to a state of almost total darkness. Then, at the instant the door clicked shut, he twisted back to the right and extended the lethal handgun out again, ready to trigger three rounds at the first sign of a muzzle flash.

No lights.

No muzzle flashes.

Nothing.

Smiling with feral satisfaction, Lightstone came up to his feet and began to move quietly around to the right in the all-too-familiar warehouse. He was listening carefully now, alert for any sound that might give him a clue as to the intruder's location, movements, and intentions.

Lightstone was prepared to shoot and kill instantly, if it came to that. But what he really wanted was to physically get his hands on the intruder. To move in, make the contact, absorb or deflect the first blows, and then take him down. Preferably with a control hold, or with a hand or foot strike if necessary. Whatever it took to bring him—or them—out into the open.

Aggressive and self-assured by nature, Henry Lightstone was perfectly willing to face down any man, woman, or creature under almost any conditions, confident in his own ability to fight, adapt, and survive. But he also knew that he was just as vulnerable as anyone else to the incapacitating fear of the unknown.

There is nothing more dangerous to you than your own imagination, his Okinawan instructor had warned. *Allow your imagination to go out of control and you will assuredly defeat yourself before the battle is ever joined.* Lightstone knew that to be especially true of himself, which was why he sought out the confrontation. Before the image of some menacing entity, drifting out there in the darkness, became a distracting handicap . . . or an incapacitating obsession.

He was barricaded against the back of one of the stand-alone walk-in freezers, less than twenty feet away from the master bank of light switches, and timing his movements to coincide with the muted sounds of the thickly insulated compressors kicking in and out, when he heard an almost inaudible click.

He froze immediately, barely breathing, as he concentrated on the sound, trying to determine the crucial elements: the source, the distance, and the direction.

Come on, go for it, he thought to himself, trying to will the intruder to move forward. To make another sound. So that he could put away the pistol and use his hands. Make the threatening illusion real.

But he couldn't see anything, and the only sounds he could hear were the cycling compressors, so he didn't dare move. Didn't dare step away from the protective wall of the freezer and expose himself to a single shot or a lethal barrage, because he would never know it was coming until he was hit.

It had come down to a matter of technology, and it was frustrating Henry Lightstone out of his mind because he couldn't do anything about it. It stood to reason that an intruder who possessed the technical capability to sneak past one of Mike Takahara's computer-monitored alarm systems would almost certainly have come equipped with night-vision gear. And if that was the case, Lightstone knew, he wouldn't stand a chance because he'd never be allowed to get close.

He was considering the extremely dangerous idea of creating his own light—by firing a 10mm round in the general direction of the office structure, and then trying to spot the figure and get off a second round in time without catching a bullet or blinding himself in the process—when he heard another sound. This one . . . where? . . . in the general direction of the small entry door. Metallic sound. Key.

Backup.

Okay, Snoopy, Lightstone thought. *Just like they taught*

you at Basic. Slow and easy with the door. Then move in as fast as you can. Right or left, it doesn't matter, just as long as you hit the floor and roll.

Lightstone had watched Mike Takahara go through the simulated exercises at the training academy several times, so he knew that the tech agent was slow on his entries. Going in by himself, against an instructor armed with a paint-pellet gun, Takahara had caught paint every time.

But you're not coming in by yourself this time, buddy, Lightstone thought as he adjusted his double-handed grip on the stainless steel Smith & Wesson pistol, reflexively brushing his thumb against the safety to verify once more that it was in the off position.

It was going to be up to the intruder. He'd either react to Mike Takahara's entry—in which case Lightstone intended to put ten of the hard-hitting 10mm rounds in the direction of the sight or sound, correcting his aim from the muzzle flashes—or he wouldn't, in which case Lightstone was going to go for the light switches in the hope that the covert team's amiable tech agent would be faster with his gun than with his feet.

Lightstone heard the door begin to slide open, and he started to come around the protective wall of the freezer with the Smith & Wesson semiautomatic coming up in both hands—when the entire warehouse seemed to erupt in an explosion of light and sound that sent Henry Lightstone stumbling backward.

Partially blinded by the sudden flash, Lightstone rolled behind the freezer. Then he twisted back around on the concrete floor with the Smith & Wesson out again, searching desperately for a target. But even as he did so, some part of his stunned brain was trying to identify the source of the familiar blaring sound that was echoing throughout the warehouse, making it impossible to hear anything over the . . . what?

Burglar alarm?

Moments later the two agents made a high/low entry

through the concealed emergency access door to the hidden surveillance room and confirmed something that, by now, they already suspected: namely, that the office, the walk-in freezers, and all the concealed operational areas in the warehouse were empty.

Whoever had disabled Mike Takahara's sophisticated alarm system and had been moving about the warehouse with a small pen light when the two agents happened to drive by, was long gone.

Chapter Eight

Branch Chief David Halahan, the supervisory special agent in charge of the U.S. Fish and Wildlife Service's Division of Law Enforcement, Special Operations Branch, sat by the door with his forearms draped across the back of an ancient office chair and glared at his agents.

To Halahan's right, Special Agent Freddy Moore, the recently appointed deputy chief for Special Ops, sat in a similar chair, wearing a perplexed expression on his normally congenial face.

At the opposite end of the small warehouse office, Larry Paxton, Dwight Stoner, and Henry Lightstone sat on wooden crates and glared back at Halahan.

The only person who seemed oblivious to the growing tension in the room was Mike Takahara. And that was only because the tech agent was completely focused on the task of running a series of diagnostics programs through the hard drive memory of the covert team's desktop computer in an attempt to figure out how somebody had managed to bypass and subvert his entire security system.

Lightstone had just finished describing the entire sequence of events from his point of view, starting from the moment he had spotted the surveillance and ending at the point when Mike Takahara had come in through the warehouse doorway and set off his own somehow reactivated alarm system. Larry Paxton was getting ready to say something else, but Halahan waved him off.

The man responsible for all three of the Fish and Wildlife Service's covert investigation teams was not happy. And neither were his Bravo Team agents.

"You guys," he began, "spent three months setting up this operation. All together, we've laid out almost fifty thousand dollars of Special Ops funds to lease a warehouse and a safe house, buy freezers, rent trucks, and establish your covers.

"Yesterday, the day before, whatever the hell day it is now, you open for business. And within what, twenty-four hours"—Halahan began to count off on his fingers—"you pick up a tail, both of whom are found dead less than an hour later; assault three city employees; create a hostage rescue scene; blow your covers; transport one of your agents to the local hospital; go out to a local crime scene with a Boston police homicide investigator, and otherwise manage to link yourselves to the deaths of five individuals, all of whom are being investigated as homicides.

"And then, to top it all off," Halahan went on, "you manage to reattract the attention of that very same homicide investigator, not to mention three more patrol units and five private security officers—and in doing so, I might add, almost certainly destroy any possibility of maintaining your covers *and* your operation—by tripping across your own alarm system at eleven-fifteen in the goddamned evening and waking up the whole goddamned neighborhood!

"Do any of you," Halahan finished, after pausing to look around at each of the four agents, "have any idea what the term *covert* means?"

As it turned out, Mike Takahara *was* paying at least some attention to the general flow of conversation.

"Our alarms are not linked to Ajax Security Systems," the tech agent muttered through clenched teeth as he kept his eyes fixed on the lines of data flowing across the monitor screen.

"Oh, is that so?" Halahan said. "Then how do you explain the fact that *their* computer log shows a break-in alarm at exactly twenty-three sixteen hours this evening, which originated from this address?"

"This building was hard-wired into an Ajax Security Systems trunk line when we rented it," Takahara explained, still staring at his computer monitor. "So we know we're in their data banks. We left it that way because Ajax Security is located here in the complex, everyone else in the complex uses them—mostly because they're cheap—and it would have looked suspicious as hell if we told them we were going with somebody else, and then didn't.

"But," the tech agent said as he turned around in the chair to face Halahan directly, "I also happen to know that our sensors are *not* hooked into the Ajax alarm board any longer, because I personally altered the wiring and reprogrammed the whole system about two months ago. I changed it so that all the intrusion alarms, freezer temperatures, the whole bit, would show up on their board as active, but the alarms would only ring at the safe house, and at the portable receivers we have in the two cars. Furthermore, I personally hard-wired every one of the sensors in this warehouse directly to this computer, which I programmed to dial specific phone numbers and send specific messages, depending upon which sensor was tripped."

"So who called Ajax Security?" Halahan demanded.

Takahara took in and then released a deep breath. "According to their readouts and the records of the phone company, this computer."

"And just how the hell did *that* happen?"

"I don't know."

"Can you replicate the sequence?"

"No."

Special Ops Branch Chief David Halahan shook his head slowly in disgust.

"So basically what you're telling me is that a little less than two hours ago that computer right there, without having been programmed to do so, dialed the phone number of Ajax Security Systems and yelled help, but now it can't?"

"No, what I'm basically telling you is that I've looked through an entire three hundred and twelve megabyte hard drive. And I can tell you right now that there isn't a single goddamned program in this computer that has the phone number of Ajax Security Systems as a piece of data, or has the coding necessary to make the goddamned dial connections and access their alarm board," Mike Takahara retorted hotly.

"Then how is it possible that it did so?"

"The only way it could happen," the tech agent said after a moment, "would be if someone added a program to this computer that included an instruction to erase itself after completing all other instructions, and go back to the original programming."

"But wouldn't that someone have to have access to the computer to do something like that?"

"Normally, yes."

"And shouldn't you be able to tell if someone *did* have access to that computer?"

Takahara nodded sullenly.

"But I take it there's nothing in any of your records or databases or whatever it is you call them that tells you somebody did that, is there?"

"No." The tech agent spoke the word as though it had to be dragged out of his throat.

"So tell me, guys, just what is it that I'm supposed to believe about all this?" Halahan asked in a deliberately calm and controlled voice.

"That somebody is fucking around with us," Henry Lightstone responded in a furious voice.

"Oh, really?" Halahan actually smiled briefly, for the first time that evening, as he turned in his chair to face the ex-police homicide officer turned wildlife special agent that

Paul McNulty had talked him into hiring. The special agent whose official performance evaluation included the words "wild-card," and "loose cannon," and "difficult to control," along with two meritorious service commendations and a fairly extensive but ultimately supportive shooting board evaluation.

The interesting part was that all this had transpired during a federal law enforcement career of less than eleven months. Even Halahan had to admit to being impressed.

"For your information, Special Agent Lightstone," the chief of special operations went on, "Lisa Abercombie and Dr. Reston Wolfe are dead. Gerd Maas, Roy Parker, and Alex Chareaux are in prison awaiting trial. Chareaux's brothers and the rest of the Operation Counter Wrench counterterrorist team are dead. There is nobody left of that entire operation that we know about. And that is also, I might add, the only significant case that you've worked in the short time you've been employed by this agency.

"So tell me, Henry," Halahan went on, his voice and his eyes taking on a cold, hard edge, "just who the hell do you think is fucking with you?"

"I don't know," Lightstone snapped, his dark eyes glittering with rage.

"Halahan, if we knew who it was, we wouldn't be sitting here jaw-boning—we'd be out getting a search warrant and taking down a door," Larry Paxton interrupted sharply before the most volatile agent on his team could come up out of his chair and go right into their branch chief's face. Paxton knew that he was still on probation as the new ASAC and acting supervisor of Bravo Team, and he also knew that he was treading right on the edge of insubordination. But at this particular point in his career he really didn't care.

Of all those present, only Freddy Moore and Dwight Stoner—the huge ex-offensive tackle for the Oakland Raiders—appeared to be calm and controlled. But Halahan knew Stoner all too well, and he recognized the expression on the huge agent's normally impassive face. By Halahan's estimate, Stoner was probably within thirty seconds or so of getting up and reaching for a fistful of bureaucratic shirt and tie with one of his incredibly strong hands.

Halahan decided that he had pushed things far enough for his purposes.

"Okay," he said, glancing down at his watch, "it's almost one in the morning, and it's obvious that we aren't going to get anywhere with this line of reasoning tonight. So where do we go from here?"

"First of all, we've got to shut this operation down," Paxton said. "Anybody in the business who hasn't figured out what we're doing here by now has got to be deaf, blind, *and* dumb." He said it without the slightest trace of hesitation, even though he knew that the blown operation would go into his personnel file as his first significant "accomplishment" as a covert team supervisor.

"Anyone want to argue that?" Halahan asked.

Henry Lightstone and Dwight Stoner shook their heads. Mike Takahara had already gone back to his utility programs and simply shrugged indifferently.

"The problem is," Halahan said, "we haven't got anything else set up to work right now. So what do we do with you guys?"

"Don't forget, they've got that rescheduled hearing coming up Thursday," Moore reminded. "Lightstone should be testifying next, with Stoner on deck."

"Right." Halahan nodded. "But after that's over, we got to get Bravo Team back on a project. Any ideas?"

"We could give the Asian medicinal market another try," Paxton suggested, visibly calming down now. "Mike looks the part, and he can speak Japanese."

"And one of the new trainee agents, Lenny Pak, is Korean," Moore added. "We're going to have to add another agent to the team anyway. We might be able to get him reassigned."

"Lenny's only halfway through his initial training assignment, but we could give it a try." Halahan nodded. "But we're still talking about a hell of a long time period to work ourselves in, especially in that area. Anything else?''

"We've heard talk about some movement in the elephant ivory trade,'' Lightstone said, following Larry Paxton's lead and forcing himself to calm down. "People are getting anxious to deal out all those buried tusks they've been holding on to while there's still a market. But I don't know how we'd work our way in on that one either. Probably take some international connections that we don't have right now.''

Halahan nodded once more. "Well—''

"Then again,'' Mike Takahara interrupted as he turned away from his computer again to face his fellow agents, "we could always do what we were talking about last week. Focus in on a couple of those live animal smugglers working out of the Bahamas, see what we can turn up.''

Paxton, Lightstone, and Stoner all blinked, but none of them responded. The tech agent turned back to face Halahan.

"This one might actually be doable right now,'' he said. "We know a few of the major players by name, we know some of the dealers they work with, and we've got a dependable contact who claims he could get us in. Better yet, we've even got a ready-made cover for the whole team.''

"What's that?'' Halahan asked.

"Charter fishing crew. Remember Henry's ex-homicide partner from San Diego, Bobby LaGrange?'' Takahara asked, gesturing with his head back at Lightstone. "The guy who got put in the hospital by Kleinfelter and his biker buddies?''

Halahan nodded silently.

"Well, what we heard is that LaGrange managed to wrangle some kind of sports fishing boat out of his lawsuit with Kleinfelter. He retired out on a medical, moved the whole family out to Fort Lauderdale, and he's setting the boat up for charters right now. All we'd have to do is hire on as his crew, learn the ropes, start to meet people, and eventually start our own 'illegal' operation on the side, once we managed to weasel a boat out of the Coast Guard.''

"The Coast Guard's going to give us one of their boats to use in a sting operation?'' Lightstone asked, finding it difficult to follow the conversation, mostly because he didn't have the slightest idea what Mike Takahara was talking about.

"Drug seizures.'' The tech agent shrugged. "The Coast Guard's got boats down there rusting away by the hundreds. Can't get rid of them. We put our minds to it, we ought to be able to work out a deal that would sound believable to the locals.''

Halahan looked around at the rest of the agent team. "What do the rest of you guys think?''

"With the contacts we've already got, it probably wouldn't take us long to set the operation up,'' Paxton conceded. "Henry would have to contact LaGrange, see if he'd be willing to take us on.''

"Bobby'll go for it, no problem.'' Lightstone shrugged.

"Given a choice, Miami in the winter ought to be a whole lot nicer than Boston, especially if you're still planning on keeping an eye on us,'' Stoner added with a meaningful scowl.

"Okay, I'm convinced,'' Halahan said as he stood up. "You guys get some sleep, then put a few details together on paper, get it to me, and I'll run it through the Washington office for approvals. And while I'm doing that, you guys get this operation cleaned up, and then get down to those hearings before anything else around here goes wrong.''

Deputy Special Operations Chief Freddy Moore waited until Paxton and Lightstone had dropped them off at their hotel and he and his new boss were alone in their room, before asking the obvious question.

"Okay, I give up,'' Moore said as he tossed his suitcase down on one of the double beds and then sat down heavily in one of the minimally stuffed chairs. "What the hell was that all about?''

"Which part?" David Halahan asked with a tired smile as he set his own suitcase down on the floor and then took the other chair.

"The whole deal. I don't think I've ever seen or heard that much bullshit being shoveled back and forth in one room since I got my first assignment to the Washington office."

"It's an interesting situation." Halahan nodded. "First of all, in case I didn't mention it, those are good agents. Smart, aggressive, self-motivated, and hardworking. All things considered, we probably couldn't ask for a better covert team."

"Oh, really? You'd never know it, the way you were ripping every one of them a new asshole back there," the special ops deputy chief pointed out.

"There was a purpose to that little exercise," Halahan said. "They got shook up pretty bad on that alarm fiasco. I wanted to get them mad and get them thinking, see how they'd react. Make sure they hadn't lost their confidence in themselves and each other."

"You did a good job on that part," Moore said. "For a minute there I thought the big guy, Stoner, was going to come up out of that chair and go after you."

"That was my mistake," Halahan admitted. "Paxton and Lightstone are easy. They rise to the bait like a couple of starved bass, which is probably a good thing, because they get all that emotion out of their systems fast. I was focusing in on Takahara, trying to break down that goddamned armor-plated computer chip he's got for a brain, and I forgot about Stoner."

"He doesn't strike me as somebody you'd want to overlook very often."

"He's not." Halahan nodded. "Stoner's got a high tolerance level for bullshit, and he'll let a lot of stuff go by before he blows. But he's also about as protective as a mother grizzly, especially where those three agents are concerned. You'll want to remember that."

"What's the story on him?" Moore asked. "I thought he

was supposed to be slated for a medical retirement.''

"He was, and probably still should be," Halahan said. "He's a damn good agent, but he came into the program with bad knees. Tore them up pretty bad playing pro ball. He managed to pass our physical, but running that mile and a half every year for qualification has been a rough deal. And that was before that asshole Maas put a couple of .22 rounds in his kneecaps out at that Whitehorse raid.''

"Yeah, I heard about that. Didn't he have to go through some kind of replacement surgery?''

Halahan nodded. "Complete knee joint replacement, titanium implants, both knees. The operations were successful, and he went through rehab fine. But he's so damn big, the medical review board examiners were afraid he'd tear the implants loose if he did anything overly active.''

"So what was the deal on his physical? I heard something about Lightstone creating some kind of flack, and that the association was all ready to get involved.''

"It was a goddamned mess," Halahan said. "The review board advised Stoner to take a medical retirement, but he refused, which meant they had to disqualify him on a physical. Lightstone and Paxton got shot up on that Whitehorse raid too, so the board decided to make the whole team go through a requalification physical. Probably figured it'd look more evenhanded that way.''

"Yeah, right." Moore snorted.

"Anyway," Halahan went on, "I guess they poked and prodded him like a goddamned experimental monkey, most of the time right there in front of his partners, which pissed them off right from the start. Made him run the mile and a half on the treadmill twice, even though he qualified the first time and had to ice-pack his knees to get the swelling down before he could continue the exam. They were going to make him run it a third time, but Paxton and Lightstone got right in their faces and threatened to file a grievance with the association. In the meantime, while those two were busy throwing a shit-fit, the new guy, Woeshack, got on the phone to some high-ranking Eskimo relative of his who works in Interior and started claiming that he was being discriminated against as a Native American because he hadn't gotten to run the test twice like the big white guys did. Between trying to deal with Paxton and Lightstone and Woeshack, the doctors forgot about Takahara, which gave him plenty of time to play with—and then accidentally erase—the software program in the treadmill. And somewhere in the middle of all that, Lightstone started making comments about breaking somebody else's kneecaps for forensic comparison purposes if they didn't hurry up and get the exam over with pretty damn quick.''

"Otherwise known as the tag-team buddy system." Moore smiled appreciatively.

"Like I said, they watch out for each other." Halahan nodded. "Anyway, the doctors apparently decided to stick with the treadmill data they had and go on to the strength tests. Which turned out to be a mistake on their part, because Stoner maxed out every machine they had, including the leg lifts and deep-knee bends. He even managed to pass the agility drills with a halfway decent score, but you know how those medical review board guys are."

"CYA, all the way," Moore commented sarcastically.

"That's about it. They went into conference, took one more look at the data, and apparently came to the conclusion that they'd be held responsible if anything went wrong with those implants, no matter what. So they called the team in and announced that the board, in their best medical judgment, was recommending a full medical retirement for Stoner. That's when Lightstone stepped in."

"You mean he actually threatened the medical review board?" the special ops deputy chief asked, clearly impressed.

"No, not exactly." Halahan half smiled. "What he did was get them aside and had a little heart-to-heart talk. Explained to the good doctors that in spite of what some idiots in the Washington office might think, it really wasn't necessary for an agent like Dwight Stoner to be able to run a mile and a half through some swamp to chase down some rabbiting suspect. The main reason being that Stoner happened to have four agent partners who were perfectly capable of chasing that suspect through a swamp for ten miles, if it came to that, and if he made it that far, right into their buddy's waiting arms. Whereupon the chase team would sit down and have a beer while their supposedly crippled partner took care of any further resistance that the suspect might be capable of offering.''

"Not a bad idea, but probably a little impractical on a routine basis,'' Moore said thoughtfully.

"The doctors mentioned that,'' Halahan nodded. ''That was when Henry suggested that if the medical review board had any further doubts on how that sort of thing might work out, he and the rest of Bravo Team would be happy to put on a demonstration, right then and there. There was even a forest nearby that would serve just as well as a swamp. Far as Henry was concerned, the medical examiners could bring all the instruments and probes and measuring gadgets with them that they wanted. They could also have a paint-gun and a two-mile head start.''

"An interesting variation of 'capture the flag,' '' Moore said noncommittally. And then, ''I take it our good doctors had enough common sense between them to take a pass on the demonstration?''

"Apparently the idea of being hunted down through ten miles of Virginia forest by four pissed-off federal agents with a hard-on for the medical profession didn't exactly appeal to their sporting instincts.'' Halahan nodded. ''Although I understand one of the younger doctors—supposedly some kind of weekend jogger, cardiovascular workout freak—did offer to take Henry up on the deal before his associates talked him out of it. Personally, I don't think he would have gotten anywhere near Stoner, even with a two-mile lead.''

"If nothing else, Takahara would have probably cheated,

taken him out with some kind of electronic dead-fall,'' Moore commented. "Actually, I'm kind of surprised the board didn't file charges on Lightstone. Threatening a federal government official, causing them to pee in their pants, screw up their golf game, something like that."

"Oh, they did."

"Really?" Freddy Moore blinked in surprise. "What did they use for evidence? Presumably it would have been their word against his?"

"No, not exactly. Turns out there was a tape of the entire conversation."

"Those bastards wore a wire to a meeting like that?"

"No." Halahan smiled. "Henry did. He sent them a copy of the tape the day after they filed, along with a set of 35mm contacts."

"Photographs?"

"Yep. It seemed that two of our ass-covering medical advisers have—or perhaps *had* is the better word—a personal preference for certain mildly addictive recreational drugs. Unfortunately for their peace of mind, not to mention their careers, they chose to do their smoking at a party in the back of a private residence where the owner had neglected to install a high fence."

"I take it that the surrounding area was public access?"

"The property butted up against a county park. Lots of trees and bushes. Nice place to hike if you happen to enjoy taking nature photos with night-vision gear."

"Ah." Moore was silent for a moment before he finally said, "Just as a theoretical question, how would you go about describing that sort of thing in terms of a personnel evaluation?"

"I don't know. Adaptive, innovative, resourceful." Halahan shrugged. "Strong sense of team loyalty. Highly developed survival skills. Unwilling to accept defeat as a viable option. Questionable use of government equipment. Pain in the ass to supervise. Something like that."

"Sounds like a description that might fit the entire team."

"That's what I'm counting on," Halahan said. "From what I've seen so far, there's every indication that Bravo Team tripped across something pretty damn serious. And whoever's involved is apparently going after them."

"The tag on Lightstone?"

"Among other things."

"You think it might be more of that Operation Counter Wrench crap?"

"I don't know," Halahan admitted. "If Abercombie and Wolfe were fronting for somebody else, they were pretty careful about keeping it hidden. We haven't found a damned thing in any of their files so far."

"What about the money angle? That was one hell of an operation for Abercombie to be funding out of her cookie jar."

"They had big-time money backers, no doubt about it." Halahan nodded. "We just haven't figured out who or where yet."

"I don't know. Considering what Abercombie and Wolfe were trying to accomplish against the environmental groups, they could have had some pretty big players out there as backers. People who don't like to lose either, and who might not mind hiring a couple more people like Maas to make sure they don't," Moore reminded.

"That's exactly what I'm afraid of," Halahan said.

"So what does that mean—you're going to dangle an entire Special Ops team out as bait?"

"That's right," Halahan said, making direct eye contact with his new deputy chief.

"You don't think that might be a hell of a risky thing to do?"

"Maybe. Might be a whole lot worse if we just sat back and did nothing. Whoever those backers are, I think they got their noses bloodied pretty bad the first time around. They might not be that careless the next time."

"So what about the team? You sure they're up to dealing with something like that?"

"Sure enough that I'm willing to let them bullshit me a little while longer," Halahan replied matter-of-factly.

Freddy Moore blinked, looking confused for a brief moment, and then smiled in sudden understanding. "That Bahamas deal?"

"They've been searching around on their own for somebody connected to Abercombie for the last three months. My guess is that Takahara found some kind of lead with that goddamned computer of his. The rest of them didn't know what the hell he was talking about, but you saw how they acted. Followed along just like they really had talked about it last week."

"Adaptive, innovative, and resourceful?"

"Exactly."

"Mind if I ask you a question?"

"Shoot."

"Why not make this an official investigation?" Moore asked reasonably. "Assign two or even all three of the special ops teams, track down every angle, see what they can turn up?"

"We already tried that," Halahan replied evenly.

"And?"

"We got turned down. The review committee decided that if the FBI couldn't find any links to anyone beyond Abercombie, then there wasn't much reason to believe that we could."

"In spite of the fact that we lost three agents on the deal?"

"That's right." Halahan nodded.

"I see."

Freddy Moore was quiet for a long moment. Then he looked up at Halahan.

"Let me see if I've got this right. Our job, unofficially, is to set the bait, let the line drift out—in this case, maybe all the way down to Miami—and then wait to see if anything shows up and starts nibbling around the hook. We feel a tug on the line, we reach for a net or a harpoon, depending on who or what shows up. That about it?''

Halahan noted that his new deputy had used the word *we* for the first time during their entire conversation. He smiled to himself. Freddy Moore had a reputation for being a tough, no-nonsense supervisory agent and a dedicated team player, but this operation has the potential to be a career-buster . . . which meant that it had to be a volunteer situation all the way. Some agents Halahan knew wouldn't have necessarily felt that being the number two in charge of the Special Operations Branch was worth that kind of risk.

"That's the way I see it."

"Halahan," Freddy Moore said, his eyes seemingly reflecting a combination of boyish amusement and deadly cold seriousness, "I'm a southern boy, and I like to fish more than just about anything I can think of . . . but it looks to me like we might be starting out a little bit skimpy in the bait department. You know what's gonna happen to Bravo Team if we don't feel that tug in time?"

"Yeah, I do," Halahan replied. "That's why we're using bait that isn't afraid to bite back."

At two-fifteen that Wednesday morning, when Larry Paxton and Henry Lightstone finally got back to the safe house—which was actually a four-bedroom apartment located on the third floor of a warehouse building across the street from their storefront operation—they found Mike Takahara and Dwight Stoner sitting at the dining room table with opened cans of beer in their hands and satisfied grins on their faces. Judging from the dirt on their faces and clothing, it looked liked they had just spent the last hour in a garbage dump.

"Okay, Snoopy, spill it," Paxton demanded as he and Lightstone fielded cold cans tossed in their direction by Stoner.

"I found out how they got into the computer." The tech agent beamed.

"Snoopy, I don't give a shit about that goddamned computer," Paxton growled as he popped open the beer. "What

I want to know is—''

"No, wait a minute, let's hear what he has to say first,'' Henry Lightstone interrupted, staring at the two smiling agents suspiciously. "I think they know something we don't.''

"The antenna system on the warehouse,'' Takahara said, his exposed teeth looking brilliant white against his dirty face. "We went back up on the roof to take a look at it. Remember when I used one of the monitor units in the car last night to make sure the alarms were set?''

Paxton and Lightstone nodded.

"Well, somebody got up on the roof of the warehouse and hooked another transmitter to the antenna. It's a real nice setup too. First-rate job. The moment I triggered our monitor, that unit automatically recorded and then transmitted a copy of the signal on a separate frequency, access codes and everything, the whole works. Somewhere nearby they had a receiver hooked up and waiting. At that point all they needed was a modem and our phone number, and they had easy access to our computer.''

"Which we gave out to at least a couple dozen people when we were setting up the buys.'' Paxton nodded.

"So there was somebody in that warehouse after all,'' Lightstone said, nodding in satisfaction.

"Whoever rigged the transmitter used a modem to plant a Trojan Horse program in our computer that they could activate to shut off the alarms,'' Mike Takahara explained. "That gave them free access to the warehouse. The noise you heard was probably the guy going out the emergency door in the office, after he activated the last phase of their little program, which was probably to wait for a few seconds and then start erasing itself.''

Lightstone nodded. "Giving the guy enough time to get out before the computer woke up, rearmed the system and scared the living shit out of both of us.''

"Exactly.'' The tech agent smiled.

"So who the hell was it, and what was he doing rummaging around in the warehouse?''

"Beats the hell out of me," Mike Takahara admitted. "A reasonable guess would be that the Boracatto brothers got pissed off when they figured out we were some kind of sting operation, but—"

"Okay, so now we *know* that somebody's fucking with us," Paxton interrupted. "We'll figure out who and why later. What I want to know is, what's all this shit about Miami?"

"Yeah, that's the best part." Dwight Stoner grinned. "Wait until you hear this."

"Come on, Snoopy, spill it. It's been a long night," Henry Lightstone snapped as he sat down at the table and took a long swallow of the cold beer.

"You know how we've been looking for some other connection to Abercombie and Wolfe?"

"Yeah, so?"

"Well, I found him."

"Found who?" Paxton demanded.

"Abercombie's boyfriend."

"You mean Wolfe? Hell, Ah *know* where *he* is," Paxton said. "They planted him six feet down in some Fairfax County cemetery."

"No." Mike Takahara shook his head. "I mean the real one."

"No shit?"

"And guess where," Dwight Stoner added, the wide smile still on his scarred face.

"Bahamas in the wintertime," Henry Lightstone whispered.

"That's right." Mike Takahara nodded.

"Well, I'll be damned," Paxton whispered, a wide smile appearing on his tired face. Then he looked over as Henry Lightstone got up, walked over to the table, began rummaging through his briefcase, then walked back toward the phone with his address book in his hand.

"Hey, who you gonna call this time of night?"

"LaGrange," Lightstone replied. "I want to find out if he's hired himself a boat crew yet."

"At two o'clock in the morning?"

"Yeah, sure, why not? He never got much sleep when we were working together in San Diego."

"I can believe that." Larry Paxton nodded, shaking his head as he watched Lightstone start to dial the phone. "And while you're busy pissing off our future employer, I'm gonna go lock myself in my room and pretend this evening didn't even happen."

"Locks? Oh, shit," Mike Takahara said, his eyes blinking open as he looked over at Stoner.

"What's the matter?" Paxton demanded suspiciously.

"Halahan got me so pissed off, I forgot to reset the alarm system on the warehouse," Mike Takahara said as he started to get up.

"Never mind, I'll do it." Paxton yawned as he walked over to the door that led to the balcony that overlooked the street in front of the warehouse. Stepping out onto the balcony, he reached into his pants pocket and brought out a small transmitter. Then he hesitated and looked back in the doorway. "Hey, man, you sure you rigged everything back up exactly the way it was?"

"It's all set to go." Mike Takahara nodded sleepily. "Just push the red button like you always do."

Nodding to himself, Larry Paxton aimed the transmitter at the front door of the building and depressed the red button.

The shock wave of the resulting high-order explosion sent the assistant special agent in charge of Bravo Team tumbling backward into the room amid a spray of broken wood and shattered glass. Moments later, as the stunned agent found himself lying dazed on the floor, a deluge of broken bricks, chunks of freezer insulation, shredded fish, and oyster shells rained down on the balcony.

Staggering up to his feet, Larry Paxton joined his fellow agents who were already out on the balcony staring down at what had once been the site of their storefront fish-dealing operation. All around the warehouse complex, burglar alarms were ringing loudly. And in the distance, the agents could hear the all-too-familiar sounds of Boston police sirens beginning to wail.

"Goddamn," the assistant special agent in charge whispered in a shocked voice, "Ah think we just woke up the neighborhood again."

Chapter Nine

Dr. Kimberly Wildman looked around her National Biological Survey field group.

"Okay," she said, "is everybody clear on who's going to be where the next few days?"

Of the thirty-one people present in the Yellowstone National Park headquarters conference room, at least two-thirds nodded sleepily. The newly assembled group had been in the field for only two weeks, and everyone was still trying to adapt to their new boss and her six-thirty A.M. middle-of-the-week staff meetings. For many of the scientist/technician teams it had been a long drive to Yellowstone yesterday evening, and it would be just as long a drive back to their individual survey sites this morning. Few of them were enthusiastic about the prospect.

"One more heads-up. The park rangers have asked me to remind all of you that they are *still* maintaining a *high* fire danger alert for most of the northwest Wyoming quadrant. So think about hot exhaust pipes when you park those trucks. And please limit your use of chain saws to emergency situations."

"How are we defining an emergency situation?" one of the field technicians asked.

"One tree drops in front of your truck, another one drops behind it, and the one in the middle is starting to go," someone said from the back of the room, which got favorable chuckles or smiles from most of the group.

"Okay, good, you're starting to wake up." Wildman nodded approvingly. "Does anybody have anything else they want to bring up before we head back out?"

"You might want to mention about that green sign we found yesterday," Wildman's field technician reminded.

"Oh, yes, that's right. Yesterday afternoon we found a metal sign attached to a Doug fir that the Fish and Wildlife Service is apparently using to mark eagle nesting sites. If you happen to run across any more of them, you should include them in your documentation data for the nest. They might make a useful cross-referencing with existing Fish and Wildlife databases."

One of the senior biologists in the back of the room raised his hand.

"Ah, Kim," he said, "could you describe that sign?"

"Yes. As I recall, we listed it as a metal plate, blank, green camouflage coating. Dimensions—uh—eighteen inches by thirty inches by three-quarters-of-an inch thick. Attached to the tree with a pair of what looked like very heavy steel lag bolts with three-inch wide, security configured heads."

"Was the sign made out of aluminum?"

"It appeared to be." The group leader nodded. "Either that or some kind of aluminum alloy."

"I don't think those are markers for eagle nests. I found one just like that last Monday, and it certainly wasn't attached to a nesting tree."

"Are you sure there wasn't a nest up there somewhere?" Wildman asked.

"Pretty sure." The elderly biologist grinned. "It was a stump about twenty-four inches high."

Laughter and a few comments about confused eagles and rapidly declining biologists immediately broke out among the suddenly reenergized group.

"Okay, okay." Wildman smiled. "I guess we can assume

that they're some kind of Forest Service marker."

"Kind of a strange way to mark a tree," the biologist commented. "Fact is, we never would have seen it if we hadn't been rummaging around in some brush."

"Yeah, we found one like that too." One of the other biologists spoke up. "Or at least it sounds like the same thing. I could only see part of it because it was nestled behind some berry brambles, and I wasn't curious enough to try to get in any closer."

"I can do you one better than that," another voice in the back said.

Wildman looked up to see one of the park maintenance men standing in the doorway.

"We damn near tore up a chain saw on one of them signs yesterday afternoon when we were taking down a diseased pine out near the north entrance. Never saw the damn thing until we made the cut. Missed it by only a couple inches, too. Lousy place to put a sign, far as I'm concerned. Gonna get somebody hurt doing dumb-ass things like that."

A puzzled and disapproving look appeared on Dr. Kimberly Wildman's face. "Have any of the other teams found similar signs in their areas?" she asked to the room at large.

Much to Wildman's surprise, a total of seven hands were raised around the room.

"All right, before you all go, would you please give Renie whatever data you have on the locations of these signs," Wildman said, gesturing with her head over to one of the computer programmers. "I want to look into this a little further."

"Want one of them signs for proof?" the maintenance man asked.

"Did you save it?" Wildman's head came back around quickly.

"Not exactly. We just cut under it, split away the wood, and then tossed the whole mess in one of the dumpsters when we came back in. I woulda just taken the sign, but I couldn't figure out how to back them damn bolts out.

Oughta still be there. Be glad to go get it for you if you want.''

"Yes, please." Wildman nodded. "And you're right, it *is* foolish to place these signs where they can't be seen. I'm going to call the Forest service right now, to see if I can find out what's going on, before somebody *does* get hurt."

At quarter after seven that Wednesday morning, just as the still irritated park maintenance man was climbing into one of the big trash dumpsters to retrieve the discarded sign, a pair of overnight campers finished cleaning up their breakfast cooking gear at a stream about twenty yards from their campsite.

"You know," one of the campers said, "I really feel kind of guilty about using an open fire like that, but there just isn't anything that tastes better on a camping trip than biscuits and coffee slow-cooked over coals."

"Hey, we made a fire ring." The second hiker shrugged. "What the hell do they expect us to do, eat cold cereal every morning?"

"Well, sort of a fire ring, anyway."

"Kind of hard to make anything other than a square out of four rocks," the second hiker chuckled. "But hey, we kept the fire small. We cleaned up the site, buried the coals, and put the rocks back where we found them. No harm, no foul, right?"

"Sounds good to me."

"Okay then, let's get going. Got some miles to go today," the second hiker said enthusiastically, leaving it unclear as to who had actually buried the coals.

As it turned out, each of them had assumed that the other had done so.

At seven-fifty-five that morning, Dr. Kimberly Wildman hung up the phone feeling even more annoyed and puzzled than before.

She had just finished making the last of seven phone

calls—to every federal agency she could think of that might have some reason to attach blank green aluminum markers to trees in the northwest Wyoming quadrant—and had come up with a complete blank.

If she saw any humor in that situation, it certainly wasn't obvious from her facial expression.

She stared for a moment at the green etched sign and the pair of steel lag bolts that the park maintenance man had just leaned against her desk, amazed at the size of the eighteen-by-three-quarter-inch lag bolts, and wondering what kind of tool could have possibly been used to drive such a huge bolt. Then she stood up and walked into the adjoining room.

"Well, Renie, how many signs did we end up with?"

The youthful computer programmer looked up from her computer.

"Seventeen, so far."

"What!" Dr. Kimberly Wildman blinked in astonishment. "Are you serious?"

"I'm afraid so."

"But why didn't they say something at the meeting?"

"Probably because most of them were too embarrassed to admit that they didn't document the locations." The shy programmer shrugged. "They told me they were going to go back and get GPS readings."

"You mean to say there are *more* than seventeen out there?"

"Apparently a lot more." The young woman nodded. "We've got global position data on nine, rough estimates on eight more, and wild guesses on the rest. They're going to go back out and try to find them again, and then call in the data."

"Have you plotted it out?"

"Just the seventeen so far."

"What's it look like?"

"All over the quadrant, for the most part, but I want to show you something."

Wildman stood behind her chair as the young programmer

called a graphics program up on the screen.

"I was looking for correlations," Renie explained as a map of northwest Wyoming area appeared on the screen. "I started with all seventeen points and basically got a random pattern."

Seventeen small purple circles suddenly appeared on the screen, spaced in a seemingly random order throughout the electronically drawn quadrant map.

"Then I separated it out into the GPS points and the rough guesses . . ."

The seventeen purple circles were suddenly replaced by eight bright red triangles and nine open green boxes.

". . . and again, basically got garbage."

Dr. Kimberly Wildman stared at the screen and agreed that she couldn't see any obvious pattern either.

"But then," Renie said, making no attempt to hide her excitement, "I decided to limit the analysis to all points within fifty miles of the Yellowstone headquarters building, and look what I got."

Dr. Wildman's eyebrows furrowed in surprise. "An arc?"

"I think so." The young programmer nodded excitedly. "But there are only three GPS points and two estimates within the fifty-mile radius, so it isn't all that much to go on. Especially since Mike said that one of his rough estimates is really a rough guess."

"That one here?" Wildman asked, pointing to one of the squares that was the farthest out from the thin yellow arc that the computer had drawn through the five designated points in a "closest fit" pattern.

"Right."

"How strange," the group leader whispered to herself.

"That's what I thought too," Renie said. And then after a moment: "You know, it's getting pretty windy out there already. Maybe you should stay here today, you know, wait to see what else we get for data."

"That's a good idea." Dr. Kimberly Wildman nodded,

seemingly preoccupied. "We need to get that sign wrapped up anyway."

"What are you going to do, send it in to headquarters?"

"No." The group leader shook her head. "I'm sending it to the Fish and Wildlife Service's forensic lab in Ashland, Oregon. Maybe they can make some sense out of all this."

At nine-fifteen that morning Dr. Kimberly Wildman, her field technician, and one of her clerks had just finished filling out all the submission paperwork and wrapping up the sign in protective layers of cardboard and nylon tape when the phone rang.

"Dr. Wildman?"

"Yes."

"This is the dispatcher. One of the forest ranger stations has reported a fire in the northeast corner of the park. Because of the wind situation, the superintendent is afraid that it's going to get out of control, so he's asking all fire-trained personnel to respond to the area immediately with their line gear."

"We're on our way," Wildman acknowledged. "I've got a couple of teams near that area right now. Can you notify them too?"

"Right away," the dispatcher acknowledged.

"Thanks."

"What's up?" the field technician asked.

"Grab your fire gear, buddy," Wildman said. "We've got a hot spot up in the northeast corner." She repeated the dispatcher's description of the situation.

"Oh, God!" The field technician rolled his eyes and then ran for the door.

Dr. Kimberly Wildman was heading toward the door herself when her clerk called out:

"Dr. Wildman, do you want me to send this out Federal Express?"

Thoroughly distracted by at least a dozen things that

were running through her mind, Dr. Kimberly Wildman made a snap decision that would have far-reaching consequences.

"Yes," she said, "you might as well."

Chapter Ten

By three-thirty that Wednesday afternoon, thanks to the sharp eyes of a resident forest ranger and the speedy response of the Yellowstone fire crews, the rapidly spreading blaze was brought under control.

But, as always, there had been a price.

Seven members of the fire crews were taken to the hospital with injuries ranging from minor burns and smoke inhalation to a broken leg suffered when a tree being cut for a fire break dropped the wrong way and rolled. More than a hundred acres of prime park land had been turned into charred trees, blackened ground, and white ash. And thousands of the park's natural residents had either been killed outright or driven from their homes in a panic to places where their chances of survival were significantly reduced.

The fire crews had managed to stop the fire in time, before it was able to take hold and cause far more extensive damage, but even so, very few of the men and women who had worked the fire lines felt that they had much to cheer about.

Dr. Kimberly Wildman staggered back into her headquarters office, covered with soot, soaked in sweat, and physically exhausted. But a long shower and a clean set of clothes quickly revived her spirits.

When she finally returned to the survey workroom, she found her computer programming assistant smiling cheerfully.

"Look at this," Renie said. "We've got GPS data now for seven of the eight rough guesses, and they found twelve more signs, for a total of twenty-nine fixed data points."

"So what does that give us—more accurate confusion?" The group leader smiled tiredly.

"I don't know, I was just about to run the correlation program," the young computer specialist said seriously. "I'm going to check the fifty-mile radius first, see if we get a better fit on that arc." Humming to herself, she hit a series of keys, and then waited as the powerful computer took a couple of million microseconds to churn through the data. Then a multicolored graphic image popped up on the screen.

"Wow, look at that, right on the money!" she exclaimed, pointing to the yellow arc that now cut through the exact centers of five tiny red triangles.

"Wait a minute, what's that?" Dr. Kimberly Wildman asked, pointing to a yellow line segment that formed the hypotenuse of a small right triangle in the far upper right corner of the screen.

"I don't know. It looks like . . ."

"Expand it out to the full quadrant," Wildman directed, but Renie's fingers were already flying across the keys.

"Oh, wow," the youthful assistant whispered as the new graphic popped into view.

"They're not arcs, they're partial circles," Dr. Kimberly Wildman said, shaking her head slowly in amazement. The screen was now displaying three almost perfectly curved yellow lines that swept through the centers of twenty-nine small scattered red triangles to form circular arcs from the left side of the screen to the bottom.

"And you know what," the young computer programmer said, talking mostly to herself as her hands flew across the keys again, "it looks like . . . yes!"

"Well, I'll be damned," Dr. Kimberly Wildman said as she stared at the five blue lines that cut through the centers of two or three of the triangles from a different direction now, forming four spokes of a wheel. Or actually three increasingly bigger wheels, she realized.

"I *thought* it looked like some of them lined up, but I

couldn't tell for sure, because all the points are scattered, and the circles were too far apart," the young woman said, her eyes flashing with excitement. "But look there, I bet that every place where the blue and yellow lines intersect, there's actually a sign out there, right at that spot. We just haven't found it yet."

"And those triangles where there isn't any blue line intersects—"

"It's probably because only one of the three signs on that 'spoke' have been found. You need at least two points for the program to draw the straight lines."

"Except now that you have a center point, you can . . . hey, wait a minute, what about that center point? Go back to the closeup view."

In a matter of seconds the young programmer had the screen displaying the intersect point of the five blue lines.

"Whitehorse Cabin?" Dr. Kimberly Wildman blinked in confusion, knowing that name meant something to her for some reason that she couldn't quite remember.

"Isn't that where the Fish and Wildlife Service had that raid?"

"That's right, it is." Wildman nodded, feeling an odd sense of being let down by the discovery. "Which means those signs are probably some sort of crime scene markers."

"Oh." Like her boss, the young computer programmer seemed disappointed that the solution was so—what?—mundane? Trivial?

"You think we ought to let them know that one of their markers almost got somebody hurt?" she asked after a moment.

"Yes, we should," Wildman answered, starting to feel the fatigue creeping back into her body, now that they had the problem solved.

"Want me to see if I can find out who the investigator was on that case, and send him an E-mail message, asking him to contact you?"

"That would be a wonderful idea, but let's do it tomorrow,'' the group leader said, smiling tiredly. "It's been a very long day."

At six-thirty that Wednesday evening exhausted fire crews were still wandering through the burn area, making sure that all the smoldering areas were safely contained and simply consuming the remainder of their fuel. As they did so, one of the men called out:

"Hey, Chief, come here, look what I found!"

Moments later the fire crew chief stood there and stared for a long moment before he whispered: "What the *hell*?"

As the other crew members gathered around, one of them turned to the others and said: "You know, something tells me it's a good thing tomorrow's our day off."

Chapter Eleven

"Would you state your name please, and spell it for the record?"

"Henry Lightstone. L-I-G-H-T-S-T-O-N-E."

"And by whom are you employed, Mr. Lightstone?"

"The Division of Law Enforcement, United States Fish and Wildlife Service."

"And during the following time periods"—Deputy United States Attorney Theresa Fletcher looked down at a list she held in her hand, and then read off a series of "from-to" dates—"in what manner were you employed with the Division of Law Enforcement?"

"As a special agent assigned to Bravo Team, Special Operations Branch."

"Basically as what you would term an undercover agent or undercover operator?"

"Yes, ma'am."

"Tell me, Special Agent Lightstone, do you have any previous experience working as an undercover operator?''

"Yes, I do."

"And what would that be?"

"I have twelve years of experience as a police officer for the San Diego Police Department. During that time I spent a total of approximately four years in varying undercover assignments."

"Vice, narcotics, burglary, that sort of thing?"

"That's correct."

"And your last five years at the San Diego Police Department, just before you joined the Fish and Wildlife Service, how were they spent?"

"As a detective assigned to the Major Crimes Unit."

"Which, I take it, would be mostly homicide and robbery?"

"Yes, ma'am."

"Your honor," Jason Bascomb III, the senior attorney in charge of the unified defense team, said, coming quickly to his feet before the African-American deputy U.S. attorney could begin her next question, "the defense will stipulate that Special Agent Lightstone is a fully trained and qualified federal law enforcement officer in all respects for purposes of this hearing."

The presiding federal judge looked over at Fletcher, who nodded agreeably.

"So stipulated," the judge said, making a note on his legal pad. "Please continue, Mrs. Fletcher."

"Special Agent Lightstone, are you familiar with an individual named Alex Chareaux?"

"Yes, I am."

"Do you see him in this courtroom today?"

"Yes, I do."

"Would you point him out, please?"

Henry Lightstone turned his head and for the second time that morning looked straight into the furiously angry eyes of Alex Chareaux. He noted that the Cajun guide remained handcuffed as a result of his outburst earlier that morning.

"He's the male subject, with dark hair tied back in a pony tail, who is sitting at the far right of the defense table."

"Is there any question in your mind as to Mr. Chareaux's identity?"

"No, ma'am."

"Did you take part in a federal undercover investigation against Mr. Alex Chareaux and his two brothers sometime during the dates I previously mentioned?"

"Yes, I did."

"For what purpose?"

"Mr. Chareaux and his brothers were suspected of conducting an illegal guiding business. We—that is, the special agents of Bravo Team, which included Special Agent in Charge Paul McNulty, ASAC Carl Scoby, and agents Larry Paxton, Dwight Stoner, Mike Takahara, and myself—were assigned to try to infiltrate their operation and obtain evidence that they were violating certain federal and state wildlife hunting laws."

"In such an operation is it typical that one or more law enforcement officers such as yourself might interact directly with the subjects under investigation, in what you might describe as a covert or undercover role?"

"Yes, ma'am, very common."

"And was there a primary covert officer who posed as an illegal hunter in this case?"

"Yes, there was."

"And who was that agent?"

"I was that agent."

"Did you use a false name and identity during the investigation?"

"Yes, I did."

"And what was the name you used?"

"Henry Allen Lightner."

"As Henry Allen Lightner, did you engage in illegal hunting activities with Mr. Chareaux and his brothers?"

"Yes, I did."

"And during the course of this covert investigation,

Agent Lightstone, did you and your fellow agents come across what you believed to be a much larger criminal conspiracy to . . .''

"Your honor"—Jason Bascomb III rose again and spoke in a professionally calm and dignified voice—"the defense would object to the use of the word *conspiracy*, unless of course the prosecution is prepared to offer proof."

"Let me rephrase the question, your honor." Deputy U.S. Attorney Theresa Fletcher smiled pleasantly. "Special Agent Lightstone, during the course of your investigation into the suspected illegal activities of Alex Chareaux, did you find yourself involved with any other subjects whom you suspected of being involved in illegal activities . . . with respect to federal wildlife laws," Fletcher added as she saw Bascomb start to rise out of his chair again.

"Yes, ma'am."

"And who were they?"

"Lisa Abercombie, Dr. Morito Asai, and Dr. Reston Wolfe."

"At the time of your covert investigation into the activities of Mr. Chareaux, did you know those individuals by their true names?"

"No, ma'am, I did not."

"What names did you know them by?"

"The names they used at that time were Reston Waters, Lisa Allen, and Morrey Asato."

"Presumably keeping their real first names, essentially as you did, for purposes of easy recognition. Is that a common ploy for people trying to maintain a false identity?"

"Yes, it is."

"Tell me, Agent Lightstone, do you see any of these people you described in this courtroom this morning?"

"No, I don't."

"Do you know, of your own personal knowledge, what happened to them?"

"Dr. Wolfe was shot and killed near the Tidal Basin in Washington, D.C.," Lightstone replied. "The incident occurred while we were attempting to track him back to his associates. I was present when he was shot and when he died.''

''And the other two?''

''At the conclusion of our investigation of Mr. Chareaux and other related subjects, I took part in a raid on underground facilities at Whitehorse Cabin in Yellowstone National Park. In the aftermath of that raid, I also assisted in a detailed search of the underground facilities. In a room identified by a sign on the door as the Command and Control Room, I personally observed the bodies of two individuals whom I then knew as Lisa Allen and Morrey Asato. Both of them appeared to have been shot in the chest with a large-caliber firearm.''

''What was it that made you suspect the weapon was a large-caliber firearm?''

''I observed a relatively small hole in the chest of each subject, which appeared to be an entry wound, and extremely large holes out the back, which were clearly exit wounds.''

''Special Agent Lightstone, in the course of your duties as a homicide investigator with the San Diego Police Department, have you had the occasion to observe entry and exit wounds in human bodies caused by a .44 Magnum pistol?''

''Yes, I have.''

''When was that?''

''During approximately fifty of the approximately three hundred autopsies I observed during my police law enforcement career.''

''And based upon this experience, and in your opinion, were these wounds on the individuals known to you as Lisa Allen and Morrey Asato consistent with having come from a .44 Magnum handgun?''

Lightstone hesitated, waiting for the expected objection that didn't come, and then said: ''Yes, ma'am, they were.''

''Were you armed with a .44 Magnum during that raid?

''No, I was not.''

"To your knowledge were any of the other federal agents or military instructors who took part in that raid armed with a .44 Magnum pistol?"

"No, ma'am, they were not."

"To your knowledge, was one of the suspects armed with such a weapon?"

"Yes, one subject *was* armed with such a weapon."

"Is this the suspect whom you observed to shoot at one or more of his fellow suspects, in addition to you and other members of your raid team?"

"Yes, it was."

"In your opinion, was that being done in order to silence them as possible witnesses—"

"Objection, your honor," lead defense attorney Jason Bascomb III responded immediately. "Calls for speculation on the part of the witness."

"Sustained."

"Special Agent Lightstone," the prosecuting attorney went on, "when you took part in this raid at Whitehorse Cabin in Yellowstone National Park how were you armed?"

"With a .223 military M-16 assault rifle, and a Model 1076 10mm Smith & Wesson semiautomatic pistol."

"Would either of those weapons be likely to produce a chest wound in a human male or female similar to that typically caused by a .44 Magnum round, or similar to the wounds you observed in Lisa Allen and Morrey Asato?"

Out of reflex, Henry Lightstone hesitated again, having no expectation that Bascomb would allow him to answer such a question, and then said: "No, they would not."

"Why not?"

"All members of the raid team carried the same ammunition for our assault rifles: .223 military ball—that is, solid-jacketed bullets that are about twenty-two-hundredths-of-an-inch in diameter. Unlike the .44 pistol round, which creates a relatively big and slow projectile, the .223 rifle round sends out a relatively small, light, high velocity bullet which is capable of penetrating the standard military issue soft body armor that we had reason to believe the suspects might be wearing. Such bullets typically create what is called a through-and-through wound. And unless the bullet tumbles—which can easily happen if it's deflected in flight or hits bone at an angle—the exit wound tends to be relatively small.''

''And what if the bullet does tumble?''

''Based solely upon my observations at autopsies,'' Lightstone said, continuing to be amazed at the latitude Bascomb was giving him as an expert witness, ''the bullet either tends to stay inside the body or tear through in a ripping manner.''

''Do those tear-through wounds look similar to a typical .44 Magnum wound?''

''No, ma'am, not at all.''

''And what about the 10mm pistol ammunition you carried?''

''To my personal knowledge, all the federal wildlife agents on that raid carried 200-grain, jacketed hollow-point rounds for our 10mm semiauto pistols. That ammunition was designed and manufactured for law enforcement officers, for the specific purpose of incapacitating or killing a human being without creating a through-and-through wound.''

''And is that primarily to prevent injury to other people in the immediate area?''

''Yes, exactly.''

''Special Agent Lightstone, did you use either of these weapons you possessed during this raid to fire a shot at either of the two individuals known to you as Lisa Allen and Morrey Asato?''

''No, ma'am, I did not.''

''What about Dr. Reston Wolfe? Did you shoot him?''

''No, I did not.''

''To your personal knowledge, did either you or one of your fellow agents at the scene at the Tidal Basin in Washington, D.C., discharge a firearm in the direction of Dr. Wolfe?''

"To my personal knowledge, I am absolutely certain that none of the U.S. Fish and Wildlife Service Special Agents at the Tidal Basin that evening discharged a firearm."

"Do you know who did discharge a firearm in the direction of Dr. Wolfe?''

Lightstone and Fletcher and nearly everyone else in the courtroom waited expectantly for the defense to rise up and object, but lead defense attorney Jason Bascomb III continued to remain seated in his chair with a pleasantly attentive smile on his face.

"Apparently you may answer the question," the judge finally said.

Lightstone nodded, and then turned his attention back to the deputy U.S. attorney. "No, ma'am, I do not."

"Your honor, if I may," Jason Bascomb III said politely as he rose partway out of his chair, "the defense has offered to stipulate—''

"Yes, I'm coming to that," Theresa Fletcher said.

The defense attorney shrugged as if to say "What can I do? I'm not the one trying to delay things here," and then sat back down. The judge motioned for the prosecutor to continue.

"Special Agent Lightstone, in the course of this extended investigation that you and your fellow agents conducted, and the raid that followed, did you ever come into contact with an individual identified to you as Gerd Maas?''

"Yes, ma'am, I did."

"And do you see him in the courtroom?''

"Yes, I do."

Henry Lightstone looked over in the direction of the defense table again and focused his attention on the man in the wheelchair. Unlike Chareaux, whose eyes were still visibly filled with undiminished hatred over his incarceration and the loss of his brothers, Gerd Maas was staring back at Lightstone with an expression that Lightstone could only describe as curious amusement.

"Would you point him out for the court, please?"

"He's the male subject with the short white hair, sitting in the wheelchair between the two defense counsels."

Lightstone found it interesting to observe that all three of the defendants, Alex Chareaux, Gerd Maas, and Roy Parker, were being kept separate from one another by representatives of the defense legal team. It occurred to him to wonder if Chareaux had any idea that Maas had almost certainly been involved in the death of his youngest brother. Probably not, Lightstone decided; otherwise the intervening presence of a single, overweight, and underexercised defense attorney wouldn't have kept Chareaux away from the German hunter's throat for more than a second or two, handcuffs or not.

The idea of two lethal adversaries like Maas and Chareaux going at each other in the middle of a federal courtroom intrigued Lightstone. He assumed that was why there were six armed bailiffs assigned to this hearing, three of whom were now sitting directly behind the three defendants.

Bad mistake, judge. You should have kept them all in custody so you could keep Maas handcuffed to that wheelchair, Lightstone thought, shaking his head. He still couldn't understand how Bascomb had convinced an experienced federal judge to set bail for men like Maas and Parker . . . or, for that matter, why. According to Theresa Fletcher, the defense team had paid the entire bail—totaling one point seven five million—in cash.

Incredible, Lightstone thought uneasily. *Absolutely incredible.*

"Thank you. Now, then, Special Agent Lightstone—"

"Your honor—" Jason Bascomb III came up to his feet again with an exasperated sigh.

"I only have two more questions of this witness, leading up to the stipulation," Deputy U.S. Attorney Theresa Fletcher said hastily.

The judge looked over at the defense attorney, who

shrugged in agreement.

"Continue."

"Special Agent Lightstone, did you prepare an official report that detailed all the events that you were personally involved in with respect to this entire investigation?"

"Yes, I did."

"May I approach the witness, your honor?"

"Go ahead."

"Special Agent Lightstone, do you recognize this document I have in my hand as being a true and representative copy of that investigative report?" The prosecuting attorney handed Lightstone a ribbon-and-grommet-sealed report that appeared to consist of about fifty typewritten pages. Lightstone examined the report briefly, verified his signature on the header page, and then nodded.

"Yes, I do."

"Your honor, prosecution would move to place Special Agent Lightstone's investigative report into evidence as people's next in order."

"No objections, your honor," defense attorney Jason Bascomb III added with only a mild theatrical sigh.

"So ordered."

"Thank you, your honor. No further questions of this witness at this time."

"Counsel?"

"Thank you, your honor," Jason Bascomb III said as he stood up and walked over to a midpoint between the defense table and the witness box.

"Special Agent Lightstone, my client, Roy Parker, whom you may recognize as being the gentleman with the crutches sitting on what would be your right side of the defense table, is recovering from a number of bullet wounds. Do you know how he acquired those wounds?"

"No, sir, I do not."

"Oh really? He seems to believe that you were the one who shot him."

"Objection, argumentative," Theresa Fletcher spoke up.

"Sustained."

"Special Agent Lightstone, is it possible that you did, in fact, fire one or more shots at Mr. Parker up near Skilak Lake, on the Kenai Peninsula in Alaska, during a time when he and his companions were legally hunting?"

"Sir, I don't know for a fact if I ever have fired a shot at Mr. Parker, and I don't know if he has ever been hunting, legal or otherwise, at Skilak Lake in Alaska," Lightstone replied evenly.

"But you shot at *someone* up at Skilak Lake during the dates and times in question, did you not?"

"Yes, sir, I did."

"In fact, according to your report, you fired quite a number of shots at at least two individuals, one of whom might very well have been my client, isn't that true?"

"That's possible, yes."

"Are you telling the court that you don't *know* whether or not you shot at two people?"

"Refuge Officer Sam Johnson and I became involved in a gun battle with at least two individuals while we were in the process of conducting a law enforcement investigation at Skilak Lake in Alaska," Lightstone responded. "I didn't—"

"You mean fishing, don't you?" the defense attorney interrupted.

"I beg your pardon?"

"I said you were fishing, not conducting an investigation. Isn't that correct?"

"Refuge Officer Johnson, Special Agent Thomas Woeshack, a civilian named Marie Pascalaura, and I were fishing on Skilak lake just prior to our conducting the investigation. Yes, that's correct."

"I see." Jason Bascomb III nodded dubiously. "And then, according to your report, you heard gunshots and decided to abandon your fishing trip and conduct a law enforcement investigation. Presumably to see if people were hunting illegally in the area. Correct?"

"Essentially, yes."

"Well, were they?"

"What?"

"Were they hunting illegally?"

"I . . . don't know."

"Actually, Special Agent Lightstone, in point of fact, you really can't prove that *anyone you ended up shooting at during this incident* was, in fact, hunting illegally in the area of Skilak Lake, isn't that true?"

Henry Lightstone started to answer and then hesitated.

"And I would ask the court to remind the witness that he is required to answer only the question being asked," Jason Bascomb III added.

"I think the witness is aware of his responsibilities in that regard," the judge responded dryly. "Agent Lightstone, do you understand the question that defense counsel has asked?"

"Yes, I believe I do, your honor." Lightstone nodded, and then turned to Bascomb. "No, sir, I can't prove that any of the individuals involved in the gun battle with Refuge Officer Johnson and myself were illegally hunting at the time."

"And, in fact, you don't even know who any of those individuals are, do you?"

"No, sir, I don't."

"Oh, and getting back to Refuge Officer Johnson for a moment. You described him as taking part in this gun battle, but in fact, he never did fire his weapon at anyone, did he?"

"No, sir, he was hit almost immediately . . ."

"By a rifle bullet that might have been inadvertently fired in his direction by my client while in the process of hunting?"

"By a large-caliber bullet that went completely through his shoulder and was never recovered," Lightstone corrected. "I don't have any reason to believe—"

"That my client was engaged in legal hunting activities and accidentally mistook you and your associate for a bear when he fired a shot in your direction, unfortunately striking

Refuge Officer Johnson in the upper-chest area?"

"That's correct."

"In your report, Agent Lightstone, you claimed that you were assaulted by two individuals dressed in military camouflage clothing and carrying military assault rifles, and—oh, yes—that in the course of the events that followed, you actually shot and killed one of those individuals at close range with . . . I believe it was Refuge Officer Johnson's pistol. Is that an accurate version of what happened?"

"It's a summarized version of what happened, yes, sir."

"Tell me, Agent Lightstone, the FBI investigated that—uh—crime scene, did they not?"

"Yes, they did."

"And did they find any evidence of this shooting you described?"

"One of their divers found a military sniper rifle and expended brass casings in the water nearby."

"And as I understand it, that diver also found your issued duty weapon, a stainless steel Smith & Wesson .357 Magnum in the same location. The weapon, I believe, that you claimed to have discarded because it was empty?"

"That I dropped on the ground because it was empty, and I had no more ammunition for it, yes."

"I see." Jason Bascomb III nodded skeptically as he began to walk slowly back and forth across the courtroom.

"And wasn't there some mention of an assault rifle that you supposedly acquired from the individual you claimed to have killed?"

"Yes, sir, a .223 Colt Commando rifle."

"Which, as you indicated in your report, was destroyed in the fire that resulted from the crash of the airplane that you and Special Agent Woeshack were flying in, is that correct?"

"Yes. The weapon was recovered from the wreckage by the FBI," Lightstone said.

"But so badly burned that the serial number could not be restored, so we have no way of knowing whether or not this weapon might have come from a Fish and Wildlife Service armory, do we?''

"Objection, argumentative," Deputy U.S. Attorney Theresa Fletcher responded.

"Sustained."

"But getting back to this individual you claim to have killed," Jason Bascomb III went on smoothly. "To your knowledge, did the FBI ever find this man's body, or for that matter, any evidence whatever to indicate that such a man might have been killed in the manner and location you described in your report?"

As Henry Lightstone's eyes followed the back-and-forth movements of the defense attorney, he noticed that the hatred in Alex Chareaux's eyes had been replaced by a look of confusion, and that Gerd Maas was openly smiling now.

"Agent Lightstone?"

Lightstone blinked, then recovered his concentration. "No, sir, as far as I am aware, no evidence of the shooting I described in my report was ever located by the FBI crime scene team, nor was the subject's body ever recovered."

"Yet isn't it also true, Agent Lightstone, during some considerable portion of the FBI investigation that followed, the supervisor of this same team of FBI agents considered you to be a primary suspect in the killing of Special Agent in Charge Paul McNulty, your own supervisor? An event that occurred at approximately the same time and location as your self-described gun battle?"

Henry Lightstone nodded silently.

"I'm sorry, I didn't hear your answer?"

"Yes, that's correct."

"Absolutely amazing," Jason Bascomb III said, shaking his head for a moment.

"Your honor—" the prosecuting attorney started to protest, but the judge waved her off.

"Stick with your line of questioning, counsel," the judge growled impatiently.

"Yes, your honor. Uh, now then, Agent Lightstone, getting back to that shooting incident at Skilak Lake, I believe you indicated you couldn't prove that any of the individuals involved in this gun battle with Refuge Officer Johnson and yourself were illegally hunting at the time the shooting started, isn't that correct?''

"Yes, it is," Lightstone nodded.

"But that didn't stop you from firing, what, sixty or seventy rounds at these same individuals, many of those from the vantage point of a circling airplane, did it?''

"I was defending—''

"Please just answer the question as asked, Agent Lightstone. Isn't it true, according to the information in your own investigative report, that you fired approximately sixty or seventy pistol and rifle bullets, from the air and on the ground, at these unknown individuals near Skilak Lake?''

"Approximately that, yes.''

"All right. Fifty or sixty." Jason Bascomb III nodded as he stopped at the defense table to make a note on a legal pad. "Now then, do you know approximately how many shots you yourself fired during the raid at Whitehorse Cabin?''

"No, sir, I don't.''

"Well, considering that you were armed at that time with an M-16 automatic assault rifle and a substantial number of thirty-round magazines, in addition to a Smith & Wesson 10mm semiautomatic pistol, with what, three nine-round magazines, shall we say approximately another hundred or so rifle and pistol shots, just to be on the conservative side?''

"That's certainly possible, yes. I wasn't counting—''

"Making a total of, what, a hundred and sixty to a hundred and seventy shots fired during this one investigation? At a minimum," the lead defense attorney added, looking up from his legal pad.

"That's possible, yes." Lightstone nodded.

"Special Agent Lightstone, do you have any idea how many times the average police officer in this country fires his duty weapon in the course of his entire law enforcement career, not counting practice at the firing range?''

"Objection, irrelevant!" Theresa Fletcher called out, standing up from her chair and glaring over at the defense attorney.

"Sustained."

"By comparison, Agent Lightstone, were you aware that the total number of shots fired by Clint Eastwood in all his *Dirty Harry* movies was only—"

"Objection!"

"Sustained." The judge sighed heavily. "Counsel is admonished to keep in mind that there is no jury in this courtroom and that the court has very little patience with this line of questioning."

"I'm truly sorry, you honor." Jason Bascomb III nodded apologetically. "I will stick to specifics from now on."

"Thank you," the judge growled.

"Special Agent Lightstone," the defense attorney went on, "did you engage in any kind of altercation with my client, Mr. Alex Chareaux, during this—uh—raid you conducted?"

"Yes, sir, I did."

"Did you shoot at Mr. Chareaux?"

Lightstone had to stop and think for a minute. "No, sir, I did not."

"Oh, really." The defense attorney smiled. "And pray tell, why not?"

"I . . . my pistol was empty at the time."

"Yes, I suppose all things considered, that's really not too surprising." Jason Bascomb III nodded.

"Your honor!" Theresa Fletcher leaped to her feet again.

"I'm sorry, you honor. My apologies. Uh, so, Agent Lightstone, I assume by your answer that you engaged my client, Mr. Chareaux, with what, your bare hands?"

"That's right."

"And in the process, successfully rendered him unconscious?"

"Yes."

"With a—what do you call it?—carotid choke hold?"

"That's correct."

"Tell me, Agent Lightstone, were you aware, at the time you were applying a choke hold to the throat of my client, that Mr. Chareaux was himself a prisoner of Miss Lisa Abercombie and Dr. Morito Asai?"

"No, I have no knowledge of anything like that," Lightstone responded. "When I first observed Mr. Chareaux, he was running directly toward me with a knife in his hand. He didn't appear to be a prisoner."

"Did it occur to you that Mr. Chareaux might, in fact, have been running from his captors, rather than running toward you?"

"No, it didn't."

"No, I suppose not." Jason Bascomb III nodded. "I take it that in addition to your considerable—uh—experience with firearms, Agent Lightstone, you have also had some martial arts training?"

"Yes, I have."

"In fact, you've had quite a bit of training, haven't you? I understand you hold a third-degree black belt in a discipline of karate?"

"Yes, sir."

"Did you acquire that training with the San Diego Police Department?"

"No, sir, it was on my own. Mostly in high school and college."

"Amazing." The defense attorney shook his head.

"Excuse me?"

"Oh—uh—that's all right, never mind." Jason Bascomb III held up his hand in apology, and then hesitated for a moment, seemingly collecting his thoughts.

"Now then, Special Agent Lightstone," the defense attorney went on, "I think it is apparent to everyone in this courtroom that my client, Mr. Gerd Maas, is still in the process of recovering from severe injuries. Do you happen to have any personal knowledge as to how he acquired those injuries?"

"Yes, sir, I do."

"Would you please explain."

"During the raid I fired four rounds from a .223 Colt Commando rifle at Mr. Maas, striking him in both shoulders and both knees."

"I see. Would that be the same model of rifle that you used at Skilak Lake?"

"Uh, yes, sir, that's correct."

"And didn't the shooting of Mr. Maas occur almost immediately after you fought with Mr. Chareaux and rendered him unconscious?"

"Yes, it did."

"But I believe you indicated previously that you were unarmed at that time. If I remember correctly, you said your pistol was empty . . . again."

"I lost my pistol during the fight with Mr. Chareaux. In looking for it, I found the Colt Commando rifle on the floor, next to the body of one of the subjects," Lightstone explained.

"I see. Well, I suppose that does explain things, doesn't it? Well, then, where were we? Oh, yes, both shoulders, both knees, four shots total. Uh, tell me, Agent Lightstone, wouldn't you say that was a rather impressive display of shooting on your part?"

"I'm sorry, I don't understand the question."

"Special Agent Lightstone, you obviously managed to hit my client, Mr. Maas, in both shoulders and both knees, at some distance, effectively crippling him, using a weapon with which you were completely unfamiliar. Well, perhaps not *completely* unfamiliar," the defense attorney added with a smile. "What I'm asking is don't you think that was rather good shooting on your part?"

Lightstone was amazed at how skillfully Jason Bascomb III had managed gradually to transform his speaking voice from almost accentless English to what was presumably his native British dialect, hereby providing the court with the irresistible image of the classic Rumpole-like English barrister: aggressive and frequently sarcastic, but at the same time, ethical, fair-minded, and determined to uphold the law at all costs. Lightstone was impressed, realizing how effective such a presentation would likely be in front of a jury. Whoever was paying the fees of Jason Bascomb III and his legal team, they were certainly getting their money's worth.

"That particular rifle was equipped with a laser sight," Lightstone explained.

"Oh, you mean one of those devices where you aim a little red dot, and then pull the trigger, and the bullet hits wherever the dot is aimed at?"

"Basically, yes, sir."

"So, in reality, it would have actually been rather difficult for you to have missed Mr. Maas with a weapon like that, especially considering that you are reasonably familiar with firearms in general, and that model of weapon in particular. Isn't that so, Agent Lightstone?"

"I suppose that's true, yes."

"So I assume that must mean you deliberately shot my client in both shoulders and both knees, is that correct?"

Deputy U.S. Attorney Theresa Fletcher started to come up to her feet, but then she hesitated and sat back down.

Henry Lightstone turned his head for a moment to look at Gerd Maas and discovered that the ex-assault group leader of Operation Counter Wrench was smiling pleasantly now, as if recalling a genuinely amusing experience.

"I fired at your client's shoulders to disarm him, to knock a pistol out of his hand, and to prevent him from killing one of my agent partners," Lightstone said calmly.

"Yes, so you said. But why then did you shoot at his knees, to disknee him also?" Jason Bascomb III asked in a calm, quiet, and utterly humorless voice.

"Objection," the prosecuting attorney said, rolling her eyes.

"Overruled. The witness may answer the relevant portion of the question," the judge responded.

"I was advised by the training coordinator at the facility,

who also took part in the raid, that Mr. Maas was an extremely dangerous individual and an expert with a wide range of firearms," Henry Lightstone said carefully. "In view of the fact that Special Agent Dwight Stoner, Special Agent Larry Paxton, and myself were all wounded—and therefore operating at a diminished capacity—when we were confronted by Mr. Maas, I made the decision to fire at his legs to put him on the ground, where he could be safely controlled."

"Oh, really? Might it also be possible, Special Agent Lightstone, that you shot my client in both knees with a .223 caliber assault rifle, because he had just done the same thing to your partner, Special Agent Dwight Stoner, with a much smaller .22 caliber pistol?" Jason Bascomb III asked in that same calm, quiet, and utterly dispassionate voice. "Tit for tat? Vengeance? Is that your job, Special Agent Lightstone? To be an avenging angel against all things that *you* perceive to be evil, as in your *Dirty Harry* movies?"

"Objection, your honor," Theresa Fletcher said firmly, shaking her head in disgust.

"I believe Agent Lightstone answered your question, counsel," the judge said. "Do you have any further cross-examination of this witness?"

"No, your honor."

"Mrs. Fletcher, anything further on redirect?"

"Just a few brief questions, your honor."

"Go ahead."

"Special Agent Lightstone, when you fought with Mr. Chareaux, with your bare hands against his knife, did you believe your life was in danger?"

"Yes, I did."

"In spite of your expertise in karate?"

"Yes, of course."

"Why was that?"

"Our background briefing materials, which included information from a number of state law enforcement officers who knew Mr. Chareaux very well, indicated that he was highly proficient in the art of fighting and killing people with knives, and that he had done so many times in the past.''

Jason Bascomb III leaped to his feet. ''Objection, your honor! That question is completely beyond the scope of the redirect! I request that the statement of the witness be stricken from the record, and that the witness be further admonished—''

''I believe you raised that issue yourself, counselor,'' the judge interrupted. ''Overruled.''

''And during that fight, Special Agent Lightstone,'' Theresa Fletcher went on with undisguised satisfaction, ''were you ever in a position to kill Mr. Chareaux with your bare hands, using your karate expertise, rather than choke him out, as you ultimately did?''

''Yes, ma'am, I was.''

''And when you confronted Mr. Maas with that laser-sighted rifle, did you believe that Special Agent Dwight Stoner's life was in danger?''

''Yes, I did.''

''And you could have certainly killed Mr. Maas with that laser-sighted rifle at any time, with a single shot to the head or heart, could you not?''

''Yes, of course.''

''But in both instances, even though you had the opportunity—and what I would suggest to the court might well have been legal justification—to use lethal force, you chose not to. Why is that?''

''My job is to arrest people and bring them to trial, not to execute them,'' Lightstone said simply.

''Thank you. No further questions, your honor.''

''Mr. Bascomb?''

The lead defense attorney hesitated for a moment, then shook his head. ''Nothing further, your honor.''

''Court will be recessed until one o'clock,'' the judge said, and slammed his gavel.

* * *

Approximately twenty-six hundred miles and three time zones to the west of the northern Virginia federal courthouse, in the latent print area of the National Fish and Wildlife Forensics Laboratory in Ashland, Oregon, the lab's senior fingerprint examiner carefully removed the last pieces of taped cardboard from a submitted evidence item.

"Well, well, look what we have here." He smiled to himself. Then he reached for the nearby phone and dialed a familiar extension number.

"Criminalistics, Dingeman."

"Roger, this is Vinny. Hey, you remember those green aluminum signs we got in from Sequoia National Park a couple of weeks ago?"

"Yeah, what about them?" the forensic scientist said warily.

"Well, you might want to drag your butt down here, 'cause another one just came in from Yellowstone. Only this one's a real brain-teaser."

"Yellowstone, huh? I didn't think they let any of the nutcases leave California. So what's this one say? 'The end is near'?"

"No, that's just it," the latent print examiner chuckled. "This one doesn't say anything at all."

Chapter Twelve

Out of habit as much as anything else, Henry Lightstone waited until almost everyone else had left the courtroom for the noon break before he walked out into the hallway. As he did so, he saw Mike Takahara sitting in one of the empty benches outside the adjacent courtroom.

"So how's it going in there?" the tech agent asked.

"Well," Lightstone shrugged as he sat down on the wooden bench—"unless Fletcher and Bascomb change their minds over lunch, it looks like Stoner's up next.''

"Already?'' Takahara blinked in surprise. "Larry and I figured you'd be on the stand at least two days, minimum.''

"Yeah, me too. Don't know what to tell you. For a guy who's supposed to be a top-dog defense attorney, Bascomb's been playing it real loose. Almost like he's going through the motions.''

"Really? Any ideas on what his strategy might be?''

"Only that if he's got one, it sure as hell isn't obvious.''

"Well, from what I know of Bascomb,'' Mike Takahara said, "if he's acting like he doesn't know where he's going, then it's even odds he's got some kind of trap waiting down the line.''

"I take it you're speaking from experience?''

"Oh, yeah, I've got my share of scars.'' The tech agent nodded. "He spent a day and a half with me on a wire tap deal, trying to convince the jury that I'd gone beyond the limits of the warrant on my entry and installation. Then, after I'd explained for the third or fourth time how careful we have to be on these deals, making sure we dot every *i* and cross every *t*, Bascomb pointed out to the jury that we apparently never noticed that the name of the street was misspelled on the warrant. The prosecutor asked for a brief recess and they worked out a plea, five felonies down to a pair of misdemeanors.''

Lightstone smiled. "Clever fellow.''

"He does make you do your homework. So what about lunch? You got time to grab a sandwich?''

Lightstone shook his head. "I've got to go pick something up from the cafeteria and then head over to the U.S. Attorney's office. Theresa wants to go over my testimony, make sure she didn't leave anything out, before she brings on Stoner.''

"Sounds like she's taking this case seriously.''

"That's why I'm heading over there right now, before she either changes her mind or somebody in the office sets her straight on how a prosecutor's supposed to treat us federal law enforcement types,''

Lightstone said, ''And speaking of which, how are you and Larry and the boss getting along?''

Mike Takahara rolled his eyes. ''Let me tell you something, given the choice, I'd rather be up here being grilled by Boy Wonder Bascomb any day of the week. You have any idea how pissed off Halahan is about us blowing up the warehouse?''

''He's blaming *us*?''

''Us in general, me specifically.''

''Why you?''

''Well, as he put it, even a rookie tech agent straight out of the Training Center should have realized that a burglar capable of breaking into a covert law enforcement operation—*without* setting off a computer-monitored alarm system—was probably capable of doing something else to the computer too.''

''As in programming the thing to detonate a bomb?''

''Uh huh.''

''Is that really possible?''

''Oh, it's possible all right,'' Mike Takahara said. ''All you'd have to do is match up the new program codes with the existing alarm sequences, copy over to the right subdirectory, and then hook up the hardware—which, from the looks of what remains of the warehouse, was probably about ten pounds of C-4 with a solenoid cutout switch between the power source and the detonator.''

''Any idea where it might have been hidden?''

''Based on the blast pattern, I'd say it was probably right behind my desk.''

''Oh.''

''You can see Halahan's point,'' Takahara said, the frustrated expression on his face conveying a sense of wounded pride and professional embarrassment.

''So how long do you figure it would take to set something like that up?''

''You mean the actual installation? I don't know, maybe

fifteen minutes at the outside. Ten if you had everything ready to go. Easiest thing in the world if you know what you're doing and you have had prior access to the alarm programs in the computer, which we know they did.''

"I take it you never got around to checking out the computer after the break-in?''

"Just the alarm sequences.'' Takahara shook his head ruefully. "Halahan's right, I should have thought about the possibilities right away and gone through the entire hard drive, just to be sure. But I was too busy getting over the aftereffects of going through that door in the dark, and then having the alarm system go off. Damn near pissed my pants.''

"Yeah, me too.'' Lightstone nodded.

"And after that,'' the tech agent went on, "there were the minor little details of my forgetting to rearm the system after the break-in, and then letting Paxton set the bomb off with one of the hand transmitters.''

"Yeah, but don't forget,'' Lightstone reminded, "if you had remembered to rearm the system when we were all down there checking things out, the bomb would have probably gone off right then and taken out the whole team, not to mention Rico and a half dozen Boston patrol officers.''

"Which is presumably what our friends, whoever they may be, had in mind when they rigged the bomb in the first place.''

"A reasonable assumption.''

"So all we have to do now is figure out who we pissed off in Boston,'' Mike Takahara muttered. "Any ideas?''

"I can think of two cops and a building inspector who are probably nursing a pretty serious grudge.'' Henry Lightstone shrugged. "But they're still in jail. And setting aside the possibility of a disgruntled cop buddy, that pretty well narrows it down to the Boracatto brothers, their muscle boys, and Halahan. Only trouble is, I can't imagine Tony or Sal or their little muscle boys having the balls to go after a federal agent. And even if they did, the four of them together barely have enough technical skills to flush a toilet. If they tried to rig a bomb like that, they'd probably blow themselves up turning on their own TV.''

"That's pretty much what Halahan thought too."

"You tell him that makes him our number-one suspect?" Lightstone grinned.

"I didn't figure he was in the mood for humor," Mike Takahara said. "As a matter of fact, the whole conversation was more along the line that if I'd done my job right, he'd have fewer people making his life difficult right now."

Lightstone nodded. "So basically, you and Larry got the old 'do you understand the definition of covert' lecture again. Only now Halahan's got a new angle to twist us with—which means he probably *is* pissed, but not necessarily at us."

"That's about it."

"You know, it always amazes me that cops and agents actually want to become supervisors. You'd think they'd know better," Lightstone said, shaking his head.

"Which reminds me," Mike Takahara said, getting up from the bench, "I'd better get back to the hotel, see if Halahan's bounced Larry as the acting team leader yet."

"So who else has he got left?"

"I imagine you, for one."

"Tell him he'd be a whole lot better off with Paxton," Lightstone advised as he stood up and stretched lazily.

"Yeah, I think he's already figured that out." The tech agent smiled. And then, after a moment: "Is this pretty much what it was like working for the San Diego Police Department?"

"No, it was worse at the PD," Lightstone admitted. "At least in the federal government they let you move to a different state when things start going downhill."

"Speaking of moving out of state," Mike Takahara said as they both started walking toward the elevators, "Rico sends his regards."

"Oh yeah?"

"He also said to tell you that as far as he's concerned, Bravo Team is a public menace, and that if any of us—and he mentioned you specifically—ever sets foot in Boston again, he's going to charge us with every unsolved homicide in their files, just so he can stand back and see who tries to kill us first."

"Good old Rico, hell of a guy." Lightstone smiled.

"Warped sense of humor, huh?"

"Who, Rico? No, not really." Lightstone shook his head. "Actually, he doesn't have much of a sense of humor at all. He just has one hell of a lot of unsolved homicides in his files."

Realizing that he was late for his appointment with Deputy U.S. Attorney Theresa Fletcher, and after making a quick detour to pick up a sandwich and a can of soda from the courthouse cafeteria, Henry Lightstone hurried over to the U.S. Attorney's office. In doing so, he decided to take a shortcut to make use of one of the small basement rest room facilities used mostly by the courthouse custodial staff.

He was just washing his hands when he heard an angry voice beyond the door, apparently using one of the pair of public phones in the little cubicle that was outside and just to the left of the rest-room door. As Lightstone began to dry his hands with a couple of paper towels, he heard:

". . . More aggressiveness from your office, I'm going to file another freedom of information request for every case that you have ever tried! That's right! Who the hell do I think I am? I'll tell you what, lady . . ." The irate talker dropped his voice down to a rough whisper just as Henry Lightstone stepped outside the door of the rest room. ". . . you just remember that you heard the word *Wildfire* from me today! You got that? Wildfire!"

Clearly startled by the sudden appearance of the federal wildlife agent, the young man's eyes bulged wide open. Then, before Lightstone could get out of the way, the young man slammed the handset back into the receiver, mumbled a brief, "Excuse me," and then quickly shouldered his way past the agent and disappeared around the corner.

When Henry Lightstone finally managed to arrive at Theresa Fletcher's office, he discovered, to his surprise, that the normally congenial deputy U.S. Attorney was in a foul mood.

"You're late!" she snapped.

Lightstone felt the blood start to rush to his face, but then he quickly brought himself back under control.

"Yes, I *know* I'm late, and I apologize," he said calmly, looking the prosecutor straight in the eye. "I was talking with one of our agents and—"

"Never mind, Henry, I'm the one who should apologize," the short and stocky federal prosecutor said quickly, shaking her head and waving her hand to interrupt his explanation. "I'm sorry, I was just on the phone having a very unpleasant conversation with one of those wonderful courthouse watchdog groups, and I haven't managed to calm down yet."

"What do they want you to do, give Maas and Chareaux a kiss on the cheek and let them walk out the door?"

"No, that was yesterday's caller. This one today apparently isn't going to be happy unless I rig up a gallows right behind the prosecutor's table."

"Really?" Lightstone chuckled. "That's a switch."

"Best I can tell, this one's from one of those ultragreen, ultraradical environmental-activist-type groups that would much prefer to see a lot more trees and wildlife on this planet and a whole lot less humans. Like maybe ninety-nine percent less."

"Sounds like a *real* good idea to me." Lightstone smiled. "In fact, I can think of a couple dozen people they could start with right off the bat. Where do I sign up?"

Theresa Fletcher's face broke out into a wide grin.

"Yes, you and me both." She nodded as she began to lay out her lunch. "Only thing is, these people are apparently pretty selective on who they want living on their 'cleansed' planet. Oh, apparently there won't be any need for us prosecutor or law-enforcement types, because everybody's going to be pretty congenial and easygoing about most things. So I guess you don't need to worry about trying to sign up, even if I knew where to tell you to go, which I don't.''

"You mean they don't even have some kind of corporate headquarters mailing address?''

"Apparently not. Or at least none that we've been able to find so far. Just an address and phone number for a one-lawyer legal firm out in Reston. And as far as we can tell, the only two legal words *he* knows are 'no comment.' ''

"Great, just what we need,'' Lightstone commented as he began to cautiously inspect his cafeteria sandwich. "A few more fruitcakes to make life interesting.''

"Based on the phone calls we've been getting so far, they're certainly capable of at least that,'' Fletcher said. "At first, we just assumed they were one of those ultraradical environmental organizations that pop up every now and then— and then quickly disappear when their backers run out of money or patience. But this one seems to be a lot more organized. Or at least organized enough to drive our office absolutely crazy the last couple of months. Letter drives, petitions, FOIA requests, 'friend of the court' briefs, the whole works. And all of it absolutely legal, so we don't have any choice but to respond.''

"Any idea what they're after?'' Lightstone asked, remembering the angry youth by the phone and wondering if that call might somehow be related. Although he couldn't imagine anyone being stupid enough to make an abusive phone call to a deputy U.S. attorney from a phone inside a federal courthouse. Even the crack dealers were smarter than that.

"You, for one thing.''

Henry Lightstone looked up from his partially unwrapped sandwich with a puzzled expression on his face. He immediately forgot about the angry young man on the phone.

"Me?''

"That's right," Theresa Fletcher mumbled through a bite of chicken sandwich. "The impression we get is that they want to find out everything they can about you, your fellow agents, your agency, and the name and address of every industrial bad guy who—as they so quaintly put it—'has ever plucked a feather off the ass of a duck.' "

"What?"

"Apparently your very words—or a close approximation thereof—when you arrested Maas and Chareaux at White-horse Cabin." The black prosecuting attorney smiled. "Which, as best we can tell from the correspondence and phone calls we've been getting from these idiots, has apparently given you the dubious distinction of being one of their current heroes."

Henry Lightstone had an absolutely dumbfounded look on his face.

"I take it this comes as something of a surprise?" Theresa Fletcher's dark eyes were gleaming with amusement.

"I—I guess I don't understand," Lightstone said, shaking his head. "I mean, I remember saying something like that when we were taking Maas into custody, but I *know* I didn't put it in my report, and it sure didn't come out in testimony. So how would some ultraradical environmentalist group, or whatever the hell they are, know about something like that?"

"As far as I'm aware, the only place those words show up in the entire case file is in Special Agent Stoner's investigative report. When I asked him about it at pretrial, he just shrugged and said he liked the comment—something about you finally understanding what it's like to be a wildlife officer instead of a cop—otherwise he wouldn't have bothered to include it." Fletcher hesitated a moment, and then said: "I take it you haven't read Stoner's report."

Lightstone shook his head. "No, as a matter of practice, we try not to read each other's reports. Just write 'em and file 'em. Makes it easier to keep things straight in our heads as to what each of us actually saw or heard or did."

"That's a good idea. But then if it wasn't one of your agents who released the information—and I can assure you it wasn't anyone in my office, because they know I'd fire them on the spot—the only other likely source would be the discovery copies given to the defense."

"Which doesn't make any sense either," Lightstone said. "Why would Bascomb want some ultraradical environmental group that he couldn't control involved with his clients?"

"He wouldn't," Theresa Fletcher said emphatically. "Jason Bascomb is much too self-absorbed and theatrical to allow any outside group, controllable or not, to be involved with one of his cases. Unless, of course, he was controlling the situation himself, which is always a possibility," she added thoughtfully.

Then, apparently deciding that enough time had been wasted on matters of little relevance, the deputy U.S. Attorney smoothly changed the topic.

"And speaking of my favorite adversary," she said after swallowing another bite of her sandwich, "you handled Jason's cross-examination extremely well this morning. He's considered one of the top criminal trial attorneys in the business, and I think you may now have a sense of why."

"He's a pretty decent actor, for one thing." Lightstone nodded.

"He majored in law and minored in Shakespearean theater, which is an interesting combination when you stop to think about it." Fletcher smiled. "Jason can be absolutely devastating in front of a jury when he gets his emotions fully engaged in the process."

"What was this today, half speed?"

"The way he was letting me ask questions, and you answer, I'd say he was barely idling." The prosecuting attorney shrugged. "But in any case, the judge wasn't buying any of it, and there wasn't anyone else to play to except his clients. My guess is that he's probably saving it all up for the full trial."

"I can hardly wait." Henry Lightstone sighed.

"You and me both. Oh, by the way, I'm sorry about letting him sneak that Clint Eastwood zinger in on you like that. My fault. I should have seen it coming."

"That's okay, I don't see that he accomplished anything, other than making me look like some kind of gun-slinging cowboy." Lightstone shrugged. "And he was right. Outside of the range, most cops never do fire their duty weapons."

"Oh, he accomplished something, all right," Fletcher said with a resigned smile, "Bascomb always lays his groundwork for some purpose, you can count on that. It's just a question of what he's going after."

"Yeah, one of my agent partners warned me about that. Any ideas on his strategy?"

"Well, I can't imagine that he's all that worried about trying to affect the trial. That's pretty cut-and-dried. The only logical assumption is that he's trying to create a useful court record. For what purpose I haven't the slightest idea. But one thing is obvious: Whoever is funding the defense effort on behalf of those three is apparently willing to spend a small fortune to have a top legal gun like Bascomb create a book on your special operations team. And if that's what they want, there's not much we can do to prevent it."

"Just out of curiosity, what do they pay a guy like that?"

"You mean for this hearing?"

"Uh huh."

"I don't know, maybe a four hundred dollars an hour, billable at about ten to twelve hours per day."

"Jesus!"

"Tends to create a bit of what you might call penal envy among his fellow sharks, not to mention us government salaried types." Theresa Fletcher smiled mischievously.

"Yeah, I'll bet." Lightstone grinned. "Any idea who might be paying the bills?"

"Not a clue."

Lightstone thought about all that for a few moments, the expression on his face turning serious. Then he said: "So we aren't going to pull it off, are we?"

"Doesn't look like it." The deputy U.S. Attorney shook her head. "The way things stand right now, there isn't a chance in the world that we're going to be able to convict any of those three on murder charges. We can't identify Parker as being one of the shooters on the island. We can't prove that Alex Chareaux was involved in the assault on Len Ruebottom. And the only really solid thing we have on Maas is an 'attempt-to-commit' on Stoner. And you know what *his* defense is going to be, don't you?"

"No, what?"

"One, that he was hired by the United States government to train a counterterrorist team, which is pretty much the case, depending on how you look at it. And we can count on Bascomb to play that angle up big. Two, that he had no idea that his team was being misused by Wolfe and Abercombie, which is a crock, but difficult to disprove. Three, that he was never involved in any of the actual field operations, which is almost certainly not true, but I'm not sure we can prove that either, unless you can testify that he was the white-haired guy on the ground who put those bullets in the engine of Woeshack's plane."

Lightstone raised his hands palm up in a hopeless gesture.

"We can link him on the ground with that mother grizzly and her cubs, right about the time all that shooting started," he said, "which puts him within a few hundred yards of where McNulty and Butch Chareaux were killed. But I can't testify that he was the one who shot us down, even though I'm pretty sure it was him. Had to be."

"Some Dirty Harry you turn out to be." Theresa Fletcher shook her head with a tired smile.

"Yeah, so much for the good old vigilante cop image." The special agent nodded sympathetically.

"Continuing on with Bascomb's probable defense," the prosecuting attorney said, "Bascomb will certainly claim that the only person Maas actually shot at during that entire raid was Stoner." She looked at Lightstone questioningly. "Anything new on that?"

Lightstone shrugged. "I talked to our lab guys this morning. They spent a week in that training facility, along with an FBI search team, collecting every weapon, bullet, and expended casing they could find. Our lab has two criminalists working on the case full time, and the FBI has one firearms examiner and one fingerprint technician working the case pretty much full time." Lightstone pulled a field notebook out of his jacket pocket. "Right now the suspect weapon count is two hundred and seventy-six pistols, consisting of 9mm, 10mm, .22, .357, .44, and .45 calibers. Fifty-two assault rifles chambered for 5.56mm, 9mm, .223-caliber or 7.65mm NATO rounds. And forty-seven assorted bolt action and semiauto long guns, ranging from one .22 long rifle to a half dozen .416 Rigby's.

"In terms of expended ordnance," Lightstone went on, flipping to the next page, "and not counting the stuff from the underground ranges packed up in cans for disposal, the crime scene teams collected a grand total of one thousand nine hundred and seventy-one expended casings, and one thousand two hundred and fourteen expended bullets, not counting all the fragments. A total of sixty-seven bullets have been removed from the bodies at the autopsies. Apparently there's still a lot of stuff buried in walls, doors, cabinets, and the pop-up targets, but they're not going to bother going after it unless we ask them to."

Theresa Fletcher waved her hand to dismiss the idea.

"So right now," Lightstone continued, "all weapons and magazines have been processed for prints, resulting in two thousand one hundred and eighty-two individual latent print cards, approximately ninety percent of which have been entered into the computers. Of the bullets, so far one hundred and seventy-two have been matched back to specific weapons, and it's been averaging somewhere around four to five hours per examination. According to the guy I talked to, most of the comparisons so far have been based on information from the reenactment tapes, which means they've done the easy ones first. Basically, they've got a long way to go.

By the way, would you like to know what the firearms examiners have to say about you, us, and the case in general?''

"Not really." The prosecutor smiled.

"That's good," Lightstone said, "because it isn't polite. However, in partial answer to your question, they've managed to match Maas's prints to one assault rifle, two 9mm pistols, and one .22 caliber pistol."

"The one he used on Stoner?''

"Yep. And the other three weapons were found cleaned and stored. The prints were basically in gun oil. None of the weapons were used during the raid."

"What about the bullets?''

"You mean the .22's?''

"Yeah.''

"The only .22 lead slugs they found in the whole damn place came out of Stoner's knees, and both of them are too badly torn up for a match, even if it mattered."

"Wonderful," Theresa Fletcher grumbled, shaking her head in irritation. "Which almost certainly means that Bascomb will claim that because Maas is an expert shot—which is absolutely true, according to Sergeant MacDonald—he could have easily killed Stoner if he had wanted to do so. And also that when you and Stoner approached him during the raid, he only fired in self-defense because he thought you were working with Chareaux, and neither of you identified yourselves as federal agents.

"Bascomb will have fun with that one too," the prosecuting attorney added, looking up at Lightstone with a sad smile, "because in a technical sense, you *were* working with Chareaux, at least for a limited time period during the covert part of your investigation, and Abercombie or Wolfe could have easily passed that information on to Maas."

"Hate to tell you this," Henry Lightstone said, "but come to think of it, I don't think that either of us ever *did* identify ourselves to Maas as federal agents when we initially confronted him. We were too busy trying to stay alive.

Although we were wearing our badges visible on our belts at the time.''

"There you go." Fletcher brought her hands up in a "What can we do?" gesture.

"What about McNulty?"

"The FBI lab's been working on the evidence from that scene for almost six months now, and they haven't found a single item that links Maas to the killing of Paul McNulty or any of the other agents."

Lightstone shook his head in disgust.

"We can put them all away on lesser counts," Theresa Fletcher said, "but in my opinion, without the murder charges as a twist, you're not going to get any of those three to roll over and give up your money man. Especially not Maas."

"Yeah, but he's the one we need." Lightstone shook his head in frustration. "As far as we can tell, Chareaux wasn't involved with Operation Counter Wrench at all, other than as a side amusement for Wolfe. And Parker wasn't involved in any of the operational planning."

"No, but we do know he was out at Skilak Lake. Bascomb all but admitted it, probably assuming that we'd be able to match that bullet fragment they took out of his leg last week to your pistol."

"Can we?"

"Not so far. Your crime lab people in Ashland are looking at it with a scanning electron microscope right now, but don't get your hopes up. As I understand it, there's not much there.''

"Wonderful," Lightstone muttered.

"However, going on the assumption that he *was* out there, that puts him in an interesting position to know something about Maas and McNulty. And also, don't forget, Parker was a member of the 'cut-out' team that got the signal from somebody to eliminate the rest of the Counter Wrench group when everything started coming apart."

"You sure the order came from the outside, that they

didn't have prearranged orders from somebody like Wolfe?''

"From what I've read about Wolfe so far, he doesn't strike me as being the brains behind that operation," Theresa Fletcher said. "When you put that together with the money angle, and the fact that they took Lisa Abercombie out right away as soon as you guys hit the door, that adds up to somebody much higher up being in control, as far as I'm concerned. Somebody with a great deal of money and possibly a great deal to lose.''

"So you really think it was some kind of big business conspiracy?"

"Well, I know a lot of perfectly legitimate and absolutely high-powered environmental lobbyist types who certainly think so," Theresa Fletcher said. "In fact, during the last few weeks I've been getting calls from several of them just about every day, wanting to know how things are going, if I need any more support, funding, toilet paper, things like that. And that's not even counting that little shit-head this afternoon who *really* wants to get involved.''

"Environmental lobbyists are calling you directly?"

"They're calling me, my boss, the U.S. Attorney herself, and probably a couple of people in the White House, for all I know.''

"Jesus!''

"Henry," the prosecuting attorney said with a tired smile, "something you need to keep in mind is that this case is a very serious deal as far as some of these environmental people are concerned. After all, don't forget that several of these groups were targets of Operation Counter Wrench in the first place. I almost hate to say it, but there are some very interesting parallels with the Watergate situation here. Paranoia can be a very powerful emotion, especially when you find out that they really *are* out to get you, just as you were telling everybody all along.''

"And with a professional counterterrorist team, no less.''

"Exactly. Their worst fears magnified by a factor of ten.

And just wait until they see Bascomb's presentation of Maas in the starring role of head bogeyman. They're going to go nuts.''

Lightstone sat there in silent contemplation for a few moments, and then said, ''I'm surprised there hasn't been a lot of pressure on you to make a deal. You know, keep this whole thing out of the public eye, let everybody work it all out behind the scenes.''

''Spoken like a man with a true grasp of the bureaucratic mind.'' The prosecuting attorney nodded approvingly. ''I take it you've spent some time in D.C.?''

''I've passed through for a couple of days.'' Lightstone shrugged. ''That was more than enough.''

''I'll bet. But what makes you think there hasn't been political pressure applied?''

''You mean there has?''

''Actually, our office has been subjected to quite a bit of it during the last couple of weeks.'' Theresa Fletcher nodded. ''One side wants full disclosure of every document and transcript in the case, public whipping of the government in general, media confirmation of the conspiracy angle, mass resignations in Congress, and hard jail time for anyone who's ever made a profit off a tree. The other side wants to hold back, play the 'I told you so' role, and then make some significant legislative gains behind closed doors.''

''And that's probably just the environmental side,'' Lightstone said sarcastically.

''Actually, you're absolutely right.'' The prosecuting attorney nodded. ''What we're talking about is a biparty, multiissue, multidimensional puzzle-solving situation on a major scale here. No such things as good guys and bad guys anymore. And you and your fellow agents are right in the middle of it.''

''Wonderful. Just wonderful.''

''In fact, from my relatively low-leveled perspective, the only thing that's kept all of this going along at a fairly steady clip, so far, is the fact that Abercombie and Wolfe keep coming across as a couple of loose cannons who went out of control on their own. Which isn't necessarily what a lot of these people want to hear.''

''So you think Bascomb is positioning himself to make a deal?''

''Why not? They've got the fall guys all in place, both of whom happen to be conveniently dead. We've got a new administration in place, so it happened on somebody else's watch. Everybody gets to posture for the media. And the surviving bad guys get a topnotch legal firm to make sure their medical expenses are covered while they recuperate at government expense for a couple of years at Lompoc. End of problem. It's our legal system at work, Henry, if you'll pardon my cynicism.''

''Except that Paul McNulty, Carl Scoby, and Len Ruebottom were murdered for being federal agents and doing their job,'' Lightstone reminded. ''And the people behind the scenes who set the whole thing into motion get to walk away.''

''If such people exist''—Theresa Fletcher nodded solemnly—''that's correct.''

''That's a lousy ending as far as I'm concerned. It needs a rewrite. So what about the money angle? The construction costs for that facility?''

''There's a lot of money floating around out there in government construction accounts.'' Fletcher shrugged. ''All you've got to do is know how to work the system. And from every indication so far, that was something that Lisa Abercombie *and* Wolfe were really good at.''

''I don't buy it.'' Lightstone shook his head.

''I don't either, but if that's the case, then you need a fall guy for the money angle too. And as far as I know, nobody's come up with a good candidate for that yet.''

''We're trying,''

''I realize that, and I can assure you that this office is going to help in any way we can. But don't forget, this is the first chance the new administration has had to crack down on government employees who haven't exactly been out there supporting the environmental movement. You put all that together with congressional budget fights, international pressures to get tough on environmental issues, world trade deficits, and a couple of upcoming elections, and you've got a lot of people paying very close attention to how the Justice Department handles this case.''

''So what are you saying, that Parker's the key?''

''Maybe.'' The black prosecuting attorney nodded. ''If he was pressured enough, he just might give up Maas on the McNulty shooting, which in turn would put pressure on Maas to cut a deal. And then too, there's always a chance that Parker knows who sent that cut-out signal to his buddy with the .44 Magnum.''

''You think Parker might crack?''

''That's the impression I'm getting.'' Fletcher nodded. ''Maas and Chareaux haven't said three words since they were taken into custody, but I understand that Parker has started to open up a little to the jail staff. The problem is, he acts like he's scared to death of Maas and Chareaux.''

''That may be what convinces him to open up, if he thinks about it long enough,'' Lightstone said. ''Do you think I could get a chance to talk with him away from Bascomb?''

''It's possible, but why don't we hold off until we get this hearing finished? By that time, we may have enough of the pieces on the table to make Parker a decent offer. One that he might not be able to refuse, in spite of his concerns.''

In a small studio apartment across the street from the federal courthouse building, the man who now called himself Riser put down the headset that was electronically connected to a professionally installed ''bug'' in the office of Deputy U.S. Attorney Theresa Fletcher, and smiled.

Chapter Thirteen

At seven-forty-five that Friday morning, the senior member of the federal marshall team responsible for transporting prisoners back and forth between the federal holding facility located on the eastern border of Washington Dulles National Airport, in northern Virginia, and the federal courthouse located approximately twenty-two miles to the east in Arlington, Virginia, handed his 9mm semiautomatic pistol over to his identically armed and uniformed driver.

Then he got out of the front passenger side of the armored transport van, walked across the completely caged parking area, and identified himself to the facility control officer.

Even though the two deputy U.S. marshalls had been playing racquetball together every Saturday morning for the last six months, the control officer still went through the ritual of comparing the team leader's face and ID card against information on his computer screen—mostly because none of them ever knew when the brass might be running a check on the system. He also verified that the facility's video recorders were functioning properly and then pressed the first release button.

The heavy exterior door came open with a loud *clack*.

After entering, and then waiting for the heavy door to close automatically behind him with another loud *clack*, the team leader walked down the thirty-foot hallway—fully lined with solid metal panels, thick bulletproof glass view panels, and ceiling nozzles capable of filling the hallway with cayenne-pepper-based tear gas in under three seconds—and stopped at the second door.

Another loud *clack* echoed through the narrow hallway,

and the team leader entered the tightly secured transfer room.

There were twelve smoothly surfaced metal chairs bolted to the floor along one side of the room, each bearing a number of strategically placed shackle rings. As expected, only one of the chairs was in use this morning.

The team leader walked over to the chair in the far right-hand corner and stood in front of the seated prisoner.

"Are you ready to go, Mr. Chareaux?" he asked in a professionally neutral voice.

Alex Chareaux looked up and glared silently at the uniformed federal officer. Even after six months in federal custody, his reddened eyes had lost none of their ferocity.

"Stand up, please, Mr. Chareaux," the federal officer directed.

Chareaux's feet were shackled together with a sixteen-inch chain. His wrists were handcuffed in front and connected to a thick chain locked snugly around his waist. His arms and legs were not secured to the completely immobile chair, so that he could have easily stood up if he had chosen to do so.

He remained defiant and sitting.

Shrugging indifferently, the transport team leader nodded to the three federal officers who stood waiting on the opposite side of the transfer room. These men were dressed in snug-fitting trousers and shirts—that revealed muscular chests, arms, and legs—soft-soled sneakers, helmets with visors, and thin leather gloves. They were a part of the elite tactical response team that the facility maintained on a twenty-four hour, seven-days-a-week basis to deal with federal prisoners who—in the view of the criminal justice system—represented a significant threat to federal investigators, witnesses, and officers of the court in general.

Coming up to either side of their uncooperative prisoner, two of the muscular officers grabbed Chareaux by the webbed straps that had been sewn at thigh and calf levels in the sides of his orange-and-yellow one-piece jumpsuit. The third officer came around behind Chareaux and power-lifted the Cajun guide up by the webbed straps sewn into the shoulders of the visually distinctive jumpsuit.

Chareaux provided no resistance as the three men easily carried him toward the first of the two exit doors. This was simply part of the ritual that he and the officers had established. He had long since discovered the futility of fighting back, but he wasn't about to assist these men in transporting him to a federal courthouse where his freedom would soon be taken away from him on what he assumed would be a permanent basis.

Something else that Chareaux clearly understood was the significance of the distinctively colored, wire and nylon jumpsuit that was locked on around his chest and shoulders. It had been explained to him in clear and simple terms when he had first entered the facility. The orange-and-yellow pattern represented a well-publicized warning to the public—and to any law enforcement officer in the greater Washington, D.C., metropolitan area—that the wearer was, one, a dangerous individual in federal custody; and, two, considered to be a serious threat to the community at large. The yellow portion of the brightly visible pattern identified vital areas of the human body. In effect, the wearers of these difficult-to-remove jumpsuits were marked targets. And any federal, state, or local officers who observed such an individual moving freely about and not in the custody of a federal marshall was authorized to shoot to kill.

Out in the caged courtyard, the van's two shotgun- and pistol-armed guards stood back as the response team members shackled Chareaux into one of the twelve seats—six of which were bolted to the floor on each side of the van—that were identical to the ones in the holding facility's transfer room. Finally the rear doors of the heavy armored van were closed, barred, and locked.

The front portion of the van, separated from the passenger area by more armor plating, was designed much like a family van in that there were four doors and four captain's chairs. Beyond those basic amenities, however, there were a number of modifications not often found in a family vehicle, such as fully armored doors, door frames, windows, and windshield; solid rubber tires; an armor-plated engine compartment; and interior racks for the shotguns, ammunition, and portable radios.

The two shotgun-armed marshalls secured themselves in the two rear seats and locked the doors. The team leader got into the front passenger seat, locked his door, accepted his pistol back from the driver, secured it in his hip holster, fastened his safety belt, and then reached for the radio mike.

"Tango-Uniform-Three to Base One."

"Base One, go."

"Tango-Uniform-Three, we are en route to Arlington Courthouse with one Poppa. Activating homer now."

Reaching forward to the dashboard, the team leader flipped a heavy-duty red switch to the on position.

"Base One to Tango-Uniform-Three, your homer is confirmed, zero-eight-zero-five hours."

"Tango-Uniform-Three, homer confirmed, zero-eight-zero-five hours," the team leader repeated. "Open the gate."

From a distance of approximately four hundred yards, the man known as Riser knelt down behind a concealing tree and watched the distinctive white van drive through the opened chain-link gate. Humming to himself, he waited until the van had disappeared through the surrounding trees on the narrow back road.

Then he picked up his spotting telescope and smiled.

Five miles east of the federal holding facility, and seventeen miles west of the Arlington Federal Courthouse, in the basement of a four-story brick and glass building located on the shore of Lake Thoreau, in the town of Reston, Virginia, Leonard Harris barely responded to a knock at the door to his large and dimly lit corner office.

"Yes, come in," he mumbled absentmindedly. He didn't

bother to look up from his computer screen.

Five seconds later, when no one walked in the main door and the knocking continued, Harris realized his mistake.

Reaching under his desk, he released the lock to the small metal emergency access and exit door in the far rear corner of his office.

The young man known as Eric entered, carefully closed the door behind him, and then walked over to the workstation where Leonard Harris had been spending most of his time during the past few days.

"Hi."

"Hello, Eric. I'm surprised to see you here this morning. I thought you were going to take a few days off to go fishing with your father."

"I still am, but I'm not leaving until tomorrow. He's going to be tied up with some business until Sunday morning, so I'm going to catch up with him then."

"That's nice." Harris nodded absentmindedly as he continued to stare at the three monitors, waiting for one of the pieces of information he needed to appear. "So where are you planning on going?"

"We're going to meet at the Hawk's Nest Marina, out on Cat Island in the Bahamas. Check out the Tartar Bank, then head out to the Bimini Islands and work our way south, see if we can hook into a couple of big blues."

"Is that so?" Harris said, his eyebrows coming up in surprise as he turned away from the monitors and stared intently at his young assistant. "Sounds like it might be an interesting trip. Are you going to be staying at the villa?"

"No, I've got a room booked at the Cutlass Bay Club. Apparently Dad's going to be using the villa for some corporate board stuff this weekend."

"Oh, *really*?"

"Yeah, bummer deal." The young man shrugged. "But that's okay, they've got a good bar down at the Cutlass. Besides, who the hell wants to hang out with a bunch of corporate types when you're on vacation?"

"Good point." Harris nodded carefully, wondering if his young assistant really *hadn't* picked up on the possibilities, or if he was just playing dumb. The latter was still always a possibility, no matter how unlikely, the veteran game player reminded himself. "So aside from all of that, how are things going this morning?"

"Actually, that's what I came to ask you," Eric said.

"Other than Crowley still being an outstanding issue, and Riser seems to be in possession of one of our computers" —Harris shrugged—"not too badly."

"What's happening with Crowley?"

"The police have contacted his parents. Naturally, they have no idea what their son could possibly have been doing to cause himself to get killed in a downtown Boston hotel room. As far as they were aware, he was just a typically rebellious twenty-four-year-old with wealthy parents who hadn't quite gotten himself settled into the family traditions yet. They are deeply shocked and saddened, of course, even though William—as they call him—had turned out to be something of a disappointment. But they are also an extremely religious family who have three other younger children to be concerned about. In essence, they seem to believe that their son's death was God's will. More to the point, they are also convinced that it had to be the result of a random hotel break-in, and that their son just happened to be at the wrong place at the wrong time."

"Which is basically true, when you get right down to it," Eric said. "Christ, what a family! No wonder Crowley seemed depressed all the time."

"Yes, but I doubt that the police are going to be willing to let it go at that."

"What can they do? From the sound of things, they can't have many leads."

"No, they don't. But they are doing all the predictable things, among which is contacting all Crowley's known associates. Somewhere along the line there's a chance that they might get to you," Harris warned.

"Crowley? Let me think a minute. Short scrawny little character? Wears those funny wire-rim granny glasses? Yeah, that sounds like a guy I used to know at Harvard." The young man shrugged. "Actually, I really didn't know him all that well. Matter of fact, I don't think I ever knew his first name. Kind of a shy type. I remember we drank a few beers together a couple of times, usually after a touch football game with a bunch of the other guys. Used to run across him on campus and occasionally at the hockey games. Haven't seen him in quite a while, so I really don't know—"

"Actually, that's not true," Harris corrected. "You saw him just recently. Four days ago, to be exact. At the airport. Remember?"

"Oh, yeah, that's right." Eric nodded uneasily.

"Do you remember what you were doing there?"

"Sure. I was there to pick up a friend. I saw Crowley sitting there at the bar and remembered who he was. We ordered a couple of beers, sat around shooting the bull until he had to leave to catch his flight."

"Do you remember the name of the friend you were waiting for? And about what time he or she arrived?"

"Uh, no, actually, now that I think about it, that must have been a different day. As I recall, I . . . shit, what *was* I doing there?"

"Waiting to pick me up," Harris said.

"I was?"

"Of course. As you recall, we've been trying to arrange a new Dungeons and Dragons Masters tournament for over a month now. I told you I would be going to New York early that morning, and then returning on the two-thirty shuttle. I had asked you to pick me up, but then I had to cancel the trip at the last minute and forgot to tell you about it. You thought I'd missed my flight, and waited around for another hour. Which is why you happened to be in the airport at the right time to see Crowley and have a beer with him, should anyone ask, which they probably won't."

"That's right, I forgot all about that." Eric nodded. Then

he smiled and said, "When did you work all that out?"

"When I realized that Crowley was dead and there would undoubtedly be an investigation."

"You think ahead."

"As should you, my young friend," Leonard Harris said in a serious voice. "There are going to be times in the very near future when Ember and I may not be in a position to provide you with an alibi. When those situations occur, you *must* be prepared to account for your whereabouts on your own. And you want to be very careful how you go about doing that," the older man warned. "The police are rarely as clever in conducting their homicide investigations as the movies and television would have you believe, but they are invariably methodical and persistent. They depend greatly upon the premise that the guilty parties will always lie to them initially, out of fear or panic if nothing else, and then be forced into telling more lies when their story starts to come apart. Eventually, those individuals become irretrievably entangled in their own deceit. At that point, it's just a matter of the formalities. You don't *ever* want to find yourself in that position."

"So I have to assume that if they ever do talk to me, and take a statement, they'll compare whatever I say with statements from other witnesses, right?"

"As a witness in a homicide investigation, you should assume that *anything* you say will be checked out, word for word." Harris nodded solemnly. "And remember, you want to try to be as vague as possible whenever you can. The police won't expect you to remember every little detail of your life, especially if you had no reason to think that those details were important at the time. But definitive statements are always dangerous, because there are hundreds of ways for an investigator to check them out. Credit card receipts, airline and hotel reservations, telephone records, security cameras . . . or statements by a witness who might have noticed the two of you arriving at the airport in the same car?"

Harris waited until his young assistant finally realized that it had been a question.

"Uh, no, it's okay. We went in separate cabs."

"Good. What about the receipt?"

"What about it?"

"Did you turn it in on a voucher?"

"No, I didn't think we'd want to have a record of that particular trip on file."

"Do you still have it?"

"Uh . . . yeah, probably, in the trash can next to my desk at home."

"Go home right now, get it, and resubmit your voucher," Harris said. "As a dedicated and hardworking member of the board of a major computer gaming association, you have every right to expect the association to cover your expenses when you offer to go pick up the president of that association at the airport. And especially when the additional expenses were the result of a miscommunication that simply wasn't your fault. Who paid for the beer?"

"I did."

"Yours and his?"

"Yes."

"Good. Add that onto the voucher also, as a business expense."

"Really?"

"Absolutely. Did you leave a tip?"

"Yes."

"Double it on the voucher. And if the police ask you about it, hesitate, and then confess."

"Misdirection?"

"That's right." The older man nodded approvingly. "Nothing wrong with exposing a little personal greed. They'll be expecting it, and it will make them feel reassured when you look and act as though you're afraid they might turn you in. The last thing you want to do is to stand out in their minds as someone who has everything covered. Or worse, someone who has something serious to hide."

"I'll get the voucher resubmitted this afternoon," the

younger man promised. And then after a moment: "Christ, do you really think they're going to dig that deep over what looks like a chance meeting and a couple of beers?"

"No, probably not. But it's important that you think ahead and that you're prepared in case they do."

"What if they ask me to take a lie detector test?"

"Say no immediately. Be apologetic and offer to help in any other way possible, but say that you've heard that polygraph machines are notoriously inaccurate. No offense meant to them as investigators, but you simply don't believe that machines should be allowed to judge humans. That's why you're so interested in computer gaming. You think humans should be able to beat machines."

"Are they?"

"What?"

"Polygraphs," Eric said. "Are they inaccurate?"

"No, they're not. They can be beaten, but only by people who have a serious pathological indifference to lying."

"I don't mind lying." The young man shrugged. "I've always figured I could do that with the best of them."

"Is that so? Are you willing to wager twenty to thirty years of your future on your expertise in that area?"

"Uh, no."

"Then don't. If the police ask, tell them no, but then immediately assure them that you want to be as open and as helpful as possible by offering them complete access to your office, your apartment, and your car. Any time they wish, day or night. Better yet, hand them your apartment and car keys right there on the spot and tell them to go to it. It's highly unlikely that they will accept, but make the offer anyway. It shows sincerity."

"Which means I'd better go through my apartment again, when I pick up that receipt, just to make sure."

"Excellent idea, but don't make any attempt to clean things up. Get rid of anything that might be compromising, certainly. But other than that, leave everything else just as it is."

"What about leaving a pair of my girlfriend's underwear on the floor in the bedroom?"

"Do you really have a girlfriend?"

"No, but I've got some underwear hanging around." The young man shrugged without any apparent sense of embarrassment.

Harris nodded. "Kicking a pair partway under the bed might be a nice touch."

"Suppose they really *do* ask to search my office or my apartment? Wouldn't I want my lawyer involved at that point?"

"Over what? The unfortunate death of some individual whom you barely remember from college? Someone who means nothing to you at all? Absolutely not. Unless the police actually start focusing in on you as a suspect, a lawyer is the last person you want to be associated with in this situation. You might as well wave a red flag that says, 'Look over here, I've got something to hide.' "

"All this over a goddamned throwaway like Crowley." The young man shook his head.

"Be grateful he's dead," Leonard Harris advised. "Try to imagine what things would be like if he were alive and anxious to talk with the police."

"But I never told Crowley anything at all about what we're really doing, and he never seemed to care much about whom I was working for," Eric said defensively. "I mean, it was like I told him, he was just going to be a go-between. Somebody to transfer things back and forth and to renegotiate the terms of a deal."

"That's right. But remember, he knew you, and he knew that the deal you were sending him out to renegotiate potentially involved several million dollars."

"I realize all that," the young man said testily. "But Crowley had a personal trust from his grandfather of over fifteen million dollars. His family is Cape Cod old money from way back. I was convinced at the time—and still am, for that matter—that the money side of the deal didn't mean a damn thing to him. The guy just wanted to do something adventurous before his family turned him into a seventh-generation investment banker. That's why I used him.''

"Suppose he talked to Riser. Did you think about that?"

Eric blinked and was silent.

"So what if he did?" he said hesitantly after a moment. "What could Crowley possibly give him that would be of any value?"

"A description of what you look like and where the two of you went to school. The model of the car you drive. Two days, three at the outside, and Riser could have your name, your home address, your parents' address, your current employer, *and* your outside interests . . . which means us.''

"But—but what—" the young man started to stammer, but Harris interrupted.

"At that point," Harris said calmly, "I can tell you that, from the 'corporate' viewpoint, you would be considered a dangerous liability to the Wildfire project.''

"Me?"

"That's right." Harris nodded. "Why, didn't it ever occur to you that if things went wrong, you might be expendable?"

The impact of the words hit the young man like a punch to the solar plexus. Harris allowed his young protégé to think about that for a few moments before he went on.

"Don't worry, Eric," he said soothingly. "If you became expendable, then so would I . . . and I'm not about to let that happen, so we need to keep Riser engaged and distracted. That's why we want him to take on the agents directly, rather than to simply leave evidence of ICER involvement as we originally planned.''

The young man nodded, seemingly able to breathe again.

"I just didn't understand," he said hesitantly, remembering the puzzled expression on Henry Lightstone's face in the basement of the courthouse, and realizing that he might be better off if Riser did kill the aggressive federal agent. "I guess I thought they were sort of on our side, and it didn't seem right.''

"Whether it's *right* or not isn't the issue," Harris said soothingly. "If you're forced to choose between principles and survival, there's only one logical choice."

"So what do *we* do now?" Eric asked quietly, the cocky and arrogant demeanor of his previous visits now long gone.

"At the first opportunity we reassure Riser that all is well, and that as far as we are concerned, Crowley was a greedy and foolish idiot who went rogue all on his own. And, of course, got exactly what he deserved."

"In other words, blame Crowley for the renegotiation idea. Like he was trying to arrange his own cut, right off the top."

"Exactly."

"You think Riser will believe that?"

"Maybe, maybe not." Harris shrugged. "The important thing is for Riser to remain absolutely convinced that he is the master of his own destiny. You must remember that Riser is a professional. If he believes that he and his organization are secure, he will concentrate on the agents *and* his mission."

"Because he doesn't get paid until he completes the job, right?"

"Until he completes each phase of the job," Harris corrected. "Yes, that's right."

Eric smiled, seemingly relieved now that the discussion was back on matters that were more familiar and far less threatening.

"You said something about being concerned that Riser might have stolen that computer we gave Crowley," he reminded.

"Yes." Harris nodded. "That computer was set up as a very temporary arrangement, to give Crowley a safe and secure means of contacting us, should something unforeseen occur."

"So what's the problem? We bought it with cash and used

a false out-of-state business name, so there's no way that the police can track it back to us. And I had Crowley pay for his own registration into the network.''

''You're forgetting something,'' Harris said.

''What's that?''

''Crowley was very unsophisticated when it came to computers. That was why we decided to program the one we gave him so that it would automatically log into a password-protected Internet bulletin board when he turned it on.''

''Yeah, I remember talking to you about that. It sounded like a good idea.''

''It was, but we didn't expect Crowley to lose the computer or Riser to acquire it.''

''Are you sure he has it?''

''Apparently.'' Harris nodded. ''At least it wasn't recorded in the listing of evidence taken from Crowley's hotel room. But there was a modem connector cord listed.''

''Has Riser tried to contact us with it?''

''No, not yet.''

''Then I don't understand the problem. So Riser has the computer. What can he do with it, other than log into the bulletin board and wait for us to answer?''

''The problem is, Eric,'' Harris said calmly, ''we know that Riser has access to some sophisticated electronics expertise. It would not be beyond such people to examine the program code, gain access through the network into the main board, and then acquire some useful information about one protected bulletin board in particular, such as the user account names and phone numbers.''

''You mean our *corporate* account?'' The young man almost choked on the word.

''That's right.''

''Why would he want to do that? I mean, he works for us, for Christ's sake!''

''The thing you must always remember about our friend Riser,'' Leonard Harris said carefully, ''is that he is extremely talented at recognizing and then immediately taking advantage of an opponent's weakness.''

''But . . .'' the youth started to protest, but hesitated when Harris raised a cautionary hand.

''Remember, Eric, Riser is *not* one of our employees. He's a private contractor. And as such, I can assure you that his only allegiance is to himself. The fact that we're the ones paying his fee right now is no guarantee—no guarantee *at all*—that he won't turn on us someday in the future for an equivalent or larger fee.''

''Christ'' the young man whispered.

''Perhaps now you understand why, up until now, we've required Riser to communicate with us through a neutral intermediary who takes a small cut of the action and supposedly provides at least a minimal enforcement of the rules. But if Riser has acquired the ability to communicate with us directly . . .'' Harris left the rest unsaid.

''So what are you going to do?''

''Wait until he calls. And when he does, explain to him that we don't mind him having the computer at all, but the system as it stands right now is awkward. Neither side knows when the other is calling. What I'll offer to do is reprogram the laptop over the modem, and put him into direct electronic contact with us for real-time communications. That way, any time he wants to contact us, all he has to do is hook up the modem, dial us up, and a bell rings at our end.''

''Why the hell would we do that?'' Eric asked. ''Sounds to me like you're making it worse than it already is. Might as well give him a key to our back door.''

''Not necessarily.'' Harris shook his head. ''The address we program into the computer will connect up here through a series of routers that *we* control. In essence, we give ourselves an electronic cutout. Once his query hits the first router, the switching equipment will transfer the link to at least one other cutout location at a very rapid speed. Ultimately we'll get the call, but Riser's electronic gurus won't be able to follow the physical connections to our facility.''

''But they would be able to find the physical location of

the switching points, right?''

''The first one, certainly.''

''But what if they just decide to go to the location, break in, examine the switching equipment, read the codes again, and then start tracking down switch site number two?''

''That's the beauty of the system,'' Harris said. ''The new routers are very small, and I have an associate who works for the telephone company. He can create these switch sites virtually anywhere.''

''So where are you going to have him put them?''

''The first one was placed in the middle of the communications center of the Fairfax County Police Department.''

Eric blinked in surprise. ''Is that a good idea?''

''If you're talking about the Fairfax County Police, their technical people would have no indication that such a device was there, and absolutely no reason to make a random search through literally tens of thousands of electronic components.''

''What about Riser? Won't that scare him off or make him suspicious?''

''From what I'm told, our Mr. Riser doesn't scare that easily. But even so, I don't think he'll be willing to risk an intrusion into a protected area of a major police facility just for the minimal advantage he'd gain in terms of communications. If anything, I think he'll simply be amused. Besides, he's got to focus on dealing with those agents. They won't be anywhere near as easy as our ICER 'friends.' ''

The young man was silent for a while, thinking. Then he said, ''We're sure going to a lot of work to protect ourselves from a guy who's supposed to be on our side, or at least for right now,'' he added.

''Believing that to be true would be the most serious mistake of all,'' Harris cautioned. ''If there's anything that's absolutely certain in this operation, it's that our friend Riser is on nobody's side but his own, no matter what.''

Eric shook his head slowly. ''Man, where did you ever find a guy like that?''

"People like Riser are always out there, Eric. It's just a matter of having the initial introduction *and* the proper go-betweens," the older man added meaningfully. "It's a delicate balance. Much like the male and female Black Widow. They need each other, but the negotiations are always perilous."

"So which one are we?"

Harris raised one eyebrow questioningly.

"Hungry or horny?" the young man grinned.

"When you get right down to it, my young friend"—Harris smiled knowingly—"that is always the question."

Harris waited until his young assistant had disappeared through the small metal door and exited into the high-rise parking garage at the other end of the narrow tunnel. Then he quickly reached for his secured phone.

"Ember," he said, "this is Eagle. It's time to fly."

At precisely eight-thirty-five that Friday morning, the driver of a specially converted light-gray van turned into the underground ramp-way entrance of the federal courthouse in Arlington, Virginia, and stopped at the guard booth. Moments later, a black sedan with smoked windows pulled into the downwardly sloped driveway behind the van.

There was a uniformed Federal Protection Service officer sitting behind an armored glass panel in the front of the booth, and a second officer in the back keeping an eye on a panel of monitors. While both of these men were classified as federal officers, they had actually received only a minimal amount of training in investigative law enforcement techniques, and were armed with relatively low-powered 38-caliber revolvers. Their primary job was to confirm the identification of individuals authorized to enter the underground parking area of the courthouse, and to raise an alarm if something went wrong.

The idea was that if such a situation should ever occur, the perpetrators who caused that alarm would suddenly find themselves facing a group of tactical response team officers who possessed a considerable amount of law enforcement training and far more lethal weaponry.

In effect, the officers who manned the guard booths of the federal facility were considered to be the trip-wire portion of the courthouse security system. It was a dubious honor at best.

The guard at the booth window first eyed the driver of the van and then the four passengers. As he did so, he casually brushed his fingers across the raised surface of the panic alarm button.

"Can I help you?"

Wordlessly, the driver held up a laminated pass that contained his photograph.

The guard checked his computer monitor, confirmed the identification of the driver and expected passengers, and then waved them on. He did precisely the same with the occupants of the black sedan.

Fifteen minutes later—after having used the van's pneumatic ramp to unload Gerd Maas and his wheelchair, along with Roy Parker, Jason Bascomb III, two assistant counsels, and two of the four highly trained security guards hired by the firm of Little, Warren, Nobles & Kole to protect their bail money—the light-gray van and the black sedan exited the underground parking area. Both vehicles turned left at the main road that led back to the adjoining town of Oakton, Virginia.

Approximately two blocks away, the man known as Riser reached forward, started up the engine of his nondescript pickup truck, and smiled.

Chapter Fourteen

Mike Takahara looked up from his cereal as Henry Lightstone walked out of one of the bedrooms of their two-bedroom, four-bed, Hyatt Regency Reston suite. Lightstone was wearing a nicely tailored three-piece suit.

"Where are you going, looking like that?"

"Court."

"I thought you finished testifying yesterday."

"Yeah, I did. Figured I'd keep an eye on Dwight, give you a chance to catch up on your reports."

"You sure you want *Henry* watching your back?" the tech agent asked dubiously, turning to the massive agent who was sitting next to him at the breakfast nook, casually finishing off an entire box of cereal.

"Why not?" Stoner shrugged as he got up from the table. "How much trouble can he get us into when we're sitting in a federal courthouse?"

"I'm not sure that's something I'd want to think about this early in the morning," Takahara said as he watched the huge agent wash out his bowl, toss the empty cereal box in the trash, and then disappear into the bathroom.

"Hey, come on, I'm just following Halahan's instructions," Lightstone protested. "You heard what he said. Until he says differently, he doesn't want any of us going anywhere by ourselves."

"Actually, as I recall, I think he was referring specifically to you and Paxton," Takahara said, patting his portable computer. "But hey, that's fine by me. I can use a little catch-up time."

"Okay, my turn in the barrel with Bascomb," Stoner

grumbled as he came back out of the bathroom, pulling on his suit coat.

"Good for your character." Lightstone smiled.

"Didn't do much for yours," the huge agent pointed out.

"Well, guys"—Mike Takahara smiled cheerfully—"if something goes wrong, give me a call."

Lightstone was starting out the door when the word *call* suddenly jarred at his memory.

"Hey, that reminds me," he said. "Does the name Wildfire mean anything to you?"

Mike Takahara shook his head. "No, I don't think so. Should it?"

"I'm not sure. It was just something I heard a guy say yesterday in the courthouse. The way he said it struck me kind of funny, like it was a threat or something like that."

"You want me to run it through some of the LE bulletin boards, see if anything pops up?"

"Yeah, I sure would, if you don't mind."

"No problem." The tech agent reached for his computer. "I'd rather play on the net than write reports any day."

At nine o'clock that Friday morning, Harold Ericson Tisbury, wealthy industrialist, chairman of the board of Cyanosphere VIII, and the current chief executive officer of ICER, walked into his son's office and sat down.

"Well, are you ready to go?" Sam Tisbury asked cheerfully.

Sam Tisbury, the CEO of Cyanosphere VIII, the one and only son of the chairman of the board, and the executive secretary of ICER, appeared relaxed and comfortable in his traditional traveling clothes: a light-blue polo shirt, sun-faded chinos, and a pair of six-year-old deck shoes. By contrast, Harold Tisbury was still in a coat and tie, although he had loosened up to the extent of exchanging his glossy-shined brogans for a pair of year-old penny loafers.

"I think so," the elder Tisbury nodded.

"Have you seen the Crucible beta units yet?"

"No, I haven't."

"I just got one in this morning. The first one off the test rack."

Sam Tisbury reached into a cabinet behind his desk and brought out a polished and hinged wooden box that was about eight inches square and sixteen inches long. He placed it on his desk, opened the box, and carefully removed a metal cylinder approximately six inches in diameter and twelve inches long, with extended one-inch knobs at both ends. The entire cylinder was covered with a chemically etched brown-and-green camouflage pattern.

The entire device appeared to be made of three subunits: two identical end pieces, the outer cylindrical surfaces of which were perforated with what appeared to be hundreds of eighth-inch diameter holes, and one center piece. The center piece was actually a hand-adjustable ring with machine-cut numbers 0, 0.1, 0.5, 1, 2, 3, 4, 5, and 10 that stood out clearly on the curved ring's chemically etched brown/green surface. The numerals had been cut into the ring at even intervals along a one-third span of the ring surface. In the exact middle of the remaining two-thirds of the ring surface, an infinity symbol had been cut.

Getting up and walking around to the front of his desk, Sam Tisbury extended the device out to his father.

"Mr. Tisbury," he said with exaggerated formality "allow me to introduce you to Crucible."

"An empty Crucible, I assume." The elder Tisbury smiled as he cradled the heavy polished cylinder on his lap with his shaky hands.

"Yes, of course."

"And these are the sensors at either end?" Harold Tisbury asked, turning the device so that he could examine the knobby structures.

"Actually, they're the new combined transmitter/sensors. That was one of the major design problems we had to resolve. Trying to come up with a detecting *and* a transmitting system that was extremely sensitive, absolutely reliable, and virtually impact-proof.''

"I gather our research team succeeded?"

"Far beyond our expectations." Sam Tisbury nodded. "The specs called for a recognition window of a thousandth of a second, with a structural impact resistance of fifty G's. As of this morning the engineers are claiming to have exceeded every one of those specs under routine manufacturing conditions."

"What's the effective range?"

"Through solid rock, the signal will travel a minimum of fifty feet before dropping off the scale of the sensor, which is fine as far as we're concerned because that's far greater than any practical separation of the units anyway."

"Have they tested them out in the open?"

Sam Tisbury nodded. "That was one of the mandatory tests, to find out how far the primed units would have to be kept from the ignition site."

"And?"

"Out in the open, the signal drops off at approximately twelve miles."

"Dear God!"

"Actually it's not that much of a problem," Sam Tisbury said. "It just means that for safety, the initial triggering device should be kept at least fifteen miles from the site until all the primed units are set into place. And, of course, you'd want to keep the units set at the infinity delay setting until they were ready to be put into place."

"Infinity delay?"

"One of the settings on the timing ring," the younger Tisbury explained. "The timing ring basically sets the time delay between the sensor receiving the ignition signal— either directly from the triggering device or remotely from another ignited unit—and the device going off." He showed his father how the infinity marking was lined up with an engraved arrowhead on each of the end pieces of the device.

Harold Tisbury tried to turn the ring and discovered that he could move it easily only in short increments, and that the ring seemed to lock into place at all ten delay-setting positions with nice, solid clicks.

"You can adjust the delay time by hand, with a little bit of effort," Sam Tisbury explained, "but it's virtually impossible for the setting to be moved from the infinity area to one of the time sequences without a deliberate effort."

"Yes, so I see." Harold Tisbury nodded approvingly. But then he thought of something.

"What if one of these devices *does* go off accidentally and then sets off all the others?"

"It would probably create a horrible mess," Sam Tisbury conceded. "But I'm not sure that's a practical concern. We've tried everything we can to set one of the Crucible units off without having it directly linked to the triggering unit—no matter what the delay setting—and we haven't been able to do it yet. And that includes crushing one under a drop press, and trying to blow another one up with ten pounds of C-4."

"Where did you do that?"

"At one of Sergio's test sites in Chile."

"I take it he didn't have to file an environmental impact report first?"

"Exactly." Sam Tisbury smiled.

"What about the manufacturing failure rate? Are we on line there too?"

"Right now we're projecting less than one unit out of a hundred at the beta level, based on the first two thousand units—the testing of which, at the rate they're going, will be completed by five o'clock this evening."

"Excellent."

Harold Tisbury sat there for a moment, rubbing his dry fingers across the bright engraved numerals.

"You know," he finally said, "it's really not as heavy as I expected."

"Part of that is due to the new alloy. The outer container has two primary functions: first, to absorb the shock of placement and protect the sensing and transmitting devices;

and second, to contain the source elements that are going to be generating a tremendous amount of heat. As it turns out, designing for one function tended to negate the other. The aluminum alloy we came up with at first really wasn't satisfactory, so our research engineers went after a completely new stainless steel/titanium alloy, and came up with a major metallurgical breakthrough.''

''Sounds expensive.''

''It is, but it turns out to be nearly as light as aluminum, but tremendously heat resistant. There should be some interesting application developments once we release the patent.''

''Why did you add the camouflage coating?''

''Apparently our engineers wanted to do some further testing of one of our new chemical etching techniques—to see how well the coating functions under extreme temperature conditions. A side benefit that will save us the cost of a separate testing program. As I understand it, the camouflage pattern wasn't intentional; it just comes out that way.''

''Incredible,'' the elder Tisbury whispered as he handed the device back to his son.

''Yes, it is. As a matter of fact, I think we should give the entire engineering department an additional bonus this year.''

''Good idea, do that.'' The elder Tisbury nodded absent-mindedly.

Sam Tisbury returned the device to its box and then waited a few moments before he said, ''So what's the matter, Harold?''

The seventy-nine-year-old industrialist sighed deeply. ''Jonathan is scared and Wilbur is deeply concerned. And so, for that matter, is Sergio. I could hear it in their voices.''

''About what? The meeting?''

''I'm sure the meeting is an underlying issue, but I believe their primary concern is with Alfred.''

''Jonathan's FBI rumors again?''

''Among other things.''

"They still don't trust him, do they?"

"No, they don't. Not at all."

"Do you?"

"I don't know, Sam," the elderly industrialist said. "I've known Alfred Bloom ever since he was born. I grew up with his father. A year ago I would never have thought to question either his courage or his integrity."

"But now?"

"I really don't know." Harold Tisbury shook his head sadly.

"I still think we have a chance to turn him back around," Sam Tisbury said. "We convinced him to buy that new boat and get out on the water by himself for a while. It was a nice long sail down to the Bahamas. Alfred's had several days to get himself refocused and to forget about Lisa. We just have to hope that it worked."

"Did you get hold of him and let him know that the time for the meeting has been moved up, to accommodate Crane?"

"No, not yet, but that shouldn't be a problem. We exchanged faxes yesterday. He was just off Freeport, in the Northwest Providence Channel, and he assured me that he would be at Cat Island in plenty of time to make the meeting. I would expect him to be somewhere between Nassau and the Berry Islands by now."

"His favorite sailing grounds." Harold Tisbury nodded. "How's the weather holding out down here?"

"Apparently not too bad. Winds are fair to moderate, five to fifteen knots, but with some erratic shifts to the northwest. I suspect that's going to give him a few problems when he gets into the Sound, but he seemed to think that it was perfect sailing weather for his new boat. I got the impression that he was enjoying the challenge."

"Good," Harold Tisbury rasped. "The weather will force him to pay attention to his sailing and keep his mind away from the past." The elderly industrialist seemed to want to continue with that thought, but then shook his head in irritation and said instead: "Are you going to make another attempt to contact him about the change in time?"

Sam Tisbury nodded. "The way he described his planned course, he's likely to be there at the villa sometime around noon tomorrow. But just in case he's still hanging around offshore, I'm going to send him another fax—confirming the new time—when I get into Nassau, which should be sometime around two or three tomorrow afternoon."

"That late?"

"I've got a couple of stops to make first."

"Part of your diversionary trip?"

Sam Tisbury nodded. "I want to check in with a couple of our friendly law enforcement types on the Royal Bahamas Defense Force, make sure that we don't have any unusual DEA or FBI activities going on in the area."

"An excellent precaution." The elder Tisbury nodded approvingly. "But don't you think you're cutting things a little too close with your flights?"

"No, I don't think so." Sam Tisbury shook his head. "The weather front is a long way off. I've arranged for a private hop from Freeport to Nassau, and then a separate plane and pilot out of Oakes Field down to the Cutlass Bay Club airstrip. Once I get there, I'll use one of the Jeeps to drive up to the villa. I figure I should be there just around five o'clock. In the worst case, if I get a flat on the way up and have to hike, five-thirty at the latest."

"What about Alfred? Do you think we're giving him enough notice about the schedule change?"

"More than enough." Sam Tisbury nodded reassuringly. "That new boat's rigged with a 75-horsepower diesel, so he can always drop the sails and motor in if need be. If he's anywhere in the Sound at all, he'll dock at the marina in plenty of time to make the meeting."

Sam Tisbury thought about how long it was going to take him to reach the southern end of Cat Island by his multistop diversionary route, including an overnight stopover in Miami, and sighed inwardly. It came out to about twenty-six hours longer than a direct flight to the Hawks Nest airstrip in one of the corporation's private Learjets, and then a short five-mile drive to the villa.

There would be a definite loss of comfort, as well as time, but Sam Tisbury had long since shrugged that sort of thing off as inconsequential. It was far more important that he and his father arrive at the Cat Island villa separately, and in as inconspicuous a manner as possible. Just like the other ICER committee members.

"Assuming, of course, that he does intend to be there," the elder Tisbury reminded.

"Yes, of course."

Harold Tisbury was quiet for a long moment, then said, "I understand that he may have someone with him on the boat."

"One of the yacht dealership employees." Sam Tisbury nodded. "A woman named Anne-Marie. Apparently it was part of the package. Delivery and shakedown cruise. She sailed the boat down to his summer home."

"By herself?" the old man asked innocently.

Sam Tisbury nodded.

"Do you think, possibly . . ."

"The broker described her as a topnotch sailor, extremely athletic and quite attractive," Sam Tisbury said. "He also assured me that they look upon Alfred as one of their special customers. Given all the extenuating circumstances, I would think it's all very possible."

"I see," Harold Tisbury rasped, and then seemed to lose himself in thought.

Sam Tisbury sat patiently, wondering—not for the first time—if his longtime mentor, partner, and father was finally starting to go senile.

"So that's why you suggested the idea of vacations as a cover," Harold Tisbury finally said.

"If the FBI is focused on Alfred, then they will see a wealthy older man on a sailing cruise to the Bahamas with a younger companion." Sam Tisbury nodded. "This time of year there should be dozens, if not hundreds of Alfreds—and their *companions*," he added significantly, "down there in the islands."

"Including us."

"Yes." Sam Tisbury smiled. "Sergio and Jonathan seemed to appreciate the added touch."

"I'm sure they did, as do I," Harold Tisbury said. And then: "What about you?"

"Sandra has a previous engagement." Sam Tisbury shrugged. "But your grandson and I are going to meet down at the Hawks Nest marina on Sunday morning. We've made arrangements to charter a boat, spend a few days fishing together."

"Excellent idea." Harold Tisbury nodded approvingly. "He's a good boy. I think you're doing very well with him."

"I still haven't managed to spend as much time with him as I would have liked, but I suppose that's the disadvantage of having children later in life," Sam Tisbury said.

"Thirty-five wasn't so old to be starting a family."

"No, I suppose not. But just the same, I was gone a lot when he was growing up, and now that I have the time to do things with him, he's the one who's not around."

"No, he's out learning the business from the ground up, just like you were when you were his age," the elder Tisbury reminded his son. "And besides, look at what we've trusted him with. Can you *imagine* what you would have done if we'd had the Crucible process then, when you were his age, and I'd entrusted the development of a test-program to *you*?"

"I think I would have been overwhelmed by the responsibility," Sam Tisbury said honestly. "I guess things were different then."

"Maybe, maybe not." The elder Tisbury shrugged. "As I recall, we took on some pretty serious situations when you were twenty-three, and we did just fine."

"As serious as this?"

"You remember how we dealt with that miners' strike in

fifty-eight? When they were going to shut down our entire South American operation, just when the market was starting to skyrocket?''

Sam Tisbury nodded silently.

''You think we were wrong?''

''Then? At first I didn't know what to think.''

''And looking back?''

''We did what we had to do.'' Sam Tisbury shrugged.

''Exactly.'' Harold Tisbury nodded with a smile. ''And I expect my namesake to do exactly the same thing. He's a Tisbury, and we Tisburys do whatever is necessary to get the job done. Just as we've always done.''

''He's a stubborn kid,'' Sam Tisbury said, shaking his head. ''We've had some pretty serious arguments. For a while there, I was afraid I'd lost him. In fact,'' the younger Tisbury added, ''sometimes I still am. I often wonder if his mother's—what should I call it, activism?—has had too much of an influence on him.''

''Your mother, God rest her soul, never really approved of my work, or yours either, but it never stopped us from doing what we had to do . . . in fact, were *destined* to do.''

''Mom was pretty persuasive, in her own way.'' Sam Tisbury nodded, a sad smile appearing on his face.

''Yes, she was, but it never stopped us, did it?''

''No, it didn't, but it still hurts every now and then.''

A pained look seemed to cross Harold Tisbury's face.

''We Tisburys have always paid a price for our dreams and our aspirations,'' the old man rasped. ''The men *and* the women. Sometimes they pay a higher price than we do, and sometimes that price seems more than we can bear, but we always go forward, no matter what, because it's in our nature . . . and our blood.''

''I remember those arguments.''

''Oh, God, yes, we had some good ones, didn't we?'' The old man chuckled, seemingly drawn out of his temporary doldrums. ''You were goddamned stubborn, and we had some hellacious arguments, but I didn't lose you, did I?''

"No, you didn't."

"And you won't lose *your* son either," Harold Tisbury said firmly. "Remember how you were after the strike, when the FBI and the trade commission started in on their investigation, and you were convinced that we were going to prison?"

"Pissed, scared, and confused, all at the same time."

"But you held together—that was the important thing. And when it was over, you remember what we did?"

Sam Tisbury nodded slowly. "Yes, we went out fishing."

"That's right," the elder Tisbury said. "We fished and we drank and we talked. We spent a lot of time talking, as I recall. Far more than we did fishing or drinking. And by the time we came back, you'd changed."

"Yes, I remember," Sam Tisbury said, a half smile forming on his lips. "You were pretty persuasive out there."

"I was just putting it all together for you." Harold Tisbury shrugged. "Telling you things you already knew. You just hadn't accepted them yet."

Sam Tisbury was silent for a few moments, staring down at the new scrambled satellite phone on his desk. Then he looked up at his father. "So who came up with the idea for this fishing trip?" he asked.

"You two get out there on that boat, get to know each other again," the elder Tisbury said with a knowing smile. "I think you'll be amazed at how much Eric has changed."

Chapter Fifteen

Deep in the bowels of the J. Edgar Hoover Building at Tenth and Pennsylvania avenues in Washington, D.C., Assistant Special Agent in Charge Al Grynard sat in conference with three of his top-ranking fellow FBI agents whose supervisory responsibilities included violent crimes, white collar crimes, and special operations for the entire bureau. Also in attendance was their boss, the assistant director in charge of the Criminal Investigations Division, and an inspector from the Office of Liaison and International Affairs.

Six identical sets of file summaries were laid out on the table in the small, secured conference room. For the past two hours Grynard had been briefing the three investigative section chiefs, the LIA inspector, and the CID-AD on his case. Finally the covert operations section chief looked up from the briefing materials.

"You know what you've got here, don't you, Al?" he said to Grynard.

"What's that?"

"A goddamned political car bomb that's all primed and ready to go."

"Why so?" Al Grynard asked. He was pretty sure he already knew the answer, but he wanted to hear it from a senior-ranking agent who had worked a number of cases just like this in his highly regarded career.

"It's obvious that these Fish and Wildlife agents tripped across one hell of an illicit operation. The way it reads here, we're talking something in the neighborhood of a hundred-million-dollar conspiracy—between some high-up right-wing types in the previous administration, and some high-up, big-money industrial types in big business—to neutralize the major environmental activist groups."

The LIA inspector and the other two investigative section chiefs nodded in agreement. The AD had a contemplative look on his freshly sunburned face.

"The trouble is, you didn't nail them all when you had the chance," he grumbled.

The man in charge of investigative operations for the FBI was not a happy man. First of all, he was irritated at having been called back to D.C. from his long-planned family vacation on the Chesapeake Bay shoreline. And secondly, he didn't like the political implications of what he was hearing from a man he considered one of the more aggressive and effective supervisory field agents in the entire bureau. But the AD hadn't risen to the directorate level of the Federal Bureau of Investigation by allowing his investigative instincts to be hindered by personal considerations, much less by politics.

"Do you all agree there has to be another layer out there that we haven't touched yet?" Grynard said, ignoring the AD's implied criticism.

"Far as I'm concerned, there's no doubt about it," the representative from the Office of Liaison and International Affairs replied. "No way in hell a couple of clowns like Abercombie and Wolfe are going to have direct access to the money and the influence it took to create that underground training center right in the middle of Yellowstone National Park."

"I assume we're still trying to track back on the money?" the AD asked.

"Yes, sir." The white-collar crimes chief nodded.

"I still don't see how somebody can build a goddamned underground training center in the middle of a goddamned national park, and we can't figure out who paid the bills," the AD grumbled.

"Actually, it turns out not to be all that difficult if you set up electronic transfers with—" the white collar crimes chief started to say, and then quickly realized that his boss didn't want to listen to any technical explanations on this particular morning. What he wanted to hear about were results.

"Besides," the AD went on, "it seems to me that for this whole deal to be strictly a government operation, you'd have to be talking Assistant Secretary level involvement at an absolute minimum."

"And probably White House connections to boot," the violent crimes section chief added.

"Goes without saying," the head of the white-collar crimes section agreed quickly.

Grynard noticed that the AD had developed a pained look on his face.

"Another thing to think about," the FBI special ops section chief added, "there's no way that Wolfe and Abercombie could have put together a team of counterterrorist types like Maas, Saltmann, and Asai without help. Which means you're talking international connections too, with possible ties to the individual national security agencies."

"Christ!" The AD shook his head.

"What's the background on those three?" the violent crimes section chief asked.

"Maas was a GSG-9 team leader in the *Bundesgrenzschutz*, the West German Federal Border Police," the special ops section chief began, and then paused when the LIA inspector raised his hand.

"What's GSG-9?"

"Basically the German equivalent of our Delta Team units," the special ops chief said. "Maas specialized in hostage situations. The unit commander describes him as one of the most lethal individuals he's ever seen in terms of tactics, aggression, technical skills, and physical reaction time. They bounced him when they discovered he was starting to take chances to get a clear kill shot. Exposing himself and his team to unnecessary risk was the way the commander put it."

"Meaning?"

"Maas had apparently developed a taste for the adrenaline thrill of coming face-to-face with imminent death. According to his commander, the closer he got to the edge, the better he liked it."

"Jesus!" the LIA inspector whispered.

"But at the same time he was effective," the special ops section chief went on. "Fourteen kills, all head shots, no officers or hostages injured . . . other than the psychological effects of having to wipe blood and brain tissue off their faces afterward."

"What the hell was wrong with that?" the violent crimes section chief asked.

"Not a whole lot as far as his unit commander was concerned. Apparently the political types decided that they wanted a somewhat less violent public image for their national headhunters. I understand that the next time a GSG-9 team was used, a couple of months after Maas picked up his retirement check and started working free-lance, they lost two hostages. One of them to friendly fire,'' the special ops section chief added.

"So much for public image," the AD snorted. "So what about Saltmann and Asai?"

"Saltmann was Secret Service, Presidential Protection Teams. His last two evaluations noted a progressive disregard for established operational procedures and minor—but increasingly frequent—acts of insubordination toward his supervisors. He was gone when an updated background check revealed an excessive amount of debt and questionable business dealings.

"Asai," the special ops section chief went on, "is simply an enigma. We have nothing on him locally, and our Japanese counterparts have been less than forthcoming."

"Doesn't matter in any case." The violent crimes section chief shrugged. "The man's dead. And so are Saltmann, Wolfe, Abercombie, and eight other members of their so-called counterterrorist team. The only survivors are Maas and one of Saltmann's men, an ex-Marine named Roy Parker. And so far, neither one of them is showing any inclination to talk."

"I wouldn't either if somebody was paying Little, Warren, Nobles & Kole to defend my ass," the AD growled. "What do we know about that?"

"Not a damn thing." ASAC Al Grynard shrugged. "Other than the fact that Maas, Parker, and Chareaux are all apparently flying free on the same ticket. And to make matters worse, they've got Jason Bascomb III as the lead attorney."

"That bastard again?"

"Somebody wants those three held real tight to the chest," the LIA inspector commented.

"Sounds like it." The AD nodded.

"Oh, by the way," Grynard said, "Bascomb got Maas and Parker out on bail."

"What!"

"One point five million on Maas, two hundred and fifty thousand for Parker."

"How the hell did he do that?" the AD demanded.

"Bascomb pointed out that Maas is crippled and confined to a wheelchair, and Parker just traded in his chair for a pair of crutches, which meant that neither of them was likely to run too far. That and the fact that neither of them has been directly linked to the deaths of the three federal wildlife agents."

"The judge went for that?"

"Apparently." Grynard nodded. "The bond was paid in cash three hours later."

"That makes about as much sense as anything else in this damn case," the AD grumbled.

"What about Chareaux?" the white-collar crimes section chief asked.

"The Louisiana Fish and Game Department filed a deposition with the court that basically said if Chareaux walked out of that courtroom a free man, they'd rearrest him on the spot . . . if they didn't shoot him on the courthouse steps first. That was on top of the fact that when the judge asked Chareaux how he pled, Chareaux called him something unpleasant in a Cajun dialect, and then followed up with a fairly graphic translation."

"No bail, I take it?"

"No bail."

"What's the story on this Chareaux character?" the AD demanded. "I thought he was a completely separate issue." He gestured at the open files on the conference table.

"That's one of the interesting parts," Grynard said. "Alex Chareaux is the surviving member of a three-brother illegal guiding outfit that Wolfe used to go out poaching on the side. As far as we know, he has no connection whatever to Operation Counter Wrench other than acting as a guide for Wolfe. Right now our best guess is that Maas executed one of Chareaux's younger brothers in the process of rigging the scene on the McNulty killing. And Saltmann killed the other one when he blew up that barn trying to nail those wildlife agents.''

"Can we prove that?''

"What, the McNulty killing? No, we can't. We can't even figure out why he and Maas should be cooperating as co-defendants. Or, for that matter, why somebody with big bucks is footing the bill. It doesn't make any sense at all.''

"Presumably nobody on the defense team has gotten around to telling Chareaux how his brothers died.'' The AD shrugged. "What's he like?''

"An absolute freak. Louisiana Fish and Game wants to prosecute him for the torture killing of two of their wardens once we're finished with him. Guy's a genuine, deep swamp Cajun boy. Deadly shot, expert knife fighter. Has a thing about going after the femoral arteries and then hanging around to watch them die.''

"Which is probably why nobody's told him about Maas and his brother.'' The violent-crimes section chief smiled. "Louisiana have a good case?''

"No, apparently not. But they don't seem to care. They just want him back in their custody.''

"I see.'' The AD nodded. "So who's the U.S. Attorney on the case?''

"Theresa Fletcher.''

"Good, she's first-rate. A real fighter,'' the AD said, seemingly relieved to hear a piece of good news for a change. "What's her read on the situation?''

"She and Henry Lightstone, the primary Fish and Wildlife Service agent on the case, have been trying to twist Maas or Parker into changing sides. So far, no go, although she thinks Parker might be starting to weaken just a little bit.''

"What about Chareaux? If they're codefendants, he might have picked something up that he could use to trade.''

"I don't think so," Grynard said. "Not with Bascomb in there running interference. And even if he does know something, it's not likely that he'd talk. According to Fletcher, Chareaux is still convinced that Lightstone killed both of his brothers. The judge has six bailiffs in the courtroom, and they've got Chareaux shackled to a chair, but they still expect him to go after Lightstone sometime during the discovery hearing or the trial."

The AD braced his forehead against his interlocked fingers and sighed heavily. He was well aware that the timing of this particular situation could not have been worse. The federal government was in a period of transition. A new administration was coming in, but a goodly portion of the old administration was still in place, not even counting the ones that had been planted deep into the civil service ranks. It was a time when careers were made or broken. And a time when a surge of bad publicity could result in wholesale change, especially at the assistant director level.

And then too, the AD reminded himself, if there really *was* another level to the Operation Counter Wrench conspiracy, then that level was almost certainly going to be comprised of wealthy and influential businessmen who, in turn, almost certainly made substantial contributions to both political parties. All of which was going to result in some serious oversight hearings if Grynard and his team of agents lived up to their reputation as aggressive and tenacious investigators.

For a brief moment, the AD let his mind drift back to his own field career, during the Hoover era, when he had been a young and aggressive agent like Grynard. Fortunately, as it turned out, he and his wife had been one of the few couples in the bureau who considered Butte, Montana, to be a desirable duty station. It occurred to the AD to wonder if there might be an open slot out there for a grouchy old agent who still had a couple of years to go before mandatory retirement.

"This is going to turn into a goddamned circus," he growled as he brought his head up and looked around the table to see if anyone cared to argue the point. Nobody did. Then he returned his attention to Grynard.

"Okay, Al, where do we go from here?"

"Two good possibilities," the assistant special agent in charge said in his characteristically calm and understated voice. "First of all, we may have a lead on an outside connection to Abercombie."

The AD's eyebrows came up.

"To the industrial community?"

"That's right."

"Is it solid?"

"No, not yet. But it looks promising."

"And the second?"

"Henry Lightstone."

"The Fish and Wildlife Service agent?"

Grynard nodded. "Right now, Lightstone seems to be the only obvious common denominator between Chareaux and Operation Counter Wrench."

"Yes, so?"

"When Lightstone and his fellow covert agents went after the Chareaux brothers for their guiding activities, Wolfe and Abercombie apparently decided that they were getting close to discovering Operation Counter Wrench and panicked. They tried to block the investigation. And when that didn't work, they arranged to get the covert team disbanded and the agents reassigned to separate duty stations. Then they turned Maas and his counterterrorists loose on the individual agents. Special Agent in Charge Paul McNulty, ASAC Carl Scoby, and Agent/Pilot Len Ruebottom were killed."

The AD nodded to indicate that he had read the summary.

"In spite of their access to Fish and Wildlife Service personnel records, and for reasons that still aren't entirely clear to us, Maas and his team weren't aware until the very end that Lightstone was a member of the covert team. That put him in a position to realize what was going on without being a primary target."

"Yes, so?" the AD said impatiently.

"I have reason to believe that, in spite of orders to the contrary," Grynard said, "Lightstone and his fellow agents are continuing to search for a lead to the people ultimately responsible for the deaths of McNulty, Scoby, and Ruebottom. And if that is the case and they do manage to find a lead, then there's every reason to believe that those people might react or even panic."

"And as a result, go after the wildlife agents . . . again?" The AD had his cold eyes fixed on Grynard.

"Yes, that's right."

The AD allowed his gaze to drift past Grynard as he considered the implications of the ASAC's answer.

"Do you fully realize what you may be setting into motion?" the AD finally asked the supervisory field agent.

"I think so," Grynard nodded. "Although, in fact, it may be more a case of our simply standing back, keeping an eye on things, and allowing a portion of it to happen."

The AD hesitated for another long moment.

"Tell me about this Lightstone."

"In my view," Grynard said, "Henry Lightstone is an extremely capable, aggressive, and innovative federal agent. I wouldn't necessarily recommend him for employment in the bureau, but he did work an Alaskan outlaw motorcycle gang *and* the Chareaux brothers at a covert level, on his own, without any backup whatever."

"So what does that make him, a fool?"

"Possibly. Or perhaps just reckless." Grynard shrugged. "But in any event, he was also directly responsible for the deaths of at least two of the counterterrorist team members, as well as the injuries to several of the others, including Parker, Maas, and Chareaux. I also understand that he fought one of the Japanese counterterrorists, a fourth-degree black belt, to a draw before one of the other wildlife agents— Paxton, as I recall—killed the man. I figure, if nothing else, that makes him a survivor."

"Wasn't Lightstone initially your primary suspect in the

McNulty killing up there in Anchorage?'' the violent-crimes section chief asked.

Grynard hesitated, then said, "Yes, he was."

"Yet one of your summary reports indicates that there was a close relationship between Lightstone, McNulty, and McNulty's wife," the violent-crimes chief pointed out.

Grynard took in a deep, steadying breath, then said: "In retrospect, Agent Henry Lightstone turns out to be a very aggressive, innovative, and protective law enforcement officer. He is also a risk taker who seems to have very little regard for the rules of the game. When he discovered that his SAC and ASAC—McNulty and Scoby—had been killed, he was clearly determined to protect the other members of his covert team. He viewed me as an obstruction to that objective. And because of some other extenuating circumstances, I viewed his evasive actions as an indication of guilt. I was wrong."

The AD seemed to view Grynard's admission as a rather startling event.

"Have you considered the possibility that Lightstone might be motivated by a desire to avenge the deaths of his three fellow agents, which just might cause him to ignore the rules once again, and thereby leave the Fish and Wildlife Service, not to mention the bureau, standing in a pile of shit?" he asked after a significant pause.

"It's possible," Grynard conceded.

"So just how do you plan to deal with that *possibility*?—which, from what I'm hearing, strikes me as pretty damned likely," the AD demanded.

"By keeping a close eye on the entire covert wildlife team, waiting for them to break something open, and then moving in on the conspirators before the situation goes out of control."

"Al, I'm not arguing with your plan," the FBI special ops section chief said, "but as I recall from your reports, didn't this Lightstone character manage to evade your surveillance team up in Anchorage, and then stay ahead of you *and* about

ten of your agents, not to mention Maas and *his* entire counterterrorist team, for how many days was it?''

The AD's eyebrows rose again. He hadn't read that part of
the report.

''As I said,'' Grynard said evenly, ''he's capable, aggressive, and innovative. But there's another factor involved
here. I have reason to believe that Lightstone and his fellow
agents have a lead on a possible co-conspirator to Operation
Counter Wrench.''

''How do you know that?'' the AD asked.

''Because I arranged for their tech agent to find it.''

''With his knowledge?''

''No.''

The AD seemed to consider the idea for a few moments.

''Are you certain that you can keep Lightstone and his
team under constant observation this time?'' he finally
asked.

''With additional agents, yes, sir.''

''How many?''

''Twenty-four.''

The special ops section chief broke into a coughing fit.

''And assuming I give you these twenty-four agents,'' the
AD said, ignoring the outburst of his section chief, ''what do
you intend to do with them?''

''Right now, which is to say right this morning,'' Grynard
added, ''I'd send at least half of them down to the Bahamas
and the other half to Fort Lauderdale.''

The FBI assistant director blinked again, and this time his
muscular shoulders seemed to sag.

''Why?'' he finally said, once he was sure he had a firm
grip on his vocal cords.

''Because the possible co-conspirator is in a sailboat
down in the Bahamas right now, and Lightstone and his fellow agents checked into a hotel in Fort Lauderdale last
night.''

The AD turned to the section chief of special ops, who
hesitated and then nodded with visible reluctance.

"Okay," the AD said, "you've got them. Anything else that I should know about this operation?"

"No, sir," Grynard lied.

"Then get out of here and get to work."

The AD waited until Grynard had disappeared out the door before turning back to the LIA inspector and his subordinate supervisors.

"All right, lay it out on the table right now," he growled. "Are we doing the right thing or not?"

"I think it's risky, but I don't see that we have much in the way of viable options," the special ops section chief said. "It's either that or back off completely."

"We don't back off on something like this," the AD said flatly.

"Actually, it may not be that much of a risk," the special ops section chief said. "You may remember what Al was like when he was a young agent?"

"Hell, yes, I remember," the AD snapped. In fact, as all the agents around the table knew, the AD had personally gone to bat for the young and overaggressive FBI agent on three separate occasions. The last one had nearly resulted in Grynard's suspension.

"Well, from what I hear, this Lightstone is worse. Makes Al look like a choir boy."

"Christ, don't tell me that." The AD winced.

"Hey, look at it this way, chief," the violent-crimes section chief said. "At least when it all hits the fan, this time Al's going to be the one standing out there holding the bag."

"You think he understands that?" the LIA inspector asked.

"You ask me." The violent-crimes chief smiled, "I think that's about the only part of this whole damn mess that Al *does* understand."

Chapter Sixteen

For a little over three hours, the man known as Riser followed the light-gray van and the black sedan in his nondescript pickup.

As expected, and much to Riser's amusement, the two professional security drivers repeated their behavior of the previous two days.

When they were ferrying their passengers back and forth between the law office, the courthouse, and the hotel, they used a nicely randomized set of routes that made it almost impossible to plan for an intercept. But once they had dropped off their charges, and were on their own, the two drivers immediately reverted to a pattern of activities that was almost embarrassingly predictable.

So far this morning, the drivers had divided their time between honing their skills, maintaining their equipment, and taking care of personal needs.

First, they had spent a half hour in the Fair Oaks Mall parking lot practicing a series of cutout techniques designed to let the van escape while the sedan blocked—and presumably dealt with—a variety of assault moves.

Next they had filled the gas tanks of the two vehicles up at the nearby Chevron station, making sure to check the oil and radiator levels and the pressures on all four tires.

After that, they had driven over to the automated car wash in Vienna and had a cup of coffee while both vehicles got the full service: wash, wax, and interior.

And then finally they had driven over to the Vienna video store, where each proceeded to spend exactly fifteen minutes searching for a movie while the other watched the two vehicles.

Riser checked his watch. It was eleven-thirty. Time for the two men to be leaving the Vienna video store and driving over to Oakton again for lunch.

He was tempted to drive on ahead to the restaurant where they had gone the last two days, arriving early enough to select a table where they could keep an eye on the two vehicles. But he didn't because Friday was the crucial day and he knew he might not have another opportunity like this. So he waited until both men were back in their vehicles and moving again before he started up the nondescript pickup and maintained a respectful distance, just in case the two men suddenly decided to act professional on their own time.

But as it turned out, he could have saved himself the effort. The drivers parked their vehicles in exactly the same spots, walked into the restaurant, and sat at exactly the same table.

As he picked up the small scrambled radio, it occurred to Riser to wonder if the men ordered the same meals every time. He suspected they did. Pausing briefly to check the parking lot one last time, he spoke into the radio briefly and then waited.

Five minutes later, a late-model dark green Mercedes entered the restaurant parking lot and parked in the open space next to the black sedan. Two curvaceous young women got out, one a blonde and one a brunette. Both wore tight dresses that exposed a considerable amount of leg and cleavage, and clearly suggested an absolute minimum in the way of underwear. Halfway to the restaurant, the blonde dropped her purse, and both of the young women squatted to retrieve the spilled contents, thereby giving the two security drivers an eyeful.

As the two women entered the restaurant, Riser brought the radio up to his mouth and spoke again.

In less than thirty seconds another vehicle—this one an ancient Volkswagen bug with a badly rusted exterior—pulled into the space next to the van. The new arrival was a white-haired man who looked to be in his late sixties. He appeared to be having a great deal of difficulty getting himself out of the little car and nearly fell to the asphalt at one point. But neither of the two security drivers seemed overly concerned. They gave him a quick glance and then turned their attention back to the two young women who were now giggling at each other—and otherwise having a good time—in the booth across the aisle from the two captivated drivers.

Eventually the elderly man managed to get himself standing upright. After carefully shutting and then locking the rusted door that looked about ready to fall off, he gingerly worked his way across the parking lot and into the restaurant. There, he slowly made his way to the empty table next to the security drivers and across the way from the two young women—where, in Riser's estimation, the old man would spend the next half hour enjoying his own eyeful of deceptively warm feminine flesh.

Once again the cold and deadly eyes of the merciless killer crinkled into an amused smile.

At two-fifteen that Friday afternoon, just as Special Agent Dwight Stoner was getting into the cross-examination portion of his testimony regarding his involvement with Gerd Maas and Alex Chareaux during the Whitehorse Cabin raid, a bailiff came forward and handed a sealed envelope to lead defense attorney Jason Bascomb III.

The defense attorney opened the envelope, read the typewritten note, frowned, read it again slowly, and in doing so missed all but the last part of the judge's question.

"Uh, I'm sorry your honor?" Bascomb said, finally looking up.

"I asked if you had any further questions of this witness," the judge repeated.

"Uh . . . no, your honor."

The judge blinked in visible surprise and then said: "Very well. Mrs. Fletcher?"

Deputy U.S. Attorney Theresa Fletcher was just as surprised as the judge, but she tried not to let it show in her facial expression. "Nothing further, your honor," she said quickly.

"Does either counsel wish to recall this witness at a later date?"

Fletcher turned around in her chair so that she could stare at Bascomb—who was in the process of reading the note for a third time—with a suspicious and distrusting look on her face. Then she turned back to look at Henry Lightstone, who as the primary investigator had been allowed to sit next to Fletcher and listen to the testimony of all the witnesses. Lightstone shrugged, as if to say, "It beats the hell out of me."

Finally, after another few moments of silent contemplation, Theresa Fletcher said: "No, your honor."

"Mr. Bascomb?"

The lead defense attorney was still clearly distracted by the contents of the note. It took him a few moments to react, and then respond: "Uh, no, your honor."

"Agent Stoner, you are excused. Mrs. Fletcher, you may call your next witness."

Deputy U.S. Attorney Theresa Fletcher looked over at her legal adversary one last time, hesitated, and then said: "No further witnesses, your honor. The prosecution rests."

"Mr. Bascomb, are you prepared to call your first witness?"

"Uh, no, your honor. Defense requests a continuance until Monday morning so that we can follow up on an unexpected lead in this case."

"Mrs. Fletcher?"

"No objections, your honor."

"Very well." The judge nodded. "Court is adjourned until nine o'clock Monday morning."

In a series of quick but still dignified movements, the judge slammed his gavel, rose out of his chair, and then stepped away from the bench—as the court clerk hurriedly called out "All rise!"—before either attorney had an opportunity to change his mind.

Then, as the surprised bailiffs moved in quickly to escort Alex Chareaux out of the courtroom, and as Theresa Fletcher, Henry Lightstone, and Dwight Stoner watched in absolute amazement, Jason Bascomb III quickly rounded up Maas, Parker, and his two assistant fellow attorneys, and headed rapidly toward the door.

Chapter Seventeen

At three-fifteen that Friday afternoon the field supervisor of the U.S. Marshall team assigned to Prisoner Transportation Unit Three watched carefully as one of the federal court bailiffs shackled Alex Chareaux into the third seat from the rear on the right-hand side of the van's isolated holding area.

"Okay," the bailiff said as he climbed down out of the van, "he's all yours. Sorry about the early callback."

"Not a problem. We might actually get home on time tonight," the team leader said as he signed the transfer form, and then walked over to shut, bar, and lock the rear door.

Once the armored door was secured, the two shotgun-armed marshalls—who had monitored the entire transfer process with their backs to the van, magnum buckshot rounds chambered in their 12-gage Remington pumps, fingers on the trigger guards, and the safeties off as they watched for any approaching vehicles or people—returned their lethal weapons to a "safe" condition. Then, still alert but more relaxed now, they walked over to the cab portion of the armored transport van.

There they opened the rear cab doors and secured their shotguns into the readily accessible racks mounted on either side of the rear wall between the rear seats and the doors. Having done that, they both climbed into the rear seats, shut and locked their doors, and then secured their safety belts.

The team leader climbed into the front passenger seat,

locked his door, and then retrieved his 9mm semiautomatic pistol back from his uniformed driver.

"Well, guys," he said as he secured the heavy pistol in his hip holster and then fastened his safety belt so that he still had easy access to the holstered weapon, "what do you say we drop this cheerful dip-shit off at the base, check out, and then stop by O'Hara's for a couple of beers, my treat?"

The two younger deputy U.S. marshalls in the back-seats—both of whom were in their mid-twenties, still single, and invariably short on cash—quickly voiced their agreement. But the older driver looked down at his watch.

"Uh, okay," he said hesitantly, "but it's gotta be a quick one. I called Sherry and let her know we'd be getting off early tonight. She's going to arrange for an overnight baby-sitter so I can take her out to dinner, hit a show, and then check into the local hotel."

"Sounds like a nice plan to me," the team leader—a married man with three children of his own—nodded approvingly.

"Hey, come on, you guys, 'fess up," the youthful deputy U.S. marshall in the left rear seat teased, "what is it that you old married farts can do in a hotel that you can't do at home?"

"I forget." The forty-five-year-old driver shrugged. "But I think it has something to do with sex."

"No shit? Guys your age still do that kinda thing?"

"With four kids running around the house all day and night? You gotta be kidding."

"At least now we know what to get him for Christmas." The young deputy marshall in the left rear seat laughed. "One of those illustrated self-help books."

"I'm not sure we should wait that long," the other rear-seated deputy marshall responded. "Sounds to me like ol' Joe's gonna need it tonight."

"Like riding a bicycle." The gray-haired driver shook his head with a broad smile.

"I think we better get this show on the road before our

driver here starts to lose his concentration," the team leader commented as he reached for the radio mike. "Tango-Uniform-Three to Base One, we are en route from the Arlington Courthouse with one Poppa in custody. Activating homer now."

Reaching forward to the dashboard, the team leader flipped a heavy-duty red switch to the ON position. On the roof of the armored transport, a small but powerful transmitter began to send out a locator signal to a grid of receivers mounted on towers and high buildings within the greater Washington, D.C., metropolitan area. The receivers close enough to detect the signal relayed directional information to the primary base receivers. These devices, in turn, calculated the triangulations and displayed the precise locations of all the activated homer units on seventeen-inch computer monitors back at the base stations. It was a very effective way to keep track of vehicles involved in sensitive or hazardous operations, such as transporting federal prisoners who stood accused of serious felonies and were thus likely to make a serious attempt to escape custody . . . with or without outside help.

"Base One to Tango-Uniform-Three, your homer is confirmed, fifteen-twenty-two hours."

"Tango-Uniform-Three to Base One. Homer activation confirmed, fifteen-twenty-two hours," the team leader repeated. "See you in a few."

"Base One to Tango-Uniform-Three. Ten-four. Base One, out."

The four deputy U.S. marshalls drove the next twenty miles in comfortable silence as the driver took Interstate 66 west to the Washington Dulles Access Toll Road, and then continued north on the toll road to the number two exit that would take them out past President's Park to the secondary road leading out to the holding facility.

As they entered the long off-ramp, the driver noted the presence of a Fairfax County repair crew working just past the shut-off gate.

"Looks like we made it just in time," he commented. "You think they're ever gonna get this road done the way they want it?"

"Not in our lifetimes," the team leader predicted.

As they headed up the long off-ramp, the driver moved over into the right-hand lane. As he did so, he reflexively noted the presence of a light-gray minivan with smoked windows taking the off-ramp right behind them and then coming up even with the transport van's rear bumper in the left-hand lane.

As the minivan came to a stop at the left-lane toll booth, the uniformed driver slowly brought the armored transport van to a stop in the right toll booth marked "Passes and Correct Change Only." Then he waited patiently for the young female attendant in the left-hand booth to raise the bar gate.

As she did so, and as the uniformed driver concentrated on slowly shifting and accelerating the heavy van up the remainder of the long off-ramp, he failed to notice in his rearview mirrors that the county working crew had closed and locked the ramp gate behind the gray minivan and were in the process of getting into their clearly marked white truck.

And as the driver continued to accelerate the heavy van through its low-range gears, he also failed to notice that the attendant was no longer visible in the window of the left-side toll booth.

In fact, the first indication the driver had that something might be wrong was when the gray minivan suddenly pulled up alongside and maintained an even pace with the larger transport van. That was when he became aware that the right front passenger side window of the minivan was rolled all the way down.

He started to yell, "Hey, watch!" when the left rear door of the van cab suddenly seemed to explode inward.

The force of the impact actually rocked the heavy transport van sideways on its heavy duty shocks, throwing the driver and the team leader over to their right.

When the driver finally managed to recover his balance,

he discovered that his view through the transport van's armored glass windshield was partially obscured by something bright red and viscous. Momentarily paralyzed from shock, the driver had only the span of a second to realize that he and the team leader and the entire interior of the cab were all covered with splattered blood.

Shaken to the point of forgetting their training, both the driver and the team leader reached for the radio mike at the same moment. They ended up knocking it to the floor. The team leader made a second attempt to grab the mike and found himself being held back by his shoulder-restraint belt.

Instinctively releasing his safety belt with his right hand, the team leader lunged downward and to his left, in a desperate effort to grab the radio mike that was bouncing around the driver's feet, just as the left driver's side window exploded in a shower of armored glass chunks.

The upper portion of the driver's lifeless body was flung sideways into the team leader just as something ripped across the top of his left shoulder behind his head and blew the right-side window out. The sledgehammerlike force of the glancing four-bore projectile, and the immediately following collision with the driver's limp body caused the team leader's unprotected head to be driven sharply against the right side door frame. At the same time, the sudden lack of pressure on the gas pedal caused the van's heavy-duty transmission to lug down, sending the armored vehicle to a shuddering halt as the engine cut out.

Stunned into semiconsciousness by the multiple impacts, the team leader stopped trying to get the radio mike and instead tried to do what he should have done immediately . . . which was to activate the emergency alarm button on the transport van's dashboard. As he started to pull himself back up in order to reach for the recessed button with his left hand, he heard footsteps outside the van, and his survival instincts sent his right hand fumbling for his holstered 9mm pistol. He had it halfway out of its holster when the mostly empty left driver's side window frame was suddenly filled with a huge and ominous form.

A pair of 10mm hollow-point bullets struck the team leader in the head and throat, killing him instantly. Three more 10mm hollow-points buried themselves in the heads of the other three deputy U.S. marshalls, all of whom were already dead.

Then, just as the heavy armored van began to roll backward, the man known as Riser reached in through the shattered window, unlocked the door, pulled it open, and set the brake with his right foot.

The driver of the gray minivan quickly accelerated up past the armored van, made a complete U-turn around the front, drove about thirty feet past the van on the right side, and then backed up until the rear doors of the minivan were within about ten feet of the rear of the van. As he did so, the driver of the newly painted and renumbered Fairfax County truck pulled up next to the driver's side door.

"Are you ready?" Riser demanded as he reached in and placed his right hand on the transport van's red "homer" switch.

The man in the front passenger side of the truck nodded.

"Now," Riser said, pausing for a brief moment for the man in the truck to turn an identically configured homing transmitter to the on position before he switched the armored van's homer to the off position. Then as the stolen Fairfax County truck began to move forward slowly up the off-ramp, Riser reached for the team leader's gun belt, removed a ring of blood-splattered keys from one of the "keepers," and then walked around quickly to the rear of the transport van.

At the top of the number-two off-ramp, the driver of the county truck turned left and proceeded to drive westward on Centreville Road, crossing over the Dulles Access Road and replicating as closely as he could the gradually accelerating speeds of the armored transport van.

Using the team leader's keys, the huge mercenary unlocked the doors, lifted the bar, quickly pulled the heavy door open with one hand, and then stepped aside—shielding himself behind the armor-plated door—with the silenced 10mm semiautomatic pistol out and ready.

But the extra precaution wasn't necessary.

As expected, the only occupant in the isolated rear portion of the transport van was Alex Chareaux, who was futilely cursing and struggling against the unyielding handcuffs and shackles that held him firmly attached to the metal seat.

Riser transferred the 10mm pistol to his left hand, and then pulled himself up into the back of the van. Ducking his head down to avoid what was to him a low ceiling, he walked up to Chareaux, smiled at the furious expression in the deadly poacher's reddened eyes, and then slammed his massive right fist squarely into the side of the helpless Cajun's exposed jaw.

Alex Chareaux's entire body recoiled from the savage blow, his jaw going slack and his eyes rolling back in his head.

After confirming that Chareaux was out cold, Riser shoved the pistol into the shoulder holster and then turned as the driver of the gray minivan tossed him a pair of heavy-duty bolt cutters. Working quickly, Riser cut Chareaux loose from the chair, leaving the waist-secured handcuffs and leg restraints in place. As he did so, the driver pulled open the back doors of the minivan. Then, in what appeared to be an effortless series of motions, Riser dragged the unconscious poacher out to the end of the tailgate and casually tossed his limp body headfirst into the back of the minivan.

Two minutes later, as the minivan first drove up to the top of the off-ramp, turned right on Centreville Road, and headed due east, the driver of the stolen county truck began to slow down as he approached the right-hand turn that would take him out to the federal holding facility.

Just as he was coming up on the turn, the driver of the truck reached forward, shut the homer switch to the off position, then continued on in a westerly direction.

By the time the holding facility control officer realized

that something was wrong, and dispatched an emergency response team out to investigate, both the minivan and the stolen county truck had long since disappeared into the Friday afternoon northern Virginia rush hour traffic.

When FBI Agent Al Grynard got the call, at six-thirty that Friday evening, he was just getting ready to walk with his wife, his sixteen-year-old son, and his fourteen-year-old daughter over to a neighboring agent's house for dinner.

Grynard's wife, who had been an FBI agent's daughter herself, handed him the phone and shook her head with an understanding half-smile. She had immediately recognized the tone in the duty agent's voice, and thereby knew that she and her children would be walking over to their neighbor's house by themselves this evening, where they would enjoy a nice dinner and cheerful conversation with a family they had first met when they were stationed in Anchorage. As usual, she would ask the hostess to wrap a plate of food in foil and put it in the refrigerator for her husband—who might be back in time to enjoy a reheated dinner, but more likely wouldn't be home until sometime in the morning, if then.

As her mother had told her more than once, with that very same understanding half-smile, this sort of thing went with the territory.

"Grynard," he said in a resigned voice.

"This is duty agent Frost. You have an alert notice on file for any event involving a subject named Alex Chareaux?"

"That's right."

"Better grab a jacket," the duty agent advised. "It could be a long night."

Less than forty minutes later, Grynard was standing on the edge of the number-two exit off-ramp number using a flashlight to examine the massive damage that the two doors on the left side of the armored transport van had sustained.

"My God," Grynard whispered, "what did they use to do that?"

"We have no idea," the supervisory U.S. marshall in

charge of the McLearen Federal Holding Facility said. "We've never seen anything like it before. Hope you guys can tell us."

There was a distinctive edge to the supervisory marshall's shaken voice that Grynard picked up on immediately. It was the voice of a man who couldn't comprehend what he could have possibly done—or failed to do—that would allow something like this to happen. Grynard had heard that sound in the voices of far too many dedicated and protective supervisors in his law enforcement career.

Moving in closer to get a better look, Grynard tried to estimate how much force it must have taken to create the deep, conelike hole in the armored van's left rear cab door. One hell of a lot, he decided.

"How many people did you lose?" he asked in a quiet voice as his crime-scene experienced eyes took in the carnage. Two slumped-over bodies were still strapped into the rear cab seats, their uniforms soaked with mostly dried blood. Grynard could see what he assumed were three other bodies lying on stretchers nearby, covered with bloody sheets.

"All four. The whole transport team."

"What about the other one?" He nodded in the direction of the three stretchers.

"The toll booth attendant. She took a round in the forehead, right between the eyes."

Grynard took a moment to absorb the information.

"Anybody get a shot off?"

"Never had a chance," the holding facility commander said. "The team leader was sitting up front. Looks like he managed to get his pistol at least partway out of his holster. That's it over there on the floor . . . fully loaded, locked, and cocked," he said, gesturing with his flashlight beam. "Everyone else had their weapons strapped in. These guys were a good team, careful *and* alert, so we figure it had to have happened real fast."

Grynard used his flashlight to examine the inside portion

of the door panel. It looked as if a sideways mounted vol-
cano had exploded, covering the inside of the cab with a dark
reddish-brown lava and rocklike chunks of armored glass.

Bigger than a fifty caliber, the FBI agent told himself. Had
to be. Which didn't make any sense, because that meant
military, and he couldn't imagine how someone could have
gotten his hands on a 20mm cannon, and mounted it in a vehicle, and driven it up a Washington Dulles Access Toll
Road exit, and somehow gotten it into a position to fire into
the side of an armored transport van without four careful and
alert deputy U.S. marshalls noticing the damn thing.

He was trying to remember how big a 20mm cannon was.
Had to be at least six or seven feet long, not counting the
base mount, he thought. So how the hell would you conceal
something like that in a civilian vehicle?

Grynard stepped away from the van, using his flashlight
to look back along the side of the roadway. He was half-
expecting to see caterpillar-tread tracks, or maybe the distinctive wide wheel base tracks of a military Humvee in the
glare of the surrounding generator-powered lights. But the
dirt along the roadway looked undisturbed.

"Any witnesses?" he asked.

"Nothing so far." The holding facility commander shook
his head. "But whoever did it locked the toll road gate at the
entrance to the off-ramp, so we figured we'd put a broadcast
out over local radio and TV this evening. Might get lucky."

Grynard nodded, then walked around to the back of the
van where the rear doors gaped open.

Moving in close, the FBI agent swept his flashlight beam
across the metal box, reflexively keeping his hands away
from any smooth surface that just might provide a useful set
of latent prints. Might, that is, if they really *were* going to get
lucky tonight, although Grynard was already convinced that
they weren't. The whole situation looked much too smooth
and professional for the perpetrators to have made that kind
of amateurish mistake.

Then he realized he wasn't seeing what he had expected to

see. Either that or the duty agent hadn't gotten his facts straight.

"Where's Chareaux?"

"We don't know."

"You mean they killed him too?"

"Apparently not. We found some blood on the floor, but we're thinking now it probably came from his nose or mouth. Probably knocked him out, keep him from causing a fuss. Looks like they used some kind of bolt cutter to cut him loose from the chair."

"Those crazy bastards. They actually took him alive," Grynard whispered, shaking his head slowly in disbelief.

"Who's they?" the holding facility commander demanded, his eyes lighting up.

"Some people we haven't got identified yet," Grynard said with audible bitterness. "That's one of our problems right now."

"You're going to let us know when you do, right?"

"I'll call you myself," the FBI agent promised as he pulled a field notebook and a pen out of his jacket pocket. "You know when these guys left the Arlington courthouse?"

"Yeah, they cleared the gate at fifteen-twenty-two hours."

Grynard furrowed his eyebrows in confusion as he looked down at his watch. It was seven-fourteen exactly. Almost four hours ago. Then he looked around the scene again and realized that the crime scene investigation was just getting started . . . what, three hours after the van would have arrived at the exit?

"Uh . . . what about the shooting?"

The supervisory U.S. marshall hesitated.

"You mean when did the shooting actually happen?"

Grynard looked up at the uniformed federal officer and realized that in addition to being shocked and angry and frustrated, the commander of the McLearen Federal Holding Facility was clearly embarrassed.

"You don't know?" Grynard blurted out before he could catch himself.

"Not exactly."

The holding facility commander went on to explain how the duty officer had left his desk at fifteen-fifty-five hours to get a cup of coffee because there hadn't been anything on the air other than periodic and routine check-in signals from Tango-Uniform-Three. The transport unit had been expected in at 1615 hours, assuming that they managed to stay ahead of Friday rush-hour traffic.

At sixteen-twenty hours, when Tango-Uniform-Three didn't show at the gate, the duty officer had gone back to his desk to call for an ETA. That was when he'd discovered that the unit's homer beacon was no longer flashing on the computer generated map.

"Is the duty officer normally allowed to leave his desk?" Grynard asked.

"Yeah, sure. In fact he has to when we're running on a short duty list. It usually isn't a problem because we have speakers mounted throughout the entire officers' block, so they can hear any emergency broadcast."

"But they can't see the monitor."

"Right." The holding facility commander nodded glumly.

"Any idea what time the beeper cut out?"

"Yeah, we were able to call it up from the computer memory. Sixteen-twelve hours. At the intersection of Centreville Road and McLearen Road. At that point they were supposedly about two minutes from the holding facility."

"What happened then?"

"Since we hadn't received any kind of emergency signal, I sent out two members of our emergency response team to see what happened, assuming that there had been some kind of mechanical breakdown."

"Does that happen occasionally?"

"Yeah, every now and then. The reason I wasn't as anxious as I probably should have been is that we had a branch break off a tree and take out both antennas on a transport unit last week. And it was windy this afternoon, so . . .'' The base commander shrugged helplessly.

Grynard wanted to tell him that it didn't matter, because his men were probably already dead by then, but he let the anguished supervisor continue talking.

''They called back in at sixteen-forty-five hours, saying they'd searched around the intersection and down to Barnsfield road—which is about three quarters of a mile south on Centreville—and hadn't found anything. At that point I sent out the full team. Six deputies in three cars. They took a loop around Sully Road, then searched the Franklin Farms area. At seventeen-fifteen, I called Fairfax County and asked for a helicopter sweep. About that time, I guess, people started calling in complaining about exit two being blocked off, and that's when the helicopter spotted the van.

''I don't know how the hell . . .'' the base commander started to say, but Grynard wasn't listening. He was starting to feel sick to his stomach, numbly aware of how much time they'd lost already and that it was probably too late . . . but he had to try.

''Bascomb. B-A-S-C-O-M-B,'' he said, speaking to the local FBI duty agent through his portable radio. ''First name Jason, common spelling. He's an attorney for the law firm of Little, Warren, Nobles & Kole. Find him, now!''

At five-thirty that Friday afternoon, Dr. Kimberly Wildman and her field assistant decided that they had put in enough overtime for one week.

They were in the process of picking up their survey gear and transferring it into the bed of their truck when one of the fire crew trucks pulled alongside their truck and stopped.

''Dr. Wildman?'' the young driver asked.

''Yes, I'm Kim Wildman.''

''My crew chief asked me to find you and give you this,'' he said as he reached down on the seat and then handed something wrapped in a burlap bag out the truck window.

"And he said to tell you he's sorry he forgot to give it to you earlier this morning."

"What is it?" she asked, realizing that the burlap-wrapped package was heavier than she had expected. She had to use both hands to hold it, and she quickly handed it over to her field technician.

"It's some kind of sign, I guess. We found it Wednesday evening when we were cleaning up some of the hot spots from that fire. It was attached to that old eagle nest tree that got burned."

"Oh, yes, one of those stupid blank signs." She nodded. "In fact, we saw this one when we were surveying that area. You'd think that whoever put it there would know better than to risk killing a nesting tree. I'm sure it must be a violation of the fish and game regs."

"Yeah, that's why my crew chief wanted you to have it." But then, with a confused look on his face, he added: "But I'm pretty sure this one wasn't blank, ma'am."

"Oh, but I'm certain it was," she said. "In fact I—"

But then her field technician interrupted.

"Uh, Kim, you'd better take a look at this."

He held up the green-and-brown camouflaged sign.

"What in the world?"

The word *Wildfire* glared back at her in bright, deeply carved, three-inch-high letters.

"That's the sign, ma'am."

"But that's not the same one that we saw attached to the eagle nesting tree," she said. "The one we saw was completely blank. I'm absolutely certain of that."

"Yeah, me too." The field technician nodded.

"I don't know what to say, ma'am," the young fire crew member said hesitantly. "I mean, I don't want to argue with you, or nothing like that, but I saw them take this sign off that tree. Fact is, I helped them do it."

"We must be talking about different trees."

"The one just off the main fire road, about a quarter mile

in? Two big granite boulders about twenty feet away, to the—uh—north?''

''That's the one.'' The field technician nodded.

''I don't understand this *at all*,'' the group survey leader said.

''Me neither, ma'am, but I'd better get back to work before the crew chief comes looking for me.''

''Oh—uh—yes, please tell your chief thank you for me. And also, if any of you see any more signs like this, would you ask him to please get hold of me immediately?''

''Yes, ma'am!''

She waited until the fire crew truck disappeared back down the dirt road. Then she turned to her field technician, who was staring at the sign as if he were still having trouble believing his eyes.

''Let's get packed up and then get back to the office,'' she said. ''I intend to find out what's going on around here.''

Chapter Eighteen

To the absolute amazement of his two legal assistants, and in spite of all his pretentious mannerisms and aggressive tactics in the courtroom, Jason Bascomb III was starting to loose his nerve as well as his patience.

''What time is it now?'' the theatrical defense attorney demanded of no one in particular, continuing, as he did so, to pace back and forth across the badly worn living room carpeting of the rented and decidedly unpretentious Warrenton, Virginia, home.

The most junior of the two legal assistants started to remind Bascomb that he had already asked that question three times during the past hour. But the young lawyer had the fortune to notice the slightly crazed expression in his boss's eyes and immediately changed his mind.

Instead, he made an elaborate show of glancing down at his expensive Rolex wristwatch.

"In precisely ten seconds," he announced to the room at large, "it will be seven-thirty-eight in the evening."

"It's pitch-black outside . . . of course it's the goddamned evening, you idiot!" the senior attorney roared, whirling around and glaring at his youthful assistant—who immediately turned pale and took a defensive step backward, but then quickly recovered.

"Hey, come on, Jason, I was just trying to be helpful." The young attorney shrugged with an uneasy grin on his face.

For a brief moment it looked as though Bascomb might lunge for the throat of the young man who was inordinately fond of advising or reminding anyone in his immediate vicinity that he had graduated in the top five of his Harvard Law School class only eight months ago. It was, perhaps, understandable that the four security guards made no effort at all to intercede on the young attorney's behalf.

But then, before Bascomb could actually cause some physical damage to his legal team, he realized that Maas and Parker were watching him with expressions of pure amusement on their smiling faces.

More than anything else that he could think of at that moment, Jason Bascomb III wanted desperately to be able to unleash all his pent-up anger and frustrations on his clients. Making it clear to them, in no uncertain terms, that they would be rotting their lives away in a federal prison at this very moment if it weren't for *his* efforts and *his* considerable legal skills. But Bascomb knew he couldn't do that, because he had long since discovered—to his amazement—that he was actually afraid of Roy Parker. And the mere thought of turning on Gerd Maas, whose chilling blue eyes seemed to have the capability of boring directly into a man's soul, was enough to turn the senior attorney's bowels to water.

So instead of venting his spleen on his clients, or following through with the equally appealing idea of strangling his unbearably pretentious assistant with the dangling end of his perfectly knotted Harvard tie, Bascomb simply looked around at the cheaply paneled walls of the rented safe house and cursed in a manner that would have done his Shakespearean mentor proud.

By this point he was absolutely convinced that this particular Friday would turn out to be one of the worst days that he had ever experienced in his entire life.

Fortunately for what little remained of his peace of mind, Jason Bascomb had no way of knowing how right he was.

Thinking back, he realized it had started to go bad from the moment that the urgent note from Leland Kole himself had sent them all hurrying out of the federal courtroom and down the service elevator to the secured underground courthouse parking lot. There, Bascomb, his two legal assistants, Maas, Parker, and their two primary bodyguards had been forced to wait for over an hour, until all the primary and decoy transportation vehicles—consisting of three identical town car sedans and three identical ramp-equipped vans—had arrived.

After a hurried consultation among the hired bodyguards and drivers, the six smoke-windowed vehicles had roared out of the underground parking lot—one after the other, with a driver and bodyguard team in each of the front seats—and then vectored away from the courthouse in six different directions.

For the next two and a half hours Bascomb had sat in the back of the town car, crammed shoulder to shoulder with his two legal assistants, while their professionally trained driver went through an extended series of tactical maneuvers designed to flush and evade anything but the most sophisticated surveillance.

Finally, at five minutes after six o'clock that evening, Jason Bascomb III and his two assistant lawyers had arrived at the northern Virginia safe house, all thoroughly carsick and with bladders about ready to burst.

Bascomb had lunged through the front door and then immediately locked himself in the one and only bathroom for a good fifteen minutes to empty his bladder and take a quick, refreshing shower. Much to the amusement of Maas and Parker—neither of whom had been the least bit hesitant to share a communal plastic jug with their driver and body-guard—this act of consummate selfishness finally forced Bascomb's two legal assistants to abandon their carefully nurtured codes of propriety and urinate in the backyard.

At twenty minutes after six, when he finally exited the bathroom with a look of numbed relief on his ashen face, Jason Bascomb learned, to his horror, that his dinner that evening would consist of sharing three tubs of greasy fried chicken, crumbly mashed potatoes, congealed gravy, soggy corn, heavy stale biscuits, and lukewarm Cokes with the four security guards, Maas, Parker, and his two legal assistants.

It was not, by any reasonable definition, a pleasant meal.

By seven-thirty-eight that evening, Jason Bascomb was in an absolutely foul mood . . . to the point that he had to be warned against going outside and searching the neighbor-hood for their late arriving and so far anonymous client, who—Bascomb assured everyone remaining in the room, two of the bodyguards having gone outside to watch and wait—would get an earful regarding the incredible absurdity of this entire situation, no matter how much money he'd al-ready paid Little, Warren, Nobles & Kole in retainer fees.

What infuriated Bascomb more than anything else was his gradual realization that Maas and Parker, in spite of their visibly painful and incapacitating injuries, didn't seem to be the least bit discomforted by the two-and-a-half-hour drive, the barely digestible dinner, or their less than luxurious sur-roundings. If anything, the defense attorney suspected, the two surviving counterterrorists from Operation Counter Wrench were probably enjoying themselves immensely at his expense.

Which, of course, was absolutely true.

At seven-forty-five one of the outside guards gave the es-tablished two-and-two knock, waited until the senior of the inside guards looked through the peephole and opened the front door, and then confirmed what everyone fully expected by now. Their anonymous money man was still a no-show.

"How's it look out there?" the senior member of the guard team asked.

"Pretty damned dark," the outside guard responded. "We're lit up here like a Christmas tree."

"Any movement?"

"Nothing. Bill's making a perimeter check, just to make sure, but the only thing we've heard or seen around here so far is a damned alley cat."

The senior member of the guard team hesitated.

"You guys feeling comfortable out there?"

"Not really."

"Me neither. You want anything?"

"We could do without the porch light."

The inside guard nodded. He reached over and shut off the bright outside light that could easily turn his outside security team into a pair of highly vulnerable silhouettes.

"Keep your eyes open," he warned as he closed and locked the front door.

Finally, at seven-fifty-eight by his own watch, when he no longer had the energy to pace back and forth across the faded and worn carpet, Jason Bascomb III pulled the typewritten note he'd received from Leland Kole—one of the senior managing partners of his law firm—out of his pocket and reread it for the fifth time since he'd left the Arlington federal courthouse almost five hours ago.

Jason,
We have been advised that Ice Chest wants to meet with you and the clients at 7:30 this evening, at the safe house. It is very important that you be there. He will be bringing an employee of the U.S. Fish and Wildlife Service who claims to have damaging information on the federal wildlife agents. I'm told that the information is likely to result in dismissal of all

charges against our clients, and may provide an opening for a viable lawsuit against the federal government through the Tort Claims Act.

Note: Ice Chest has received intelligence information that you and our clients are under visual and electronic surveillance. Leave the courtroom immediately and meet your drivers in the underground parking lot. Wait for the decoys to arrive, then proceed immediately to the safe house, using maximum evasive techniques and separate routes for each vehicle.

Important: Until we have better information on this electronic surveillance, all communications between you and me and any other members of the office staff are to be in written form and delivered by bonded messenger. Do not call the office, do not use cellular phones or any other transmitting devices, and do not make any other stops until you reach the safe house. Ice Chest will monitor your arrival, verify that you have not been followed, and then meet with you at 7:30 sharp.
　　Leland.

"Why would anyone with the slightest shred of dignity choose to call themselves 'Ice Chest,' " Bascomb muttered to the room at large. "And if this is such an important meeting, why the hell didn't they—"

"He's here," one of the bodyguards announced from the front window where he had been watching the front yard and driveway through a gap in the closed drapes.

"Thank *God*!" Bascomb snarled, elbowing one of his assistants aside as he hurried over and peeked through the edge of the drapes. He was starting toward the front door when the bodyguard grabbed his arm.

"Sir, you'd better let us . . . just in case," the muscular young man advised.

Bascomb started to argue and yank his arm loose. But he quickly realized that his strength was no match for a twenty-eight-year-old body builder. Besides, Bascomb quickly rationalized, there was no reason to appear anxious. Especially after what he'd been through during the past five hours.

"I'll meet with him in the kitchen. In *private*," the pompous defense attorney added with a theatrical toss of his head.

Bascomb turned and was starting to walk back to the kitchen when he heard the now familiar two-and-two knock. Unable to ignore his sense of curiosity, he turned back to watch as the senior member of the security team walked up to the door.

The muscular guard started to look through the peephole, hesitated, shook his head irritably, and then unlocked and opened the heavy wooden door.

Two loud thumps echoed through the small room as the impact of the two 10mm hollow-point bullets, throat and head, sent the bodyguard staggering backward in a spray of blood.

In the moments that followed, the theory that a human being responds in an emergency situation in the exact manner that he or she has been trained was demonstrated once again.

As the huge form of Riser filled the doorway, the one remaining bodyguard who was still alive—his two outside associates having been quietly dispatched with a knife three and two minutes earlier, respectively—whirled around into a crouched position as he brought his 9mm semiautomatic double-action pistol out of his hip holster with blinding speed. As an ex–Secret Service agent who had spent five years assigned to a Presidential Protection Team, the now privately employed bodyguard had been thoroughly and relentlessly trained to stop a bullet with his vest first and to kill only as a secondary action.

He stopped the first 10mm bullet in his groin—three inches below the lower edge of his vest—which diverted the upward movement of his hands and caused an explosive

9mm round to be discharged through the worn carpet. Bent forward by the impact, the crippled bodyguard died when the second 10mm slug tore through the top of his head.

Roy Parker had been trained in the U.S. Marine Corps to move in, take cover, kill, and keep moving. He reacted to the sudden and violent death of the senior bodyguard by diving forward and scrambling for the man's weapon. Had he not been hampered by a crippled leg, which had been caused by a bullet fired by Special Agent Henry Lightstone six months earlier, he might have made it. Instead, Parker's outstretched hand was less than six inches away from the butt of the bodyguard's 9mm pistol when a 10mm hollow-point punched through the side of his head, just in front of his left ear. A second unnecessary bullet severed his spine at the base of his skull.

Jason Bascomb's two legal assistants had no military, police, or survival training at all, which meant that they both simply stood there, paralyzed and with mouths agape, during the four seconds it took for Riser to kill the two inside guards and Parker. They were still standing there, looking for all the world like highly realistic pop-up targets, when Riser—in a one-two manner that was almost as casual as it was fast—sent two more 10mm bullets tearing into their completely exposed and vulnerable hearts.

Of all the men in the room, dead or alive, Gerd Maas possessed the greatest amount of very practical training and experience in killing and staying alive. Accordingly, he spent those four seconds verifying with a sweep of his cold blue eyes that he had no access to a weapon that would be of any use against a professional killer like the man who had just walked in the doorway and calmly dispatched Jason Bascomb's entire protection team.

So Maas simply sat there in his wheelchair and stared calmly back at the huge man—who, in spite of his size, was so incredibly fast and accurate with his hands and with the sound-suppressed 10mm semiautomatic pistol—with an almost gentle and curious smile on his face.

Like his fellow lawyers, Jason Bascomb III had never fired a gun in his entire life. And the idea of actually having to defend himself against a man with a gun was so foreign and so unlikely for a man in his position that he'd never even given it a moment's thought. And even though he had observed hundreds of bodies shot and stabbed in hundreds of ways, it had always been through videos of crime scenes and photographs of autopsies. The noise and the blood and the smell and the shock had never been real. Thus, aside from his legal education and courtroom practice, the only other halfway useful training that Bascomb had ever acquired was on a stage.

So, like everyone else in the room, Bascomb responded instinctively to his training by stepping forward in a mindless daze, extending a pointed finger out at the huge man who had just killed five people before his very eyes, and declaring in a loud, Shakespearean voice:

"You cannot do this!"

In his last moments the ever-theatrical defense attorney had the dubious pleasure of knowing that he had nailed his entire audience with his final performance, because both Riser and Maas had responded to his loud declaration in an identical manner . . . and their laughter was the last sound— but one—that rang in his ears.

Chapter Nineteen

Henry Lightstone stood at the end of the main dock of the Windbreaker Marina with his hands on his hips and a perplexed expression on his face.

"Any sign of them?" Larry Paxton asked in a quiet voice, trying hard not to wake up anyone who might be sleeping in one of the nearby boats.

"Nope."

"You *sure* we're at the right place?" the assistant special agent in charge asked for the third time, making no attempt to smother a deep yawn as he stared out across the dark glistening expanse of dock-light-illuminated yachts, cruisers, and sailboats.

"Windbreaker Marina. Fort Lauderdale, Florida. Saturday morning, oh-two-hundred hours," Lightstone replied. "Said not to worry, he'd be real easy to find."

"Yeah, well, you couldn't prove that by me," Paxton grumbled, rubbing his eyes in an effort to wake up.

Following the directions provided by Bobby LaGrange, Henry Lightstone's ex-homicide detective partner at the San Diego Police Department, the five federal wildlife agents had arrived at the Windbreaker Marina at one-forty-five in the morning. A half hour later, and after having checked every one of the one-hundred-and-ninety-two boat slips at the marina, they still hadn't found any sign of LaGrange or his brand-new sports fishing boat.

"This isn't like Bobby," Lightstone said, growing concern evident in his voice.

"What, you mean he never got you up in the middle of the night before, or he never left you standing around waiting for him when you guys were working cases together?"

"People always kill each other at one o'clock in the morning," Lightstone said. "It's practically an American tradition. But I was always the one who was late. Bobby always got to the scenes on time."

"Maybe we ought to try the Windsong Marina," Mike Takahara suggested. "The names are similar and it's down the coast a couple of miles." And when Lightstone started to argue, the tech agent added: "Hey, don't forget, it was two o'clock in the morning when you woke him up. And as I recall, you even said he mumbled a lot."

"Yeah, I know, but he was pretty clear about the name of the marina. He even made me repeat it."

"Now Ah understand why he told us to meet him here at two in the friggin' morning." Paxton nodded in sudden understanding. "He probably just wanted to get back at your sorry ass for waking him up like that."

"Yeah, but did he say anything at all about what the boat looks like or what slip he was in?" Takahara pressed.

"Not that I recall. If he did, I must have forgotten."

"That's wonderful, Lightstone, just absolutely wonderful," Dwight Stoner muttered.

"All right, people," Larry Paxton said with a noticeable lack of enthusiasm, "let's give it one more try. And this time try to keep your eyes open for somebody who just might know what the hell's going on around here."

According to the one half-awake and barely functional night shift employee that they'd managed to find so far—a nineteen- or twenty-year-old youth dressed in ragged white overalls and a pair of decomposing open-toed sneakers, who seemed to know absolutely nothing about a boat named the *Lone Granger,* and to care even less—there were exactly one-hundred-and-ninety-two boats registered in the Windbreak Marina, with about seventy-five anxious applicants on the waiting list. Not having a key to the office where the register was kept (an understandable precaution on the part of the management, as far as Paxton and Lightstone were concerned), or any idea where anyone with such a key might be at two A.M. on a Saturday morning, the scroungy-looking dockworker had been less than helpful.

But in trying to convey what little he apparently knew, the young marina employee *had* managed to explain why the idea of someone going out and buying a brand-new boat, and only *then* going around trying to find a slip to put it in, was one of the standing jokes in southern Florida.

"Trust me," the youth had said with what presumably passed for a sincere expression in Fort Lauderdale. "Unless your buddy's got *really* big bucks, it just ain't gonna happen in his lifetime. No way."

Paxton and Lightstone couldn't decide whether they

found this explanation to be mildly reassuring or just plain unnerving.

In any event, as best the agents could tell from their dock-level position, approximately half of the Windbreaker Marina's hundred-and-ninety-two slips were currently empty, which should have made the task of checking names on the remaining ninety-some sailboats, yachts, and ocean cruisers a relatively easy task. Or at least it would have been, had it been light out, and had all the remaining boats been bunched together. But, of course, it wasn't and they weren't.

And not only were the remaining boats not all together, but most of them were tied up bow first, which meant the agents had to work themselves around to the outer edge of each slip, and then hang out over the water with flashlights in order to read the names painted on the stern plates. The three apparently insomniac boat owners they met in the process of doing this were reasonably friendly and understanding, but none of them professed to have ever heard of a fishing boat named the *Lone Granger.*

At two-forty-five A.M. the four agents were back at the far end of the main dock, hungry, sleepy, dripping with sweat, and glaring at one another.

"What did you say the name of that boat was again?" Thomas Woeshack asked from his sitting position on the pile of duffel bags. Aside from mentioning that the sweat was starting to make his cast itch—a complaint that failed to elicit the slightest degree of sympathy from his fellow agents—the diminutive Eskimo agent was the only member of the covert team who appeared to be enjoying himself.

"The *Lone Granger.* G-R-A-N-G-E-R," Lightstone said absentmindedly, squinting as he continued to search with a growing sense of unease for some sign of the familiar figure of his long-time friend.

"What'd he call it that for?"

"Probably because he's got a warped sense of humor," Mike Takahara suggested.

"I don't understand." The Eskimo agent shook his head.

"What's so funny about being a lone granger, whatever that is?"

"What, you mean you never heard about the Lone Ranger when you were a kid?" the tech agent asked in a disbelieving voice.

"No, I don't think so. Who was he?"

"Just one of your average everyday white-hat cowboy law enforcement types," Larry Paxton said. "Usually spent his days riding the range and taking unfair advantage of his ethnically disadvantaged partner . . . which has pretty much turned out to be a tradition down here in the lower forty-eight," the supervisory agent added with a meaningful glare at the members of his covert team.

"Aye aye, *kemo sabe*," Mike Takahara chuckled.

"Now I really don't understand," Woeshack said, looking even more confused than before. "How come they called him the Lone Ranger if he had a partner?"

"Tell you what, Thomas," Henry Lightstone said, patting the Eskimo agent on his shoulder, "first we'll explain what *kemo sabe* really means. *Then* we'll tell you about the Lone Ranger. It'll make a lot more sense that way."

"Speaking of things not making any sense," Dwight Stoner reminded.

"Yeah, I know, I'm starting to feel real uneasy about this whole deal." Lightstone nodded. "I could be wrong about the name of the marina, but Bobby's always been real sharp on making his connections, no matter what. And the way things have been going downhill the last few days. . . ." He left the rest unsaid.

"You think somebody might have gone after him, on account of us?" Mike Takahara asked.

"I don't know." Lightstone shrugged. "But you said it yourself. Whoever it was who broke into that warehouse up in Boston knew a hell of a lot about electronic communications, not to mention locks and burglar alarms. And if they were that sophisticated, who's to say they didn't have our phone tapped at the safe house?"

''You did run a check on that, didn't you?'' Larry Paxton turned and asked his tech agent.

''Not after the break-in.'' Mike Takahara shook his head ruefully. ''Never thought about it. I was too busy trying to figure out how the S.O.B.'s got into our alarm system.''

''So what you're saying is that whoever was messing with us up there in Boston could have front-tailed us down here, knowing we're going to link up with Bobby?'' Dwight Stoner asked.

''If they tapped into the phone line, they'd have both sides of the conversation, plus Bobby's area code and phone number.'' Mike Takahara nodded. ''You give a professional that much information, he'd have been down here a long time ago.''

''Shit,'' Henry Lightstone muttered.

''Listen, before we go off half-cocked, let's first work on the assumption that we might be at the wrong marina and go check out the Windsong,'' Larry Paxton said.

''Sounds good to me.'' Lightstone nodded.

''But before we do that,'' Paxton said, ''I want to make damn sure nobody around here knows anything about the *Lone Granger*.''

''So how are you going to do that, wake everybody up?'' Thomas Woeshack asked.

''By going over and having a little chat with the owner of that boat,'' Paxton said, gesturing with his head.

The four agents all turned around and seemed to notice for the first time the huge luxury yacht tied up along the extended L-shaped end of the main dock. There was obviously a light on in the upper-deck cabin.

''Christ, is that thing really a boat?'' Henry Lightstone exclaimed, staring at the huge craft through the glary dock lights.

''Looks more like one of those Star Destroyer space ships in *Star Wars*,'' Mike Takahara commented as he and the other agents picked up their bags and began to walk toward the sleek, white multidecked craft that—from their angled, bow-end perspective—looked as if it had been designed more for racing than deep water cruising and sports fishing. The sharp angles formed by the superstructure gave the glistening yacht a visual sense of being in forward motion in spite of being securely lashed to the dock.

"Either that or a floating hotel," Dwight Stoner suggested as the five agents stopped at the edge of the chained-off gangplank and stared up at the massive triple-decked cruising yacht.

"Wow," Thomas Woeshack whispered softly.

"You really think a guy with the dough to run a boat like that is going to be the least bit interested in any of the other smaller boats around here?" Lightstone asked dubiously.

"Oh, I don't know, I'll bet you these boat-owner types are all pretty much alike, no matter what size boat they've got," Mike Takahara said. "Probably spend at least half their time keeping an eye on each other. You know, who's fishing where, who's using what, and who's got the latest in gizmos and gadgets."

Larry Paxton looked up at the enclosed bridge of the huge yacht and then cupped his hands to his mouth.

"Ahoy up there, anybody home?"

The agents waited for about thirty seconds. There was no answer and no indication that anyone was aboard, in spite of the light shining through the closed curtains.

"Windsong Marina?" Lightstone said.

"Might as well," Paxton nodded.

As the agents started to gather up their gear again, they realized that Thomas Woeshack was still staring at the over-sized cruiser, his dark eyes wide with amazement and curiosity.

"What's the matter, Woeshack? Don't you guys have boats like this up in your village?" Paxton asked, looking up from his duffel bag.

"Not that I ever saw." Thomas Woeshack shook his head. "Man, I bet it'd take at least five hundred walrus hides to build a boat like that."

Henry Lightstone turned to stare at the young Eskimo agent. "Woeshack," he said after a long moment, "how in God's name did you ever manage to pass that pilot's exam?"

"Hey, it sounds reasonable to me," Dwight Stoner said, winking at Paxton. "Bet they only needed a half dozen walruses and a couple rubber bands to build that piss-ant little plane these turkeys crashed up by that glacier."

Thomas Woeshack really didn't understand that his native Alaskan naiveté had provided the necessary spark to regenerate the flagging spirits of his fellow agents. But Larry Paxton certainly did, and as the acting team leader, he took immediate advantage of the opportunity.

"Woeshack," he said, "don't you let these ignorant crackers bother you none. Fact is, if I really thought you knew how to turn an igloo full of rotten walrus hides into a fine boat like this, I'd retire right now and hire you on as my business partner. Hell, Ah'd even split the profits even, all the way down the line."

"And in doing so, immediately start taking advantage of your ethnically disadvantaged partner?" Mike Takahara suggested.

"Hey, fair is fair." The supervisory agent smiled cheerfully.

"Does that mean I'd get to call you *kemo sabe* too?" Woeshack asked.

"You bet."

"So how big do you think this thing really is?" Stoner asked as the agents continued to stand there at the extended edge of the dock and stare up at the huge, white fiberglass and stainless steel boat.

"Beats me." Paxton shrugged as he swung the heavy duffel bag over his shoulder again. "Have to ask the owner next time we're by this way.

"And just what makes you think the owner's gonna be interested in talking to a bunch of ignorant landlubbers like you guys?" Bobby LaGrange inquired as he leaned out over the side of the high top deck of the *Lone Granger* and glared down at his late-arriving crew.

At a public phone booth near the entrance of the Wind-breaker Marina, a disreputable-looking young man in ragged white overalls and a pair of slowly decomposing open-toed sneakers dropped a quarter into the coin slot and carefully dialed a number that had been block-printed in pencil on what was now a thoroughly worn and water-soaked three-by-five card.

"Mr.—uh—Jones?"

"Yes?"

The man on the other end of the line sounded alert, re-freshed, and wide-awake. There was no indication at all that—in the span of the last twelve hours—he had killed a total of twelve law enforcement officers, security guards, lawyers, and federal witnesses, kidnapped two professional counterterrorists, and then transported those two captives in a private jet down to Fort Lauderdale.

Instead, the voice on the other end of the line sounded alert, awake, cold, gravelly, and malicious, causing the young man to shiver in spite of the indigenous southern Florida heat and humidity.

"You said you wanted to know if anyone came around asking for the *Lone Granger*," the young man reminded.

"Yes, so?"

"Five guys just showed up."

"When?"

"About fifteen minutes ago."

"Describe them."

"Uh, there's one tall black guy. He acts kinda like he's the leader. And one huge bastard, looks like he mighta played pro ball somewhere. And one little guy who kinda looks like he might be an Indian or maybe a—"

"Fine, thank you," the cold gravelly voice interrupted, and the phone went dead in the young dockworker's hand.

* * *

At a quarter to four that Saturday morning, while Bobby LaGrange was patiently demonstrating the entertainment package in the master stateroom of the *Lone Granger* to a gleefully incredulous Larry Paxton and his disbelieving fellow agents, a rented green van with dark tinted windows drove into the entrance of the marina, pulled around back, and came to a stop next to the trash dumpsters, and then flashed its headlights.

Ten minutes later a disreputable-looking young man in ragged white overalls and a pair of slowly decomposing open-toed sneakers hurried over and got in through the front passenger side door.

"What's happening now?" Riser demanded, the expression in his cold and foreboding eyes nearly causing the terrified dockworker to void his bladder.

"Uh . . . th-they're still out there on th-the extension dock," he stammered.

"Are they fueled up already?"

"Uh—y-yeah, sure. I—uh—f-filled his tanks early this morning." The youth was so terrified that his entire body was trembling now.

"Good." Riser nodded. "When are you due to go off duty?"

"Uh—uh—at s-six-thirty."

"When are you due back?"

"Uh . . ."

"When are you due back?" Riser demanded impatiently.

"W-Wednesday!" the youth blurted out.

"Good."

The man known as Riser looked out both side windows of the rented van, checked the rearview mirrors, and then—in a motion too fast to follow with the human eye—slashed the hardened edge of his right hand into the youth's throat.

The young dockworker's head snapped back against the rear cab window as he gurgled in shock. Then, as the youth's sagging body started to fall forward, Riser quickly reached across with both hands to grab and twist sharply his loosely hanging head. The crack of snapping neck vertebrae signaled the end of the night-shift dockworker's thankless career.

After checking the windows and mirrors one last time, Riser grabbed the front of the youth's overalls with his right hand and then—with no apparent effort—lifted the lifeless body out of the seat and tossed it into the back of the van like a leftover sack of trash.

". . . so my lawyer and Kleinfelter's lawyer got their little shyster heads together, and they came up with this deal . . . thanks, Justin," Bobby LaGrange said, accepting a steaming mug of hot coffee from his fifteen-year-old son who had just come up from helping Mo-Jo—the elder of the two part-time Jamaican crewmen—load the rest of the supplies for their planned shake-down cruise. Justin LaGrange handed out identical mugs to the five agents, all of whom were either sitting casually on the salon's incredibly comfortable starboard side couch, hanging around the control station of the bridge, or—in Paxton's case—sitting next to LaGrange in one of the newly designated commodore's chairs.

"Justin, you're starting to look and act more like your dad every day," Henry Lightstone commented as he took a careful sip of the hot beverage.

"Is that good?" the slender T-shirted youth asked.

"Not necessarily. I'll talk to you about that later."

"Dad said I'm not supposed to listen to anything you tell me until I turn twenty-one, and if I'm smart, not even then," Justin LaGrange said, which got the expected laugh out of everyone on the deck.

"Son," Bobby LaGrange said after the laughter and side comments had died down, "if we're going to get out of this place before oh-five-hundred, you'd probably better go give Mo-Jo a hand storing all that food and gear."

"Yes, sir."

Looking only mildly disappointed, the youth quickly disappeared out the sliding glass door leading to the aft deck.

"Quite a kid you got there." Larry Paxton nodded approvingly. "How'd you get him to turn out that polite and hardworking?"

"Real simple." Bobby LaGrange shrugged. "I told him it was either going to be 'yes, sir' and 'no, sir' and working his ass off the entire weekend or I'd leave him at home with his mom and sister to help with chores."

"Which might not have been a bad idea anyway," Henry Lightstone said hesitantly.

"Yeah, I know, I remembered you said something about you guys getting into some kind of trouble." LaGrange nodded. "Anything new on all that?"

"Not that we know of, but we're keeping our eyes open."

"Okay, well, I figured we'll take Justin along on the first trip, spend a couple of days giving him a chance to show you guys some of the ropes, and then put him back on shore when we get down to serious business. Besides, he's got to be back in school Monday anyway. What do you think?"

"I guess that sounds okay," Lightstone said uneasily.

"Henry's always been a worry wart." LaGrange smiled, winking at the surrounding agent team. "He was like that every single day we worked together. Don't know how you guys put up with him."

"We generally don't," Larry Paxton said. "But before we start asking you personal questions about our wild-card buddy here, Ah want to hear some more about Kleinfelter and his lawyer."

"Oh, yeah, Kleinfelter." Bobby LaGrange nodded, looking ruefully down at the numerous scars that covered both of his hands and bared arms. Similar scars were visible on the retired homicide investigator's face and neck—reminders of the severe and nearly fatal beating he had received from Brendon Kleinfelter and the members of his outlaw motorcycle gang. "I don't have many fond memories of the gentleman, but I do remember somebody at the hospital telling me that some federal wildlife agent managed to rearrange his ugly face with a bat."

"You can thank Stoner for that," Henry Lightstone said, motioning with his head in the direction of the huge agent who had discovered that he was much more comfortable sitting on the thickly padded carpeting with his massive back and arms propped against the extended couch. "He was the one with the oversized strike zone. Also managed to save my butt at the same time, *after* he put it into jeopardy in the first place," Lightstone added.

"Just happened to be at the right place at the right time." Dwight Stoner shrugged modestly.

"With a Louisville slugger and a love of the game," Paxton reminded.

"Well, yeah, I guess that probably helped some too." The huge agent grinned.

"Stoner, I want you to know that you have my undying gratitude," Bobby LaGrange said seriously. "Far as I'm concerned, from this day on, any time you set foot on the *Lone Granger*, the beer and the grub are on the house. Beyond that, I'm going to see what I can do about hooking you up with a walk-in freezer full of big blues, some night dives off Bimini and The Wall, and maybe even a pretty young native gal to run off and make babies with in your declining years. How's that for a start?"

"Gawd *damn*, LaGrange, don't treat him *that* nice," Larry Paxton protested. "The man's a dedicated government employee. You're gonna ruin him! Besides," the acting team leader warned, "if you're planning on feeding him for free for the rest of his life, you might as well go out and sell this thing right now for whatever cash you can get, 'cause you're gonna need it."

"And speaking of money, not that we're nosy or anything," Mike Takahara said, looking up from the bridge control station where he was deeply involved in exploring the *Lone Granger*'s computer-controlled electronics systems.

"Ask away." Bobby LaGrange shrugged. "What do you want to know?"

"Well, for a start, what kind of boat is this, and how much?"

"Well," LaGrange said after a moment's thought, "technically, she's an eighty-two-foot luxury cruiser that got converted over into what you might call a custom sports fishing yacht. In addition to all the stuff you already saw, she's got dual props, upgrade engines, a computer-designed racing hull, dual stabilizers, a matched set of fighting chairs we can mount in place on the aft lower deck, refrigerated bait tank, holding freezers, extended swim platform, radar, loran, top-of-the-line electronics package—which I assume Snoopy over there knows a whole lot more about by now than I do— and probably a couple of torpedo tubes I haven't discovered yet." The retired homicide detective grinned. "Guy who paid the bill spent a little over one-point-eight million to rig this gal for deep-sea fishing and pleasure cruising. Apparently, he had more money than he knew what to do with. Or at least he did until he ran across Kleinfelter and his boys." LaGrange shook his head sadly.

Henry Lightstone turned to Thomas Woeshack, who still seemed to have trouble accepting the fact that he was actually on a boat that had cost somebody one-point-eight-million dollars.

"So how many walrus hides did you figure now?" he asked.

"I don't know, might have to pick up a couple dozen moose and bearskins too," Woeshack replied cheerfully. "This boat's a whole lot bigger inside than I thought it was."

Bobby LaGrange looked as if he were tempted to ask one or both of the agents what the hell they were talking about when Larry Paxton interrupted.

"So who was this ex-owner character, one of Kleinfelter's Florida connections?"

"That's what it sounded like." Bobby LaGrange nodded. "I don't know what all happened, and apparently nobody else does either. Or at least nobody who's willing to talk. All

I know is the guy signed the pink slip over to Kleinfelter, and then sometime shortly thereafter disappeared off the face of this earth.''

"Convenient."

"Yeah, no kidding. I figure by now he's probably bouncing along the bottom of one of those deep water canyons off the Bahamas with three or four hundred pounds of anchor chain wrapped around his neck. Anyway, my lawyer spotted the boat when he filed a discovery motion looking for Kleinfelter's assets, and got a copy of all the papers you guys seized out of . . . what was it, some place called the High Horse Bar up in Anchorage?''

"You mean to tell me Brendon Kleinfelter just *gave* you this thing, willingly?" Henry Lightstone blinked.

"Well, actually, it was his lawyer and my lawyer who cut the deal." Bobby LaGrange shrugged. "Apparently, it was either that or go back to court and risk losing the bar, the château, and a couple of other big pieces of property just north of Anchorage along with it. Guess he figured he could always strong-arm some poor slob out of another boat. Of course, the fact that you guys already had him nailed on attempted murder of a federal officer—not to mention watering down the draft beer in that bar—probably helped some too.''

"Probably didn't figure he had much hope of finding a sympathetic judge or jury in Anchorage, especially after his beer policy came to light," Lightstone chuckled. "Man, would I have loved to have seen ol' Brendon's face when he signed that pink slip.''

"He still had his jaw all wired together at the time, so I never got to hear what he really thought of the deal''— LaGrange grinned—"but he didn't look too happy. Didn't look all that pretty either," the ex-homicide detective added. "Never saw a man that black-and-blue before.''

"Which is probably a real good reason you and Henry shouldn't do too much traveling up in Alaska for the next few years," Larry Paxton suggested.

"Yeah, I reckon you're right." LaGrange nodded. "Which is just fine with me. No sense going all the way up there and freezing to death, just to make myself feel better hunting the son of a bitch down, when I can make a real nice living down here where it's sunny and warm."

"Speaking of which, how *do* you make a living with this thing?" Mike Takahara asked, looking up from one of the thick owner's manuals. "Just filling up those diesel tanks alone must cost a small fortune."

"Yeah, it does," LaGrange said, "but you'd be surprised what some of these New York, Boston, and Washington, D.C., types will pay for a week out on the water with a couple of their buddies. No troubles, no cares. Just eat, drink, fish, drink, and sleep."

"Eskimo way of life." Woeshack nodded approvingly.

" 'Course, it always helps when you latch on to one of the big boys," LaGrange added.

"What'd you do, find yourself a repeat customer? One of them sugar-daddy types?" Paxton asked.

"I got a couple of good ones, include one character that we're going to work when we get out to the islands." The retired homicide investigator nodded. "But when it comes down to sugar daddies, there's nothing quite like hooking up with the federal government if you really want to make a killing in this business."

If it had been physically possible, Larry Paxton's dark complexion would have turned a pale white. "Oh, my God . . ." he whispered.

"Hey, that's right, Larry," Henry Lightstone said. "I bet Halahan's gonna be real surprised when he finds out you signed—what was that you and Snoopy were faxing back and forth yesterday?"

"Uh . . . I don't exactly remember," the acting team leader tried hopefully.

"Actually, I think Larry's just being modest." Bobby La-Grange smiled. "But as a matter of record, I distinctly remember that it was a six-month lease—with a verifying cosignature from some little purchasing clerk in Washington, D.C.—for full-time use of the *Lone Granger*, as is, not including all fuel and docking charges, which Larry generously agreed to pay separately," the retired homicide detective added with undisguised cheerfulness.

"Yeah, that's right, I remember now," Lightstone nodded. "A six-month lease for a one-point-eight-million-dollar yacht. Man, oh, man, wait until the United States government hears about this one."

"Actually, I believe the lease described the *Lone Granger* as a mid-sized sports fishing boat," LaGrange corrected.

"Which might have been halfway accurate if you were comparing her to a goddamned commercial trawler," Paxton grumbled accusingly.

"But if we'd gone out and leased a trawler, then we wouldn't have all those guest and owner staterooms," Lightstone reminded, "not to mention a salon *and* a galley, complete with entertainment packages."

"And also not to mention all those fuel and docking charges," Mike Takahara added, "which, based on my initial rough estimates, ought to cost us a small fortune, even at government rates."

"Which is really pretty cheap when you consider that you're talking about experiencing the true Eskimo way of life," Woeshack put in.

"That's right, Paxton." Lightstone grinned. "Don't forget to tell Halahan about that. The Eskimo way of life. He's gonna *love* that part."

Special Agent Dwight Stoner simply leaned back against the overstuffed salon couch and stared at Paxton with what might have passed for a sympathetic expression on his meaty and scarred face.

"Halahan's gonna kill you for sure this time," he offered.

Bobby LaGrange turned to his ex-police homicide partner. "So who's this Halahan character you guys are talking about?"

"Our real boss," Lightstone said, "as opposed to the dip-shit commodore over here.''

"Oh, yeah, so what's he like?"

Lightstone thought about the question for a moment. "First, picture Gengis Khan with a suit and a shave."

"Okay." LaGrange nodded agreeably.

"Then give him an attitude problem."

"I see. In other words, your standard-issue law enforcement brass."

"Pretty much."

"Except Henry forgot to mention that he's actually said, 'Yes, sir,' to Halahan twice this week already," Mike Takahara corrected.

"Oh, really?"

Bobby LaGrange looked back at Lightstone with a disbelieving expression on his suntanned face. "What's going on here, Henry? You starting to go soft on me now that you've become a fed?"

Lightstone smiled. "Nah, just trying to get in good with the new management."

"Yeah, I'll bet." Bobby LaGrange nodded knowingly. He seemed to consider the whole situation for a couple of moments, then smiled to himself and turned his attention back to Paxton, who still appeared to be in a state of mild shock.

"So, Larry, if I understand the situation correctly, not only do you get to have a modern version of the Mad Cossack for a boss; but as a bonus they made you responsible for all Henry's shit too. Sounds like one hell of a deal." The ex-homicide investigator shook his head sympathetically. "So who'd you piss off?"

"I don't wanna talk about it," Larry Paxton grumbled. "You got anything stronger to add to this coffee?"

"As a rule, I usually don't let my clients start dipping into the sauce until at least oh-nine-hundred hours," LaGrange said as he levered himself up out of the comfortable chair, walked over to the galley, reached into a cupboard, and pulled out a corked bottle. "However, taking into account the nature and the magnitude of the responsibilities that you are about to undertake, and all the support you're likely to get from your crew, I think we can make an exception on this fine Saturday morning. How about some cognac?''

"It any good?" Paxton inquired.

"Costs me seventy-nine a bottle, wholesale." LaGrange shrugged. "I keep it around for my real picky customers."

"Shit, that's me," Paxton said, extending his mug.

"Probably ought to give him the whole bottle," Henry Lightstone suggested. "Might keep him quiet for a while."

Larry Paxton accepted a generous slug of the expensive brandy from Bobby LaGrange, sniffed cautiously, and then took a sip of the potent mixture. The other agents observed the blissful smile that suddenly broke out on their acting leader's face and immediately extended their own mugs. La-Grange complied and then added about a quarter slug to his own mug. After returning the bottle to the dubious security of the unlocked cupboard, LaGrange held up his mug in a toast. "To good buddies."

"And six-month leases."

"And the Eskimo way of life."

"And a new ASAC."

"Amen t' that!"

Setting his mug aside, Bobby LaGrange turned back to the five federal wildlife agents.

"Okay," he said, "if you guys are ready to sack out for a few hours, we'll take her out on the first leg. And then, after you get up and get some decent grub in your stomachs, somebody can start this whole deal out by telling me everything you know about this character named Alfred Bloom."

At precisely five minutes after five on what would soon turn out to be a beautiful Saturday morning, Bobby LaGrange and his able assistant Mo-Jo stood at the bridge controls and skillfully piloted the eighty-two-foot *Lone Granger* out of the Windbreaker Marina harbor and into the main channel, her twin Detroit diesels rumbling smoothly. And as they did so, four men and a young boy settled into their bunks and beds, already soothed into a peaceful sleep by the gentle rocking motions of the deep-water craft.

As the *Lone Granger* cleared the first set of channel markers, a huge man pulled himself out of the water and up onto the dock. Then he sat there, salt water dripping off his huge, deeply tanned, and muscular body, as he watched the departure of the customized yacht with a look that was overwhelmingly cold, malicious, and foreboding.

But because of the surrounding darkness, the man who called himself Riser had no way of knowing that on the rear deck of the *Lone Granger*, in a place where the running lights left only dark shadows, Henry Lightstone sat cross-legged in quiet solitude, staring back in the direction of the marina with an expression of uneasy awareness and protective fury in his equally cold and unforgiving eyes.

Chapter Twenty

Alfred Bloom would have been absolutely panic-stricken had he known that at ten-fifteen that Saturday morning his fate was being contemplated by at least four dozen professionally trained and extremely dangerous individuals—one of whom happened to be sitting by himself in a far corner of the cafeteria of the J. Edgar Hoover Building in downtown Washington, D.C.

It had been a long night for FBI agent Al Grynard.

After three hours out at the Dulles Access Road crime scene, the FBI special task force commander had spent another hour on the phone talking back and forth with two of the senior partners from Little, Warren, Nobles & Kole, in an effort to locate Jason Bascomb III and his two counterterrorist clients. At one-thirty A.M., Grynard had taken his field notebook down to the communications center and had begun contacting the senior members of his task force and the night-duty agents working out of the local FBI field offices, sharing with them what little the two senior law partners knew about Jason Bascomb III's security arrangements. Then, at four-thirty A.M., he had begun digging through the FBI's computerized central records files, searching for that elusive connection that no one else had managed to find yet.

And after all that, the fatigued supervisor of the thirty-two-agent special task force realized, he was no closer to making any sense out of the entire confused Operation Counter Wrench fiasco than he had been forty-eight hours earlier.

So what do I do, Mr. Alfred Linneas Bloom? Al Grynard thought to himself. *Pull you in or let you run?*

Grynard was tired, hungry, irritable, and absolutely frustrated. He had been on the go for the last twenty-eight hours, and he had long since given up any thoughts of dinner, rewarmed or otherwise. Instead, he'd finally settled for a quick breakfast of coffee and a couple of bran muffins in the FBI headquarter's cafeteria before allowing himself to decide whether he should make an attempt to set an emergency meeting with Alfred Bloom—and in doing so, possibly either save the wealthy industrialist's life, or put him at much greater risk—or simply go home and go to bed.

It was turning out to be a far more difficult choice than Grynard would have ever imagined.

The veteran agent was sleepily contemplating the last cold dregs of his coffee, having just about convinced himself that Alfred Bloom would get along just fine for another twelve hours or so without the assistance of the FBI, when he happened to glance up and see a young man who looked a great deal like his teenage son enter the cafeteria.

Except that as far as Grynard knew, his sports-minded and government-hating son didn't even own a pair of gray slacks and a navy blazer—the standard uniform of the Washington, D.C., bureaucrat.

As he continued to sit there, caught up in a sense of uneasy anticipation that he couldn't quite define, Grynard watched the neatly dressed young man stop just inside the entrance to the cafeteria and begin looking around at the scattered faces of the agents and technicians and clerical staff who were either coming on or going off duty. Then it hit him.

Oh, Christ, no, he thought to himself.

Grynard froze in place, trying to convince himself that if he didn't move, didn't look up, and didn't meet the young man's searching gaze, then it just might not be . . .

But then, out of the corner of his eye, Grynard saw the navy-blazered young man suddenly stop his visual search and begin to move forward in the direction of his corner table. At that moment Special Agent Al Grynard realized that pausing for breakfast at the J. Edgar Building had been a mistake.

Should have just gone home and gone to bed, he told himself, knowing of course that it wouldn't have made much difference one way or the other, because they would have found him no matter where he went. That was what FBI agents were good at, finding people who didn't want to be found, he thought with a morose sense of irony.

For a brief moment Grynard tried to convince himself that the young man was looking for someone else—another agent who had futilely sought a few moments of peace and escape from the pressures of the job—and that he would get to go home to his incredibly patient and understanding wife after all. But the numbness in his stomach and the visible relief on the young agent's face had already warned him that it wasn't going to work out that way.

Not today.

And they had to send one of the young ones, too, Grynard mused; realizing, of course, that the brass knew better than to send one of the old-timers for a notification like this. It was a common understanding in the bureau that the "dinosaurs" all watched out for each other. If they had dispatched one of his forty-eight-year-old peers with the news, Grynard knew, that agent would have taken one look at him and told him to go home—let someone else handle it—because there were always other agents available on standby, and they'd all been through the same thing hundreds of times in their careers.

No, Grynard thought, *they wouldn't send an old-timer. They'd send one of the new ones who would hunt you down until they dropped, because they were young and dedicated and trained to never give up, no matter what.*

"Uh, Agent Grynard?"

Al Grynard looked up with tired and reddened eyes, and immediately decided that the young man in the navy blue blazer who was standing hesitantly in front of him couldn't possibly be an FBI agent, because he looked much too young and healthy and rested.

Where the hell are they recruiting these new ones, right out of high school? he asked himself, and then decided that he really didn't want to think about that particular topic right now.

In fact, Grynard wasn't even sure if he wanted to identify himself. Not that it mattered, he immediately realized, because the rookie agent undoubtedly possessed 20/20 vision, and therefore would have no trouble whatever in reading the ID badge secured to the breast pocket of Grynard's suit coat from where he was standing. For Grynard to read the small print on the young agent's laminated ID badge, he would have to retrieve his glasses from his coat pocket. And for some reason that he couldn't quite define at that moment, he really didn't want to do that.

"Yes?"

"Sir, Supervisory Special Agent Whittman asked me to find you and to advise you that they've located a Mr. Jason . . . uh . . ."

"Bascomb the Third?"

"Yes, sir, that's correct."

"Is he alive?"

"I don't know, sir. I was directed to find you and to transport you to the scene if you'd like a ride.''

Al Grynard sagged heavily in his chair. Whether he knew it or not, the young rookie agent had just answered his question. Or at least one of his questions.

"Yes." Grynard nodded tiredly. "I think I'd like that very much.''

It was nearly quarter after ten in the morning by the time Al Grynard and his rookie agent driver arrived at the Warrenton safe house.

"Uh, doesn't look too good, does it, sir?" the young agent said as he brought the brightly polished late-model sedan up alongside one of the Fauquier County patrol units.

"No, it doesn't," Grynard agreed.

He didn't bother to tell his youthful escort that he had been reading the scene from the moment they'd come around the corner and he had seen the number of marked units and uniformed officers surrounding the outside of the yellow scene tape. Four patrol cars and six uniforms outside, manning the perimeter. Four unmarked units, all locals, and three distinctive bureau cars inside, along with at least a half dozen plain-clothed figures, none of whom seemed to be in any particular hurry at all. And most telling, no ambulances or paramedic units parked outside with their rear doors open and ready.

Either they've already been here and left, or nobody bothered to call them, Grynard thought, not allowing himself to develop any hope because he was pretty sure he knew which way it had gone. The people who had hit the U.S. Marshall transport team back at the Reston off-ramp had been much too professional to leave any living witnesses behind.

"Grynard?"

A trim and hard-looking man sporting a graying crew cut, pressed new blue jeans, rubber-soled field boots, a maroon polo shirt, and a 10mm Model 1076 Smith & Wesson semiautomatic pistol worn high in a snug-fitting hip holster, walked up to the passenger side of Grynard's car and bent down to look in the passenger side window. Grynard noted the distinctive creases and sweat marks that a Kevlar vest had recently made in the tight-fitting polo shirt. A vest that had undoubtedly been tossed in the trunk of one of the bureau units out of pure frustration, not to mention outright defiance of standing bureau regulations.

"That's right."

The man stuck a muscular hand in the window.

"Jim Whittman," he said. "Thanks for coming."

Whittman, Grynard knew, was the supervisory agent of one of the FBI's highly regarded hostage recovery teams. He had never met Whittman before, but he had certainly heard a number of rumors about the ex-Marine combat veteran. One of the more interesting ones was that Whittman had somehow managed to subvert personnel rules and recruit all twelve of his young agents from Army Ranger and Marine Recon teams. Another had it that his operational tactics were based on the simple principles of conditioning, intelligence, and planning—and then split-second controlled aggression when they got the ''go'' signal to extract a hostage.

True or not, Grynard reminded himself, there was one thing that was definitely not a rumor: the fact that in a little over three years Whittman's team had never lost a hostage or sustained a single agent casualty.

For a brief moment Grynard wondered how the Whittman aggressive fire-team tactics might fare against an unknown adversary armed with a four-bore rifle and the element of surprise, and then decided that he didn't want to think about that right now. Not after the Waco incident, or after what had just happened to one of the U.S. marshall's elite prisoner transport teams.

"I take it the scene's secure?" Grynard said evenly as he stepped out of the car, making it clear to Whittman that he had noted the vest transgression, but was not pushing the issue. It was Whittman's scene, Grynard reasoned. The hostage recovery team commander could argue rules and regs with his own supervisor.

"Oh, it's secure all right," the lanky FBI agent said disgustedly. "If it was any more secure, we could invite the goddamned White House press corps in for a barbecue."

Grynard allowed the casually dressed team commander to escort him into the house, thinking to himself that the FBI had certainly changed since he'd been a rookie agent.

"The two outside were part of the security team," Whittman said mechanically as he led Grynard through the scene. "Each of them took a knife in the kidney, and then got their throats cut. Military recon style," the ex-Marine added with a distant and professional casualness.

"Were they private?" Grynard asked as he stood inside the doorway and observed the neat bullet holes in the forehead and chest of the third body.

"Yeah, but they all had federal law enforcement backgrounds. Two DEA, one Secret Service, and one from the bureau."

Grynard's eyebrows came up in surprise.

"Stanley Woodson," Whittman went on. "Good man. Too damn good to have let himself get caught up in a situation like this. Put in his twenty and decided to see if he could spend more time with his kids before they got too old," the hostage recovery team commander said in a voice that was filled with tightly controlled anger.

"Which one is he?"

"You're looking at him." Whittman gestured with his crew-cut head at the sprawled body.

"What about the others?"

Whittman began to use the index finger of his extended right hand like a lecture pointer. "Roy Parker, one of the defendants . . . and an ex-Marine." He half-smiled. "Apparently made a try for one of the security guard's pistols when everything broke loose. Looks like he damn near made it too," he added approvingly.

The right hand shifted over to the next two bodies. "Calvin Green and Williston Fordham, attorneys at law for the firm of Little, Warren, Nobles & Kole. Far as we can tell, neither of them made any attempt to defend themselves. All they did was shit and piss their pants, probably before they got nailed. Whoever did it didn't even bother to double-tap them," Whittman said with a disdain that clearly bespoke his opinion of anyone who would chose to give up his life without a fight.

"And last but not least," Whittman added, bringing his arm around in what might have been a deliberately theatrical sweep, "Jason Bascomb the fucking Third."

It took Grynard a moment before he realized the significance of the hostage recovery team commander's comment.

"You said 'last but not least'?"

"Man was an asshole." Whittman shrugged indifferently, not understanding Grynard's question. "Didn't necessarily deserve to die this way, but he was still an asshole."

"No, I mean what about Maas?"

"You mean the Kraut in the wheelchair?"

That's right, Whittman, you'd know all about a guy like Gerd Maas, wouldn't you? Grynard thought to himself. *Man after your own heart. Probably already tried to talk Headquarters into recruiting the bastard if Bascomb ever figured out how to work the whole deal down to a misdemeanor.*

"Yeah, right."

"Don't know, haven't found him yet." Whittman shrugged again. "Kinda hoping we would. I don't like to see a guy like that running around loose, even if he is in a wheelchair. Idiot who let him out on bail ought to be disbarred."

"Any sign of the chair?"

"Nope. Some wheel marks in the carpet. That's about it." Whittman shook his head. "You ask me, I figure whoever hit this place probably came here with the direct intention of scooping him up rather than killing him."

"Why do you say that?"

"Because if that wasn't the case," Whittman said, his eyes taking on a cold and distant expression as he turned to stare at Grynard, "I really doubt that the situation here would have ended up anywhere near this one-sided."

"I see." Grynard nodded thoughtfully. And then after a moment: "Any make on a weapon?"

Whittman nodded. "Oh, yeah, you'll love this part. Based on the ejected casings, we're looking at a Model 1076 using restricted law enforcement ammo."

"What? Are you sure?"

The hostage rescue team commander didn't even bother to answer that question. Instead, he simply stared back at Grynard.

"Okay, I believe you." Grynard shrugged. "So who has access to that stuff?"

"You mean besides us law enforcement types?"

"Yeah, I'm assuming we're not dealing with a rogue agent here," Grynard responded sarcastically.

"Don't be too sure," Whittman said. "Whoever took this place down knew a hell of a lot about federal procedures for operating a safe house. Besides, a lot of federal and state law enforcement agencies have switched over to the 10mm round in the last couple of years. Hell, even the bunnies and guppies guys are starting to carry 'tens.' "

"The who?"

"Fish and Wildlife Service Agents," Whittman translated.

Al Grynard's eyebrows furrowed in confusion.

"Wait a minute," he said, starting to feel that familiar numbness in his stomach again. "I thought those wildlife guys carried short-barreled stainless steel .357's, because they were out in the water all the time."

"Yep, Smith & Wesson Model 66's." Whittman nodded. "Or at least they did until a few years ago when about two-thirds of their force switched over to 9mm's. The Model 66 and the 'ten-seventy' were put out as authorized options. What I hear now is that most of their agents have gone to the Model 1076 as their basic duty weapon, and use the 66's as a backup option when they're out in the boats."

"Shit," Grynard muttered.

"Why, does that make some kind of difference with this deal here?"

"I don't know, maybe."

"Oh, that's right," Whittman said, "this whole deal started out as some kind of federal wildlife investigation, didn't it?"

"A covert investigation of the illegal guiding activities of the Chareaux brothers just outside of Yellowstone." Grynard nodded. "And it ended up with the deaths of three federal wildlife agents, ten of the twelve counterterrorists, two of the three Chareaux brothers, and a pair of dead-on-arrival co-conspirator types from the Department of the Interior; the destruction of an underground counterterrorist training center—built right under the noses of the federal government in Yellowstone National Park—that would make you drool—and a whole bunch of pieces still missing from the puzzle."

The hostage recovery team commander stared at Grynard for a long moment.

"So what's the deal here, Grynard? You thinking that maybe the buddies of those dead wildlife agents went after Maas on their own, and took out four security experts, and a handful of sleazy defense attorneys on the side, just to even things out? Or maybe hired somebody to do it for them?"

Grynard shook his head. "No, I don't believe that."

"You could say that with a whole lot more conviction," Whittman commented.

"Christ, I don't know what I think anymore," the exhausted FBI agent muttered. "Nothing about this whole deal makes much sense."

There was a long pause while the two supervisory FBI agents watched members of the FBI crime-scene team begin to work around the body of their fallen ex-comrade.

"So tell me, Grynard," Whittman asked in a conversational tone of voice, "how is it that an FBI ASAC out of Anchorage ends up getting involved in a wildlife case originating out of Yellowstone?"

"One of those dead wildlife agents, a guy named Paul

McNulty, got nailed up in Skilak Lake. Probably by Maas, although we haven't been able to prove that so far. McNulty was the special agent in charge of the covert team that tripped across Maas and his counterterrorist group in the course of investigating the Chareaux brothers, which was right before they walked into a political hornet's nest and got disbanded as a team. McNulty got reassigned to the SAC position at the Anchorage Regional Office and then got hit a few weeks later. The team's ASAC, Carl Scoby, was shot and killed down in Arizona, and attempts were made on three of the other covert team members shortly thereafter. Beyond that, it gets a little complicated.''

"Yeah, I'll bet it does." Whittman nodded. And then, after a moment: "Mind if I make a suggestion?"

"No, go ahead."

"The guy who hit this place—you *are* going after him, right?"

Grynard blinked and then stared at the tall, casually dressed agent. "You said 'the guy.' You mean as in singular? One guy?"

"That's right." Whittman nodded.

"Wait a minute, Whittman, let me get this straight. You're telling me you think that one individual took out a four-man, professionally trained security team, and an ex-Marine with counterterrorist training"—Grynard nodded toward the body of Roy Parker—"and then physically *captured* a guy like Gerd Maas?" he added incredulously, ignoring Whittman's question for the moment.

"About three hours after he took out a four-man U.S. Marshall transport team on the Dulles Access Road with a four-bore rifle, right in the middle of rush-hour traffic, and made off with your buddy Chareaux." The hostage recovery team commander nodded. "Yes, that's exactly what I'm telling you."

"Assuming for the moment that there really was only one shooter involved in each incident, and I'm not conceding that by any means, what makes you so sure it was the same man?'' Grynard demanded, feeling his heart start to pound heavily as he realized that Whittman was basically confirming his own growing fears.

"Two professional hits that result in the escape or kidnapping of two highly trained killers like Maas and Chareaux, both of whom are linked to the same federal conspiracy case? Come on, Grynard, give me a fucking break.''

"Still, it doesn't have to be one man. Whoever pulled these hits off could have had help," the Anchorage-based FBI agent argued.

"With the planning and setup, sure, I'd buy that. But not with the hit itself. I'm telling you, buddy, you're looking for the Lone Ranger on this one.''

"Based on what evidence?''

"Hell, take a look at the scene." Whittman shrugged. "Whoever this bastard is, he might just as well have choreographed his moves out with a piece of chalk. You can walk your way through it, step by step, just as plain as day. And when you do, you get a real sense that the guy had plenty of time to figure out exactly where everybody was at, and exactly what he was going to do next, every step of the way. And let me tell you something, he moved goddamned fast when he did it, too.''

"But how did he know where—'' Grynard started to ask, but Whittman was way ahead of him.

"We found a transmitter attached with a magnet under the transport van. I had it checked out, and it wasn't chirping on any of the local law enforcement frequencies. So I figure the bastard found some way to get access to the van, slapped on a transmitter, tracked them to this place some time after the U.S. Marshall hit, and then took his sweet time checking things out while Bascomb and his buddies ate their take-out fried chicken dinner . . . none of which answers my original question, Grynard. You *are* going after him, aren't you?''

Grynard nodded silently.

"How about doing yourself a favor then,'' the hostage recovery team commander said quietly as he stared down at the body of Roy Parker, the ex-Marine who had refused to give up.

"What's that?"

"Give us a call when you spot him. Let us give you a hand."

"Whittman, I've got twenty-four agents from Special Ops, in addition to my eight," Grynard said. "If you're right, and we really are dealing with only one individual, then thirty-three experienced agents ought to be capable of dealing with him, no matter how good he is or how well he's armed. Especially since we're baiting him in," he added.

"Oh, really?" Whittman's head came up. "With what?"

"A five-man covert team of federal wildlife agents."

"The same guys?"

Grynard nodded. "The surviving members of the original team."

"You're shitting me."

Grynard shrugged but said nothing.

"So that's why you spooked when I mentioned the 10mm stuff."

"Let's just say that it adds another dimension to a case that's already too damned confusing as it is," Grynard replied.

Whittman hesitated for a moment, staring down at the floor as he seemed to be working things out in his head with respect to the scene and what few rumors he'd heard about the raid on the Whitehorse training facility at Yellowstone National Park. Then he looked back at his fellow supervisory agent.

"Where are these agents now?"

"They were up in Boston, setting up some kind of storefront operation. We're not sure exactly what happened, but they apparently blew their cover and got roused by the Boston police. According to our surveillance team, they may have pulled up stakes and transferred their operation to the Miami area."

"Do they know this bastard's coming after them?"

Whittman asked in a quiet, raspy voice.

"No, not as far as we know."

"Christ, Grynard," the hostage recovery team commander exclaimed angrily, "why don't you just go ahead and take them out yourself! Make it easier on the poor sons of bitches!"

"Hey, it's not like I'm staking them out like a bunch of goddamned goats!" Grynard bristled.

"Bullshit, that's exactly what you're doing!"

"Look, Whittman, six months ago these wildlife guys took out ten members of an international team of counterterrorist experts that included Parker and Maas. They're a good group of agents. They can take care of themselves."

"Doesn't matter how good they are. You set them out in front of a guy like this," Whittman said, gesturing with his hand at the surrounding scene, "you're gonna lose them. And you're gonna lose good agents trying to protect them, too."

And then, before Grynard could respond, the hostage recovery team commander said: "Look, Grynard, I understand what you're trying to do. And the truth is, in your position, I'd probably try to do the same thing myself. But honest to God," Whittman added in a voice that, to Grynard, sounded almost pleading, "you get a line on this guy, at least call us in on standby. That way, if it all goes to shit, at least you'll be able to sleep at night."

Fifteen minutes later, Grynard was back outside with his rookie agent driver.

"Back to headquarters," he snapped as he got in the front seat of the polished vehicle and slammed the door. "Fast as you can get there."

"But—"

"Don't talk," Grynard ordered in a cold voice. "Drive."

Chapter Twenty-one

It was two-forty-five that Saturday afternoon by the time Al Grynard and his young FBI agent driver returned to the Hoover Building.

After thanking the rookie agent, and then badging his way through security, All Grynard took the elevator to the third floor, then walked down the corridor until he came to an open double door that led into a maze of interconnected work spaces and offices. He paused at the door of the occupied corner office.

"Ready to go to work?"

"You back again?" Reggie Blackburn, the supervisory agent in charge of the electronics support unit, blinked sleepily. "I thought you went home."

"Got work to do." Grynard shook his head. "I need a fax linkup to Bloom."

"The one in the sailboat?"

"Yep."

"Okay." Blackburn nodded agreeably. "Let's go see where the man's got himself to now."

Humming to himself, the supervisory electronics specialist led the way over to an adjacent workshop where every flat surface was covered with computers, keyboards, monitors, and an incredible array of miscellaneous electronics tools, instruments, and parts—all scattered about in a seemingly randomized order. From the back of the computers and electronic devices, dozens of shielded cables and antenna wires rose to and through the ceiling panels, many of which had either been punctured with multiple holes or simply lifted and moved aside.

Selecting a desk-height workbench area that held two separate computer systems, Reggie Blackburn sat himself down in a well-worn secretary's chair and reached behind one of the computers to flip a recessed switch.

In a matter of moments the larger of the two screens—a huge color monitor that Grynard judged was at least twenty-four inches on the diagonal—came to life.

As Grynard watched in fascination, the powerful Pentium-based computer began to rapidly draw a detailed map of the Bahamas Islands, showing Walker Cay at the top of the screen and Great Inagua at the bottom. The islands were outlined in dark green, filled in with a lighter shade of green, and the surrounding ocean was displayed in gradient shades of light to medium blue, indicating the approximate depth of the water.

Next, at the upper-left-hand corner of the screen, the computer displayed southern Florida from Lake Okeechobee down to the Florida keys.

"Wow," Grynard whispered.

"Don't get too excited yet," Reggie Blackburn cautioned. "We're just starting to have fun here. Watch this."

A few more key strokes, and a number of small colored and numbered geometric shapes appeared on the oversized monitor.

"We're talking state-of-the-art transmitters hooked directly into the Defense Department's global positioning satellites, with no downgrade in accuracy, along with a CART—computer-aided recognition and tracking—capability that is absolutely unbelievable," the supervisory electronics specialist said proudly.

"You mean the computer can track a ship by remembering what it looks like?"

"That's right."

"Incredible." Grynard shook his head in amazement. "So what do all those symbols mean?"

"Well, first of all, the one you're interested in is that orange rectangle just about in the exact center of the screen. The one marked number one. See it?"

"Yeah, sure."

"Okay, that's the *Sea Amber*."

"Bloom's boat?"

"That's right. And at this very moment we're showing Mr. Bloom—or at least Mr. Bloom's boat—to be right smack dab in the middle of the Exuma Sound."

"Can you get a fax message to him out there?"

"Easiest thing in the world, assuming he's got his fax machine turned on. Either that, or we can just hand-deliver it on a silver platter if you *really* want to mess with the man," Blackburn chuckled.

"It's a tempting idea," Grynard said. "Why, you guys have him on that short a leash?"

"No, not really. But I did arrange to set up some resources for you on standby, like you asked me to—just in case our bird happens to go down, or you folks decide you want to do some of that genuine gung-ho agent stuff. Oh, and by the way, I can guarantee you right now, Owens ain't gonna be happy when he finds out, either."

"Who's Owens?"

"Hal Owens? He's the SAC for the Special Bahamas Task Force. You mean to tell me you two never met?"

Grynard shook his head. "Not that I can recall."

"Take my word for it, you'd remember the man," Blackburn said. "Real grouchy old bastard. Just like you, come to think of it."

"If he's just like me, then he'll get over it," Grynard said indifferently. "Now what kind of resources are we talking about?"

"Start with a sixty-foot sailer and a fifty-five-foot fishing boat for cover, and a thirty-six-foot cigarette for fast intercept. And as backup, a pair of Blackhawk assault/transport choppers, along with one of them little bitty surveillance jobs that look more like some kind of demented insect than a real, honest-to-God helicopter. The boats are designated as gold triangle one, gold triangle two, and gold triangle three, in that order, and the choppers are gold circle four through gold circle six.''

''All that just for us?''

''No, not exactly. Seems like Owens and his DEA counterpart down there have a little narcotics deal cooking. But not much is happening just yet, so you can probably get access to just about any part of it, long as Owens doesn't have you shot first.''

''Nice.'' Grynard nodded appreciatively. ''What do we have for crews?''

''Genuine U.S. Coast Guard boarding-team types in the boats, FBI agent/pilots and FBI SWAT crews in the choppers. All of them are familiar with the area and the locals, so we shouldn't run into any confusion about who the good guys and the bad guys are.''

''You're a good man, Charley Brown.'' Grynard smiled tiredly, patting the supervisory electronics specialist on the shoulder.

''Hey, I just used your name and credit card.'' Blackburn shrugged. ''When it all hits the fan, I'm not going to be the one they come looking for.''

''Yeah, thanks,'' Grynard said with cheerful sarcasm.

''Sit down a spell. Long as you're here, I might as well show you some of our new tricks.''

''You mean there's more?''

''Oh, sure. Lots more. For example, one thing we can do is zoom in or out, depending on how much detail you want to see.''

As Blackburn demonstrated the zoom capability of the computerized satellite monitoring system, Grynard noted that longitude and latitude coordinates immediately appeared next to each of the enlarged and numbered symbols.

''I'm impressed,'' Grynard admitted.

''Hell, you ain't seen nothing yet. You want to know where your buddy Bloom's been the last seventy-two hours''

''You can do that too?''

" 'Course we can. What the hell kind of operation do you think we're runnin' down here?'' the supervisory electronics specialist demanded indignantly.

"From what I've seen so far, a goddamned playground with lots of expensive toys and very little supervision,'' Grynard responded, looking around the cluttered electronics and computer shop.

"You got that right.'' Reggie Blackburn nodded cheerfully. "Now look here, watch this.''

Blackburn hit a series of keys, and suddenly the orange rectangle reappeared, sporting a long dotted orange tail that started up at the top of the screen and then zigzagged back and forth, from north to south, in and around the island chain.

"Looks like he's been gradually working his way south, more or less, in a pretty casual manner, except right here, which was—oh, let's see—about six o'clock this morning, when he started straight down into Exuma Sound,'' the supervisory electronics specialist said.

"What's the update rate?''

"I've got it set on an every-half-hour basis right now. I could make it more frequent, but then I'd end up using a goodly portion of our computer processing resources on just one boat.''

"Oh, yeah, why so?''

"We haven't been able to get a transmitter installed on the *Sea Amber* yet,'' the technical agent explained, "so we have to use the computer recognition system exclusively. And since she's a relatively small boat to begin with, that means we tie up a big chunk of our processing capability every time we try to fix her location. Figured every half-hour would be enough for what you wanted.''

"More than enough.'' Grynard nodded as he noted the surrounding locations of the golden triangles and circles. "And it looks like we've got everybody staying back out of the way too,'' he added approvingly. "Bloom ought to feel real comfortable right about now.''

"Just like you said, if the man's gonna do something stupid, we want to give him plenty of room to do it in."

"So what are all those red and white and gray and green rectangles?" Grynard asked

"The red ones are DEA boats, the whites are regular Coast Guard patrol craft, the dark gray are U.S. Navy ships, and we use the green to designate the miscellaneous stuff. Since it's peacetime, they're all squawking their locations with their SSRS transmitters, which eliminates the need for CART processing," Blackburn said.

"SSRS? What does that mean?"

"Standard Ship Recognition System. A transmitting device built into every military ship's radio communications system. Which ones do you want to know about?"

"How about that one right there," Grynard said, pointing with a finger to a rectangle along the fishtail-like southern edge of Eleuthera Island.

"Man, we've got to start using a different color for them miscellaneous objects. Can't hardly see the damned things," Reggie Blackburn said, squinting at the screen. "Let's see what we've got there." Using the zoom capability of the computer program, the supervisory tech agent enlarged the area around New Providence, Eleuthera Island, and the northern end of the Exuma Sound to three times normal size.

"Okay," Blackburn mumbled to himself as he continued to enter commands into the keyboard, "that's green rectangle number three, which is . . . the *Lone Granger*."

"The *Lone Granger*? What is that, a boat?"

"If it's a rectangle, it damn well better be a boat."

"And just what, may I ask, does a boat named the *Lone Granger* have to do with this operation?"

"I don't know, let's go take a look and find out." Leaving the large color screen in place, Blackburn shifted over to the second computer on the workbench, the one with the normal-sized color monitor, and began entering commands.

Moments later Reggie Blackburn had the relevant information up on the smaller monitor.

"Hmm, according to this, you ordered a full-press surveillance—tags, taps, the whole works—on some people named, uh, Lightstone, Paxton, Stoner, Takahara, and Woeshack working out of Boston? Fish and Wildlife Service agents, according to this. Does that sound right?"

"Yeah, so?"

"Well, according to this, they left . . . uh, let me see, the Windbreaker Marina down in Fort Lauderdale at approximately oh-five-hundred hours this morning on the *Lone Granger*. That's why the boat shows up on our satellite scan."

"For Christ's sake!" Grynard exclaimed, his eyes widening as images of the eight dead bodies at the Warrenton safe house, and Whittman's comments about the restricted 10mm law enforcement pistol ammunition flashing through the back of his mind. "What the hell are those guys doing out there?"

"How should I . . . hey, wait a minute. Takahara. I thought that name rang a bell. Isn't that the name of that tech agent you had me feed information to a couple of weeks ago?" Reggie Blackburn asked.

"Yeah, it sure was. So what did you tell him?"

"Not much, far as I recall," Blackburn said, his fingers flashing across the computer keyboard as he called up another program on the smaller monitor. "Okay, here we go," the supervisory electronics specialist whispered. "Yeah, now I remember. When I went looking for him, on the sly—you know, electronically—I found him digging at that Abercombie broad, rummaging around the billings for her credit cards for the past two years. So what I did is I got out ahead of him and had Ms. Lisa Abercombie pay for some diesel fuel with one of her gas cards at a little marina on North Bimini. Then I had Bloom pay for a couple of bottles of expensive wine with a Mastercard at the same place about two minutes later."

"That's *all* you gave him?" Grynard blinked in surprise.

"That's it." The supervisory electronics specialist shrugged.

"Jeese, that's not much."

"Looks like it was more than enough, as far as I can see," Blackburn countered. "Look where they're at now."

"How are you identifying them?" Grynard asked, staring at the big screen with increased interest now. "With that CART-computer recognition stuff?"

"Don't have to with this baby," Blackburn chuckled. "Nowdays just about all the big private boats—and by 'big,' I mean the expensive ones—get rigged with a civilian version of the SSRS transmitters too, either when they're built or when they're refitted."

"So what does that mean? That the *Lone Granger* has her own identifying transmitter?"

"That's right." The FBI tech agent nodded. "And it looks like she's squawking real pretty out there."

"Yeah, but what are they doing over there by—what is it?—Eleuthera Island, instead of picking up the trail around Bimini?"

"Damned if I know. Let's see if we can figure out how they went about getting there," Blackburn said as he went back to the larger computer screen and started to key up the history of green rectangle number three. "Okay, if they started out from Fort Lauderdale at five this morning, which we know they did, then we only have to calculate back about what—oh, say ten hours, which won't take long at all because we've got squawk data, so . . ."

"Christ, look at that!" Grynard exclaimed as a thinly dotted and nearly straight green line suddenly appeared on the screen, connecting the city of Fort Lauderdale and the green rectangle in a long sweeping curve that dropped right down into the northern end of the Exuma Sound. "They never even went near Bimini."

"And from the looks of things, if they stay on the same course, it's gonna take them right along the western shore of Cat Island. Which means they're going to end up right on top of your surveillance target,'' Blackburn noted.

Al Grynard cursed, and then asked: ''About how far away from Bloom are they right now?''

''Hmm, I'd say they're maybe about fifteen miles northwest of the *Sea Amber* at the outside. Doesn't look like they're moving all that fast right now, but based on the distance between those half-hour location points on the first part of their run, it looks to me like they could close in on the *Sea Amber* pretty damn fast if they had a mind to. Man, whatever that *Lone Granger* is, she can really scoot!''

''Do you have any information on her from the tag?''

''I don't know, let me check.''

Blackburn switched back to the second computer monitor.

''Ah, no wonder,'' the electronics specialist muttered. ''She's described here by your surveillance team as a brandnew eighty-two-foot sports cruiser slash luxury yacht, multimillion dollar value, which means she probably has a pretty fast hull and one hell of an engine package.''

''What?'' Al Grynard exclaimed, not sure he'd heard Blackburn right.

''Hey, I'm just telling you what the agents reported in,'' Reggie Blackburn reminded, ''but if they're right—and based on those early tracks, they probably are—those wildlife guys aren't going to have any trouble *at all* catching up with that little forty-five-foot sailboat. Fact is, if they're not careful and they keep cruising around when it's dark, they're liable to run right over her.''

''What I want to know,'' Grynard said with forced restraint, ''is how a bunch of wildlife agents got their hands on a boat like that. And I also want to know how they managed to get a line on Bloom that fast.''

Al Grynard was frustrated by the realization the twenty-four agents he'd just wheedled out of special operations were now useless because it was too late to set them into position. That and the fact that he was now forced to play catch-up behind Henry Lightstone and his wildlife agent buddies again, just like the last time up in Anchorage.

And there was something else in the back of his mind that he really didn't want to think about—the presence of all those restricted issue 10mm law enforcement ammunition casings, and the possibility that Henry Lightstone and his buddies really were intent on avenging the deaths of their fellow agents.

"I don't know what to tell you about your first question," Reggie Blackburn replied, "but I'm about to answer that second one right now."

"Oh, yeah? And just how are you going to do that?"

"You just watch."

As Al Grynard stood there glaring at the large color monitor displaying the haphazard course of the *Sea Amber*, and the seemingly locked-on path of the *Lone Granger*, the supervisory electronics specialist settled down to work with his keyboard.

"Okay, Special Agent Takahara," Blackburn muttered as his rapidly moving fingers started calling up file access sets and requesting search patterns, "Abercombie's gas credit card got you Bloom's Mastercard, based on the store code, which you . . . what? You looked it up? How the hell . . . Oh, okay, sure, that gets you there, but it doesn't do you any good unless you've got a security . . . oh really? I'll be damned . . . and then you discovered that it was a corporate account, which gave you a name and address of the corporation, but not . . . oh, okay, yeah . . . nice, *real* nice . . . so you went in that direction instead . . . I see . . . and then . . ."

"How the hell do *you* know he did all that?" Al Grynard demanded, having no idea what Blackburn was mumbling about or doing with his computer.

"I can follow his tracks because he uses an undercover eight hundred number to access the 'net,' " Reggie Blackburn explained. "It's a good idea because that way he can stay hooked up for extended time periods, but his connections don't show up on his hotel bills. But see, that also turns out to be his basic weakness because—oh, yeah, of course . . . sure, once you have that . . ." The supervisory electronics specialist nodded, still watching the monitor. "Then . . . sure, right—he still has to pay his bills, even if it's through an undercover business account, and the eight hundred number turns out to be the easiest way to do it without getting into a bunch of hassles with the phone company. But see, when he does that, he creates this beautiful electronic trail, so all I have to do is just tap in behind and follow along— just like one shark following another one, only he doesn't know I'm back here—using his starting location, which *I* know from the beginning, and all his network accounts and access codes, which I was able to get because—oh, man . . . just look at that!"

"What?"

"So that's how he did it." Reggie Blackburn laughed delightedly, ignoring Grynard completely now. "Look at that! The son of a bitch cheats, and he's pretty damned clever about it too. See, what he did is track back though Bloom's bank account to this guy, who must be his accountant, because he uses electronic mail to pay Bloom's bills, which gives him . . . yeah, right there. *Damn*, that's nice!"

The supervisory electronics specialist remained silent, staring intently at his computer screen as the data elements flashed before his eyes, until Grynard finally cleared his throat.

"Uh, Reggie."

"Huh?" Blackburn blinked. "Oh, yeah, sorry. What was I saying? Oh, right. See, what he did was finally work himself all the way back into the database of the travel agency that Bloom's corporation uses to book their trips. And then he used one of the corporate computers instead of his own network access codes, so the travel agency doesn't show an intrusion."

"You mean he took over one of Bloom's corporate computers remotely?"

"Yeah, essentially, that's exactly what he did." Blackburn grinned. "See, right there, first thing he did was match up a couple of hotels with Abercombie, which just confirmed his suspicions about the two of them being a linked-up pair. Then he started digging around a little bit, and discovered that Bloom has a room reservation for two nights—uh, tonight and tomorrow night—at the Cutlass Bay Club on Cat Island, which,'' the supervisory electronics specialist said, turning back around to point at the large screen monitor, ''is right about there.''

''Right down at the southern tip of Cat Island,'' Grynard nodded. ''Which means the *Lone Granger* might not be following the Sea Amber as we thought. It might be they're both just going in the same direction.''

''Yeah, maybe.'' Blackburn nodded skeptically. ''But you want to make sure that . . . Oh, shit!'' the supervisory electronics specialist screamed as he glanced down at the front lights on the computer's hard drive, and then lunged forward, nearly knocking the huge monitor to the floor, as he reached around and wrenched a cable loose from its connection at the back of the computer.

''Jesus Christ, Blackburn, what the hell's the matter with you?'' Grynard demanded, startled by Reggie Blackburn's sudden violent actions.

''That son of a bitch,'' the supervisory electronics specialist whispered, a furious look appearing on his dark face as he stared at the torn end of the computer network cable.

Grynard looked around the workshop and realized that about half the monitors in the workroom had suddenly gone blank.

''Blackburn, talk to me,'' Grynard said in a softer voice. ''What just happened in here?''

''Remember what I told you about the two sharks, one following the other without the one in front knowing about it?''

''Yeah, so?''

''Well, figuratively speaking, we just bumped into the guy up front, and in doing so, we may have just got a chunk of our nose chewed off.''

''Reggie''—Grynard shook his head—''try to speak English. I haven't the slightest idea what you're talking about.''

The supervisory electronics specialist let out a deep, exasperated sigh. ''In simple terms, what the man did was set a bear trap, just in case somebody like me started to follow along that electronic trail I told you about.''

''Yeah, so now he knows somebody tried to tap into his system. So what?''

''No, that's not it.'' Blackburn shook his head. ''He didn't just set a little trip wire and let us bump into it—he *reversed* the damn thing.''

''You mean he got into *your* computers?'' Grynard said in a disbelieving voice.

''Maybe.'' The supervisory electronics specialist nodded unhappily. ''Leastwise, it sure *looked* like that was what was happening.''

''So what do you do now?'' Grynard asked, realizing that the huge color monitor that the computer had used to draw the satellite monitoring map of the Bahamas was one of those that had gone blank.

''Well, right about now I've got two choices, and neither of them is what you would call good. First choice is to sit down and repair this cable, and then hook it back up to the computer, and then turn everything back on, and risk the chance that Special Agent Mike Takahara just might have dropped a virus program in one of our memory disks.''

''If he did, what would that do?''

''That's just the problem. I don't know. It would do whatever he programmed it to do. Probably the first thing it would do is make a couple of copies of itself, hide them away somewhere, and then just sit and wait for a while. And then, just at the right moment—for him, not for us—it would jump out and cause holy havoc.''

''Can't you find it?''

''Maybe, maybe not. Might be worse if I tried. Kind of like one of those cancers you don't want to start cutting on, because sometimes they start going berserk.''

"So what's your other choice?"

"Play it safe and reformat every one of these goddamned hard disks, four of which are in the gigabyte range," the supervisory electronics specialist said with an exasperated sigh. "After that, I'll have to start reloading all the programs and databases back in from the original disks and the hopefully protected backups, which is going to take one hell of a long time, even if I back up the data from mirrored drives—which ought to be safe, but might not be because, as you may recall my mentioning, the son of a bitch cheats."

"I take it you don't have much of a choice," Grynard said quietly, having at least a vague idea—based on some stupid mistakes he'd made with his own home computer—of how much work might be involved in what Blackburn had just described.

"Not really." Reggie Blackburn shook his head. "I can't take the chance. I'll have to reformat and start all over again. It's the only way."

"So what does that mean in terms of our surveillance?" Grynard asked, having a horrible feeling that he already knew what the answer was going to be.

"Well, as far as the CART surveillance goes, there's no doubt about it. You're going to be blind for a while."

Grynard muttered a silent curse, and then: "How long?"

"I'm guessing maybe eight, nine hours, at a minimum." Reggie Blackburn looked at his watch. "Might be able to get the system back on line by midnight if I'm lucky. If not, figure sometime tomorrow morning."

"Can't you just rig up another system?"

"Not without knowing exactly what he did." The supervisory electronics specialist shook his head. "Whatever it was he left there, waiting for us, managed to access that hard drive for sure," he said, pointing at the now silent computer. "But this cable links up about fifteen other hard drives too, including those four giga-monsters, which means he could have created all kinds of mayhem."

"Such as?"

"Well, if I was doing it, I'd have given these computers instructions to wait until someone queried any suspect or agent name on a list that I provided, which—if we're talking about this case—would damn sure include you and Bloom, and then have them send me a message telling me who, what, when, and where."

"Jesus!"

"And that's just me thinking," Blackburn reminded. "This guy's mind is on a whole different level."

"And in the meantime, I don't know what's going on down there in Exuma Sound."

"Not as far as the *Sea Amber*'s concerned, you sure don't. Not unless you guys can get an SSRS transmitter attached to her somehow."

Grynard thought for a moment. And then: "What about the fax?"

Blackburn looked around. "The fax system is physically isolated in here, in terms of the computer links, and it works off of a different satellite, so it shouldn't have been affected by all this. You still want to send Bloom a message?"

"Absolutely."

The supervisory electronics specialist allowed the torn network cable to drop out of his hand as he walked over and sat down in front of another bank of computers.

Three minutes later he got up and gestured for Grynard to take the chair. "Okay, she's all yours."

The assistant special agent in charge from Anchorage, Alaska, sat down and stared at the display for a moment, thinking. Then he began to type:

```
TO:     ALFRED BLOOM
        C/O SEA AMBER
FROM:   SA AL GRYNARD


WE NEED TO TALK. VERY IMPORTANT. NO
MORE GAMES. IT'S TIME TO FISH OR CUT BAIT.
I'LL MEET YOU AT THE CUTLASS BAY CLUB BAR,
```

ELEVEN O'CLOCK THIS EVENING. I'LL HAVE A
U.S. ATTORNEY WITH ME. YOUR LAST CHANCE.
BE THERE.

"That the way you want it to go out?" Reggie Blackburn
asked.

Grynard nodded, then hesitated. "How will I know if he
got it?"

"Hey, Grynard, we're talking state-of-the-art here, my
man. Anybody on the Faxsat system has to be wired up with
a FBX transceiver. Basically what happens," Blackburn
hurriedly explained when he saw the glazed look in Al Grynard's eyes, "is we bounce a recognition signal up to the
bird and down to the boat. If the fax system on the boat is on,
then the boat bounces a confirmation signal back up to the
bird and down to us, which tells our computer that it's okay
to send the message."

"All that just to send a fax?"

"You can do it a lot simpler if all you want to do is send
and hope." Blackburn shrugged. "Getting a confirmation
back up the link is a whole lot more complex." Reaching
across Grynard's shoulder, he pressed a quick series of key
codes.

Immediately, the computer screen flashed a message:

ATTEMPTING UPLINK FBIHQTS5 CNX FAXSAT/
S12 DOWNLINK DESTINATION: SB4454/SEAAM-
BER UPLINK CONNECTION CONFIRMED

Then, moments later:

DOWNLINK CONNECTION CONFIRMED

And then finally:

TRANSMISSION COMPLETED

"Okay, looks like he's got it. Anything else I can do for you?"

"No," Grynard said as he looked around the workshop, "it looks to me like I've caused enough damage around here for one day."

"Yeah, that's a fact." Blackburn nodded. "But just the same, there is one thing you could do for me."

"Yeah, what's that?"

"You're gonna go down to the islands, right? Try to keep up with Bloom and those wildlife agents the old-fashioned way?"

"Just as soon as I can get hold of a U.S. attorney and get us on a plane." Al Grynard nodded.

"Well, when you get there, if you run across this Mike Takahara, I want you to do something for me."

"Yeah, what's that?"

"Sign him up."

"You really want a guy like that working here?"

"Not necessarily." Reggie Blackburn shrugged. "It's more like I don't want him working against me anymore."

"And suppose he's not interested in being recruited into the FBI?"

"Then you just feel free to stomp his devious little ass," Reggie Blackburn said as he looked around at the staggered array of dead computer monitors in the workshop, "with my compliments."

Chapter Twenty-two

It was fifteen minutes to three that Saturday afternoon when the flashing light on the center cockpit instrument board warned Alfred Bloom that another fax message was about to be beamed aboard the *Sea Amber*.

"Christ, is there no escape?" he muttered.

He started to unhook himself from the safety line, intent on going below and finding out who was sending him all these fax messages and what it was they wanted. But the heat of her hand caused him to pause.

"Ignore it," she whispered in his ear.

"But—"

She silenced him with salty yet amazingly warm and soft lips as her hand moved slowly up his bare thigh.

"Pay attention to me instead," she whispered again.

"You mean like this?"

He slid his free hand inside her open windbreaker, feeling the swelling nipples and the heat of her full, firm breasts through the tightly stretched, ultrathin fabric of her single-piece bathing suit. A sound originating deep in her throat, somewhere between a whimper and a moan, escaped her lips.

"Yes, exactly like that," she murmured. She started to bring her hand farther up Bloom's loose-fitting bathing suit, but then hesitated as she sensed a shift in the wind. Glancing up at the telltales, she quickly made a slight adjustment to the steering wheel and then returned her full attention to the task at hand.

The powerful sailing craft responded immediately, heeling over to an angle of maximum efficiency as the flexible mast and tautened sails sent the computer-designed hull slicing though the moderate chops in a hiss of fine salt spray.

Incredible, Bloom thought as he allowed himself to be overwhelmed by the combined sensations of wind-driven speed and slow, unhurried sex.

Absolutely incredible.

She was a Freedom 45 with 990 square feet of sail, less than five feet of draft, an easily accessible back-porch swim platform, a carbon-fiber mast that rose sixty-three feet off the water, and a huge, teak-lined main salon that bordered on the sybaritic. Equipped with an electric winch, oversized gears, and every modern navigation device known to man, the *Sea Amber* was the perfect boat for an experienced sailor with time on his hands, memories to escape, and money to burn.

Which had turned out to be a perfect description for an incredibly wealthy and yet—at the time—fearfully angry and despondent industrialist named Alfred Bloom.

Responding to the encouragement of his fellow ICER Committee members, who had good reason to be deeply concerned about his emotional stability, Bloom had begun to spend his weekends prowling yacht dealerships. A skillful deep-water sailor from his childhood days on Martha's Vineyard, he had been infatuated immediately with the graceful yet visibly powerful lines of the *Sea Amber.* She needed a complete refit on top and a lot of work below deck, but the dealer had been amiable. They negotiated a price of $350,000 in cash, with extended sea trials included in the package. So when all of the committee members finally agreed to an offshore meeting, Bloom decided that the Bahamas would be just the place to put his new forty-five-foot toy through her paces.

He had planned on taking her out alone on that first day, hoping—somehow—to lose himself in a battle of winds and currents and high seas until the image of Lisa Abercombie no longer appeared in his memories.

But Anne-Marie, the blue-eyed, dark-haired skipper who singlehandedly delivered the expensively renovated sailboat to his private dock that next Saturday morning, and stood there waiting for him in a pair of loose white coveralls, had caused him to make a radical change in his plans.

She had walked him through all the minor adjustments to the topside gear, and then took him down into the main salon, pointing out the luxurious amenities, the upgraded navigation station, and the easy accesses to the engine, battery, and generator compartments.

Then, after making sure that Bloom was completely familiar with all the various accessories that one might expect to find on a $350,000 racing yacht, she had led him into the master stateroom.

There, standing in front of the queen-sized berth, Anne-Marie had stepped out of the loose coveralls to reveal a surprisingly full, visibly muscular, and incredibly enticing body that wasn't the least bit concealed beneath her thin, blue, single-piece bathing suit.

Staring straight into his eyes without the slightest trace of a smile, she had quietly asked if he had reconsidered his decision to take the *Sea Amber* out on her shakedown cruise by himself.

That had been three days ago, and during that time he had almost managed to forget about Lisa Abercombie and ICER.

Almost, but not quite.

Taking turns at the wheel and winches, Bloom and his new companion had spent the entire morning and the better part of the afternoon off the western shore of Cat's Island, exploring the outer limits of his new boat. Secured to the center cockpit by nylon safety lines, and braced against sudden yawls and pitches, they had tacked the wing-keeled craft into the surging winds time after time, deliberately heeling her out well past the recommended angles as they sought the worst that the Caribbean waters could provide.

And when their arms and shoulders began to tire, they simply sat shoulder to shoulder in the center cockpit and extended the sloop-rigged boat out on long reaches under the deep blue sky. All the while kissing, caressing, smiling, whispering, and gazing fondly at each other as the blazing sun and the shifting breezes and the splashing whitecaps scorched and cooled and soaked the fabric of their light windbreakers.

It had been a magnificent day. One that they both agreed they would remember and savor for the rest of their lives. But the hours of exertion and exposure had begun to take their inevitable toll even before they had allowed themselves to be caught up in their latest sensual diversion.

The wind shifted again, and they were forced to break away from their increasingly heated and impatient caressing.

"I think I'm going to die if I don't get something to

drink," Anne-Marie said in a shaky voice as she gave him one last, lingering kiss before she relinquished control of the forty-two-inch steering wheel. "Want me to get you something?"

Bloom nodded gratefully as he made an adjustment of the main winch with the foot pedal. "Anything, just as long as it's warm and alcoholic."

She hesitated at the top of the companionway and looked back, the muscles of her full hips and buttocks flexed enticingly beneath the glistening fabric of her thin bathing suit.

"A couple of Navy Grogs, my way? Or maybe I could interest you in something a little warmer?" Beneath the dark sunglasses, her suntanned face dimpled into a mischievous smile.

"The grog sounds wonderful, and yes, you could." He smiled. "But—"

"Yes?"

"One of us would have to steer, and I honestly don't think I'd have the strength to do both," he replied with a look of sincere regret on his sun-and-wind-burned face.

She stared out across the glistening water for a few moments, seemingly lost in thought.

"About how far do you think we are from Old Blight?" she finally asked.

He noted their compass heading, glanced at his watch, thought about the distances for a moment, and then made a couple of quick mental calculations.

"I'd say maybe a couple of hours if we really worked at it."

"I'll tell you what," she said in a slow, sultry voice. "Why don't I get us something to drink first. Then we can both work at it, and the first one who sets the anchor gets to chose?"

"Chose what?" he asked, although he was pretty sure he already knew the answer.

"Everything," she replied as she pulled the windbreaker over her head, offering him a tantalizing view of the superbly conditioned and barely concealed torso that his hands had been busily exploring only moments before. She tossed the windbreaker at his head, stepped back onto the companionway ladder, removed her sunglasses, and then raised a single eyebrow expectantly.

Once again Alfred Bloom marveled at the way the reflective, cerulean-blue fabric of the tightly stretched bathing suit precisely matched the color of her penetrating eyes. Not to mention the thick, quilted cover of the queen-sized main berth, he remembered with a smile, wondering if she had been involved in the selection of that too.

"Well?"

"You, my dear, are on."

She was down below in the teak and stainless steel galley, humming to herself as she filled spill-proof mugs with a warmed lethal mixture of dark and light rums and assorted citrus juices, when she remembered the fax warning light.

Moving across the varnished teak deck to the navigation station in her bare feet, she picked up the top piece of curled paper in the drop tray and began to read.

Her eyes widened as soon as she saw the words U.S. Attorney.

Forcing herself to relax, she read the brief message slowly, word by word. She was starting to read through it a second time when her eyes were drawn to the earlier message that had arrived over three hours ago—the one that they'd ignored because they'd been much too busy with the wind and the sails and each other.

She stood there for a long moment, bracing her muscular body against the rounded edge of the teak desktop as she continued to read. A frown appeared on her beautiful tanned face as she slowly absorbed the import of the two messages.

She paused for a moment, not at all convinced that what she was about to do was right. But then she remembered once again the incident that had occurred—how many weeks ago now? It was so hard to remember—when she had been Valerie, instead of Anne-Marie, and hesitation had cost her a job and very nearly her life.

It had been an easy decision then, she reminded herself. So why should it be any more difficult now?

Don't think about how much you've changed, inside and out. Think about staying alive.

Nodding decisively, she quickly picked up the warm mugs and the two pieces of paper and hurried back up the companionway to the cockpit.

"You got two fax messages. One of them's from some company called ICER," she said. She handed him one of the mugs and then started to hold the printed messages up for his inspection. But before she could do so, the wind caught the pieces of paper and yanked them out of her fingers. In spite of her seemingly desperate attempt to catch them in midair, both messages fluttered out of reach, and out over the water.

"Oh, shit!" she muttered, raising a smoothly tanned arm to shield her eyes as she and Bloom watched the rolled pieces of paper disappear, one after the other, beneath the choppy surface. Then she turned to him with a look of chagrin on her beautiful face.

"Alfred, I'm so sorry. I didn't—"

"Don't worry about it." Bloom shrugged. The troubled expression that had suddenly appeared in his eyes was hidden by the dark sunglasses that were speckled white from the dried saltwater. "They probably weren't important anyway."

"Actually, I think they were," she said, and then paused to take a sip of her rum grog. "The one from the ICER company said something about the time of the meeting being moved back. Everyone is supposed to meet at the villa at nine o'clock this evening, instead of seven. Also, if you need a ride, someone will be at the marina to pick you up at . . . uh . . . eight-thirty."

"Eight-thirty? Are you sure?"

"Twenty-thirty hours. Yes, I am sure." She nodded. "There wasn't all that much to it."

Bloom glanced down at his watch. "Okay, that will work

out fine. We've got plenty of time now, so we can just take things slow and easy.''

''Hmmm, that sounds fun,'' she said, moving forward and kissing in his ear.

Bloom grinned and started to make an appropriate rejoinder when he suddenly remembered that there had been two messages. ''What about the other one?'' he asked. ''Do you recall who it was from?''

She paused to think. ''No, I can't remember his name. Just that whoever it was wants to talk with you real bad. It said he wants to meet you tomorrow afternoon at the . . . uh, the wharfside bar on Rum Cay.''

''Oh, really? Did he say why?'' Bloom asked with apparent indifference, his darkly tanned face glistening from the saltwater spray. He made a slight adjustment of the elk-hide-covered wheel, turning the bow of the *Sea Amber* a little tighter into the wind.

''No, just that it was very important. Something about no more games, fish or cut bait. It didn't make much sense.''

''Doesn't sound like it. You sure it was for me?''

She nodded. ''It was like a telex, you know, on plain paper, to Alfred Bloom from . . . wait, that's right, now I remember.'' She smiled. ''There was a name. Sal Grin? Sal Grinnerd? Does that sound right?''

Bloom furrowed his eyebrows for a moment as he stared down at his feet, thinking back. Then he brought his head up in sudden understanding.

''Could it have been SA Al Grynard?''

''Yes, that's it! Al Grynard. I'm sure that was the name,'' she said with a satisfied smile. ''So what does the SA stand for?''

''Special Agent.''

Her eyes opened wide in surprise.

''Special Agent?''

Bloom nodded solemnly. ''Grynard's from the FBI.''

''So why does the FBI want to talk to you?'' she asked,

the expression on her beautiful face now a mixture of curiosity and concern.

"I don't know." Bloom shrugged, a distant look appearing in his eyes. "My secretary said he tried to contact me at the office, but I'd already left." He hesitated for a moment. "Do you remember if he provided a local phone number, or if he wanted any kind of acknowledgment?"

"No, I'm sure it didn't. It was a very brief message."

"What about the time? Do you recall what time tomorrow afternoon he wants me to meet him at the bar?"

She shrugged her muscular shoulders helplessly.

"I'm really sorry, Alfred," she whispered, staring down at her bare feet. "I guess I was thinking about how little time we had left today, and I didn't see anything that seemed to involve a schedule change for us on that one, so I guess I just didn't pay much attention to it."

But then she brought her head up suddenly.

"Wait a minute, I just thought of something," she said. "Let me look down below and see if there were any cover sheets with either of those faxes that I might have missed."

"How could you possibly miss something like that?"

"Sometimes the first pages on those faxes don't feed through the machine right, especially if the leading edge of the paper has absorbed too much moisture," she explained. "And when that happens, they tend to fall out of the tray. And with all the tacking we've been doing, it could have easily rolled under the table."

"But even so . . ."

"A cover sheet will have their fax number on it. We can contact them and have them send us another copy!"

Before Bloom could protest and tell her not to worry about it, because he really didn't care, she disappeared down the companionway again.

The first thing she did was to shut off the radio fax before the damned thing started churning out any more unnerving messages.

Then, after looking over her shoulder to make sure that

Bloom was still up on deck, she quickly began to unlatch the front panel of the navigation station. Once she got the panel off, which took about fifteen seconds, she carefully reached in among the maze of wiring and found the pair of colored switches, one blue and one red. She snapped the blue switch to the down position, hesitated for a brief moment, and then—her face set in an unreadable expression—snapped the red switch into the same down position. After that, she found and pulled loose the wire that ran from the antenna to the fax machine. Then, after returning the external on/off switch for the now disconnected fax back to the on position, she quickly began to relatch the console panel back into place.

Thirty seconds later she was back up on deck.

"Nothing," she said, shaking her head. And then, after a moment: "You know, if you want, I could try using the ship-to-shore to call your office, see if copies were sent there too."

"No, no, that won't be necessary." Bloom shook his head quickly. "If Grynard is expecting a confirmation, and he doesn't get one, he'll just send another fax."

"Okay, if you're sure."

"It's not going to be a problem," he said reassuringly. "It's a little less than fifty miles from the Hawk's Nest marina to Rum Cay. If we get up early tomorrow, we'll get there by noon easily. Then we'll just wait for him to show."

Bloom was certain that Special Agent Al Grynard of the FBI would not have sent a copy of the fax to his office, because Grynard *knew* that he was on the *Sea Amber*. And knowing the FBI, the wealthy industrialist thought morosely, they wouldn't care whether he acknowledged their faxed message or not, because they probably received an hourly update on the *Sea Amber*'s exact position by some kind of satellite image monitoring. He'd heard that they had been actively developing that technology in conjunction with the DEA a couple of years ago.

He tapped his fingers absentmindedly against the steering

wheel, knowing that he couldn't put the decision off any longer. Finding himself caught up in the exhilaration of a new
boat and a new lover, he had been putting the whole thing
off, hoping somehow that it would all go away. But it hadn't,
and now the time had come when he had to decide . . . one
way or the other.

But not right now, he told himself, caressing the hide-
wrapped steering wheel with a callused hand as he allowed
his tired eyes to travel down the incredibly erotic surface of
the stretched bathing suit, feeling a renewed sense of lust
and adrenaline surge through his deeply fatigued body.

Not until he savored two of the ultimate pleasures in life
just a little bit longer.

If the FBI wanted to talk to him that badly, they would
force the issue anyway, and there wouldn't be much that he
could do about it. He just hoped that they'd wait until tomorrow, at Rum Cay, and not show up at the Hawk's Nest marina instead . . . or at least not until much later this evening,
after the ICER Committee meeting, when he returned to the
Sea Amber.

The trouble was, Bloom knew, if they could track the *Sea
Amber* by satellite, then they were just as likely to have
agents there at the marina too, watching his arrival. And that
could mean serious trouble, even if they didn't try to contact
him there. Especially if they spotted his pickup ride and followed him out to the villa. To where the ICER Committee
would be meeting for the first time in six months, reasonably
confident that they had managed to avoid any possible surveillance by federal law enforcement authorities.

Bloom felt his chest start to tighten in panic, knowing how
much effort the committee members had put into finding a
place where they could come together once again without
fear of exposure. And knowing, too, how they would react
when they learned that he, Alfred Bloom, had led the FBI to
their island retreat.

For a brief moment the memory of his phone call to Saltmann at Whitehorse Cabin—and the mental image of Lisa

Abercombie lying on her back with a .44 caliber hole through her chest—flashed through his mind.

Bloom realized now that he didn't dare dock at the marina this evening as he'd planned. He'd have to anchor the *Sea Amber* offshore near Cutlass Bay and use the rubber Zodiac to row out and back without being seen . . . which would be dangerous, because of the shallow reefs and strong currents in the area. But it was either that or skip the meeting entirely. And he didn't dare do that, because then the rest of the committee would be convinced that he was about to betray them.

And if that was the case, Bloom knew, feeling his mouth go dry, someone would make a phone call, and within the next twenty-four hours—or a week at the outside—he'd be dead. No matter where he went or what he did.

For a brief moment and for the first time in his entire life Alfred Bloom felt absolutely helpless and completely alone.

Considering the fragile state of his current mental health, it was probably just as well that Bloom had no way of knowing how far Al Grynard and his team of FBI agents had progressed in their unrelenting investigation during the past six months.

In digging into the curious and fascinating past of Lisa Abercombie, Grynard's investigators had managed to unearth rumors of a hidden relationship with a wealthy industrialist who liked to sail in the Bahamas. Six agents had immediately descended on the islands, and had returned two weeks later with long printouts of possible subjects who had stayed in the same hotels on the same dates as Abercombie. Predictably, there had been several hundred wealthy industrialist types on the lists, but Bloom's name was one of the few that had appeared more than once. And when the agents started digging deeper, they quickly discovered that Bloom and Abercombie had checked into adjoining rooms during their last two visits to the Islands.

That had been enough to generate an early morning phone call to Grynard, who, at the time, was still working out of the

Anchorage field office. Grynard had been on the next military flight out of Elmendorf with the nonstop destination of Andrews Air Force Base just outside of Washington, D.C.

Bloom had managed to avoid the pair of agents who had come calling at his corporate headquarters, but Assistant Special Agent in Charge Al Grynard turned out to be a different kind of adversary entirely.

Grynard had listened patiently to his agent's explanations of why they hadn't been able to interview Alfred Bloom yet. Then he reached for a nearby phone and put in a direct call to Bloom's secretary. Ignoring her protests, he had advised the protective assistant that she had exactly one hour to contact her boss and have him call Special Agent Al Grynard at the following Washington, D.C., number. And if Mr. Bloom failed to make that call within that allotted time, Grynard had gone on, continuing to ignore the woman's increasingly frantic assurances that Mr. Bloom was out of town and simply could not be reached, then a warrant would be issued for his immediate arrest.

When Bloom had called exactly fourteen minutes later from the yacht dealer's office, Grynard had been just as blunt and to the point. Bloom could either sit down and explain to the FBI, in some detail, his past relationship with a woman named Lisa Abercombie; or he could do his explaining to a federal grand jury. It was his choice, but he had to make it now.

Unable to resist the experienced agent's pressure tactics, Bloom had agreed to meet Grynard at some remote site in the Bahamas when he arrived there the following week. But that was before he had fallen in love with a new boat and a new woman who made him forget—at least temporarily—all of his pain and anger . . . and fear.

"Alfred, are you all right?" Anne-Marie whispered.

Bloom blinked and then shook his head, realizing that in his emotional turmoil he had completely lost track of where he was and what he was doing. But now, in addition to the fear and the ache of desire, he felt a familiar gnawing in the pit of his stomach.

"I'm sorry." He smiled weakly. "I guess I just realized, in the midst of everything else, that we haven't eaten anything since breakfast . . . and in addition to being tired and horny, I'm absolutely starving."

The blue-eyed and dark-haired woman who, in the brief span of a few days, had given Alfred Bloom a new lease on his deeply troubled life, blinked in momentary confusion and then burst out laughing.

"What's the matter?"

"You," she whispered in a husky voice, and was starting to reach for him again—with a mischievous expression on her face that caused Bloom to experience another surge of desire—when the wind shifted again.

This time they both had to work at the winches and the rudder, fighting the sail and the currents to maintain their approximate heading.

Finally, after several minutes of energetic tacking, they got the *Sea Amber* into a position of relative stability into the wind. A nearly exhausted Alfred Bloom glanced up at the telltales, checked the compass and his watch, and then sighed audibly as he stood with his back braced tight up against the railing and accepted another steaming cup of Navy grog from his voluptuous sailing companion.

"What's the matter?" she asked as she braced herself against the opposite side of the steering well and sipped cautiously at the hot brew.

"It looks like we're going to be dead to windward most of the way back," he replied, keeping one aching hand tight on the wheel. "And the way it's blowing right now, I don't think that's going to leave us enough time . . ."

He let the sentence hang unfinished.

"Do you really have to be there by eight-thirty?" she asked, staring at Bloom with a thoughtful expression in her deep-blue eyes.

"Yes, I'm afraid so." He nodded. "I'm really sorry."

"Don't be, I haven't given up yet," she responded in a raspy voice that was barely audible over the sharp hiss of the water against the *Sea Amber*'s smooth fiberglass hull.

"Oh, really?" Alfred Bloom's tired eyes crinkled with amused interest. "And just what, exactly, did you have in mind?"

In answer, she set the steaming mug aside. Then she slowly came forward, wrapped her arms around the wealthy industrialist's neck, and pressed her thinly covered upper torso tight against his chest.

Bloom could feel her swollen nipples through his windbreaker and wished desperately that he was forty years old again. Or even fifty, he thought wistfully, aware of the fatigue that had left his arms and legs feeling numb and almost useless.

"There's a seventy-five-horse marine diesel down below that we haven't gotten around to testing yet," she whispered, her breath hot against his ear. "If we open her up to full throttle, she can do eight knots easy."

"Eight? In this weather? Are you sure?" He looked out at the choppy water skeptically.

"Uh huh." She bit softly against his ear lobe as her right hand moved down to the waistband of his shorts.

Incredibly Bloom could feel the surge of adrenaline coursing through his veins once again. For a brief moment it occurred to him to wonder if this was the way that men of his age died—out of pure exhaustion. But then he decided that he didn't care.

"At eight knots," he calculated, ignoring the purposeful actions of her hands for the moment, "that would give us—"

"Plenty of time," she murmured. "Depending on how long it takes you to set that anchor. And then after that you've got just one more important decision to make."

"Oh, yeah, and what's that?" he asked, trying not to think

about important decisions that needed to be made as he felt his pulse quicken and the familiar sense of desire starting to build in his chest and groin.

"Which are you? Hungry or horny?"

Chapter Twenty-three

Less than fifty yards away from the *Lone Granger*'s idling position, a creature very similar in nature to a predatory shark settled down onto the sandy bottom of Exuma Sound and maintained a still watchfulness as Dwight Stoner released the fearsome great hammerhead he had fought for an hour and had finally subdued and brought alongside the yacht.

Although, in truth, the actions of this newly arriving creature were far more tactical and instinctive than precautionary.

For example, he didn't even appear to react when the shark—in its determined effort to put depth and distance between itself and the powerful yacht that had provided such a tantalizing blood trail to follow—suddenly dove to the bottom and began a fast and visually aggressive run in his direction.

For a brief moment it appeared as though the great hammerhead were about to unleash its primitive angers and frustrations upon this new creature. But then, in a process as ageless as it was practical, one fearsome predator recognized another, and the shark turned away in search of a less dangerous source of food to satisfy its never-ending hunger.

Riser, on the other hand, continued to wait patiently on the sandy bottom until the *Lone Granger* had once again taken up her southerly course.

Then, after checking the display of the tracking device on the control panel of his underwater "scooter," to make certain that the transmitter he'd attached behind the keel of the *Lone Granger* at the Fort Lauderdale marina was still functioning, he brought the electrically powered underwater vehicle up off the bottom and once again began to follow.

Fifteen minutes later, while Mo-Jo—Bobby LaGrange's Jamaican crewman and right-hand man—maintained a leisurely course along the eastern shore of Cat Island, the five federal wildlife agents of Bravo Team settled into comfortable deck chairs and enjoyed a well-deserved break from their afternoon exertions. As they did so, Bobby LaGrange explained the setup that his son had used to lure in the huge hammerhead.

"As I understand it, the ex-owner was supposed to be some kind of avid shark fisherman, only he apparently never had much luck in hooking the big ones," LaGrange said as he sipped a glass of iced tea. "So one day I guess he must have decided that he wanted to change the odds in his favor. What he did was to have one of the boat repair yards install a little plastic tube from the engine compartment down through the hull and into the keel. Then all he had to do was attach a two-quart reservoir and a little cycling pump that puts out a drop or so every couple of minutes, fill the reservoir with diluted fish blood, and bingo, he had himself one hell of a shark lure system."

"So basically what Justin was doing was creating a very long and very diluted scent trail." Mike Takahara nodded. "That's why the shark stayed down below the surface the whole time, because he was looking for the source that should have been right under the boat. Must have been real frustrating for him, not to be able to find anything to chew on."

"Yeah, but the thing is, the big sharks around here are real patient," Bobby LaGrange said as he bit into one of Mo-Jo's tuna fish sandwiches. "They'll follow a trail like that for a long time, I guess figuring that eventually they'll find something good to eat at the front end."

"Which also explains why we weren't catching anything else all afternoon," Stoner said. "With a creature like that following along behind, there probably wasn't another fish within a half mile of this boat."

"Anybody want to buy a kid?" Bobby LaGrange asked hopefully.

"Better watch yourself, buddy," Henry Lightstone warned, standing up as he reached out and messed up Justin LaGrange's hair. "The way these guys are going, they're probably going to end up turning you into a wildlife agent. Although, come to think about it," he added thoughtfully, "we can always use another devious mind on this team."

"If I haven't taught him better than that by now, he can suffer the consequences just as I did," LaGrange laughed. "Hey, where are you going?"

"Didn't sleep too good last night," Lightstone said. "Figured I'd check out the owner's cabin, catch a couple of winks before dinner."

Larry Paxton's eyes opened wide and his head snapped up. "Hey, now, I'll thank you to keep your raggedy-ass butt outta mah cabin and off mah clean silk sheets. You hear?"

Lightstone laughed and then winked at Paxton before disappearing through the sliding glass door into the salon.

"Looks to me like Henry's feeling a whole lot better," Dwight Stoner mumbled from behind his third tuna fish sandwich.

"Too damn good if you ask me," Larry Paxton grumbled. But it was obvious that he too was relieved to see the positive change in his moody and unpredictable wild-card agent.

"So what do you think that earlier business was all about?" Mike Takahara asked.

"If you're asking me," Bobby LaGrange responded, "I think he sensed there was something out there he didn't like, something threatening, but he didn't know what it was."

"Say what?" Larry Paxton blinked.

"One of your basic instincts: fear of the unknown." LaGrange shrugged. "And Henry's a classic case. As long as

I've known him, I don't think I've ever seen him act like he was afraid of anything he could see or touch. But''— LaGrange held up his hand for emphasis—''you let something hide out there in the darkness, where he can sense it but not see it, and he goes nuts.''

''So that's why you rigged that game with the masks and fins,'' Mike Takahara said. The tech agent referred to LaGrange's offering to go into the water with Lightstone before the great hammerhead struck Dwight Stoner's line— and Henry, without explanation but with a look in his eye, refusing.

''Yeah, I wanted to see if he still had that ol' sixth sense, or whatever the hell it is.'' Bobby LaGrange nodded.

''That's right,'' Mike Takahara said, ''before we got distracted by that shark, you were starting to tell us that you'd seen him act this way before.''

''Oh, yeah, I sure did,'' Bobby LaGrange admitted. ''It happened back when we were going to high school together, sophomore year, down in San Diego.'' The ex-homicide investigator went on to describe how he and his childhood buddy, Henry Lightstone, had gone out body-surfing off La Jolla, as they'd done a hundred times before, and how this time they'd stayed out past the breakers much too late, wanting to hit that last big wave.

''It was really something. One of those absolutely beautiful sunsets you'd see down there on the coast every now and then,'' LaGrange said. ''The clouds would turn a real bright reddish-orange and then gradually go dim, shifting into the purples and grays. Absolutely breathtaking. Well, anyway, Henry and I were out there floating in the water—which by then had turned kind of a glassy dark green, not that it really mattered, because unlike this place, the water was always so cold and murky that you could never see much past the end of your arm anyway out there—and you could feel the smaller swells going past. You know, kinda lifting you up and then dropping you back down. Decent swells, but not the one we wanted. Not the really big one that keeps building up momentum as it heads in toward shore, until the water being drawn back underneath drives the entire swell upward, and then all of a sudden you feel this absolutely bitchin' wave forming all around you that, with a couple of kicks, you could get right out front of—your head and chest completely out of the water—and ride that baby all the way into shore.''

Bobby LaGrange sat there in his deck chair, looking as if he'd gotten lost somewhere in the vivid emotions of his memories.

"So that's where the term 'bitchin'' came from." Mike Takahara smiled. "I always wondered about that."

"Actually, as I recall, it also referred to just about any young woman in a bathing suit, and definitely any car that didn't look like it belonged to your parents." LaGrange nodded, blinking his way back to reality. "But yeah, a hot wave was your basic definition of bitchin', no doubt about it. I take it you must have grown up somewhere inland?"

"Flagstaff, Arizona," the Japanese-American tech agent said.

"Too bad." The ex-homicide investigator shook his head sympathetically.

"Ah think Ah missed something," Larry Paxton said. "Just what exactly do all these teenage fantasies of yours have to do with Henry?"

"Yeah, I'm coming to that." LaGrange smiled. "So anyway," he went on, "Henry and I are out there in the swells, wearing fins and light wet suits, and still waiting for that last big one to show up. Only the sun's pretty well gone now, and the sky's starting to turn this dark gray color—which means we really shouldn't be out there—when all of a sudden Henry gets this funny look in his eyes and yells at me not to move.''

"What?"

"Yeah, I'm telling you, I just about crapped in my trunks." Bobby LaGrange nodded. "So there I am, treading water as slow as I possibly can, trying not to move my legs or arms, with my nose and eyes just barely out of the water.

But, man, I'm looking everywhere I can, looking for a fin, barracuda flash, something, trying to see what it is he saw. Only I can't see a damn thing. And then I see Henry turn around in the water so that he's facing south, you know, parallel to the shore. And now I'm *really* looking, only I *still* can't see anything, and my heart's got to be doing at least a hundred and twenty. And then''—LaGrange paused for effect—"I hear him say—and he was about ten feet away from me when he said it: 'It's coming right at us, Bobby, right now. Don't move.' Just like that."

Bobby LaGrange looked around at the faces of the four agents and his son, all of whom were sitting there in stunned silence.

"And you still didn't see anything?" Paxton finally asked, his eyes wide.

"Not a thing." Bobby LaGrange shook his head. "But then all of a sudden I felt it—felt something, a change in the pressure, whatever—like something big, and I mean *really* big, was going by somewhere down there below my feet."

"Jesus!" Dwight Stoner whispered.

"And, man, I'm telling you, my brain is numb and I'm so scared now I can't even move, even if I wanted to. And then I look around with my eyes—because I'm afraid to move any other part of my body, because I know if I do it'll come at me, whatever and wherever it is—and I can't see Henry."

"I mean to tell you he's gone, nowhere in sight. So there I am, out there by myself, and it's really getting dark and cold now, and I can't even *think*, I'm so scared. And then ten, maybe fifteen seconds later—whatever it was, it seemed like a goddamned hour—up pops Henry's head, and I'm screaming at him—'What the hell is it?!'—only he doesn't know because he couldn't see it either, but at least he had the guts to go down there and look, which I couldn't have done if somebody'd put a gun to my head. And then''—LaGrange paused for effect again—"he gets that funny expression on his face again, and he says, 'Oh, God, it's turning. It's coming back.' "

Bobby LaGrange paused to take a sip of his iced tea, aware that five sets of eyes were locked on his every movement.

"So right then I knew we were gone. Dead. Nothing we could do about it, 'cause we didn't know what it was or what direction it was coming at us from—only that it was coming back. And right then both of us felt it. The swell building up, the one we'd been waiting for. And I remember we looked at each other, eyeball to eyeball, and then we went for it. Two kids, what?—fifteen years old, swimming like it was the Olympics finals, trying to catch a wave like it was the last thing we were ever going to do in our entire lives."

"And you caught it, right?"

"Caught it?" LaGrange laughed. "Hell, Paxton, we didn't just *catch* that wave, we outswam it. Me, I think I was up on shore and ten yards past the lifeguard station before I stopped clawing and kicking my way through the sand. Henry, I don't know how he got there or who beat who, but the next thing I knew he was right there on the sand next to me, pounding on my shoulder and coughing up saltwater. All I remember after that is both of us shaking and choking and laughing and hugging each other like we'd just decided to go steady; and then getting yelled at by the lifeguard, who was really pissed 'cause he'd thought everybody was out of the water, and we were so far out in the swells that he hadn't even noticed us until we went for that wave."

"Christ almighty!" Larry Paxton said softly.

"So what was it? Did you ever find out?" Mike Takahara asked.

"No, we never did. And to tell you the truth, I'm not real sure that either of us ever wanted to know. But one thing I *do* know is that a week later, a twenty-foot white nailed an abalone diver off La Jolla Cove, which was about a quarter of a mile south of where we were swimming. The guy diving with him saw him pop up screaming and then disappear. When he got there and looked down, he saw his buddy hanging out of both sides of the shark's mouth and both of them heading west. As far as I know," LaGrange said after a moment, "that was the last time that either of us ever went out body-surfing. Fear of the unknown, Snoopy, my man. It'll get you every time."

"So what—" Larry Paxton started to ask when they all heard and then saw Henry Lightstone appear on the lower deck with a mask, fins, snorkel, and a diving knife in his hands.

"Hey, Mo-Jo!" Lightstone called up to the bridge.

The Jamaican crewman looked back over his shoulder.

"Yass, sir?"

"How about cutting the engine for a few minutes?"

"Yass, sir!"

Moments later, the *Lone Granger*'s diesels rumbled to a stop.

"And just where the hell do you think you're going?" Bobby LaGrange demanded from his sitting position on the main deck.

"I think Mo-Jo just hit something," Henry Lightstone said as he stepped out onto the swim platform and began strapping the diving knife around his leg.

"What?"

"I heard something clank against the bottom."

"What do you mean, 'clank'?" Bobby LaGrange demanded. "This thing's got a fiberglass hull."

"Yeah, I know, didn't sound right, so I figured I'd go down and take a look," Lightstone said as he reached down and began pulling the fins onto his feet.

Bobby LaGrange stared at his ex-partner and childhood friend as though he'd lost his mind.

"Henry, by any chance do you happen to remember what it was we were all doing about a half hour ago?" he asked in an incredulous voice.

"Oh, yeah, sure. No big deal. I'll keep an eye out for that critter." Henry Lightstone shrugged as he stood up again.

At that moment Bobby LaGrange saw it again—that unforgettable expression in his ex-partner's eyes.

"Hey, wait, hold on a minute. I'll go with you," La-Grange said hurriedly, trying to work himself up out of the confining deck chair. But by the time he managed to get into a standing position, Henry Lightstone was already sitting on the swim platform and pulling the mask on over his head.

"Henry, you dumb—" LaGrange started to yell, but it was too late. With a small splash Henry Lightstone disappeared beneath the surface of the turquoise-green water.

"For Christ's sake!" Bobby LaGrange raged as he fumbled around on the main deck, looking for his mask and fins. Then he realized that Lightstone had taken his set that he'd left by the door to the crew's quarters.

"Mo-Jo!"

The Jamaican crewman looked over the back side of the bridge again.

"Yass, sir?"

"Get a diver's flag out, and then grab that shark rifle and keep an eye out for that damned hammerhead!"

"Yass, sir!"

"What do we do?" Larry Paxton demanded.

"Go get anything you brought with you that'll shoot a bullet and help Mo-Jo stand watch for that shark."

"You got it." Paxton nodded as the four agents disappeared into the salon.

"Justin."

"Yes, sir!"

"Go get me your diving gear and your spear gun right now," LaGrange ordered. "And, son," the ex-homicide investigator added in a softer voice.

"Yes, sir?"

"Hurry."

Chapter Twenty-four

The first thing that struck Henry Lightstone was the incredible clarity of the water.

Accustomed to the blue-green murkiness of the relatively cold and dark Pacific Ocean along his native Southern California coastline, he had expected to find himself peering through gloomy depths in an effort to spot the hammerhead or other lurking predators. Instead he immediately experienced an overwhelming sense of vertigo—of being suspended forty feet in midair above an open expanse of pristine ocean floor ringed with rocky crags and coral formations and seaweed.

It took a few moments for his jarred survival instincts to accept the fact that he was actually floating, rather than hovering, above the spectacular aquatic vista.

And even though it was late in the afternoon and difficult to judge distances in any case, Lightstone was convinced that he could easily see at least a hundred yards in all directions before the azure-blue waters of the western Atlantic Ocean began to turn opaque out in the distance.

At the same time, he was also aware of being able to hear a multitude of sounds through the ocean water with a similar degree of clarity. Most of these sounds, he quickly realized, were being made by Larry Paxton and his fellow agents as they scrambled to retrieve their weapons from the below-deck storage lockers of the huge white and red hovering object above his head that was the *Lone Granger*.

Caught up in the incredible beauty of the turquoise-tinged panorama, as he made a quick three-hundred-and-sixty-degree turn to make certain that the hammerhead shark *wasn't* in the immediate vicinity, Lightstone almost missed the movement off to his right. And when he did finally notice it, out at the edge of his visibility, he had to blink and look again before he was able to recognize the distant blurry object as a diver moving away . . . on what? Some kind of underwater sled?

And then another movement caught Lightstone's attention, something dark and moving fast out in the far opaque distance to his left, and he suddenly became conscious of the fact that he was starting to run out of air.

Rising quickly to the surface, he forcibly expelled the remaining air in his lungs, took in another deep breath— ignoring as he did so the cursing of Bobby LaGrange, who was still waiting for his son to find his diving gear, and the yelling of Larry Paxton and Dwight Stoner, both of whom had pistols in their hands and were pointing off to the distance in the direction where Lightstone had briefly observed the rapidly moving dark shape and then immediately went back under again because he suddenly remembered why he'd gone into the water in the first place.

That barely audible clanking sound.

It took him almost a full minute to find it because Bobby had said the hull was fiberglass, so he'd started at the stern where the stainless steel propeller shafts and manganese bronze rudder were located, and found nothing. It was only as he moved forward along the eight-two-foot craft, ignoring the splash behind him, that he realized that the leading edge of the keel was also made of stainless steel.

But even then he almost missed it, because the design appeared to have been based on the shape of a small manta ray: thick in the middle and then flaring out into two progressively thinner winglike extensions that were folded across the leading keel edge and attached with some kind of adhesive bond to the smooth broad keel surfaces on either side. The color was a perfect match for the protective marine-red coating on the keel of the luxury sports fishing yacht, and he might not have seen it at all if it hadn't been for the visible break in the protective metal keel edge.

Even the texture of the material—smooth and flexible and giving, and somehow very familiar—felt manta-ray-like.

What the hell . . .

The movement of the water had warned Henry Lightstone of the approach, even before he felt the impact. But he had ignored the warning because his senses told him that the threat wasn't coming from that direction. It was the other movement that he had to be concerned about, the dark, fast-moving shape out in the distance.

That, and this thing—whatever it was—that was stuck to the keel of the *Lone Granger.*

Bobby LaGrange had given up waiting for his son to bring up the scuba gear, and had simply gone into the water with the diving mask and knife he'd found in one of the lower-deck storage cabinets. Finally catching up with Henry Lightstone under the keel of the *Lone Granger,* he grabbed his ex-partner's shoulder, shook it, and pointed with the diving knife in the same direction that Paxton and Stoner had been pointing.

But Lightstone shook his head and ignored him, already starting to feel the tightening in his lungs, as if they were going to explode if he didn't hurry up and—

Explode.

The word jarred Henry Lightstone's mind like a fist strike.

Twisting around in the water, Lightstone wrenched the diving knife out of Bobby LaGrange's hand. Then, pulling himself back around again, he quickly jammed the point of the blade underneath the flexible, rubberlike flap. In doing so, he ignored the damage that the knife blade was causing to the glass-smooth keel because he understood now why the soft, flexible material had felt so familiar.

It was plastic explosive.

He could feel Bobby LaGrange pulling on his shoulder, insistently now. Lightstone continued to ignore his boyhood friend because he was running out of air and he was terribly afraid that if he went back up for another breath, they'd run out of time too.

It took the struggling wildlife agent almost ten seconds to pry the tightly bound and incredibly resilient flap loose, and another three to get a grip on the slippery material and wrench the entire device loose. In doing so, he managed to expose the metallic timer and detonator that had clanked ever so slightly when it had come into contact with the stainless steel keel edge and given them a chance.

And in doing *that*, he also managed to trip a cleverly designed tamper-protect switch specifically engineered to *prevent* people like Henry Lightstone from peeling the device off boat keels prematurely.

In the time it took Lightstone to understand what he had done, the exposed red numerals on the timer counted down from twenty to thirteen.

He had a brief second to see the sudden, horrified look of recognition and awareness in Bobby LaGrange's eyes. Then Lightstone turned away and dove downward, kicking hard with his fins—two, three, four times—before he shoved the device toward the bottom, confirmed that it was drifting down instead of up, and then kicked hard for the surface.

Bobby LaGrange had already pulled himself up onto the swim platform and was screaming for Mo-Jo to get the engine started when Lightstone reached the platform.

Henry Lightstone felt the powerful diesels rumble into life, and he scrambled desperately to get his legs away from the stainless steel propellers. He had one leg up onto the platform and was starting to pull himself out of the water when Bobby LaGrange grabbed his arm, pulled him clear, and then yelled up at the bridge:

"Mo-Jo! Full speed! Right now! Go! Go!"

Grasping the stainless steel railing with his right hand, Lightstone shoved Bobby LaGrange up over the railing and toward the deck-mounted fighting chair. Then he was forced to grab onto the railing with both hands as Mo-Jo slammed the throttle all the way forward.

At that moment, as the *Lone Granger* lunged forward in a desperate effort to escape the imminent explosion, the concussive shock of a high-order underwater detonation drove hundreds of tons of saltwater upward and outward, sending the two hundred-and-twenty-thousand-pound luxury yacht twisting violently into the air.

Chapter Twenty-five

The enormous forces generated by the detonation of ten pounds of C-4 about thirty feet beneath the stern of the *Lone Granger* had two immediate effects on Henry Lightstone:

The first involved the initial shock wave created by the explosion, which—in addition to breaking almost every one of the light bulbs on the *Lone Granger*, and loosening most of the ROM and RAM chips on the yacht's control station circuit boards—caused the wildlife agent to strike his head with a resounding *thunk* against the reinforced fiberglass rail separating the yacht's lower deck from the extended swim platform.

The second occurred approximately one second later when hundreds of tons of displaced seawater took the path of least resistance and surged upward, catapulting Lightstone high up into the air.

Partially dazed by the sharp blow to his forehead, Lightstone was still tumbling head over heels in midair, trying to figure out up from down—while at the same time, somewhere in the back of his semiconscious mind, trying to understand why two resonating *thunk* sounds, instead of only one, actually meant something—when he suddenly landed on his back in the water with a cannonball-like splash.

The unexpected impact drove the remaining air from his lungs, and it was all he could do to keep himself from trying to draw a breath underwater. But it wasn't until he finally managed to claw and kick his way back to the surface, realizing only then that he was still wearing the swim fins, that

Lightstone remembered why that second *thunk* sound had seemed so important a few moments ago.

He started yelling, "Bobby!" as he twisted around in the water, searching for some sign of his ex-partner. But then a second series of massive waves—caused by the impact of a hundred-ton sports fishing yacht dropping back down and striking the water—sent him tumbling backward in a rush of sand-and-debris-filled saltwater that left him coughing, gagging, and cursing.

Bobbing up and down in the smaller after-swells, Lightstone suddenly remembered the source of that second *thunk* sound: the nauseating "hollow gourd" sound of Bobby La-Grange's head ricocheting off the stainless steel fighting chair.

He heard splashing and a familiar voice yelling for help, but some analytical portion of Henry Lightstone's dazed mind decided that anybody who was capable of splashing and yelling wasn't completely helpless yet. Then his hands found the face mask that was still hanging around his neck. Without really being aware of what he was doing, he cleared the mask and adjusted it to his face and tightened the strap, and then dove down, searching for his ex-partner and childhood friend.

Got to be somewhere close, because . . . there!

Lightstone could see Bobby LaGrange now: about twenty yards away, and drifting down toward the bottom, his arms and legs waving about loosely in the churned and cloudy water.

He started to go down after him and quickly discovered that the diving mask was a hindrance to any kind of rapid swimming. Wrenching the mask off, he continued his dive, kicking hard with the powerful swim fins to propel himself downward. But even so, it seemed to take minutes—instead of seconds—to reach his unconscious ex-partner and then drag him back up to the surface. There Lightstone's instincts and training immediately took over as his hands began to go through the familiar motions.

Right hand under the chin, forearm into the shoulder. Pull back. Left hand across the chest. Hold him tight. Now scissor-kick and stroke! Goddamn it, Lightstone, kick!

In the back of his mind Henry Lightstone could hear the demanding voice of his high school lifeguard instructor calling out the cadence as he worked to get Bobby LaGrange's limp upper torso tucked in tight under his left arm. Then he held on tight with his left arm and began to stroke hard with his right and scissor-kick with his legs. He was trying desperately to reach the still floating *Lone Granger* as quickly as he could, because he knew that LaGrange wasn't breathing and he didn't think he could perform CPR successfully in the water.

He paused once in his strokes, to realign himself with the boat, and he saw the huge form of Stoner, blood pouring down the side of his face from a cut over his right eye, reaching down over the side of the boat for somebody in the water.

Who? Somebody with black hair and dark brown skin. Larry? Yes, and somebody else. Woeshack? Okay, right, the familiar voice. Had to have been Woeshack yelling for help because he doesn't know how to swim. And even if he did, he'd still have a hell of a time of it with that plaster rock wrapped around his arm, Lightstone remembered, breathing hard now as he continued to stroke with his right arm. *Good man, Paxton. Gotta take care of your troops.*

He kept on stroking and kicking with everything he had, until his head hit the side of the *Lone Granger* and he felt Dwight Stoner's thickly muscled arms reach down and snatch the limp form of Bobby LaGrange out of his weakening grasp.

"Gotta hurry! CPR! He's not breathing!" Lightstone gasped, and then tried to work himself back to the swim platform.

Still groggy from the head blow and nearly exhausted by his desperate swim, it took Henry Lightstone three separate attempts before he was finally able to pull himself up out of the water and onto the wooden platform. He remained there on his back for a few moments, trying to control his breathing and regain his strength. Then he heard someone coughing violently.

Woeshack?

Lightstone pulled himself up to his knees, with his arms resting on the railing and his chin resting on his arms. He immediately saw the diminutive agent at the far left-hand corner of the lower deck, crouching down on one forearm and both knees as he tried to clear the burning saltwater from his spasmodically heaving lungs.

Knowing that there wasn't much he could do for Woeshack that the tough Eskimo agent couldn't do for himself, Henry Lightstone turned his attention back to Bobby La-Grange, who was lying on his back on the lower deck, surrounded by Paxton and Stoner. From his swim platform position he could see that both Stoner and Paxton had sustained bleeding head wounds, presumably from the concussive effects of the underwater explosion . . . which immediately caused Lightstone to think about the others.

Mike and Mo-Jo and Justin? Where the hell . . .

As Lightstone tried to look around for the three missing crew members, wincing both from the effort and the pain in his throbbing head, Stoner and Paxton continued to work on Bobby LaGrange.

They had started by trying to drive as much of the saltwater out of LaGrange's lungs as possible. Stoner thrust down hard on the boat captain's back with both hands and shoulders as Paxton turned and held his face to the side, giving the expelled liquids an easy pathway. Then, after additional back thrusts failed to produce any more water, Stoner quickly flipped LaGrange over, crossed the palms of his huge hands over the unconscious boat captain's sternum, and then began to drive his extended and locked arms down hard in steady, shoulder-driven strokes.

At the fifth stroke Larry Paxton tried to use his left arm to lift Bobby LaGrange's neck and to clear his throat, and discovered to his amazement that his left arm wouldn't function properly. So he used his right arm instead, leaning forward to force air into the unconscious boat captain's lungs.

Thomas Woeshack had managed to get himself up to his feet and was now leaning over the side, throwing up. Henry Lightstone was starting to lean forward to pull the swim fins off his feet, and the two wildlife agents were starting on the third series of strokes and breaths—having worked themselves into a steady rhythm without having any noticeable effect on LaGrange—when a distant voice that was both youthful and familiar suddenly began to scream in panic.

Henry Lightstone's head came up instantly, and he yelled out, "Justin?"

When he didn't get a response, Lightstone staggered up to his feet on the swim platform. He had to steady himself against the railing as he looked back around to his left.

"Help!"

Whirling back around to his right, Lightstone immediately spotted Justin LaGrange in the water, off the starboard beam of the boat, some fifty yards out. Then his eyes caught movement out in the distance to his far left, and he saw what had caused the youth to start screaming.

The distinctive high curved dorsal fin of the great hammerhead, about a hundred yards out off the starboard bow, circling around and coming fast.

"Justin, swim for the stern of the boat!" Lightstone screamed. Then, without stopping to think about how dazed and weak he still was, he dove off the swim platform in a flat racing dive.

The impact of the cool water had at least a minimally reviving effect. Lightstone began to stroke hard at a full-on, energy-draining, finishing-kick pace—left, right, left, right, left, right, and *then* breathe—kicking hard with the fins with every stroke, because it wasn't a question of endurance now, but rather one of distance and timing and triangulation.

He had already figured out the likely intercept points: calculating them the moment that he saw the shark coming around in a wide sweeping turn, and just before he dove off the platform. And he knew that it was going to be very close. A question of who or what got there first.

Lightstone tried several times to spot the shark when his face was down and under water, but his vision was blurred without the mask, and his increasingly heavy arms were churning up the water that was still clouded from the explosion. So he had to wait for the next breath, turning his head to the left this time, instead of to the right, to take a quick look.

That was when the frantically swimming wildlife agent realized that Justin LaGrange had thrown all his intercept calculations to the winds by turning and swimming desperately toward him—and thus back in the direction of the oncoming shark—instead of toward the more distant stern of the *Lone Granger.*

Henry Lightstone had less than half a second to reestimate the new intercept points, which told him that he couldn't possibly make it in time. Refusing to accept that answer, he lunged forward in an all-out effort anyway—no breathing now, just furious stroking and kicking with every ounce of his rapidly dwindling strength—just as spouts of water began to rise around the zigzagging dorsal fin.

Lightstone never heard the heavy splash far behind him, and he was barely aware of the loud gunshots that Larry Paxton was triggering off, one by one, as the supervisory agent tried to adjust his aim and timing to the bobbing movements of the boat, while at the same time, trying to brace the 10mm pistol in his partially crippled right hand with his apparently broken left arm. Nor did Lightstone see the shark react to the two mushrooming 10mm bullets that punched ragged holes through its high dorsal fin, by pausing to slash out at this new and invisible enemy, before continuing in its aggressive charge.

All Henry Lightstone knew was that suddenly the desperately swimming form of Justin LaGrange was less than a dozen feet away to his right, and a dark blurry streamlined shape was coming in fast from his left, aiming straight for the midpoint of the youth's slender and extended body.

Thrusting himself forward with a final desperate kick of the fins, Lightstone shot his right arm out, caught the rasplike leading right edge of the shark's mallet-shaped head with his bare hand, felt himself being dragged around to his right by the irresistible strength and momentum of the nine-hundred-pound shark. He quickly brought his left hand around to double his grip, then wrenched the shark's wing-like head back around—and away from the boy—with every bit of strength and energy he could muster.

Lightstone experienced a brief moment of elation when he realized that he'd succeeded in turning the shark's attention away from the boy. But then everything around him turned into a mindless series of actions and reactions as he desperately twisted his lower body away from the shark's slashing jaws, felt the rasplike surface of the shark's thrashing body tear away patches of skin from his arms and legs and hands as he gouged with his fingers at the shark's eye, and then lost his grip in the savagely churning mélée as the shark's powerfully sweeping tail slammed into his hip and knocked him away.

Then, in the next instant, the shark was gone, leaving a turmoil of swirling water in its wake.

When Lightstone came up, coughing and gasping for air, the first thing he saw was the panicked face of Justin La-Grange.

"It's okay, Justin! Everything's okay," he yelled, grabbing at the youth and pulling him behind his back, knowing even as he spoke the words that everything was definitely *not* okay. He could feel the burning of the saltwater on his savagely torn and abraded skin, and could see streaks of blood in the water—his, presumably, because he knew that he hadn't made *that* much of an impact on the predatory shark with his bare hands. "Just stay behind me and you'll be fine."

Looking up, Lightstone saw the distinctive dorsal fin pop

up to the surface out in the distance. He watched it for a few seconds and then breathed a temporary sigh of relief when it didn't get any closer. If the shark decided to circle them for a while, they might have a chance to get back to the boat.

But then he looked back over his shoulder and discovered to his dismay just how far he'd managed to swim from the distant *Lone Granger*.

Spotting the small figure of Larry Paxton bracing himself against the railing as he struggled to reload the heavy double-action pistol one-handed, Lightstone yelled out across the water: "Hey, Larry, can you get that boat over here?"

"No, not yet! Something's wrong with the electrical system," the acting team leader yelled back, "The engine won't start. Mike's working on it."

"What about the Zodiac?"

"We're working on that too!"

"Well, tell Snoopy to get his ass . . ." Lightstone started to yell, and then flinched when he saw Paxton suddenly bring his pistol up and begin firing again.

Turning back around quickly, Lightstone looked out across the water, saw the scythelike dorsal fin cutting back and forth, spouts of water rising up all around it, and realized that the shark had turned away from its wide circling pattern and was coming back around in their direction.

Justin LaGrange saw it too.

"Oh, no," he whispered in terror. Lightstone could feel the trembling of the boy's arms and torso behind his back.

"Listen to me, Justin," Lightstone said, keeping his eyes fixed on the shark's movements, "we're going to keep moving backward, toward the boat."

"But the boat's too far away," he protested.

"It's not *that* far, and it doesn't matter anyway, because I'm going to keep fending that thing off until we get there, okay?"

"Are you sure?"

"Yes, of course I'm sure," Lightstone lied. "But listen to me, when I tell you to swim for the boat, you do it. And you don't hesitate and you *don't* stop, not for anything, no matter what. You understand?''

"I'm scared," the youth whispered, staring out wide-eyed at the approaching dorsal fin.

"Yeah, me too, but do you *understand*?''

"Yes."

"Okay, Justin, we're going to be fine," Lightstone said soothingly, watching as the high dorsal fin seemed to vector in on their position. "You just be ready."

The rapidly approaching hammerhead was less than thirty feet away when Lightstone heard the start-up roar of the small outboard motor that LaGrange had purchased for his inflatable Zodiac boat.

But the shark was too close and coming too fast, and he knew it was too late for a boat rescue now. So he told the boy to get ready to swim, because he'd already made the decision to go straight in after the other eye. Either to blind the shark or at least keep it occupied long enough for Justin La-Grange to make a desperate swim back to his father's boat. He was determined to give the boy at least that much of a chance, no matter what he had to do.

But then—before he could drop down below the surface and ready himself for the final seconds of the shark's charge, and to his absolute astonishment—Henry Lightstone saw the front half of the great hammerhead suddenly rise out of the water and then go thrashing backward under the propelling force of Dwight Stoner's massive shoulders and arms.

Henry Lightstone had a moment to blink in disbelief, unable to comprehend—until he realized that Stoner was wearing a pair of scuba tanks from the *Lone Granger*'s diving locker—how the huge agent had managed to get between them and the shark without being seen. But then he quickly realized that the enraged hammerhead had now shifted his predatory focus onto Stoner.

"Go for the boat, Justin, now!" he yelled, and then dove forward underwater, intending to do whatever he could to help his fearless partner. He was just in time to see the hammerhead launch itself forward in a head-on attack at Stoner with a savage sweep of its tail—and then come to a jarring halt in midlunge when the ex–Oakland Raider drove his gloved fist squarely into the center notched area of the malletlike head where a normally configured shark would have had a nose.

Seemingly more surprised than hurt by the unexpected assault, the shark immediately jerked away; started to sweep around to the left, to come at Stoner from a different direction; jerked back to avoid a straight-fingered gouge to its left eye from Lightstone; and was jarred again when Stoner put every ounce of his considerable strength into a second punishing blow that caught the shark right in the center of its now extremely sensitive ''nose'' area.

For a brief moment, as they all began to sink downward in the rapidly clearing water, the two humans and the shark warily faced each other. But then, before the cautious hammerhead could regather itself for another charge, the engine roar of the rapidly approaching Zodiac sent the predatory fish turning away into a full-fledged retreat.

Three minutes later, with his two agent partners on board, Mike Takahara brought the small inflatable craft alongside the swim platform of the *Lone Granger*, where a decidedly pale and unsteady Thomas Woeshack was waiting. As he did so, acting team leader Larry Paxton braced himself against the lower deck railing, holding onto the heavy Model 1076 stainless steel pistol with his one reasonably good arm as he glared down at his returning agents.

''If you two are all done playing with that goddamned fish,'' Paxton said, a mixture of relief and furious anger plainly visible on his bleeding face, ''I'd be grateful if you'd get your sorry asses back on board so we can take care of a little unfinished business.''

''Where's Bobby and Mo-Jo and Justin?'' Lightstone asked in a barely audible voice. He remained sprawled out on his back in the Zodiac, blinking in confusion as Stoner first handed the borrowed scuba tanks up to Woeshack and then helped Mike Takahara tie the inflatable boat up to the stern of the *Lone Granger*.

"Got 'em down in the cabins. Come on, Henry, get your ass up here before that damned thing comes back!" Paxton snapped, maintaining an uneasy watch on the surrounding water with the 10mm pistol still clenched in his poorly functioning right hand.

Moving slowly and carefully, the three agents pulled themselves out of the unstable Zodiac and onto the extended wooden swim platform.

"Paxton, are they okay?" Henry Lightstone said insistently. He had paused at the latch door that separated the swim platform from the lower deck.

"Ah don't know," Paxton said, his cold, dark eyes still searching the water surface in the futile hope that whoever it was who had gone after his team this time would pop their heads up. Just once. Just for a second.

"What do you *mean* you don't know?" Lightstone demanded as he pulled himself up to the lower deck and balanced himself unsteadily against the reinforced fiberglass railing. His leg and arm muscles were trembling uncontrollably now—from the exertion and the injuries and the overload of adrenaline that was still churning through his bloodstream.

"Means we're gonna have to get Bobby and Mo-Jo to a hospital before too long," Paxton responded in a cold, gravelly voice, ignoring Lightstone's anger because he knew it didn't mean anything. Or at least nothing personal. He and Lightstone were much alike in their personalities: easygoing and irreverent by nature, but quick to anger and protective as hell when someone went after one of their friends or partners. And right now he also knew that both of them were furious and just barely in control.

Lightstone's head came up sharply.

"Henry, they're both banged up pretty bad," Paxton said. "Kinda drifting in and out. Looks to me like they both got concussions; but they're breathing steady, and their color looks okay."

"Thank God for that," Lightstone whispered in relief as he and Stoner collapsed gratefully against the starboard side railing of the lower deck, ignoring the blood that was seeping from their numerous sharkskin abrasions. Mike Takahara and Thomas Woeshack joined them on the deck, leaning their backs against the port-side railing.

"I sent Justin down there to stay with them," Paxton went on in a calmer voice. "Told him to keep an eye on everybody till we get things figured out."

"How's he doing?" Lightstone asked after a moment.

"Who, Justin? Outside of being half-scared out of his mind, and probably needing a change of shorts, he's fine," Paxton said. "All things considered, he's probably doing a whole lot better than the rest of us put together," the supervisory agent added, looking around at the battered and bleeding remnants of his covert agent team.

Lightstone and Stoner were sprawled out on the deck, dazed, bleeding, and exhausted. Woeshack looked exactly the way Paxton would have expected someone to look who had nearly drowned and was now deathly seasick from ingesting a couple of gallons of saltwater. And the front of Mike Takahara's shirt was covered with dried blood, the result of the tech agent smashing his nose against one of the stainless steel ladders when the underwater explosion had gone off.

Christ, and we haven't even gotten our hands on anybody yet, Paxton thought.

"Glad to hear Justin's all right," Henry Lightstone rasped. "So what's the matter with your arm?"

Paxton looked down at his left arm and observed that it was now swollen to about twice its normal size.

The acting team leader shook his head in disgust.

"Tell you what," he said after a few moments, uneasily aware of how vulnerable they were, sitting around in a disabled boat in the middle of the Bahamas, and having little or no idea who or where the bad guys were, "if you characters are up to moving, and I don't have to carry anybody up or down any ladders, why don't we go check on Bobby and Mo-Jo again. Make sure they're doing okay. Then we'll go up top, see what we can find in the way of medical supplies, and get everybody patched up while Snoopy here figures out how to get this here boat going again."

Ten minutes later, while Mike Takahara was down on his knees in front of the control station, pulling circuit boards out of the main panel, the four agents carefully brushed aside fragments of broken glass, settled themselves into the couches of the *Lone Granger*'s thoroughly trashed flying bridge, and then surveyed the damage.

In Paxton's words, which he had uttered in a dismayed whisper when he saw the damage to the salon downstairs, it looked as though the bomb had gone off *inside* the eighty-two-foot yacht, rather than thirty-some feet beneath the hull.

"Hate to think what the owner's cabin must look like," Dwight Stoner commented as he helped Lightstone apply antiseptic and bandages to the painfully oozing abrasions that covered an impressive amount of his bare skin.

"Probably looks a whole lot worse than the salon," Lightstone said, looking even more glassy-eyed than before from the cumulative effects of his medical treatment.

"Ah don't want to hear about it," Paxton growled. "Fact is, Ah don't even want to *think* about it."

But he smiled when Lightstone erupted into another burst of fervent cursing as Stoner swabbed a particularly deep abrasion with the Mercurochrome-based disinfectant.

"Better give him the rest of the bottle on that one, Stoner, mah man," the supervisory agent suggested. "Wouldn't want one of them bad-ass wounds to get infected now, would we?"

"Hate to do this to you, Henry, but I think he's right," Stoner said sympathetically as he easily deflected the wide-eyed agent's instinctively protective hand, and then poured the rest of the bottle into the palm-sized hip abrasion.

Henry Lightstone's reply was lost in yet another agonized explosion of profanity.

Paxton waited until his wild-card agent had calmed down and blinked the tears out of his eyes.

"Good thing ol' Bobby believes in being prepared," the supervisory agent said as he selected another bottle of the fiery antiseptic out of the box he had tucked against his crudely splinted left arm, and tossed it over to Stoner.

"Paxton, you son of a bitch," Henry Lightstone rasped, "I'm going to—"

"Thank me kindly, and then *listen* the next time I tell you to shoot a goddamned hammerhead shark instead of patting it on the head and cutting it loose?" Larry Paxton suggested with a cheerful smile.

Lightstone simply glared at his acting team leader.

"And speaking of dumb-ass stunts in general," Paxton went on, his voice turning serious, "I don't suppose you happened to notice anybody else swimming around down there, before that bomb went off?"

"Yeah, as a matter of fact, I did," Lightstone said. "A diver in one of those aqua-sleds, heading out that way." He gestured over his shoulder with his thumb in the general direction of Cat Island, the top of which was barely visible off in the distance.

"Anything useful for ID?"

"He might have been wearing a yellow diving suit, but I'm not even sure of that." Lightstone looked around and then suddenly realized the distant boat that had been anchored was no longer visible. "But I bet I know how he got out here." Lightstone explained his theory about the dive boat being used as a transport for the diver and his sled.

"Anybody remember what it looked like?" Paxton asked hopefully.

Everyone shook their heads.

"Shit," the supervisory agent muttered.

"Thing is, though," Lightstone said thoughtfully, "whoever these people are, I think we might have screwed up their plans this time.''

''Oh, yeah, and just what gave you that idea? The fact that we're still alive and complaining, instead of being fish food?'' Paxton asked sarcastically.

''Yeah, I suppose.'' Lightstone smiled in spite of himself. ''But I'm pretty sure that bomb had some kind of antenna wire sticking out of it.''

He described how he'd peeled the device off the keel of the ship, and what it had looked like when he'd exposed the timing mechanism.

''Do you remember about how far away that diver was when you saw him?'' Mike Takahara asked, sticking his head up over the pilot chairs in the front of the enclosed flying bridge.

''I'd say maybe a hundred feet, hundred and fifty feet at the outside, but that's a guess.''

''Did you ever see him look back?''

Lightstone thought for a moment. ''No, not that I recall. To tell you the truth, I think he was going pretty fast the other way, but I wasn't paying that much attention.''

''About how long would you say that wire was?''

''Eight, ten inches. Something like that.''

''Kind of thick, not real flexible?''

''It was about as thick as that Romex stuff we used to wire the warehouse.''

''Sounds like a transmitter detonation system to me.'' The tech agent nodded. ''And from the way you described it, the guy on the sled was too close to the boat to have set the bomb off deliberately, so you probably *did* trigger some kind of antitampering switch that started the timer. You said the red numbers started counting down from twenty?''

''That's right.''

''Which makes it even less likely that whoever was on that sled set the bomb off intentionally,'' Takahara said.

''Oh, yeah, why's that?'' Paxton asked.

''Because you always want to build a delay sequence into

an antitamper switch, just to make sure you have time to shut the whole thing off and start over again if you accidentally trigger the switch during installation,'' the tech agent explained.

Paxton shrugged. "Makes sense."

"I don't know about you guys, but I'm getting tired of people trying to blow us up all the time," Thomas Woeshack muttered. "I think I want to go back to flying planes."

"No offense, Woeshack," Lightstone said. "But the way you fly, I think you've got a lot better odds with bombs."

"And speaking of taking chances," Stoner said, looking out through the amazingly still-intact side window of the flying bridge, "what do you think about the idea that the guy on the sled might still be hanging around, instead of taking off with that dive boat?"

"I kind of doubt it," Mike Takahara said after a moment. "If I were in his place and I saw Henry trying to peel that thing off the keel with a diving knife, I'd have taken off as fast as I could get that sled to go. And if he didn't, and stayed close, I guarantee you that the initial shock wave blew him *and* his sled ass-end over teakettle."

"Along with about ten thousand fish." Paxton nodded, looking out one of the amazingly unbroken bridge windows. The water surface around the *Lone Granger* was now covered with thousands of floating fish carcasses for about a hundred yards in all directions. As the agents watched, a half dozen more dorsal fins—all of them much smaller than that of the fearsome hammerhead—cut back and forth through the water all around the yacht.

"Maybe he's out there right now, bleeding out his ass and ears, and trying to figure out how to get that sled going again before he gets eaten alive," Dwight Stoner commented hopefully.

"That's a nice thought," Lightstone said, grimacing as the huge agent taped a big patch of gauze over his hip abrasion. "In fact, if we didn't need to get Bobby and Mo-Jo some medical attention pretty soon, I'd want to go back out there in the Zodiac just to look. But since we *are* in a hurry,'' he reminded, ''where are we going to find a hospital around here, and how do we get to it?''

Paxton looked over at Mike Takahara.

''The only real hospitals are at Nassau and Freeport,'' the tech agent said, looking up from the circuit board he held in his hand. ''Almost all the main islands are supposed to have clinics, but most of them are probably going to be just a nurse on call and some basic first-aid gear.''

''How far is it to Nassau?'' Paxton asked.

Takahara thought for a moment. ''Figure maybe about a hundred miles. Too damned far to paddle in an eighty-two-foot yacht, if that's what you're thinking.''

''What about the Coast Guard or the Royal Bahamas Defense Force,'' Woeshack asked. ''I bet those guys could get a seaplane out here pretty quick.''

''Is the radio working?'' Paxton asked Takahara.

''Not right now, but I could get it rigged up to the main batteries without much trouble. But do we really want to attract that kind of attention?''

''Yeah, that's a good point.'' Paxton nodded.

''There's a small airstrip near Arthur's Town, at the north end of Cat's Island.''

''How far's that?''

''Maybe fifteen at the outside. We could make it in the Zodiac if we had to, then charter a plane to Nassau.''

''Okay, good.'' Paxton smiled.

''I don't understand. Why wouldn't we want to call the Coast Guard?'' Woeshack asked, looking confused.

''Because if we put out a radio signal right now,'' Henry Lightstone explained, ''the bastards who've been putting all this effort into trying to blow us up will figure out we're still functioning out here, and try again. Only this time they're liable to use a submarine and a goddamned torpedo.''

''Oh.''

''What do you think?'' Lightstone asked Paxton.

The supervisory agent hesitated and then looked over at his tech agent.

"So how long's it gonna take you to get this thing started again?"

"I don't know." Mike Takahara shrugged. "Maybe four or five minutes, maybe four or five hours. Depends."

"On what?"

"On which parts just got shaken loose and which parts got broken," he said, holding up a circuit board. "This, for example, is broken."

"What is it?" Paxton demanded.

"SSRS transmitter board."

"And just what the hell is *that*?"

"Satellite locator system. Standard on all big boats."

"You mean somebody could be tracking us by satellite?" Henry Lightstone asked.

"If anybody was, they're not doing it anymore." Mike Takahara shrugged as he tossed the circuit board into a nearby trash can.

"What about all the other stuff?" Paxton asked. "How we looking so far?"

"So far, all things considered, I'd say we're looking pretty good."

"Okay, keep at it."

"So what now, boss?" Lightstone asked as Mike Takahara disappeared back behind the pilot chairs again.

"Like Ah said, it's about time we took care of some business around here."

"What's that mean? You got some kind of plan?"

"Damn well better have one," Dwight Stoner growled as he examined the shredded remains of the leather glove that had partially protected the bleeding knuckles of his right hand from the abrasive skin of the hammerhead. "So far, all we've been doing is reacting and improvising and getting our ass kicked in the process."

"Oh, Ah got a *plan*, all right." The supervisory federal

wildlife agent nodded. "And it's a good one too."

"I'm listening," Henry Lightstone said as he gingerly applied some of the antiseptic to a relatively small abrasion on his knee.

"You're gonna like this one, Henry, mah man, 'cause it's real simple," Larry Paxton said in a voice that was amazingly calm and controlled, considering the intensity of the anger that was still churning around in his aching head.

Whoever these people were—the ones who had tagged their operations and screwed with their computers and blown up their warehouse and tried to blow up their boat—as far as acting Bravo Team leader Larry Paxton was concerned, they had gone after his people, his team, for the last time.

"Ain't gonna *be* no more this 'good guys playin' by the rules, and bad guys doing whatever the fuck they please,' " Paxton went on in his deep, gravelly voice, " ' 'cause we already tried that, and it ain't worked. Only thing that happened is they damn near blew us up twice, and fucked up mah boat."

Henry Lightstone cocked his head and looked over at the acting leader of Bravo Team, a pleasant smile appearing on his deeply scraped face in spite of the fact that he was still having to control an almost overwhelming desire to take someone apart at the seams. Anyone. It didn't matter who. Just as long as it was one of the people responsible for the only son of his lifelong friend having to try to outswim a goddamned hammerhead shark to save his life.

Those people, whoever they were, and wherever they happened to be right now, were going to pay.

"Yeah, so what's the plan?"

"Real simple," Paxton said. "First we get Bobby and Mo-Jo to a hospital, however we have to do it. Then once we do that, we're gonna go down to the other end of this Cat Island, and find ourselves this fellow named Alfred Bloom and have a little heart-to-heart talk with the man."

"And if that doesn't work?"

"Then," the supervisory agent said, his voice turning deadly cold, "we're gonna start doing a little ass-kicking of our own."

Chapter Twenty-six

The FBI-leased jet touched down at the San Salvador airport landing strip at precisely seventeen-thirty-two hours that Saturday afternoon.

The pilot taxied in close to the knee-high rock wall surrounding the small airport terminal building, and then shut down the screaming engines. As he did so, he noted that the wind sock had changed directions, a sign that the predicted norther might not hit this evening as expected.

When Special Agent Al Grynard stepped out of the plane, casually dressed in jeans, tennis shoes, and a maroon polo shirt, he immediately observed two similarly dressed men sitting in a Jeep next to a sign that read: Welcome, San Salvador Bahamas, Site of Columbus Landings.

The man in the front passenger seat removed his sunglasses, stuck them in his shirt pocket, and sighed to himself. Then he stepped out of the covered Jeep and walked across the rough tarmac toward the waiting plane.

"Al Grynard?" he asked as he stopped in front of the waiting agent.

"That's right."

"Hal Owens. Welcome to the Bahamas." The two men shook hands. Owens was about five-ten, balding, heavyset, thick in the shoulders and arms, and looked to be in his early fifties. As Reggie Blackburn had said, one of the FBI's old-timers. Grynard interpreted the firm handshake as saying, "Welcome, but I sincerely hope—for both our sakes—that you're not here to cause me grief or screw up my operation."

"I understand you're the SAC out here?" Grynard said as he turned back to help Theresa Fletcher down the jet's short drop-down ramp, and then take their two carry-on bags from the copilot. He put the bags on the tarmac and looked back up at Owens.

"That's right," the supervisory field agent acknowledged in a neutral voice.

"Appreciate your taking time out to meet with us on this deal." Grynard nodded. "This is Deputy U.S. Attorney Theresa Fletcher. She's been handling our initial prosecutions in this case."

"Ms. Fletcher." Owens extended his hand in a similar but much less forceful greeting.

"Theresa will do just fine," the federal prosecutor said, offering one of her more beaming smiles as she clasped the agent's hairy and muscular hand in both of her own. "I'm sorry we had to drop in on you like this with so little notice."

"Not a problem, ma'am. I'm happy to do it," the supervisory field agent said, finding himself warming to the amiable prosecuting attorney in spite of his instinctive wariness. In Hal Owens' thirty-two years of experience as an FBI agent, surprise visits from the Washington office that included a U.S. Attorney almost never worked out to the benefit of the supervising agent involved.

Then the significance of Grynard's statement registered. Blinking his eyes in confusion, Owens turned back to his visitor with a puzzled expression on his deeply tanned and crinkled face.

"Did you say 'case'?"

"That's right." Grynard nodded. "I'm the SAC out of Anchorage, in charge of a special task force investigating the murders of three federal wildlife agents on a covert assignment. Not internal affairs."

"But Blackburn—"

"I know." Grynard nodded. "And I apologize. I was the one who asked Reggie to set things up like that, to make it look that way."

"Mind if I ask why," Owens asked, his practiced neutral voice now tinged with irritation, if not outright anger.

"Did you guys get the word on those two boats: the *Sea Amber* and the *Lone Granger*?" Grynard asked, ignoring the question for the moment.

"Be alert to the presence of a three-hundred-and-fifty-thousand-dollar sailboat and a multimillion-dollar yacht? Observe and monitor, but do not approach? Oh, yeah, we got the word all right," Owens replied sarcastically.

"Your agents give them plenty of room?"

"Like they were the original plague ships."

"Let me guess," Grynard said. "Because you and your agents figured they were part of some kind of internal affairs honey trap? Checking to see if you guys might have been out here too long? Starting to get susceptible to easy money, drugs, women, something like that?"

Special Agent in Charge Hal Owens started to say something, saw Grynard's slight smile, and then shook his head in sudden understanding.

"Jesus, Grynard, couldn't you have just picked up a goddamned phone and *told* me that this was some kind of sensitive operation?" the supervisory agent demanded.

"Yeah, I could have," Grynard acknowledged, "but the thing is, I've got five federal wildlife agents floating around out here somewhere in that goddamned yacht, and I think they tripped over something pretty damned serious. Something that's liable to get them killed too, if I screw this thing up."

"*Wildlife* agents?"

"Let me put it this way," Grynard said. "Right now, I'm looking at an eighty-million-dollar terrorist training facility built right under our noses in Yellowstone National Park; ten dead international terrorists who were planning on taking out a bunch of environmental activist groups for some reason that I haven't completely figured out yet; two high-up Department of Interior co-conspirators who got blown away before they could talk; some commando freak with a four-bore rifle who kills four deputy U.S. marshalls so he can break a homicidal Cajun poacher out of a transport van; and then, the same day, takes out one of the surviving terrorists, three members of the bar, and four bodyguards in a safe house in Warrenton, just so he can run off with a GSG-9 trained counterterrorist; not to mention a warehouse in Boston—a wildlife sting operation, mind you—that's going to have to be put back together with broom and dustpan.''

"Woodson," Owens said, nodding to himself.

"What?"

"Stanley Woodson, ex-FBI agent. One of the four bodyguards they found at the Warrenton scene," the supervisory field agent explained.

"You knew him?"

"Oh, yeah, I knew old Stanley, all right. Woodson and Whittman and I graduated out of the same Academy class. Jim sent me a fax a couple of hours ago.'' There was a sad, distant tone to his voice.

"Sorry to hear that."

"Yeah, me too." Owens nodded morosely. But then he shook his head and seemed to refocus his attention on the reason that he'd driven down to the airport personally instead of sending one of his agents. "So what's all this have to do with you and me and a bunch of wildlife agents?"

"As best I can tell, this whole situation, the escaped prisoners, the guy with the four-bore, and whoever's behind him, are all focused on one thing: five federal wildlife agents who—as of about three hours ago—were heading this way in a yacht named the *Lone Granger.*"

"Christ!" Owens whispered.

"And there's one more thing," Grynard said. "For the last three months those wildlife agents have been trying to find a lead to the boyfriend of one of those DOI conspirators who helped blow away their three buddies. A guy who turns out to be one of our major industrialists."

"Alfred Bloom, the guy in the sailboat?"

"That's right."

Owens thought about that for a moment.

"You think he's doing all this by himself?"

"He could be, but from the scope of the operation—just the resources that went into that training facility alone—I'd say we're probably looking at two or three co-conspirators at a minimum. Maybe more."

"Any good suspects?"

"For starters, any major industrialist or developer who wouldn't mind seeing some of the environmental activist groups take a nosedive into an empty pool."

"That's a pretty long list."

"Yeah, tell me about it."

"And every one of them connected like a telephone switchboard. Congressmen, senators, governors, heads of state," Owens added knowingly. Then he turned his head and looked back at the small San Salvador airport terminal. "Customs officials too, most likely."

"That's part of the problem."

Hal Owens stared down at his dirty tennis shoes, deep in thought, for almost a full minute. Then he looked up at Grynard, his eyes filled with understanding.

"So it really *is* a honey trap after all."

"In a manner of speaking."

"Except that what you're *really* doing is trolling for a bunch of rogue alligators, and those five agents are the bait."

"That's right," Grynard said in a soft voice. "Which is why I need your help. I've got thirty-two agents assigned to my task force, but this all broke loose in the past twenty-four hours. We're still trying to get them reassembled and sent down here. But trying to move thirty-two agents and a support staff into position down here this fast—"

"It wouldn't take long for somebody to figure that you're up to something." Owens nodded.

"Right."

"So what do you need?"

"Your team. Every agent you've got. Maintaining their

positions on a twenty-four-hour standby. Nothing out of the ordinary, just ready to go.''

"You've got them," Owens said. And then after a moment: "You got a deputy for this task force of yours?''

"No.''

"You do now.''

Grynard nodded in a gesture of unspoken appreciation.

"So what about these wildlife agents?'' Owens asked. "Do they know they're the bait?''

"No, I don't think so," Grynard replied, a grim expression appearing on his tired face.

"You going to tell them?''

"No.''

"Why not?''

Grynard took in a deep breath and then let it out. "Because if we do, it's likely that they'll react to that information in some manner that will alert the people involved and cause them to break away and go to ground, where we'll never find them. I don't want that to happen. And,'' he added, "it's my impression that the wildlife agents don't want that to happen either. That's why they're down here.''

Owens turned to Theresa Fletcher.

"Mind if I ask how the U.S. Attorney's office feels about that?''

"Would you like the official opinion?''

"Sure, why not.''

"Officially, the U.S. Attorney's office has complete faith in the ability of the FBI to conduct their investigations and bring violators to justice without putting innocent civilians or any other law enforcement officers at unnecessary risk.''

"Ah," Owens said noncommittally. "And the unofficial opinion?''

"Agent Owens, over the past few months, I've managed to become very fond of those wildlife agents," the black prosecuting attorney said, a steely expression appearing in her dark eyes. "If any of them *do* come to harm, I fully intend to bring the responsible individuals to justice, even if I have to do it with my bare hands.''

The self-appointed deputy to Al Grynard's newly acquired task force nodded in apparent satisfaction.

''In that case, ma'am, I think you and I are going to get along just fine.''

Reaching down, Hal Owens picked up the two carry-on bags and then stared at Grynard.

''What do you say, Al? Ready to go meet your new team?''

''You don't have to do that, you know,'' Grynard said seriously as they all started walking toward the Jeep.

''What's that?''

''Turn your task force over to me. They're your agents. I'm perfectly willing to go along as an adviser. Supplemental case, however you want to handle it.''

Hal Owens stopped in his tracks.

''Al,'' he said, a gentle smile crossing his tanned and weathered face, ''let me explain something to you. About thirty years ago some bureaucratic old fart of a training officer sat Stanley, Jim, and me down in a room and explained to us how every well-planned FBI raid has a command post and a team leader who mans that post until every suspect is in custody and every agent is accounted for. 'There's the wrong way to do something, and then there's the FBI way,' is, I think, the way he put it.''

''Yeah, sure, but . . .''

''So the thing is, Al,'' Owens went on, the expression in his eyes changing from gentle amusement to something that wasn't gentle or amusing at all, ''when that guy with that four-bore—the guy who nailed my old buddy Stanley and all those other folks—pops his head up around here, gunning for those wildlife agents, and Bloom and all his little cockroach buddies start scurrying around looking for some place to hide, *you're* going to be the one doing things the FBI way: manning that command center until everybody's accounted for.

"And while you're doing that, Jim Whittman and I, and maybe even Ms. Fletcher here"—Owens smiled warmly at Theresa Fletcher—"we're going to be the ones kicking the goddamned doors."

Chapter Twenty-seven

It was the first time in nine long months that the ICER Committee had dared to meet—the first time since the deaths of Lisa Abercombie and Dr. Reston Wolfe and the downfall of Operation Counter Wrench had sent these wealthy and powerful conspirators scrambling for their private sanctuaries.

But even now, out of a fear that bordered on paranoia, they could only agree to meet on a Saturday evening at Harold Tisbury's Cat Island villa—a remote site on the toe end of a bootlike strip of land widely considered by the local inhabitants to be possessed by an uneasy gathering of mismatched Christian and Obeah spirits—as if the weekend, and the superstitions and the distant offshore location might somehow shield them from the terrifying specter of plodding bureaucrats and self-righteous zealots who tirelessly sought their total destruction.

Incredibly and ironically, for these were men of immense power, influence, and self-confidence, the self-imposed isolation of the ICER Committee had caused them to fall prey to that one element of human nature which seemed to have no known antidote or remedy:

The overwhelming nature of their greed had finally, and inevitably, overcome their fear of the unknown.

As planned, Sam Tisbury was the last to arrive.

But he did not arrive as planned.

Whether it was the certain knowledge that his father had been monitoring his movements with private detectives, or the simple—and understandable—belief than *none* of his fellow conspirators could be completely trusted, a sudden sense of intuition had caused Sam Tisbury to change his travel plans at the last minute.

Instead of taking his reserved commercial flight from Nassau's Oak Field airport to the Hawk's Nest Creek airstrip at the southern end of Cat Island, Sam Tisbury hesitated, considered some unpleasant possibilities, and then withdrew his pilot's license and his American Express card from his wallet.

It didn't take the owner and chief pilot of the small Air Shuttle Service long to decide that the offered fee of ten times his normal rate for a round-trip flight to Cat Island, plus a signed and verified insurance transfer on the plane, plus a five-hundred-dollar tip under the table for his trouble, represented a more than fair rental rate for a five-year-old twin prop that was long overdue for a scheduled overhaul.

Sam Tisbury's twin prop piloting skills were rusty—mostly because most of his flying the last couple of years had been limited to copiloting one of the corporation's Learjets—and he found himself caught up in the adrenaline-rich sensation of being at risk again, so he ended up taking a low-level sight-seeing course along the eastern shore of Eleuthera Island that extended what would have normally been a one-hour flight into almost two. Thus it was nearly five-thirty in the evening by the time he touched down at the small airstrip at Fernandez Bay, which was located just above ankle level on the Cat Island boot.

Which was another last-minute decision, because his flight plan had him landing at the Cutlass Bay airstrip some fifteen miles to the south.

It cost him a hundred-dollar bill to acquire the services of the local mechanic—who promised to tie the plane down, fill the gas tanks, and forget to mention the minor matter of an altered flight plan to the local customs official, who was busy tending to matters of a more personal nature and probably wouldn't have cared anyway—and another hundred to rent a battered red Jeep for the weekend. But that was okay, because now he had a hidden and remote escape route that no one else knew about.

Smiling to himself for the first time in several weeks, Sam Tisbury pulled out of the airport parking lot and began driving south along the narrow undivided asphalt road.

At precisely three minutes to six that Saturday evening, Sam Tisbury turned north off the main road about a mile from Devil's Point, then, about four miles later, made a sharp right turn into a narrow and mostly concealed driveway.

About a tenth of a mile up the winding dirt driveway, he stopped at a gate control box, identified himself to the hollow-sounding electronic voice, and then waited patiently for the freshly painted and lubricated iron gates to swing open.

He parked in one of the two remaining spots along a rock wall, and then allowed a pair of politely alert young men, both of whom were wearing casual clothing that effectively concealed their muscular bodies and lethal 9mm automatic pistols, to escort him up the rough-finished pathway to the open elevator.

Harold Tisbury was waiting for him on the third-floor foyer.

"I was beginning to get worried," the elder Tisbury said, the concern evident in his watery eyes. "Were there any problems?"

"No, just reliving a few pleasant memories," Sam Tisbury said. Then he noticed a pair of familiar figures standing a dozen feet away, next to the wide foyer window.

It was immediately apparent to Tisbury that the two men had been waiting for his arrival with growing impatience. Something also apparent, from the furtive glances that each of the men made into the empty elevator and the somber expressions on their faces, was the fact that they had been obviously expecting—or perhaps *hoping* was the better word, Tisbury decided—to see someone else also.

He had a brief moment to wonder *who?* before the two men turned in his direction.

"Hello, Nicholas, it's good to see you again," he said as he stepped forward and took the hand of the European Community's chief representative for the oil and gas industry.

"Yes," Nicholas Von Hagberg said in his inevitably cold and formal manner, the overhead lights reflecting off his high forehead and titanium-rimmed glasses. "It is good to see you also."

If there was any sincerity to his words at all, it was not the least bit evident in his voice.

"And Sergio," Sam Tisbury turned to Sergio Paz-Rios, the mercurial chairman of Amazon Global, a conglomerate of South American timber and wood products industries. "You're looking well, my friend."

Sergio Paz-Rios responded with a grunt and a curt nod as he shook hands. There was a flash of fear and accusation in his dark, piercing eyes before he turned back to stare out through the huge single-pane foyer window to the distant water below.

Proud, vain, manipulative, and absolutely ruthless by nature, the sixty-two-year-old Chilean industrialist presented himself as a man of supreme self-confidence, and one who was in complete control of his destiny. But in this case outward appearances were deceiving, Sam Tisbury reminded himself. Of all the ICER committee members, Sergio Paz-Rios had been the last to agree to the meeting.

Sam Tisbury had only a brief moment to consider all those factors when two more men emerged from the spacious sitting room of the luxurious three-story villa. "Jonathan. Wilbur. Thank you all for coming."

Then he looked around for the last familiar face, and immediately understood the expression he saw in Sergio Paz-Rios' dark eyes. He felt his heart sink.

"Has anyone seen or heard from Alfred?" he asked in a quiet voice. He glanced over at his father and saw the elder Tisbury shake his head slowly.

The other four looked at each other, their unspoken concern now open for all to see. It was the thing that every one of these incredibly wealthy and powerful men had come to fear during the last nine months of their suddenly confused and tortured lives: the terrifying possibility that at any moment one of them might suddenly lose his nerve.

It was a perfectly understandable fear, because each one of them possessed enough information on ICER and on each other to bring the entire conspiracy down around their heads . . . and to put them all in prison for the rest of their lives.

All, perhaps, except one, Sam Tisbury mused, knowing full well that every man in the room had long since experienced similar thoughts.

"We exchanged faxes early this morning," Wilbur Lee Edgarton, CEO of the Moss Mariner Mining Group, offered in a neutral voice after a moment. "He said he was in the sound, sailing a few miles offshore. He assured me that he would be here."

"He'd damn well *better* be here," Sergio Paz-Rios muttered darkly.

There were muttered nods of agreement all around.

"Perhaps we should adjourn to the dining room," Harold Tisbury suggested soothingly, having to work hard to conceal his own shaken nerves and anger. "Jean-Pierre tells me he's found an exceptional Chardonnay to complement his chowder this evening."

After a momentary hesitation he added: "And I'm sure that Alfred will be here momentarily."

The six industrialists walked across the sitting room, ignoring the wide expanse of window glass that provided a beautiful panoramic view of Exuma Sound and the distant Conception Island. They entered the huge formal dining room with a visible sense of apprehension, as if half expecting to see the ghosts of their ill-fated counterterrorist team waiting for them within the lavishly paneled walls.

Or, even worse, a team of Special Agents from the Federal Bureau of Investigation.

But instead the only person they saw as they took their seats around the solid teak and rosewood table was a man whose familiar face and invariably calm demeanor was immediately reassuring.

Walter Crane was the chief investigator for the firm of Little, Warren, Nobles & Kole, a very expensive Washington, D.C., legal firm whose primary mission in life during the last nine months had been to keep the ICER Committee members completely isolated from the judicial process.

To date, the firm had submitted billings to the International Commission for Environmental Restoration to the tune of three-point-two million dollars, mostly for work performed by Crane and his highly trained, talented, and motivated team of criminal investigators. The committee members had authorized their share of the payments without so much as a blink. But they were impatient men who expected results for their money. Harold Tisbury knew that they would only be put off for so long by fine wine and spicy chowder.

Deeply disturbed by the absence of one of their fellow conspirators, the men took their accustomed seats around the table. Harold Tisbury's serving staff took their cue and were immediately attentive. Bowls were filled from a steaming cauldron by Jean-Pierre himself as the wine steward personally opened and sampled each bottle. Second helpings were offered as the conversation gradually shifted to more pleasant topics, such as corporate profits and future holdings. Empty bowls and glasses were being replaced with mugs of hot tea and rich Colombian coffee when Harold Tisbury rapped a polished silver spoon against the side of his mug.

"Gentlemen," he acknowledged in a quietly dignified voice that hardly matched the chill in his cold, dark eyes. "I don't think we can wait for Alfred any longer."

The resulting silence was chilling, but Harold Tisbury went on.

"I believe we all know why we are here tonight. Apart from Alfred, there is only one item on the agenda this evening. A vote to either terminate the International Commission for Environmental Restoration or to go forward with a mission that we have all agreed is vital to the very survival of our nations, not to mention our own industrial enterprises.''

Harold Tisbury allowed his cold eyes to scan each of the six familiar faces seated around the table.

''I think it goes without saying that our first operation against the environmental extremist groups was an unmitigated disaster. Not only did we fail to meet our objectives and waste a fifty-million-dollar investment,'' the CEO said in a voice leaden with fatigue and disgust, ''but in doing so we may have alerted the authorities to ICER and to our activities, and thereby exposed ourselves to legal jeopardy.''

There were murmured nods of agreement around the table.

''We have many things to discuss,'' Harold Tisbury went on. ''However, before we begin that discussion,'' he said with a significance glance over at Walter Crane, ''I think we should listen to what our guest has to say.''

The murmuring was immediately hushed and they all turned their attention to Crane, who slowly stood up.

''Thank you, Harold.'' Crane nodded pleasantly to his host before turning to the table at large.

''Gentlemen,'' he began as his cool, penetrating eyes slowly swept around the table, ''Harold has invited me here today to present a synopsis of what we have discovered, to date, on the events leading up to the raid by federal authorities on Whitehorse Cabin. And also, to provide you with an estimate of the legal difficulties which the members of ICER may be facing as a consequence of that raid.''

Crane was well aware that he had their undivided attention.

''But before I do so, let me begin by saying that, *to date*,'' Crane emphasized those words with his voice and an upraised index finger, ''there is nothing to indicate that the FBI, or any other law enforcement entity, for that matter, is aware of the existence of this committee.''

There were sighs and murmured words of relief around the table.

''As far as we know,'' Crane went on, ''the FBI's investigation was effectively halted by the untimely and unfortunate deaths of Lisa Abercombie and Dr. Reston Wolfe, along with ten members of their Operation Counter Wrench team.''

While every man in the room was well aware of the underlying irony to Crane's words, there was no evidence of that in any of their faces.

''But there are still two members of that team in federal custody,'' Sergio Paz-Rios interrupted.

''Gerd Maas and Roy Parker.''

''Yes, exactly.'' the Chilean industrialist nodded. ''What if they decide to talk?''

''Maas will never talk, no matter what they do or what they say,'' Nicholas Von Hagberg said. There was a sense of chilling confidence in his voice.

''I have no doubt that Mr. Von Hagberg is correct,'' Crane replied easily. ''And you needn't worry about Mr. Parker either, because he's dead.''

''What?''

To Walter Crane's experienced eyes, every one of the ICER Committee members appeared to be surprised and shocked by the news. He shrugged inwardly. He really hadn't expected the matter to be resolved that easily.

''Mr. Parker is dead, and therefore no longer a concern,'' Crane repeated patiently. ''I'll explain the circumstances of his death in a moment. But before I do, I want to make certain that every one of you understands the sequence of events that led to the failure of Operation Counter Wrench.

''In essence, and as all of you are certainly aware,'' Crane began when no one interrupted, ''the initial failure occurred when Dr. Wolfe chose to spend his free time hunting—how shall we put it?—without benefit of a license or a legal hunting season. In order to do so, he engaged the services of three hunting guides, Mr. Alex Chareaux and his two brothers, who saw to it that he had ample opportunity to shoot at whatever he pleased, whenever and wherever he pleased.

"For reasons that are not entirely clear to us, Dr. Wolfe chose to take Ms. Lisa Abercombie and Dr. Morito Asai on one of his illicit hunts; unaware that a Mr. Henry Lightstone—whom they and apparently Mr. Chareaux knew then as Henry Allen Lightner—would also be involved in the hunt.''

"You told us all this the last time we met, and I don't see—'' Wilbur Lee Edgarton started to interrupt, but Crane held up his hand.

"Mr. Lightstone, as it turns out, was—and still is, I might add—a federal agent for the United States Fish and Wildlife Service.''

"Oh, dear God!'' Jonathan Chilmark whispered.

"Did anyone know of this?'' Nicholas Von Hagberg demanded, looking around the table at his fellow conspirators.

"Special Agent Lightstone's true identity was withheld by the U.S. Attorney's office until two weeks before the trial,'' Crane said calmly. "At that point they were obligated to release a copy of his investigative report to our attorneys through the discovery process.''

"But—'' Von Hagberg started to protest. Crane ignored him and continued.

"As of this morning, Agent Lightstone's identity in this case is a matter of public record, at least in the *Washington Post*. Up until last week I'd been keeping Mr. Harold Tisbury aware of our findings on an intermittent basis. I thought it''—Crane hesitated for a moment, as if searching for precisely the right word—"*unwise* for me to make similar contacts with the rest of the committee. I assumed that you would all prefer to wait until you were all together again.''

"And although I certainly kept Sam fully informed, for reasons of continuity if nothing else,'' Harold Tisbury said, making obvious reference to his poor health, "I chose not to say anything during our brief telephone conversations, for similar reasons. There was always the possibility that one of us might have been the subject of an authorized wire tap.''

He didn't have to mention a name. Everyone in the room, with the possible exception of Walter Crane, knew whom he was talking about: the one person on the committee with clear and irrefutable links to Lisa Abercombie, if the FBI dug deep enough.

Alfred Bloom.

"Yes, I agree, it was a wise decision all the way around.'' Von Hagberg nodded quickly.

"But it does get worse, I'm afraid,'' Crane went on. "It seems that when Special Agent Lightstone and the members of his special operations team effected an arrest of Mr. Chareaux and his brothers, for illegal guiding and assorted violations of the Endangered Species Act, Ms. Abercombie and Dr. Wolfe panicked.

"Now you must understand,'' Crane said, "that at this point, neither Ms. Abercombie nor Dr. Wolfe nor Dr. Asai were looked upon as suspects in this particular investigation. And in all likelihood, none of them would have ever *become* suspects, because these wildlife agents had no reason to view them as being anything other than illegal hunters. And as best we can tell, the agents weren't *interested* in pursuing charges against mere illegal hunters. One, because they were aware that the hunters were almost certainly using false names, and two, because they were completely focused on putting the Chareaux brothers out of business.

"But because Lisa Abercombie and Dr. Reston Wolfe believed otherwise,'' Crane said, adjusting his facial expression into a sad smile, "they made an attempt to block the agent's investigation.''

"What!'' Sam Tisbury exclaimed.

"Oh, yes.'' Crane nodded. "And when their bureaucratic approach didn't succeed, they simply turned Mr. Maas and his counterterrorist team loose on the agents, which—to no great surprise, since the agents didn't know they were being hunted—resulted in two of them being killed in rather short order.''

''Mother of Mary!'' Sergio Paz-Rios whispered.

''Indeed.'' Crane nodded in agreement. ''But the truly incredible part is that up until the final day—that is, the day of the raid on the Whitehorse Cabin training facility—Ms. Abercombie and Dr. Wolfe and apparently even Mr. Maas were under the impression that they had successfully eliminated the entire covert agent team. They had no idea that Henry Lightner—who was, in fact, Henry Lightstone, an ex-homicide investigator from the San Diego Police Department—was also a federal wildlife agent *and* a member of that covert team.

''The result of that error,'' Crane said, ''was the loss of an extremely expensive training facility; the deaths of Abercombie, Wolfe, ten members of the counterterrorist team, *and* both of Alex Chareaux's brothers; and ultimately, the complete failure of Operation Counter Wrench.''

''Not to mention the current prosecutions of Maas and Parker and Chareaux for the deaths of those three agents,'' Harold Tisbury added bitterly.

''Yes, I was about to get to that.'' Crane nodded. ''At the request of Harold Tisbury, we assigned one of our top attorneys, a Mr. Jason Bascomb III, and two of our leading associates to their defense.''

''Was that wise?'' Wilbur Lee Edgarton interrupted.

''In retrospect, perhaps not,'' Crane said with an ironic twist to his smile, ''but we *are* a large and well-known legal firm in the District, and it wouldn't be unusual for someone with Mr. Chareaux's presumed wealth to engage our services.

''However, in the meantime,'' Crane went on, ''we decided that it might be useful to keep track of the whereabouts of Mr. Henry Lightstone and his fellow agents—who, as it turned out, were engaged in setting up another covert operation in Boston, Massachusetts. So we engaged the services of what I will describe here as a pair of streetwise surveillance experts whose names, if you don't mind, will remain anonymous for the time being.''

''Why is that?'' Nicholas Von Hagberg asked suspiciously.

''Among other reasons, because both of them were found dead in a Boston alley four days ago.''

''The agents killed them?'' Jonathan Chilmark, the president of the Northwest Timber Alliance, blurted out.

''Perhaps.'' Crane shrugged. ''To tell you the truth, I seriously doubt that they would have done any such thing. However, given their notable success with the Operation Counter Wrench team, it's hardly a possibility that we can safely ignore.''

''You said 'initially'?'' Sam Tisbury noted.

''That was before an attempt was made—last Wednesday—to kill the entire wildlife agent team, Mr. Lightstone included, by blowing up the warehouse that they were using for their 'sting' operation.''

Crane paused to look around at each of the ICER Committee faces individually.

''You think one of *us* did something like that?'' Wilbur Lee Edgarton exclaimed.

''I would certainly *hope* that none of you made an attempt, either as individuals *or* as a group, to resolve your problems with these agents in such a manner,'' Crane said with pointed emphasis on the word *or*. ''Because if one of you *did*, and we find out about it, I can assure you that your relationship with the firm of Little, Warren, Nobles & Kole will be terminated immediately.''

''But why in the *world* would one of *us*—'' Jonathan Chilmark started to say, but Crane cut him off.

''I'm not suggesting that any of you here actually *did* it,'' Crane said, ''I'm simply saying that it would be an incredibly stupid thing to do. Especially now.''

''Mr. Crane,'' Wilbur Lee Edgarton interrupted in his deepest southern accent, ''I may not be the smartest man in this room, but I seem to recall that the firm of Little, Warren,

Nobles & Kole has been perfectly willing to take our money to defend two individuals who were certainly *involved*—directly or otherwise—in a great deal of killing about nine months ago. Now I'm just curious, Mr. Crane, why this large and well-known Washington, D.C., law firm of yours has suddenly gotten so gawddamned self-righteous about the deaths of a couple of street bums, or surveillance experts, or whatever the hell it was you called them?''

"You make a perfectly valid point, Mr. Edgarton," Crane said with apparently unflappable calm. "Like any law firm, we make no inferences as to the actual guilt or innocence of our clients. We simply endeavor to provide them with the best possible legal defense—"

"That money can buy?" Sam Tisbury finished.

"Yes, of course." Crane nodded. "It's no secret that our legal system has always provided certain, shall we say, *advantages* to the wealthy? That's a given. But it's also not the point."

"Then just what *is* the point, Mr. Crane?" Wilbur Lee Edgarton demanded with thinly veiled sarcasm.

"The point is that our law firm takes a dim view of having three of our attorneys murdered by one of our clients."

"What?"

A chair and a water glass went crashing to the floor as Harold Tisbury lunged to his feet, his face reddened with shock and rage. All the other ICER members stared at Crane and each other in silent disbelief.

"I suggest you sit down, Mr. Tisbury . . .." Crane said with amazing calm.

"This is an outrage!"

". . . before you have a stroke," the legal investigator finished.

"And yes, you're absolutely right," Crane went on as the elder Tisbury stumbled back into his chair with the assistance of his son, "it *is* an outrage. It's just a question of who and why."

"Would you care to explain yourself, Mr. Crane?" Sam Tisbury demanded.

"Certainly. I'll begin by advising you that last Friday, yesterday, at approximately four-fifteen in the afternoon, someone managed to remove Alex Chareaux from federal custody; and in doing so, managed to kill four deputy U.S. Marshalls."

"Chareaux is loose?" Sergio Paz-Rios blinked, showing no apparent concern for the federal law enforcement officials.

"Oh, yes, he *is* loose, Mr. Paz-Rios, I can assure you of that. And so, by the way, is Mr. Maas."

Had a small pin been dropped on the huge rosewood table, every one in the room would have heard it.

"How did Maas escape?" Nicholas Von Hagberg finally rasped.

"We're not sure, Mr. Von Hagberg," Crane said evenly. "It seems that at seven-thirty yesterday evening, someone— very possibly the same individual, from what we've learned of the investigation so far—managed to track or follow Mr. Bascomb to a house in Warrenton, Virginia, where we were keeping Mr. Maas and Mr. Parker in protective custody. That someone broke into the residence, killed all four body-guards—all of whom, by the way, were retired federal law enforcement officers—killed Mr. Parker, Mr. Bascomb and both of his associates, and then apparently left with Gerd Maas."

The overwhelming reaction of the ICER Committee to this news was for the individual members to shake their heads and blink in stunned disbelief.

"But even worse, if such a description has any possible meaning in this situation," Crane went on, "whoever was responsible for these killings apparently left evidence to suggest that the murders were committed by other federal law enforcement officers."

"I don't understand any of this." Nicholas Von Hagberg shook his head. "Are you suggesting that these federal wildlife agents did in fact kill your surveillance employees, your bodyguards, and Roy Parker, *and* your attorneys? And then kidnaped Maas and Chareaux?''

"No, Mr. Von Hagberg." Crane sighed. "I'm suggesting nothing of the sort. What I *am* suggesting is that someone tried to make it look that way. Only they didn't do a very good job of it. Which raises the interesting question of who might stand to gain by removing Maas, Parker, and Chareaux from federal custody and trying to make it *look* like these wildlife agents committed these murders."

"You mean one of us? Do you think we are that *stupid*?" Von Hagberg demanded, incredulous.

Crane remained silent for a good ten seconds.

"I certainly hope not," the legal investigator finally said, his voice deadly serious now. "Because, at the risk of being repetitive, if one or more of you gentlemen *did* set any of these incredible events into motion, then I'm here on behalf of Little, Warren, Nobles & Kole to advise you that you are a committee of fools. And we have no intention of representing fools, no matter how wealthy and influential they may be."

"Then on behalf of my associates here," Nicholas Von Hagberg said, his Teutonic features reddened with rage, "let me be the one to tell you that your services—"

"*Before* you vent your anger, Mr. Von Hagberg," Crane said in a firm voice, raising his hand as his eyes flashed with anger for the first time that evening, "and *before* you expose your fellow committee members to further risk, you might be interested to learn one final thing. Those wildlife agents that we've been talking about? Well, it's very likely that they're somewhere in the Bahamas right now. And so, I might add, is Grynard, the FBI agent who was initially responsible for the Alaska investigation into the death of wildlife agent McNulty."

The ICER Committee members were too far gone to be shocked anymore.

Finally Nicholas Von Hagberg managed to speak.

"Do you know where?" he rasped in a shaken voice.

"Yesterday, at two o'clock in the morning, Henry Lightstone and four of his associates arrived at the Windbreaker Marina in Fort Lauderdale. They boarded a large sports fishing yacht apparently owned by a man who makes a living running charter fishing trips in the Bahamas. The boat was observed leaving the marina at five o'clock yesterday morning, heading in an easterly direction. That's the last we've seen of them."

"Do you know the name of the boat?" Von Hagberg asked.

"No. The one boat owner our investigator was able to talk with before the body was found and the police arrived had only met the yacht owner once, and they'd only had a casual conversation about good fishing areas out in the islands."

"What body?" the Teutonic industrialist whispered.

"A young man who worked at the dock. He was found in a van with his neck broken."

"The agents?" Von Hagberg asked in disbelief.

"We don't know yet, but we are continuing the investigation." Crane shrugged. "As far as Special Agent Grynard is concerned, he was observed approximately"—the private investigator looked down at his watch—"ninety minutes ago, meeting with a pair of FBI agents at the San Salvador airport, which I believe is approximately sixty miles from our current location."

Sergio Paz-Rios muttered a fervent curse.

"But . . . but do you know why they would be coming *here*, to the Bahamas? And why now? I mean, they . . . they can't possibly know about our meeting," Von Hagberg stammered, seemingly unaware that he was still standing.

"Yes, I *do* know," Crane said, pausing dramatically to look around the room one last time.

"They're looking for Alfred Bloom."

The only sound in the dining room was that of an absolutely stunned Nicholas Von Hagberg collapsing back down into his chair.

Crane was starting for the door when Harold Tisbury finally found his voice.

"Walter," he rasped hoarsely, "please . . . don't leave just yet."

"Why not?"

"Because . . . because we—or at least I—wish to continue making use of your services."

Crane looked around the room and observed that all six heads were nodding solemnly now.

"All right," he said finally, with what Harold Tisbury and all the others could only think of, in the circumstances, as incredible calm, "what would you like me to do?"

Chapter Twenty-eight

"So what's the deal?" Henry Lightstone asked as he watched the beautiful Arthur's Town nurse carefully wrap the soaked plaster bandage around Larry Paxton's still swollen right forearm.

"Negotiations seem to be getting a little complicated," Mike Takahara replied.

"What's that mean?"

"He wants a demonstration flight first."

"Oh, yeah? What kind of demonstration?" Paxton asked suspiciously.

"You know, the normal stuff." The tech agent shrugged. "Turn the engine on, takeoff, landing, that sort of thing. Say, are casts supposed to be that thick?"

"Oh, yes." The exceptionally attractive but suspiciously youthful nurse nodded. "My father always says: big arm, big cast." She gave Paxton another one of her heart-melting smiles and then walked slowly over to the counter, her firm hips and legs stretching the thin fabric of her tight skirt, to begin soaking another plaster bandage.

Larry Paxton rested his head back against the wall, closed his eyes, sighed, and shook his head slowly.

"What's the matter, Paxton, starting to feel your age?" Lightstone suggested with a certain degree of sympathy, because he too was finding it difficult to ignore the eye-catching movements of the muscular young woman. If pressed, he would have guessed that she was either fifteen or sixteen, but he wouldn't have been at all surprised if she turned out to be considerably younger or older. It occurred to him to wonder how and where she had managed to obtain her medical training.

"Maybe, but I'm not *about* to start feeling my son's age," the acting team leader muttered.

"Glad to hear it." Lightstone smiled, and then winced as he glanced down at his watch.

Henry Lightstone was starting to get uneasy because they'd been at the small Cat Island airport—which, as best he could tell, also served as the local customs office, police station, clinic, and island rental agency—for over half an hour now, trying to arrange a flight to Nassau. And the realization that they were leaving themselves exposed and vulnerable to whoever had been dogging their trial the last five days was beginning to work on his nerves.

It had taken Mike Takahara nearly a half hour to get the *Lone Granger* up and running again. Then it took the agents another forty-five minutes—with Takahara at the helm, Paxton monitoring the sonar screen, Lightstone and Stoner hanging out over the railings watching for reefs and coral heads, and using the red flashing lights on Arthur's Town's two-hundred-foot Batelco tower as a reference point—to cautiously approach and then anchor the huge boat in close enough to the northernmost town on the narrow forty-eight-mile-long island so that they could motor in to the dock with the much smaller Zodiac.

Figuring out how to anchor the massive yacht offshore, with only the owner's manual and Justin LaGrange's inexpert help as a guide, had been one of the more challenging problems of the entire trip. They finally solved it by sending Stoner down with the scuba gear again to move the forward and aft anchors into position with his bare hands and muscular shoulders. But in doing so, he managed to wrench one of his knees—which immediately began to swell—which meant they now had one more candidate for the Nassau hospital trip.

So now they were trying to negotiate a rental agreement for a fifteen-year-old, single-engined Cessna that was visibly held together in some places with strips of gray duct tape. And they hadn't seen any sign of anyone watching their movements yet. But just the same, Lightstone didn't want to push their luck any more than he had to.

"You know, Paxton, Snoopy's got a point about that cast," Lighthouse said thoughtfully. "If you guys end up having to ditch that plane in the water, you're gonna go down like a rock."

The young nurse turned around with an alarmed look on her face.

"No, that's all right, nothing to worry about. He's just making a joke," Paxton said hurriedly, giving his youthful nurse a reassuring smile that sent her happily on her way to check on Bobby LaGrange and Mo-Jo, both of whom were lying on a pair of cots in the back of the terminal building.

And probably to continue her flirtation with Justin, Lightstone thought to himself with a smile, wondering if there had been any young women around like that when he had been Justin's age. He found it depressing to realize that he couldn't remember.

"And a bad one at that," Larry Paxton muttered, after the girl had disappeared through the door.

"Think maybe we ought to go back to the boat and get him one of those scuba tanks, just in case?" Mike Takahara suggested.

"Better pick up a couple. It's still a long way to walk," Lightstone smiled.

"Ah don't want to hear about it," the acting team leader growled.

But then, after a moment, Paxton brought his head forward, opened his eyes, and looked over at Lightstone. "What about it, Henry?" he asked. "You think Woeshack can pull it off?"

"What, you mean the demonstration?"

"Uh huh."

"Well, actually, all things considered, he's really not all that bad on takeoffs," Lightstone said.

"How many did you guys do when you were up there in Alaska?"

"A couple."

"They work out okay?"

"Yeah, sure."

"What about the landings."

"You *really* want to know?"

"Probably not, but tell me anyway."

"Well, first of all, we were in a float plane, which probably isn't the same thing," Lightstone hedged.

"Come on, Henry."

"The first time we tried to land"—Lightstone shrugged—"we basically skipped like a stone for about half a mile before the engine cut out, or he shut it off, I'm not sure which. The second time we ended up in a tree and had to pull ourselves out before the plane burned. But that's only because he was going to try to hit the bad guys with the prop if I missed with the rifle," he added with a cheerful smile.

Paxton stared at his wild-card agent for a long moment.

"Tell me you're shitting me," he finally said.

"No, I wouldn't do that to you, Larry," Lightstone said with a straight face. "That's no way to show respect for a boss who really tries to do the right thing."

"Respect, mah ass," Paxton whispered hoarsely. "The last boss you had, you and LaGrange floated out in the middle of the ocean, in the middle of the night, in an exploding coffin." Larry Paxton had never gotten over hearing Rico

Testano tell the story of what Henry and Bobby LaGrange had done to their boss on the San Diego PD at the homicide investigator's convention where Rico had met Henry Lightstone. Lightstone and LaGrange had launched their inebriated and unconscious boss out in the San Diego Harbor in a coffin packed with ice and Mexican firecrackers on a delayed fuse and had both been demoted for it.

"Well, yeah, but that was more a sign of affection than anything else."

"Henry, listen to me, serious now," Paxton said, looking over his shoulder to make sure that neither the resident manager of the airport or his daughter the nurse were within hearing distance. "Tell me the truth. You *really* think this is a good idea?"

"I wouldn't necessarily use the word *good*," Lightstone admitted, "but I think it's probably the best choice we've got. The next scheduled flight isn't until Monday, and I don't think we can wait that long to get Bobby and Mo-Jo to that hospital in Nassau. And Stoner's knee's looking worse every hour.

"Besides," he added in a quieter voice, looking around to make sure that the nurse was still gone, "I want to get Justin out of here as fast as I can, before that asshole on the aquasled starts trying to blow us up again."

"We could still try to make it with the boat," Paxton said.

"What do you think, Snoopy?" Lightstone asked, looking up at their tech agent. "Any second thoughts?"

"Same deal, no guarantees we'd ever get there." Mike Takahara shrugged. "We're talking about a hundred-mile run with an electrical system that's cut out on us twice already. Besides, with Mo-Jo and Bobby out of operation, none of us knows anything about all the tides and buoys and coral heads and crawfish traps around here. And the thing is, if we try to make it tonight, at any kind of speed, there's a real good chance we'll end up running aground, even if we stay clear of the shorelines."

"Which still leaves us the Coast Guard," Paxton reminded.

"Yeah, but if we contact them, everybody with a radio and a scanner around here is going to know about it, which means we're going to lose Bloom *and* our link to all those other assholes who had McNulty and Scoby and Ruebottom killed," Lightstone argued.

"Who are also probably the same people who've been trying to knock the rest of us off ever since," Mike Takahara added. "Thing is, you gotta figure if they can rig a bomb like that, then they've probably got at least a couple of people monitoring the radio frequencies around here."

"Just means we'd have to start over again," Paxton said unconvincingly.

"Which one of you guys is going to tell that to Bobby?" Takahara asked. "The last time I mentioned the Coast Guard, he told me to either forget it or get the hell off his boat. You try to strap him into some Coast Guard chopper, knowing that we blew the investigation on his account, he's *really* going to be pissed."

"Not to mention the fact that the Coast Guard will probably want to see some proof that one of us actually knows how to operate an eighty-two-foot fishing yacht," Lightstone added. "By the time we work our way through all that crap, Bloom's going to be long gone. And if he learns we're on to him, then he's just going to disappear for good."

"Although that's not always so easy to do these days," Takahara said. "We found him this time."

"Yeah, but what are you going to do if he switches to cash?" Lightstone asked. "Major industrialist. Shit-pot full of money. If he gets a head start, he could probably go a long time before he had to cash a check."

The tech agent shrugged his wide shoulders.

"Okay, I'm convinced," Paxton sighed, starting to get up. "Let me see if I can talk this guy into—"

"Wait a minute," Henry Lightstone said. "Let me try something first."

Lightstone walked over to the far side of the terminal where Special Agent/Pilot Thomas Woeshack and a tall, slender Bahamian native who looked to be in his late forties were involved in an animated discussion.

"Sir, can I talk with you a minute?" Lightstone said to the tall man.

"Yes, mon, of course. I am Sidney Bordeaux, manager of the airport. How can I help you?"

"Excuse me just a second, Mr. Bordeaux. Ah, Woeshack, why don't you go over and kick the tires a couple of times, make sure everything checks out okay so Larry doesn't have a seizure up there, while I work out the details with Mr. Bordeaux here."

Lightstone waited until the cheerfully agreeable agent had disappeared into the cockpit of the ancient plane before turning back to the airport manager, who immediately began the conversation by saying in a hopeful manner, "You are happy with my daughter, how she takes care of your friends?"

"Uh, yes, she's a beautiful child, and a very good nurse too, I'm sure, but—"

"She *is* a good nurse, and as you say, very beautiful too. Very fair, just like her mother, God rest her soul." The man nodded sadly. "And that, of course, is my problem, because all the young men . . . well, you know how it is."

"I, uh—"

"So what I must do is find her a husband quickly, before it is too late. A good 'Conchy Joe' who will give me many fair and beautiful grandchildren, just like her. Perhaps you are looking for a good wife?"

"Uh, actually—"

"It is obvious, of course, that my daughter is attracted to your friend, and my sense is that he is a very good man, even if he is a little dark—which would not be so good for the children here in the Islands as the other way around, you understand. But then I am dark like that, too, and as you saw, my daughter was born fair, so who can know how things will work out, yes?''

''Uh, Mr. Bordeaux, the last time I checked, Larry was still married and had two children about your daughter's age.''

''Ah, then that settles that.'' The airport manager smiled with some evident relief. ''But perhaps the young man in your party is interested?''

''I'm sure he is *very* much interested.'' Lightstone smiled. ''But the reason I came over here is that I wanted to explain to you that we are with the United States Federal Government.'' He held his government ID card out for inspection, but kept his thumb over the law enforcement insignia.

''Oh, so then it is *you* who are here to help *me*, instead of the other way around!'' The Bahamian native grinned widely. ''A good joke, yes?''

''A very good joke,'' Lightstone nodded, ''but what I was going to say . . .''

But the manager wasn't paying any attention, because he was peering more closely at the card in Lightstone's hand.

''It says on your card that you are also from the Fish and Wildlife Service? Is that true?''

''Uh, yes. Actually, the Fish and Wildlife Service is a part of the federal government, I guess.''

''Wonderful.'' The man smiled widely again. ''Because that means you *can* help me.''

Before Lighthouse could say anything else, the Bahamian native disappeared, then quickly reappeared with a rusty wire basket attached to a long rope. He handed the dripping basket and rope to Lightstone.

''I would like another one,'' he said.

''You want a new basket?''

''Oh, no, mon.'' The manager waved his hand impatiently. ''Not the basket. The peter.''

''The *what*?''

''Another one of these, mon.''

The manager reached into the basket and lifted up a large

moss-covered turtle that—from Lightstone's nonexpert point of view—had clearly seen better days.

"You want me to get you another turtle?"

"Yes, mon, I do. Very badly. Can you do that for me?"

"I suppose I could, but—"

"I will make you a deal. You sign a contract and promise to bring me a new peter, a big one, your word of honor as a representative of the United States Fish and Wildlife Service, then the plane is yours. You pay for the fuel, and one hundred dollars an hour, flight time only. No demonstration of skill is necessary. If your pilot crashes the airplane, your federal government will replace it and you will still owe me the peter."

"On behalf of the United States Fish and Wildlife Service," Lightstone said, taking the manager's hand in a firm handshake, "you've got yourself a deal."

Two minutes later, as the manager took the hastily scribbled contract out of Lightstone's hand and hurried over to help Woeshack top off the fuel tanks, Mike Takahara appeared at Lightstone's shoulder.

"I understand we are now the proud renters of what might actually be a flyable airplane," the tech agent said. "How'd you do it?"

"Simple." Lightstone shrugged. "I promised to get him another one of these." He held up the still dripping basket for inspection. "It was either that or marry his daughter."

"You mean the kid nurse?"

"Uh huh."

"You might want to see if she's still a viable option," Mike Takahara said as he cautiously examined the unmoving creature.

"What are you talking about?" Lightstone demanded. "We're the Fish and Wildlife Service, for Christ's sake. So I have to go find the guy another turtle. How hard can that be?"

"Probably a lot harder than you think. Unless I'm mistaken, that looks like a Cat Island turtle."

"Yeah, so?"

"Cat Island turtles are on the Endangered Species list. And as I recall, they're pretty near extinct."

Lightstone blinked, and then stared at the tech agent in disbelief.

"The Bahamians like to keep them in their wells for good luck," the tech agent explained. "And also as a source of food if things start getting a little tight, which I gather must have happened fairly frequently. Either that, or they're a lot better eating than anyone around here is willing to admit."

"Christ, I just signed a contract with this guy. How the hell am I going to get him another turtle like this if there aren't any?"

"Well, I suppose you could always try sneaking into some of the neighboring wells late at night," Takahara said thoughtfully. "But I wouldn't be surprised if these folks know every Cat Island turtle on the island by name and serial number. Probably not a good idea."

"So what can he do if I don't pay up?"

"Well, I suppose he could sue you, for a start."

"Over a *turtle*?"

"A very *valuable* turtle," the tech agent corrected. "For which we clearly received valuable payment in kind, namely one more or less functional airplane. All things considered, he'd probably have a pretty decent case."

"You're a lot of help."

"Science can do only so much."

"Hey, that's right. What about our lab? You think if I sent them this one, the DNA people could make some more?"

"I don't know, Henry. If it was that easy, these little guys probably wouldn't be on the endangered list in the first place. But thanks for reminding me—I've got to check in with the lab anyway. I'll ask about the DNA, but I wouldn't get my hopes up if I were you."

"So what do I do with this one, put it back in the well?"

"No, I wouldn't recommend you do that, unless you're planning on giving it CPR first."

"You mean it's dead?" Lightstone stared down into the basket and then poked the immobile creature with his finger. It still didn't move.

"That would be my guess."

"Why the hell didn't he tell me that before we signed the deal?"

"Probably because he expected a member of the Fish and Wildlife Service to be able to tell a dead turtle from a live one," Mike Takahara suggested. "And besides, if you stop to think about it, that's also probably why he wanted a new one."

"Ah."

"Pig in a poke, turtle in a basket. Sounds like it's pretty much the same thing." The tech agent shrugged.

"Tell you what," Lightstone said as he gingerly lowered the basket into a nearby trash can, "you check in with the lab and I'll help Woeshack get everybody loaded up. Then we can figure out how to solve our turtle problem."

"You mean *your* turtle problem," Takahara corrected.

"Yeah, right."

Fifteen minutes later all six occupants were securely fastened in the Cessna: Woeshack and Stoner in the pilot and copilot seats, Paxton and Bobby LaGrange in the rear seats, and Justin LaGrange and Mo-Jo tucked in the rear storage area next to the mandatory inflatable life raft.

"Everybody got their life jackets on?" Lightstone asked, standing next to the Cessna's left rear door.

"You're acting pretty damned cheerful for somebody who's being left behind to fight off the bad guys and take care of my boat in the process," Bobby LaGrange said suspiciously.

"Hey, if I let you guys hang around here much longer, probably you'd end up being a grandpa and it would be my fault, 'cause the turtle died."

"*What?*"

"Never mind," Lightstone said, winking at Justin who

had an embarrassed grin on his face. "I'll explain it all to you later."

After helping Bobby LaGrange to secure the door, Henry Lightstone walked around behind the plane to the open right rear door and slapped Larry Paxton on the shoulder.

"Mike and I are going to try to park ourselves somewhere off Devil's Point, see what we can stir up," Lightstone said. "You guys get clear, you ought to be able to find us on channel two."

Paxton nodded glumly.

"And don't forget to remind Woeshack about the floats on this thing before you land."

A perplexed expression appeared on Larry Paxton's face. He stuck his head out the door, looked down at the Cessna's ancient but still serviceable rubber tires, and then stared back up at his wild-card agent.

"Henry, what the hell are you talkin' about? Look for yourself. There ain't no floats on this plane."

"That's right." Lightstone smiled. "Have a nice flight."

In a series of very slow and deliberate motions, Larry Paxton worked his tall, lanky body out of the small plane. Then he turned around and stuck his head back into the rear cargo area.

"Mo-Jo," he said, "why don't you sit up here. It'll be a lot more comfortable for both you and Justin."

Once the Bahamian native had repositioned himself, Paxton shut and secured the door, and then slapped the side of the plane and said, "Woeshack, get your sorry pilot's ass out of here before Ah change my mind."

Nodding his head agreeably, the Eskimo special agent/ pilot engaged the starter and throttle and then began to rev up the engine.

"You really think it's a good idea to trust the kid nurse with your arm *and* your will power?" Lightstone asked as he and Paxton backed away from the slowly taxiing airplane.

"No, Ah don't." The acting team leader shook his head. "But Ah don't think it's a good idea to trust Woeshack with mah ass, or you two with mah boat neither."

Chapter Twenty-nine

They remained anchored in the small protective cove for over an hour, alternately allowing the slow rocking of the boat to guide the motion of their oiled and sweaty bodies against each other, and then losing control again and again as they both sought to release the sexual tension they had purposefully allowed to build up all afternoon.

Finally, their urges temporarily sated and exhaustion nearly complete, they lay together side by side in the semi-darkness, letting the warm air from the open, stainless steel ports flow over their naked bodies until Alfred Bloom suddenly blinked his eyes open.

"What time is it?" he whispered weakly.

Anne-Marie turned her head toward the starboard-mounted dressing table. "Seven-forty-six. I think it's about time we got going."

Bloom groaned loudly and started to sit up, but then changed his mind and dropped his head back onto the pillow.

"What's the matter, lover? Getting a little tired?" She giggled in that exotic, deep-throated voice that suddenly made Bloom want to reach for her again. But she easily evaded his grasp.

"Make up your mind, buddy-boy," she warned. "Do you have to be at that meeting or don't you?"

Bloom closed his eyes, sighed, and nodded his head slowly. "I have to be there."

"Tell you what," she said as she brought herself up onto her hands and knees, and then leaned over and placed a gentle kiss on his forehead, "since you're probably going to have to be awake for this meeting, and I'm not, why don't you catch a couple of winks while I take us in?''

Bloom started to protest, but she shifted her position and quickly silenced him with a much longer and far more passionate kiss. ''It's okay,'' she said. ''I promise I'll stay in the middle of the sound and take it nice and slow and easy.''

''Like you do everything else?''

''No, *not* like I do everything else,'' she responded with a breathless laugh as she evaded his fondling hands again. ''And besides, that way I can take a nap and be wide-awake when you get back.''

''Wide-awake, huh?''

''And ready to go.'' She nodded, her lips forming that familiar mischievous smile as she sat up, allowing the dimmed cabin lights to reflect across the oily curves of her full breasts and illuminate the small matched pair of Scarlet Macaws that Bloom had found so enticing.

''You never did tell me how you got those,'' he reminded, gently running his forefinger in an oily circle around the intricately etched parrot tattoo on the inner curve of her right breast that was a mirror image of the one on her left.

''Later,'' she whispered, ''but only if you're good.''

''Okay.'' Bloom nodded, surrendering to the enticement of the soft mattress and the equally irresistible promise of more sex later. ''You're on.''

By the time he closed his eyes, he had completely forgotten about Special Agent Al Grynard and the scheduled meeting the following morning.

Alfred Bloom was already starting to drift away when she stepped into the master cabin head and turned on the shower. He never heard the woman he knew as Anne-Marie go back up the companionway, nor did he hear the clanking sound of the anchor being raised by the electric windlass.

He was snoring steadily when the muffled sound of the Yanmar starter turning over caused him to jerk half awake. But the pitch of the powerful marine diesel quickly evened out into a steady, bubbling rumble, and Bloom sank back directly into the dark abyss of a deep and needful sleep as the

368 ◆ *Ken Goddard*

bow of the *Sea Amber* began to slice through the calm water once again.

Fifteen minutes later he was jarred awake by a violent wrenching motion that slammed his head into the teak bulkhead surrounding the sides of the berth.

His first conscious thought was that they had struck another boat.

He tried to move and was immediately aware that his head and arms hurt, and that the rumbling sounds of the marine diesel had changed to a high-pitched shrieking. Then, suddenly, the engine shut off and the boat rocked silently in the darkness.

He stumbled up the companionway ladder, only vaguely aware that he was completely naked.

"What happened?" he gasped as he saw her working quickly at the cockpit controls, checking gauges and shutting off switches. Her face was just barely illuminated by the dim lights on the control panel. He realized immediately that she'd been motoring with just the running lights on the bow and stern, to protect her night vision.

"I don't know," she replied, her voice sounding shaky but still controlled. "But I think whatever we hit is probably tangled up in the prop."

They both climbed down to the swim platform that encompassed the full expanse of the stern, and he held her arm as she used a gaff to probe around the skeg-hung rudder and propeller.

"Oh, shit," she said as she felt the hook catch on something.

"What is it?"

"A goddamned net," she muttered as she pulled a portion of what was clearly a large expanse of dark fish net to the surface.

"Can you get it loose?"

"I don't know, I'm trying," she grunted as she leaned outward and thrust her arm deeper into the dark water, trying to work the gaff back around the rudder to the propeller.

After a few minutes of fruitless effort, they switched places and Bloom attempted to use his longer arms to some advantage.

They finally gave up when it was apparent that the net was tightly wrapped around the propeller shaft. Bloom set the gaff aside and they sat shoulder to shoulder on the swim platform.

"Aren't they supposed to have markers or lights on those damn things?" Bloom muttered as he stared out across the water at the still distant harbor lights.

"They're supposed to," she acknowledged, "but they didn't, or I would have seen them in the running lights."

Bloom was thinking about the faxed messages now, wondering for the first time why the ICER Committee had decided at the last minute to change the time of the meeting to nine o'clock in the evening, when everyone knew that Harold Tisbury was rarely able to stay awake past ten. And why FBI agent Al Grynard would pick Rum Cay—of all places— for an early morning meeting, unless he knew for sure that Bloom would have the *Sea Amber* anchored somewhere nearby.

The possibility that Grynard knew about his planned overnight stay with his new companion at the Cutlass Bay Club—or worse, much worse, the ICER meeting at the Devil's Point villa—caused Bloom to shudder in spite of the warm weather.

He was also remembering, much too late now, that he hadn't tried to get word to Grynard through the ship-to-shore, as he'd intended, because he'd been distracted. Which meant it was all too possible that the FBI Agent might be waiting for him at the Hawk's Nest marina.

"I felt something hit the keel," she went on as they both stared out over the water, "and I tried to back her off, but it was too late, and then . . . aw, shit," she whispered in frustration.

"Not your fault," he said consolingly. "Storms probably

tear them loose from their moorings. No way you could have seen it.''

''I suppose, but that doesn't help you any.''

''Why's that?''

''You've got a meeting to be at in about half an hour, remember?''

Bloom nodded. ''That's all right, I'll still make it. We'll just have to go down there and pull it loose.''

He felt her body stiffen.

''What's the matter? Does diving at night bother you?''

She shook her head. ''No, not normally. But I—uh—just started my period, so . . .'' She hesitated and looked out over the dark surface of the water again. ''. . . I'm not sure it's a good idea.''

''No, it's not,'' Bloom agreed as he got to his feet and then climbed back up into the cockpit. A few moments later he was back on the swim platform with a face plate, swim fins, a diving light, and a sheath knife in his hands.

''You sure you're going to be okay under there by yourself?'' she asked hesitantly as he strapped the knife sheath around his waist and then sat on the edge of the platform and began to pull the swim fins onto his feet.

''I've been taking midnight swims off boats ever since I was a kid.'' He shrugged. ''I'll be fine. Why, did you see any activity on the way in?''

By activity, he was referring not only to the obvious dorsal fins, but also to schools of fish that might draw the presence of some of Exuma Sound's more dangerous predators.

''No, but that doesn't mean it isn't dangerous.''

She realized, as soon as the words left her mouth, that she might have gone too far; but she tried to reassure herself that it was all part of the act. How would it look if she didn't act concerned, she told herself.

But that rationalization didn't stop a cold chill from running down her back.

''I'll stay in close to the boat,'' he said reassuringly as he reached for the face mask. ''You stay up on top and keep a lookout. You see anything just rap on the hull three times. I'll be back on board in a flash.''

"Uh—speaking of flashing . . .'' she reminded.

Bloom glanced down at his exposed genitals and shrugged his shoulders as he cleared the face plate and then adjusted the mask and snorkel over his head. "I doubt that I'm going to shock anybody down there, especially at this time of night.''

"That's not exactly what I was worried about.''

"Well, then, how about if I promise not to get bit in any vital area?'' he teased.

"They're your goodies, buddy-boy, not mine,'' she smiled back, "but try to be careful anyway. We may need them later on this evening.''

Alfred Bloom winked in reply, took a deep breath, and then eased himself over the edge of the swim platform and into the dark water.

The water was relatively warm, and the visibility wasn't too bad with the diving light. But in spite of his brave talk, Bloom wasn't all that enthusiastic about diving under a boat at night by himself. He looked around quickly to convince himself—to the extent possible—that there really *wasn't* some nightmarish creature lurking out there in the dark shadows. Then, momentarily reassured, he used the slippery six-and-a-half-foot rudder as a guide to work himself carefully through the overlapping folds of torn fish netting until he could see the propeller. Thirty seconds later he surfaced next to the swim platform.

"I can't pull it loose,'' he gasped. "Wrapped around the shaft too tight. Going to have to cut it loose.''

"Just make sure you don't get caught up in that netting,'' she warned.

"Right,'' he acknowledged, and then slipped beneath the surface again.

It was easier to find the propeller this time because he knew how the netting was twisted and he knew where he'd have to cut to get it loose.

He held onto the diving light and the net with his left hand, and was reaching for the knife when he felt a sudden surge of water pressure at his back.

The impact caught him from the side, just beneath his lower ribs, and slammed the air out of his lungs in an explosive gasp. He tried to respond, to fight back, but the shock was too great; his mind was numb with terror and his legs and arms suddenly seemed distant from his body. He had a brief moment of awareness, of being dragged down beneath the boat into the cold darkness, and of being unable to do anything about it.

Then his lungs filled with water, and the darkness became everything.

Chapter Thirty

The team of FBI agents had been cruising along the northern edge of the deep Tartar Bank—along a line about twelve miles off the southern shore of Cat Island—for over an hour, watching for any sign of the *Sea Amber* and Alfred Bloom, when the Coast Guard radioman stuck his head up through the rear bridge hatch.

"Agent Grynard?"

Al Grynard turned around. "Yes."

"Got a guy calling in from the FBI crime lab. A tech agent Reggie Blackburn. Says he needs to talk with you real bad."

Grynard hurried down the ladder and went over to the port side of the main stateroom where the Coast Guard had set up a fairly elaborate communications center on the converted sports fishing trawler.

"Can you put it out on an open speaker?" he asked, aware that Hal Owens, special agent in charge of the FBI Special Bahamas Task Force, and Jim Whittman, the commander of the FBI's recently arrived hostage recovery team, had followed him down the ladder.

"Yes, sir." The radio operator reached forward on his console and flipped a pair of switches. "Go ahead, sir."

"This is Grynard."

"Hi, Al, this is Reggie."

"I've got Hal Owens and Jim Whittman here with me. You got any good news for us?"

"Well, yes and no," the supervisory electronics specialist said, his voice sounding rough and scratchy over the marine radio link. "The good news is I got my computers reprogrammed, and the CART system back on line. The bad news is that the *Sea Amber* and the *Lone Granger* are gone."

"What? What do you mean, *gone*?" Grynard demanded.

"Just that. They've disappeared. I can't find them anywhere."

"How can that be?"

"I don't know," the FBI tech agent confessed. "We're still having to use the computer recognition system for the *Sea Amber*, so she could be hiding someplace where the satellite can't spot her. But the *Lone Granger*'s a different story. Her SSRS transmitter just ain't squawking anymore."

Grynard cursed fervently and looked around at Owens and Whittman with his hands held palm up in disbelief. But then he remembered something.

"Reggie, can you give us a fix on their last known positions before your system went down?"

"I can do better than that. I can give you all the tracking data. You guys got a fax out there?"

Grynard looked down at the Coast Guard radioman who gave a thumbs up signal.

"Yes, we do."

"Okay, let me talk to the radio operator again, and then give me about five minutes."

Seven minutes later, the radioman handed Grynard a faxed map of Exuma Sound that showed one dotted line with the hand printed designation *"Sea Amber"* and a second dotted line marked *"The Lone Granger."*

"Looks to me like they were both headed in the same direction," Owens commented. "Southern tip of Cat Island."

"Which would be just about right, if Bloom really is on his way to your eleven o'clock meeting, and they're hot on his tail," Whittman added. "All we have to do is stake out the Cutlass Club and wait for everybody to show up."

Al Grynard stood there shaking his head slowly as he stared at the faxed chart.

"What's the matter?" Owens asked.

"I don't know, I guess I'm suspicious because it's too goddamned pat," Grynard muttered. "Nothing about this case has worked out this easy from day one."

"You complaining?" Owens asked, raising an eyebrow.

"No, not really." Grynard shrugged. "Probably just getting old and crotchety and tired of things going to shit every time I turn around."

"Probably can't do much about that other than offer you a beer." The special agent in charge smiled. "But the thing is, even if it doesn't sound right, I'm not sure we have any choice. We can't run any kind of aerial surveillance until daybreak. And even then, once we put those choppers in the air, everybody in the Islands is going to know that we're up to something down here."

"What about the response units?" Whittman asked. "Want to keep everybody back until we know what's going on?"

"I think we'd better," Owens said, looking to Grynard for confirmation, who nodded in agreement.

"Tell you what," Hal Owens said. "The three of us are dressed just about right for a night on the town, Cat Island style. Why don't we have the captain let us off outside the reef with the dinghy. We can motor in to the harbor, sit ourselves down in the bar, and wait to see who shows up. If it's just Bloom, then Jim and I'll make ourselves scarce and if that idiot with the four-bore shows up, then Al and I are the ones who are going to disappear,'' he added, smiling at Whittman.

"Sounds like a plan to me.'' The hostage recovery team commander nodded agreeably.

"Al?''

"Let's do it.''

"Okay, Cutlass Club it is. Oh, and make sure you guys check out a life jacket,'' Owens added with a smile. "It's been a long time since I tried to navigate those reefs at night on my own.''

Three and a half hours later, having safely navigated not only the offshore reefs and the unmarked entrance channel, but also several trips to the men's room of the Cutlass Bay Club, SAC Hal Owens contemplated the latest pot of fresh coffee with a definite lack of enthusiasm.

Then he looked up as Jim Whittman sat back down at the table.

"Well?''

"Starting to get pretty dead around here,'' the hostage recovery team commander muttered. "Couple of hard-looking types sitting in that little cubbyhole on the other side of the bar drinking beers. Aside from them, pretty much the same drunken assholes who've been here all evening.''

"The two hard types look like they might be setting up on anybody?''

"If they are, they're pretty casual about it.'' Whittman shrugged. "Younger guy sounds like he's from Louisiana, Mississippi, or Arkansas. Talking about how nothing out here compares with night fishing for 'gators with his daddy. And if they're carrying, they've got it all hidden pretty good.''

"Anybody outside?''

"Nope.''

"Well, folks,'' Owens said, looking past Al Grynard and

Theresa Fletcher as he surveyed the mostly empty lounge that had long since been abandoned by most of the early-rising fishermen, "I hate to say it, but I think we've been stood up."

Chapter Thirty-one

At four o'clock that Sunday morning, a native boat captain, who had taken the same route from Old Bight out to the northwestern edge of the Tartar Bank for the past twenty-three years, cursed. He first heard and then felt the impact of a submerged object against the underside of his small boat.

Using a long gaff, he quickly discovered that the object in question was not a rock or a coral head—as he had feared—but rather, the aluminum mast of a large sailboat.

Five minutes later, the boat captain quickly pulled himself back into his boat, tossed his mask and fins aside, and reached for his radio.

An hour and a half later, a pair of divers from the Bahamas Air-Sea Rescue Association pulled the bodies of Alfred Bloom and his sailing companion out of the water. A sleepy uniformed officer from the Royal Bahamas Defense Force was on hand to monitor the process.

The officer waited until the divers had laid the two bodies out on the deck of their dive boat. He stepped forward, examined both bodies for a few moments, and then yawned.

"So what do you think?" the officer asked the older of the two divers, a man with whom he had worked for several years.

"Looks to me like they got tangled up in a net. He went down first with a mask, to try to cut it away, and got caught. She went in after him, and in their panic, both of them became entangled and they drowned."

The uniformed officer nodded and made appropriate facial expressions to imply that he found such an explanation to be perfectly believable. Writing slowly, he filled a half page of his notebook.

"The name of the boat is the *Sea Amber*," the diver offered.

The Bahamian officer's head came up quickly.

"Are you certain?"

The diver nodded. "Read the name off the stern. We'll go back down, see if we can find some ID for the victims, after we change tanks."

The uniformed officer seemed to contemplate that information for a moment. Then he said: "Did you happen to see anything to explain why a brand-new sailboat would sink by itself?"

If the diver happened to wonder why an official of the Royal Bahamian Defense Force would know anything at all about a sailboat that he hadn't even seen yet, much less that it was brand-new, he didn't say anything.

"Saw what looked like a pretty good-sized hole in the bow." The diver shrugged. "My guess is that after they got caught in the net, the boat drifted into the reef back there, holed the hull, and then continued drifting to about here where it finally sank."

"In other words, an accident?"

"Looks like it to me," the diver said.

The uniformed officer made one more entry in his notebook, then nodded in apparent satisfaction.

"All right," he said, "call me at my office when you find some identification."

"Aren't you going to wait?" The diver blinked in surprise.

"For an accident? No, of course not. I have much better things to do with my time."

Chapter Thirty-two

Harold Tisbury, chairman of the board of Cyanosphere VIII, and CEO of the ICER Committee, was trying to ignore his son, who was shaking his shoulder insistently and saying—over and over again, like a skipping record—that "sometimes the Tisbury women pay a higher price than we do, and sometimes that price seems more than we can bear," when the shaking became even more insistent.

"I'm sorry to wake you, sir," the butler said, "but Mr. Crane assured me that it was urgent."

"Mr. Crane?" The elderly man blinked, trying to focus his thoughts.

"Yes, sir."

"All right," Harold Tisbury nodded groggily, "Tell him I'll be right out."

Five minutes later Harold Tisbury emerged from his bedroom, teeth brushed, hair combed, and bathrobe tied, to find his son and the rest of the committee members sitting around the living room. Apart from Sam Tisbury and Walter Crane, both of whom were fully dressed, all the other men were similarly attired in bathrobes and slippers.

Crane waited until Harold Tisbury settled himself into one of the high-backed chairs.

"I apologize for the rude awakening, gentlemen," Crane said in a voice that suggested he was not the least bit sorry and would actually have preferred to have arrived an hour earlier, "but I thought you'd all want to be told, as soon as possible, that Alfred Bloom is dead. His body was recovered at five-thirty this morning about a mile off the tip of Hawk's Nest."

There were gasps of astonishment and dismay throughout

the room. Crane noted, with no great surprise, that some of the ICER members seemed far less dismayed than others.

"Walter," Harold Tisbury said hesitantly, acting as though he still wasn't sure if he was dreaming or not, "What happened?"

"There is some indication that he and his sailing companion both drowned when they attempted to disentangle themselves from a net that had become wrapped around their rudder and propeller."

"Oh, dear God, that's terrible," the old man sighed.

"Yes, it is," Crane agreed. "Especially since Mr. Bloom's 'accidental' death will undoubtedly be viewed by the law enforcement authorities with a considerable amount of suspicion."

"What do you mean, suspicion?" Sergio Paz-Rios, the fiery chairman of Amazon Global, demanded.

"He means that the only known link between Operation Counter Wrench and our committee is now severed," Nicholas Von Hagberg said in his characteristically cold and haughty manner.

"Which isn't necessarily a bad deal, when you think about it," Wilbur Lee Edgarton reminded.

"Hold on a second, Walter. You assured us yesterday that the FBI isn't even aware that our committee exists," Jonathan Chilmark pointed out.

"As of yesterday afternoon, that was true to the best of our knowledge." Crane nodded. "However, as of this morning, I can tell you that thirteen agents of an elite FBI hostage rescue team departed from Quantico, Virginia, en route to an unknown destination in the Bahamas. And I have some reason to believe that they landed on San Salvador."

There was dead silence around the room.

"But what would a hostage rescue team from the FBI possibly have to do with us?" Sam Tisbury asked reasonably. "We certainly don't have any hostages in this villa, or anywhere else, for that matter."

"As far as the FBI is concerned," Walter Crane said

calmly, "the terms 'hostage recovery' and 'S.W.A.T.' are synonymous."

Sergio Paz-Rios muttered something in his Chilean dialect as an argument broke out between Jonathan Chilmark and Nicholas Von Hagberg.

"Gentlemen!" Walter Crane spoke sharply, raising his hand for silence.

In spite of the emotional turmoil that seemed to fill the room, all eyes turned in Crane's direction.

"Before you become overly alarmed," Crane said calmly, "I would repeat what I said yesterday. There is still no evidence that the FBI or any other law enforcement entity is aware that the ICER committee exists or that you are here on this island. As far as I am aware, Mr. Bloom was the only member of the committee under investigation.

"However," the legal investigator emphasized with a single raised forefinger, "the fact that the attentions of a thirteen-agent S.W.A.T. team, approximately seventy-five FBI and DEA agents of the Special Bahamas Task Force, FBI Agent Al Grynard, *and* a covert team of Fish and Wildlife Service special agents, now seem to be focused in this isolated part of the world is certainly good reason to be *concerned*."

"I think we should terminate this meeting and leave the Islands immediately," Jonathan Chilmark said.

"I agree," Wilbur Lee Edgarton nodded.

"But if they don't know . . ." Harold Tisbury started to say when Nicholas Von Hagberg interrupted.

"I disagree, we should not run like terrified rabbits," Nicholas Von Hagberg said emphatically. "And besides, we *cannot* leave before we decide about the future of this committee."

"But if we don't leave right now, we may be trapped," Jonathan Chilmark protested.

"That's right." Sergio Paz-Rios nodded, his dark eyes widened with emotion. "Too many people have died already. The FBI will not be satisfied with just one of us. They will keep looking until they find us all. Killing Bloom was a stupid idea!'' He glared accusingly at Von Hagberg.

''You think *I* had him killed?''

''Why not? It's obvious that you had others killed to free your precious Maas. Why should you stop there!?'' Sergio Paz-Rios yelled, coming to his feet.

''You are an imbecile!'' the Teutonic industrialist exploded, knocking aside a lamp as he too came up out of his chair, his face beet-red beneath his titanium-rimmed glasses.

Incredibly, before the two furious ICER committee members could take a swing at each other with their clenched fists, the sharp tinkling of a knife blade against a glass instinctively caught everyone's attention.

Walter Crane paused to make certain that he did, in fact, have everyone's attention. Then he set the glass and knife back down on the lamp table and continued. ''Nicholas has a point,'' he said in an absolutely calm and controlled voice. ''If you run now, you will attract attention.''

''But—'' Jonathan Chilmark started to protest again, but Crane shook him off.

''No, listen to me,'' he said firmly. ''If a hunter has no idea where his prey is, the age-old tactic is to create a disturbance. Drum-beaters, a show of force, whatever. But the important thing to remember,'' he emphasized, ''is that once the animal breaks cover, it is almost always doomed.''

Crane allowed his gaze to pass slowly from face to face.

''If the arrival of the FBI team and the activities of the wildlife agents are just that, a show of force to cause one or more of you to run, when you can be assured that they are watching every possible means of leaving these islands.''

The silence went on for almost thirty seconds.

''Then you are advising us to stay here, together, at the villa?''

''Or wherever it is that you are staying,'' Crane nodded. ''What I'm advising you *not* to do is to get on board a boat or a plane and try to leave.''

Sam Tisbury raised his hand hesitantly.

"Yes, Sam?"

"Walter, my son and I were planning on going out fishing this morning." Tisbury looked down at his watch. "In fact, he should be waiting for me down at the marina right now."

"Have you already chartered the boat?"

"Yes."

"Then I would strongly recommend that you go down to the marina right now and continue on as if none of this"—Crane waved his hand to indicate the general atmosphere of the room—"had ever happened."

"But he must come back, yes?" Nicholas Von Hagberg demanded.

"Oh, yes." Walter Crane nodded. "Under the circumstances, I think that would be highly advisable."

Crane waited until Sam Tisbury had departed and then turned his attention back to the assembled group.

"Gentlemen, I understand that breakfast will be available in the dining room. Perhaps all this will look better after we eat?"

Nodding in agreement, the emotionally exhausted ICER Committee members rose to their feet and followed their legal adviser into the dining room.

Where they found themselves staring into the cold blue eyes of Gerd Maas.

Chapter Thirty-three

With Larry Paxton at the helm, Mike Takahara at his side with the ship's manual and a copy of *The Yachtsman's Guide to the Bahamas,* and Henry Lightstone acting as lookout and general deckhand, it took the inexperienced crew of the *Lone Granger* three separate tries before they finally managed to snag the yacht's ninety-pound bow anchor, with some uncertain degree of permanence, to the relatively shallow ocean floor off the Hawk's Nest inlet at the tip of the Cat Island "boot."

Then, while Paxton and Takahara continued to consult on the bridge, Henry Lightstone tied one end of a fifty-foot line to one of the stern cleats, the other end to one of the ship's seventy-five-pound spare anchors, dropped the anchor into the water, and then dove overboard.

A little under a minute later, Lightstone's head popped up off the starboard side of the yacht.

"Are we hooked up?" Paxton yelled out the bridge window.

Lightstone extended his arms in an exaggerated palms-up shrug.

"I'm going to interpret that as a definite 'maybe,' " Paxton said. "What do you think?"

"Other than being extremely grateful that Halahan and Moore are waiting for us about ten miles away at Cutlass Bay, and not out here at the Hawk's Nest, you don't want to know what I think," Mike Takahara said seriously.

"That bad?"

The tech agent nodded.

"What's the worst that can happen?"

Mike Takahara gave Paxton a long look. "Offhand, I'd say the two most likely possibilities are that the anchors pull loose and the boat drifts out to sea, or the anchors pull loose and the boat breaks up on the reef."

Larry Paxton blinked.

"What the hell's the matter with 'the anchors *don't* pull loose, and the boat stays right where it is'?" he demanded.

"Yeah, I suppose that's always a possibility too," the tech agent conceded.

Larry Paxton was about to say something else when Henry Lightstone climbed up the outside ladder to the bridge, water still dripping from his bathing suit.

"So how are things looking up here?" he asked Takahara—who was busy doing something behind the control console panel—as he stripped out of his bathing suit and started to towel off.

"You don't want to be asking the prophet of doom a question like that," Paxton advised.

"Larry's starting to worry that we might not know what we're doing," Takahara explained, looking up from the console as he slipped something into his shirt pocket.

"He's right, we *don't* know what we're doing. But there's not much we can do to change that right now, so why worry about it?" Lightstone shrugged philosophically as he rummaged around in his equipment bag for a clean set of underwear, jeans, and a short-sleeved shirt.

"Exactly." The tech agent nodded.

"But as long as we're on the subject of not knowing what we're doing," Lightstone said as he got dressed, "you think next time we stop somewhere, we could just try motoring up to the dock? This business of dragging seventy-five-pound anchors around, looking for something to hook them to, is starting to get a little old. If we're going to keep this up, we need to get Stoner back into the game."

"I guess we could *try* coming in to the marina," Mike Takahara said dubiously, "but I'm not too sure how well that would work out."

"Oh, yeah, what's the problem?"

"Well, first of all, you *do* know we lost all our charts of Cat Island in the explosion, right?"

"Yeah, sure, but you guys managed to find this place okay with that yachtsman's guidebook."

"Yes, we did, but if you'll take a look at what it says here," Takahara said, pointing to the bottom of the line sketch titled Cat Island Harbours and Creeks.

" 'Caution: Not for Navigating,' " Lightstone read out loud. He looked up at the team's tech agent. "Does that mean what I think it means?"

The tech agent nodded. "Pretty much. Actually, if you want to know the truth, the only reason Larry and I managed to find the Hawk's Nest marina is because we kept on heading south, parallel to the shoreline, and never lost sight of the island. Had to hit the end of it eventually.''

"Ah.''

"And there's one other problem with the docking idea,'' Mike Takahara went on. "First of all, you need to understand that, according to the ship's manual, the draft of the *Lone Granger* is exactly six and a half feet.''

"What's that mean?'' Larry Paxton asked.

"The draft is basically how much water you need so that the boat doesn't scrape on the bottom,'' Takahara explained. "Now if you'll look at the numbers here on this sketch, you can see—roughly—how deep the water is at the entrance to the Hawk's Nest marina.''

"What's that, four to six fathoms?'' Lightstone asked.

"No, four to six *feet* . . . plus you've got to add or subtract a couple, depending on whether the tide's coming in or going out.''

"And just how are we supposed to know *that*?''

"Well, as best I can figure out, we start with the Nassau tide tables at the back of the Guide, subtract twenty-five minutes for Cat Island time, add or subtract a half foot depending on how far the moon is from the earth—''

Henry Lightstone turned to Larry Paxton. "He's bullshitting us, right?''

Paxton just rolled his eyes to the ceiling and shook his head, as if to say, "How the hell would I know?''

"—and then cross our fingers real tight,'' the tech agent went on, "' 'cause if we guess wrong and the tide's going down instead of up, then we get to try to drag a hundred-ton boat off the rocks instead of a seventy-five-pound anchor.''

"I think I just changed my outlook on anchor-dragging,'' Lightstone said. "Sorry I asked.''

"That's pretty much the way I figured it too.'' The tech agent nodded. "Especially since I wasn't sure if Bobby had this thing fully insured.''

"Knowing Bobby, I imagine he's got full coverage on this tub,'' Lightstone said. "But I don't think that's one of his big concerns right now. As I recall, the lease Larry signed says the federal government will cover any unusual wear and tear.''

"You mean like if the anchors come loose and the boat breaks up on the reef?" Takahara asked, looking cheerfully over at Paxton.

"I guess. Sounds like unusual wear and tear to me." Lightstone shrugged. "And besides, if the government backs out on the deal, Bobby can always garnishee Larry's paycheck for the next fifty, sixty years."

"Don't know what I'd do without you guys," Paxton muttered.

"Actually, from here, it doesn't look like you've been doing all *that* good *with* us," Lightstone said, gesturing with his head at the oversized cast on Paxton's left arm.

"Ain't that the truth." Paxton nodded, looking down at his badly scarred right arm and the huge cast on his left arm that he'd been forced to put into a sling because of the weight. And then: "Okay, everybody ready to load up?"

Mike Takahara pulled a dark blue backpack out of a storage cabinet, withdrew his 10mm Model 1076 double-action pistol, spare magazines, and agent credentials from his tool kit, and then accepted Lightstone's and Paxton's pistols, spare magazines, and credentials. He carefully wrapped the weapons, magazines, and badge cases in T-shirts and light windbreakers, and placed them in the backpack, along with his portable computer, a pack-set radio, a pair of binoculars, and some other electronic gear.

"So what's the plan?" the tech agent asked. "We hit the marina, maintain our cover by trying to keep Bobby's charter business alive for a few more months, and then track down our buddy Alfred Bloom?"

"Sounds good to me," Lightstone responded.

"I don't know," Paxton said uneasily. "I'm still not sure it's a good idea for all three of us to be going in and leaving the boat unattended."

"Under anything resembling normal circumstances, I'd

have to agree with you.'' Mike Takahara nodded. ''But seeing as how just about everything of any value on this boat has been pretty much destroyed anyway, the possibility that somebody's going to be stupid enough to try to row out here, try to jump-start the engine of an eighty-two-foot yacht, and then run off and try to hide it somewhere, is probably the least of our worries right now.''

''*You* managed to get it started,'' Paxton reminded.

''Yeah, but I've got a degree in electrical engineering,'' Takahara said. ''And I also had this,'' he added, reaching into his shirt pocket and pulling out a small circuit board.

''What's that?'' the acting team leader asked.

''The starter relay board.''

''Which they won't have, I take it?''

''According to the manual, there's only one spare.''

''Yeah, and where's that?''

''Right here. The original's in three pieces in the bottom of the trash can. One of the many reasons the engine wouldn't start in the first place.''

''You needed a degree in electrical engineering to figure *that* out?'' Paxton asked.

''No, not really. I just looked on the floor under the electrical panel and then tried to figure out where all the broken parts came from.''

''But it *will* start up again once you put that board back in, right?'' Paxton asked in clarification.

The tech agent nodded. ''Most likely.''

''Well, in *that* case,'' Paxton said, looking visibly relieved, ''why don't you raggedy-ass crew types get down there and pump up mah dinghy so we can go cancel Bobby's charter. And we do that,'' he added, a dangerous glint appearing in his dark eyes, ''then we're gonna take a ride over to the Cutlass Bay Club, find this asshole Bloom fellow, and start making somebody else's life downright miserable for a change.''

* * *

Aside from being nearly swamped by the bow wave of a thirty-two-foot cabin cruiser, whose owner seemed to be in a hurry to get out into open water, the trip in through the narrow channel entrance to the Hawk's Nest marina was uneventful.

Lightstone steered the Zodiac straight into the shoreline adjacent to the far northeast corner of the landlocked marina, and then waited until his two partners managed to get themselves out of the flexible, rubberized craft and onto shore.

"Okay," Paxton said to Lightstone, "why don't you go get the gas tank filled and find someplace to tie this thing up, while Mike and I track down Bobby's charter and then see about renting a car."

"Aye, aye, boss," the lanky agent agreed.

A couple of minutes later, while Henry Lightstone was cautiously guiding the Zodiac over to the gas dock, and Mike Takahara was starting to negotiate with an elderly Bahamian native who was sitting under an umbrella that had the words "Jeeps for Rent" stenciled on it in bright green letters, Larry Paxton walked into the marina store.

"Help you?" the proprietor asked from behind the counter.

"Actually, I'm looking for a Mr. Tisbury—"

A slender gray-haired man looked up from the nearby pay phone. "Mr. LaGrange?"

"Well, actually, I'm one of Bobby LaGrange's crew," Paxton said hesitantly.

Sam Tisbury said something into the phone, quickly hung up, and then hurried over.

"I can't tell you how glad I am to see you," he said, reaching out to shake Paxton's hand. "I'm Sam Tisbury, and this is my son, Eric."

"Sam, Eric. Larry Higgins," Paxton nodded, shaking both their hands. "Sorry we're late, but we ran into some unexpected difficulties."

"That's perfectly all right. To tell you the truth, I was afraid we were the ones who had missed the connections."

The gray-haired executive paused when he suddenly seemed to realize that there might be a connection between Paxton's sling and cast, and his comment about "unexpected difficulties."

"Did something happen to your boat?" Tisbury asked, staring down at the huge cast, and then up at the cuts and bruises on Paxton's face.

"I'm afraid so," Larry Paxton nodded, easily dropping into his preplanned role. "We were coming in from a run off San Salvador last night when we got broadsided by one humongous ground swell. The boat was pretty badly damaged, and we ended up having to have the Coast Guard transport Bobby, his son, and one of our clients to the hospital."

"Dear God!" Sam Tisbury said, shaking his head sadly. And then: "Are *you* all right?

"Oh, I'm fine, just a little banged up." Paxton shrugged, gesturing with the heavy cast. "The problem is, though, it doesn't look like we're gonna be able to take you fellows out until we have a marine engineer and an electrician go over the boat from bow to stern. She's under way, but that's about all. We would have called and tried to leave a message here at the marina, but the radio started going out on us on the way in. The way things have been going, we figure we were going good just to get here in the Zodiac."

"Murphy's Law strikes again." Eric Tisbury smiled.

"If that's the one that says everything that *can* go wrong *will* go wrong, Ah sure can't argue with you none," Paxton nodded.

"Apparently it's been one of those weeks," Sam Tisbury said cryptically, shaking his head.

"Real sorry we messed up your plans like this, Mr. Tisbury," Paxton went on, "but Bobby said to tell you that he owes you a free trip, once he gets back in operation again."

As he was talking, Paxton saw Henry Lightstone enter the store, and got ready to make the additional introductions. But then he saw the lanky agent turn away suddenly and start looking through the beer cooler.

"Please tell Mr. LaGrange that we appreciate his concern *and* his generosity," Sam Tisbury said, "and that my son and I will be sure to get hold of him before our next trip."

"You know, Ah might be able to help you guys locate another charter if Ah call around," Paxton offered hesitantly as he gradually shifted over into a deeper version of his South Carolina accent, "But Ah—"

"Don't worry about it." Sam Tisbury shook his head. "I'll simply call my booking agent who gets paid to handle this sort of thing. We'll let him earn some of that money for a change."

"Appreciate your understanding, Mr. Tisbury," Paxton said, shaking hands with father and son. "Hope the rest of your week turns out a whole lot better." He stood there politely as the two vacationers turned and walked back outside.

Lightstone waited for a count of twenty, and then came up beside Paxton.

"Where's Snoopy?" he asked.

Paxton immediately picked up on the sense of urgency in Lightstone's voice.

"Outside, renting a car. What's the matter?"

"That kid."

"Yeah, what about him?"

"Remember the young guy I told you about, down in the Arlington Courthouse basement, yelling on the phone?"

"You mean that 'wildfire' business?"

"That's right."

"You *sure*?"

"No question about it." Lightstone nodded.

"Did he recognize you?"

"I don't think so. He was looking at one of those fishing rods, and I turned away as soon as I saw him."

"What the hell's he doing *here*? And for that matter," Paxton added, "who the hell *is* he, anyway?"

"Interesting questions."

"Damn right they are," Paxton muttered. "And too damn much of a coincidence, as far as I'm concerned."

"Let's go find Snoopy," Lightstone said as they looked cautiously out the door and then hurried over to where Mike Takahara had just finished signing a rental agreement and a credit card charge slip.

"You see 'em?" Paxton asked, looking around.

"Yeah," Lightstone said, "over there to your left, in the far parking lot, getting into that red Jeep."

"You guys ready to—" Takahara said, and then found himself being hustled away from the smiling rental car dealer. Paxton and Lighthouse quickly explained the situation.

"You know, we should probably notify Halahan," the tech agent said hesitantly, watching the red Jeep backing out of the dirt parking spot.

"We don't have time for that." Lightstone shook his head. "Look, they're taking off right now. If we don't get going, we're gonna lose them."

Both agents turned to Paxton, who sighed deeply and then reluctantly nodded.

Moments later all three agents were climbing into their newly rented bright green Jeep.

"Don't worry about it," Lightstone advised Paxton as Mike Takahara awkwardly shifted the gears with his left hand and then accelerated the open Jeep toward the narrow asphalt road. "You never really figured you were going to get to keep that promotion anyway."

Sam Tisbury sat in the front right-hand passenger seat of the open Jeep and tried to block everything except the beautiful scenery out of his mind as his son skillfully maneuvered the rented vehicle down the road leading away from the Hawk's Nest marina.

Coming up to the McQueen junction, the younger Tisbury turned south, drove a few more miles, and then turned left onto a narrow and partially concealed dirt road about four miles north of Devil's Point.

About a hundred yards from the road, they stopped at the

gates where Sam Tisbury leaned past his son and spoke into the microphone.

After about thirty seconds, when nobody responded, Eric Tisbury fed his father's coded access card into the slot and then waited impatiently for the gates to open.

As he did so, his eye caught a flash of bright green in the right side-view mirror.

"Looks like we've got some company," he said to his father, who turned back around in his seat and leaned out around the roll bar to look back down the road.

"It appears to be that black fellow from the charter boat," Sam Tisbury said.

Eric looked up into the rearview mirror and recognized Larry Paxton—and his plaster-casted arm—sitting in the middle of the rear seat. Then his gaze shifted over to the figure sitting in the front passenger seat of the rapidly approaching Jeep, and he blinked in disbelief.

Unable to comprehend what he was seeing in the Jeep's rearview mirror, Eric Tisbury whirled around in his seat.

"Oh, my God, it's Lightstone!" he gasped.

"Lightstone?" Sam Tisbury said, turning back around to stare at his son. "You mean *agent* Lightstone?"

"What is he doing *here*?" Eric Tisbury whispered, ignoring his father's question as he continued to stare in horror at the oncoming Jeep. His normally tanned face had taken on a deathly ashen pallor.

"How do you know about—" Sam Tisbury started to demand, but before he could finish his question, he found himself being flung sideways and backward out of the front seat as his son suddenly released the clutch and then accelerated the Jeep through the opened gates.

Sam Tisbury landed hard on his back, the impact driving the air out of his lungs.

Mike Takahara brought the bright green Jeep to a dust-billowing halt at the open gateway just as Sam Tisbury managed to bring himself up to his knees and yell out: "Eric, stop! Come back!"

But his efforts were to no avail.

Eric Tisbury was almost halfway between the gates and the villa when the explosive roar of a double-barreled, four-bore rifle blew the front windshield completely out of the red Jeep and tossed the panicked youth out of the driver's seat like a broken rag doll.

An instant later, as Sam Tisbury continued to kneel there in the dirt in absolute shock, Henry Lightstone, Larry Paxton, and Mike Takahara scrambled out of their rented Jeep and dove for cover.

Chapter Thirty-four

The members of the ICER Committee who were still in the villa—Harold Tisbury, Sergio Paz-Rios, Nicholas Von Hagberg, Wilbur Lee Edgarton, and Jonathan Chilmark—and Walter Crane all heard the concussive boom of the four-bore rifle from inside the dining room. And then several smaller-caliber shots.

To a man, they all wanted desperately to do *something*—to go to the window and see what was going on, or to dive beneath the table, or to flee for their lives—but they didn't dare. Not with Gerd Maas sitting there in his wheelchair, holding a sound-suppressed 10mm semiautomatic pistol in his hand, and staring at them with his cold blue eyes.

Then they all turned to look when a figure holding a deadly looking fighting knife in his right hand came running through the living room and stopped in the entrance of the dining room.

"The fools brought Lightstone with them," Alex Chareaux said, a crazed expression appearing in his reddened eyes.

"Ah, *Herr* Lightstone, *sehr gut*!" Gerd Maas grinned widely.

"He killed my brothers, so he's mine. You remember that," Chareaux snarled, which made the German counter-terrorist laugh out loud and then level his cold gaze on his Cajun poacher accomplice.

"*Ja*, he can be yours first, but you must try harder to kill him this time."

Alex Chareaux's reddened eyes flashed with anger, and he started to respond with an explosive curse when Sergio Paz-Rios interrupted.

"Henry Lightstone, the wildlife agent, is *here*?" The Chilean industrialist blinked, his eyes widening in shock as he stared at Alex Chareaux.

"*Stupide enfant*," Chareaux snarled. "Shut up."

Driven by blind and thoughtless rage, as well as his male macho-dominated upbringing, Sergio Paz-Rios lunged to his feet and then went down immediately in a fit of spasmodic gurgling and kicking when Chareaux slashed the razor-sharp edge of the knife across his exposed throat.

"Ah, *gut*! You practice." Maas smiled.

More shots rang out below the villa, followed by another loud, concussive boom as Sergio Paz-Rios's legs made one last spasmodic kick and then grew still.

The remaining ICER Committee members and Walter Crane sat frozen in their chairs.

The front door on the first floor exploded into a shower of wood fragments, and Maas cocked his head.

"I think it is time we go," he said, his cold blue eyes glittering with anticipation as he wheeled himself past the dining room table and then stopped beside Walter Crane.

"You find this amusing?" he asked the private investigator.

"No, I don't," Crane said evenly.

"*Gut*, then I give you something better to do," Maas said, and in a movement almost too quick to see, he slammed the butt of the heavy double-action pistol against the side of Crane's head. The investigator sagged and then dropped to the floor with a loud thump.

"Bring him with us," Maas ordered as he began to roll his wheelchair into the living room.

"Bring him yourself," Chareaux snapped.

"You wish to have your chance with *Herr* Lightstone again?" Maas inquired calmly, making only the slightest gesture with the silenced pistol. The implication was absolutely clear. No matter how fast and skilled Alex Chareaux might be with a knife, a 10mm bullet would be just as lethal and much, much faster.

Having no choice but to bow to the balance of power that Riser had deliberately established in arming his two new employees, Alex Chareaux nodded in silent agreement. He began to drag the unconscious form of Walter Crane into the living room.

One of the 1900-grain slugs aimed at the approaching agents ricocheted off the bumper of the rented green Jeep, and a sheared-off fragment struck Mike Takahara just above the right knee.

Grimacing from the pain, the tech agent used his pocket knife to cut away the pants leg. After verifying that the freely bleeding wound was shallow and therefore not life-threatening, Takahara quickly used the remnants of his pants leg to make a crude bandage.

Then, as Henry Lightstone and Larry Paxton maintained a forward covering fire up ahead, Takahara and Sam Tisbury managed to crawl forward to the red Jeep. There they found Eric Tisbury lying on his back amid hundreds of fragments of safety glass, bleeding from the chest and mouth.

From his barricaded position against the side of the Jeep, the tech agent could see at least four large buckshot holes in the youth's blood-soaked shirt.

Sam Tisbury reacted by grabbing his son and mumbling, "No! No!" over and over again, until Mike Takahara finally pulled him away to see if there was anything he could possibly do in the way of first aid.

As he did so, Eric Tisbury opened his eyes and whispered something.

"What?" Takahara said, and then tucked his head in close so that he could try to hear what Sam Tisbury's dying son was trying to say. But before the youth could finish, his eyes glazed over and his head rolled to one side.

Takahara started to say something to the father when they heard the four-bore again, the concussive blast echoing across the island as Riser blew the front door of the villa off its bronze hinges.

Staying as low to the ground as he could, Mike Takahara hobbled back to the bright green Jeep, grabbed the pack-set radio out of the backpack, and switched it on.

"Foxtrot Whiskey Three to Foxtrot Whiskey Five, do you read me?"

"Foxtrot Whiskey Three, I read you!" Woeshack's distinctive voice crackled across the airwaves.

"Foxtrot Whiskey Five, where are you?"

"This is four." Dwight Stoner's deep voice came over the radio. "We're over Exuma Sound, heading straight toward the Hawk's Nest marina, about thirty miles out. What's going on?"

"We followed a pair of suspects to a villa about four miles northeast of Devil's Point. We have multiple shots fired, one suspect down, and at least one guy running around with what sounds like a cannon. Notify Halahan and get us some backup—whoever you can find, and make it fast."

"Ten-four," Stoner acknowledged. "Backup is on the way. Is anybody hurt?"

"Just me, I think, and it's minor."

"Well, keep your goddamned head down until we get there!"

Maintaining his low profile with the ground, Mike Takahara hobbled his way back to where Henry Lightstone and Larry Paxton were crouched down behind a pair of what looked like extremely small palm trees. A third tree lay shattered and toppled on the sandy ground a few feet away, the victim of another 1900-grain rifle slug.

"You okay?" Paxton asked, looking back and seeing the blood-soaked bandage on Takahara's muscular leg.

"Yeah, fine. Where the hell is he?" the tech agent asked, just as a pair of concussive explosions blew a shower of glass flying from the third story of the villa, and causing all three agents to duck down behind the minimally protective trees.

"I'd say he's up there," Larry Paxton said.

"Any idea what that thing is?" Takahara asked.

"Some combination of 20mm cannon and long-range blunderbuss, from the looks of things around here," Lightstone said. "You get hold of anybody?" He gestured with his head at the radio in the tech agent's hand.

"Woeshack and Stoner." Takahara quickly described their brief conversation.

"You know, I hate to admit it, but I think Stoner's right," Larry Paxton commented, glancing over at the shattered palm tree. "The smart thing to do would be to stay right where we are, keep our heads down, and wait for help."

"Sounds like one hell of a good plan to me." Lightstone nodded.

At that moment a familiar voice rang out.

"*Herr* Lightstone! You are coming for me, *ja*?"

Henry Lightstone blinked, and then looked over at Paxton in disbelief. "Maas?"

"I wait for you too, Henry!"

"And our buddy Chareaux," Paxton said, his dark eyes starting to narrow dangerously.

"McNulty died very badly, *Herr* Lightstone. Perhaps you and your friends can do better, *ja*?"

"Well, so much for good plans and intentions," Lightstone muttered as he slowly and cautiously began to move forward beyond the protection of the small palms.

Chapter Thirty-five

Henry Lightstone, Larry Paxton, and Mike Takahara moved forward in a rapid series of crossover maneuvers designed to give the person out in the open as much cover as possible, knowing, as they did so, that they were still leaving themselves horribly vulnerable to a lethal blast from whatever kind of weapon it was that had been making the cannonlike explosions.

As they approached the blown-open front door of the villa, they observed the bodies of what appeared to be four security guards sprawled next to a pair of gray-painted Jeeps. A brief glance told the wildlife agents what they wanted to know: Three of the casually uniformed men had bullet holes in their foreheads, and the fourth had his throat cut.

Lightstone waited until Paxton and Takahara were in position, signaled a two count with his left hand . . . and then dove in through the doors, rolling and ending up flat on the floor with the 10mm semiautomatic extended out in both hands. At the same instant, Takahara barricaded himself low against the right side of the door frame, and Paxton barricaded himself high on the left, both agents aiming their weapons in a crossing direction over Lightstone's prone body, and all three ready to shoot at the first sign of movement.

Nothing.

Stopping frequently to look and listen, the three agents slowly and cautiously worked their way up the wide staircase until they reached the third floor.

Still nothing.

"Where *are* those bastards?" Larry Paxton whispered as the three agents arranged themselves in a triangulated, back-to-back protective position, watching and waiting.

"I don't know," Lightstone replied in a soft voice, "but they've got to be around here somewhere."

Finally Henry Lightstone began to move carefully forward toward the far bedroom, as Paxton sifted over toward the living room, and Takahara slowly inched his way into the dining room.

"Oh, Christ, look at this," Takahara whispered, gesturing with his head to Paxton as he maintained a covering watch over Henry Lightstone, who was still moving toward the far bedroom.

"Man, oh, man," Larry Paxton said softly as he took a quick look into the dining room and saw the sprawled and shattered bodies of Harold Tisbury, Nicholas Von Hagberg, Wilbur Lee Edgarton, Jonathan Chilmark . . . and Sergio Paz-Rios, who lay on his back in the pool of blood that had formed around his slashed neck and head, his empty dark eyes staring up at the ceiling.

Then Larry Paxton froze as he saw Lightstone bring up a warning hand.

Moving as carefully and quietly as they could, the two wildlife agents came up beside Lightstone.

"I think I can see the edge of a wheelchair in that mirror," he whispered, motioning with his head to the far wall where an angled mirror gave the agents a very limited and cropped view of a small portion of the darkened bedroom.

"Maas?" Paxton asked.

"I think so." Lightstone whispered. "You ready?"

They both nodded.

Keeping a loose grip on the heavy double-action pistol and his finger through the trigger guard, Lightstone got down on his hands and knees and slowly moved over toward the open door. Then he looked back at his two partners.

"On three," he mouthed silently, and then held up a single finger.

One.

Two.

At that moment, the roar of a rapidly approaching single-engined plane; the sound of three Jeep engines revving up, two close and one more distant; and a pair of thundering explosions outside the villa jarred the three agents.

"Foxtrot Whiskey Four," Stoner's deep voice crackled softly from the radio attached to Mike Takahara's belt. "They're getting away!"

As the single-engined Cessna with Special Agent/Pilot Thomas Woeshack at the controls roared directly over the villa in a series of desperately evasive maneuvers, Henry Lightstone dove inside the bedroom with the Model 1076 pistol outstretched in both hands—ready to send the 10mm hollow-pointed rounds into the body of the wheelchair-bound terrorist as fast as he could pull the trigger.

Then he remained stretched out on the carpet, staring uncomprehending at the slumped figure of Walter Crane who—based upon the visual evidence—had been quickly secured to the wheelchair with multiple loops of duct tape before someone cut his throat too.

At eight-thirty that Sunday morning FBI agent Al Grynard responded groggily to the pounding on his door and was startled to see U.S. Attorney Theresa Fletcher standing there wide-eyed in the hallway.

"I'm sorry to wake you, but I've been hearing what I think are gunshots and—"

At that moment two more distant explosions from Riser's four-bore rifle echoed through the open window of Grynard's Cutlass Bay Club hotel room.

"Holy shit," Grynard muttered, and then: "Call Owens and Whittman while I get dressed."

Grynard grabbed his black nylon equipment bag and disappeared into the bathroom as Theresa Fletcher ran over to the bed and reached for the phone. She let the phone to Hal Owen's room ring six times before hanging up with an unladylike curse. She was just getting ready to dial Whittman's room when somebody knocked on the door.

After cautiously checking the peephole, she quickly opened the door to Hal Owens and Jim Whittman. Both agents were wearing dark green military camouflage clothing and black webbing gear. In addition, hostage recovery team commander Whittman was carrying an assault rifle, and trying to strap himself hurriedly into his black Kevlar vest. Moving forward quickly, the prosecutor grabbed at the back of the vest and helped him readjust the Velcro straps.

"Where's Grynard?" Owens demanded.

"Here," Al Grynard said, strapping on his pistol as he came out of the bathroom. "What's going on?"

"Sounds like we got some kind of firefight in progress, somewhere to the northwest of us," Owens said. "Which probably has something to do with a call for backup that the radio operator on one of our boats just picked up on a scrambled law enforcement channel. The location described is a red-tile-roofed villa about four miles northwest of us. Whoever was calling for help used the call sign Foxtrot Whiskey."

"Foxtrot Whiskey?" Grynard blinked, and then it hit him. "That's got to be Fish and Wildlife."

"Oh, Christ," Owens said, "let's get going. I've got one of our choppers en route to pick us up."

When the three FBI agents and deputy U.S. Attorney Theresa Fletcher got outside in the parking lot, the first thing Jim Whittman saw was the two men who had been in the bar the night before. Only now the two casually dressed men were hurrying to get into a rented car, and one of them clearly had a pack-set radio in his hand.

"Hey!" Whittman yelled, leveling the assault rifle and thumbing the selective-fire lever to "Auto," just as the second man whirled around fast in a low crouch with a stainless steel semiautomatic pistol extended in both hands.

"Federal Agent, drop—" Freddy Moore, the newly appointed FWS special operations deputy chief, started to yell, and then instinctively shifted the point-sight of his pistol away when he saw the FBI insignia on Whittman's vest. At the same moment, the tensed and focused hostage recovery team commander backed his finger off the trigger of the M-16 assault rifle.

David Halahan, the chief of the Fish and Wildlife Service's Special Ops Branch, was reaching for his own weapon when he spotted and immediately recognized FBI agent Al Grynard.

"What the hell are you guys doing here?" Halahan demanded as the five federal law enforcement officers cautiously approached one another.

"If it involves Henry Lightstone, probably the same thing you are," Grynard said as the rotor noise of the rapidly approaching Blackhawk assault helicopter started to drown out their voices. "You want a lift?"

Chapter Thirty-six

Henry Lightstone was scrambling to his feet when Larry Paxton entered the bedroom.

"What the hell . . ." Paxton blinked, staring uncomprehendingly at the slumped and bloody figure of Walter Crane.

"Looks to me like Maas's sense of humor and Chareaux's knife," Lightstone said. "That goddamned kraut's been playing with us all this time, pretending he couldn't get out of that chair."

"Must have gotten himself a couple of them fake knee jobs, like Stoner did," Paxton commented.

"Yeah, probably . . . did you see which way they went?"

"No, but maybe . . ." Paxton started to say when Mike Takahara appeared in the bedroom doorway with the packset radio in his hand.

"They went out the back and then took off in those gray Jeeps," the tech agent said. "According to Stoner, Maas and

Chareaux are in one, and the big asshole with the cannon in the other. He said it looked like they were getting ready to set up on us outside when they saw the plane coming.''

"Thank God for that crazy Woeshack," Lightstone smiled.

"Yeah, well, according to Stoner, it looked like they were arguing about something before they took off. Like maybe Chareaux wanted to stay, but Maas and the big guy either talked him out of it or threatened his ass, Stoner couldn't tell which. But he did say that Maas has some kind of black nylon bag with him. Oh, yeah, and that guy in the red Jeep— Tisbury, whatever his name is—he took off too.''

"Any idea where they're going?"

"The airstrip at Cutlass Bay would be my guess." The tech agent shrugged. "Woeshack and Stoner are going to try to keep them in sight from a safe distance.''

"Okay, great, let's go get 'em," Lightstone said, and the headed for the door.

"Snoopy, do we have another radio in the Jeep?" Paxton asked Takahara.

"Nope, this is it," the tech agent said, handing him the small pack-set radio.

"Okay, you're not going to be able to run very far with that leg," Paxton said, "so why don't you come down to the Jeep with us, get what you need out of the backpack, then stay here, get hold of Halahan, tell him what we're doing, then check around and see if you can figure out what's going on around here.''

When Takahara nodded in agreement, the two agents took off after Lightstone.

Thirty seconds later Henry Lightstone and Larry Paxton were racing down the road in the bright green rented Jeep with Lightstone at the wheel.

"How's that arm holding up?" Lighthouse asked, glancing over at Paxton, who was busy trying to reload 10mm magazines from a box of ammo he'd retrieved from the backpack.

"Jes' great," Paxton muttered darkly, having to work at not bouncing out of the seat or losing the magazines and ammo. He glared ahead at the rising cloud of dust coming off the sand-and-dirt-covered road. "Can't you drive any faster?"

"Sure, but I'm afraid the wheels will fall off if I do," Lightstone said as he reached down for the radio and brought it up to the side of his face.

"Stoner, this is Henry," Lightstone said, ignoring radio procedure. "We're in the bright green Jeep. Is that them up ahead of us?"

"Okay, I see you," Stoner's deep voice acknowledged. "The two gray Jeeps are about a quarter mile ahead of you, and the red one's maybe a couple hundred yards beyond that. We're pretty sure Maas and Chareaux are in the rear Jeep, with Chareaux driving, but who are the other guys?"

"The guy in the red Jeep may be one of the money men linked in with Bloom," Lightstone said. "Forget about him, it's Maas and Chareaux and the other guy we want. We figure they're heading for the airstrip at Cutlass Bay. There's a decent chance that the other guy by himself is the bastard who keeps trying to blow us up. Watch out for him—he's got some kind of souped-up shotgun that takes down doors like they were made of cardboard."

"Yeah, no shit," Stoner acknowledged. "We've already got one hole the size of my fist in the right wing."

"Well, tell Woeshack to stay the hell away from him! You guys just circle around up there and spot for us."

"Ten-four, we're . . . wait a minute, they just drove past the turn for Cutlass Bay. Looks like they're headed north."

"Are there any airstrips up that way?"

"Hold on, let me check the map."

Lightstone stuck the radio between his legs and then tried to accelerate the elderly Jeep an extra couple of miles per hour while he waited for Stoner to get back on the radio.

"Okay," Stoner said, "it looks like there's one airstrip between New Bight and Fernandez Bay, which is about ten to twelve miles north of your location. The only other one is at Arthur's Town, at the far north end of the island.''

"Ten-four. Stay close enough so they don't disappear on us," Lightstone said. Then he stuffed the radio under the seat so that he had both hands free to drive.

Driving like a madman, Lightstone gradually gained ground on the two gray Jeeps until the distance between the three vehicles was reduced to about a hundred yards. They had just passed a sign that said:

NEW BIGHT
COMMISSIONER'S
OFFICE

THE HERMITAGE

NEXT RIGHT

when Lightstone yelled to Paxton: "Can you hit one of the drivers or the tires from here?''

"I don't know. I'll try," Paxton yelled back.

Bracing his right arm against the Jeep's roll bar, Paxton began firing 10mm rounds at the rearmost of the two gray Jeeps. The first four rounds appeared to have no effect other than to cause Alex Chareaux to hunch down at the wheel. Maas simply looked back with a smile on his Teutonic face.

The fifth round punctured the fuel tank mounted on the underside of Maas and Chareaux's Jeep, causing gasoline to start flying around in all directions.

Gerd Maas looked back, immediately assessed the situation, and snapped out an order. Responding instantly, because he could not accept the possibility of being captured and put in prison again, Alex Chareaux made use of the evasive-driving skills he'd learned in the narrow winding bayou roads of southern Louisiana to send the small off-road vehicle into a rear-end sliding right-hand turn up a narrow dirt road. The spinning tires sent a huge cloud of dust and dirt flying into the air, partially concealing the road.

Henry Lightstone had less than three seconds to make a decision.

He hesitated, not wanting to have to choose. But finally, at the last possible moment, he jammed on the brakes and downshifted into the turn.

They were still sliding sideways, the spinning tires trying to get a grip on the loose dirt, when Paxton suddenly screamed "Look out!" and used his right foot to shove Lightstone out of the driver's seat. Then he twisted sideways out of the left-side passenger's seat just as the cloud of dust cleared enough to reveal Riser swinging around in his stopped Jeep with the four-bore rifle up to his shoulder. The two massive "shotgun" rounds blew out the entire front window and dashboard of the bright green Jeep as Paxton and Lightstone tumbled head over heels across the dirt road.

Stunned by the double jolt of his head hitting the ground, and the heavy cast being gouged deep into his ribs, Larry Paxton lost his grip on his Smith & Wesson, but Lightstone's pistol somehow managed to stay stuck inside the waistband of his jeans. Dazed and bleeding, the enraged agent pulled the double-action pistol out and sent five rounds streaking in the direction of Riser's rapidly disappearing Jeep.

Then, staggering to his feet, Lightstone stumbled over to where Paxton was cursing, and trying to sit up, and at the same time, trying to fumble around for his lost weapon.

Bending over stiffly, Lightstone retrieved the dirt-covered semiauto, shook the dirt and debris out of the barrel as best he could, and then handed the pistol back to his still dazed partner.

"Try holding it in your teeth next time," he suggested, coughing to clear his lungs of the dust and dirt as he helped Paxton get to his feet. Then he took a closer look at his partner's glazed eyes.

"You still in there?"

"Oh, hell, yes." Paxton blinked groggily, looking as if he

night fall back down at any moment. "Which way'd the bastards go?"

"That way and that way. Take your pick," Lightstone said as he helped guide Paxton over to the stalled Jeep that was amazingly still upright.

Then he saw the inside of the shattered vehicle.

"Shit," he muttered, observing that in addition to the dashboard and windshield, both seats had been torn to shreds by the double fusillade of buckshot. "Good thing you decided we ought to jump."

"Man's really beginning to piss me off," Larry Paxton mumbled to himself as Lightstone tried to restart the engine, with no success.

Slamming his hand on the steering wheel with a curse, Lightstone reached under the seat and retrieved the radio, hoping that its sensitive innards were still intact.

"Stoner, you still there?" he said, keying the mike.

"Yeah, you guys okay?" Stoner's voice came back immediately, scratchy but still clearly audible.

"We're fine. Just took a tumble and got our Jeep shot up. Maas and Chareaux are on foot, too, somewhere around this Hermitage area, whatever that is."

"Copy," Stoner acknowledged. "You guys need help?"

Lightstone looked over at Paxton, who was leaning against the Jeep, looking as if he were finally starting to regain most of his senses. The acting team leader shook his head firmly.

"Negative," Lightstone responded. "What's your situation?"

"We're circling around the airstrip out here just north of you guys. Both the red and the gray Jeep are parked in front of what we assume is the main airport building. Haven't seen either of our suspects yet. We're going to stay up here, keep an eye on things until the FBI gets here."

"The FBI's got an office in the Bahamas?"

"Not exactly an office," Stoner chuckled. "More like a thirteen-agent hostage recovery team, a combined FBI-DEA

task force, three choppers, Halahan and Moore and our old
buddy Al Grynard, all on account of us.''

"Well, I'll be damned." Lightstone smiled. "When are
they getting here?''

"Be a few," Stoner said. "The command chopper just
touched down at the villa, and they're waiting for the rest of
the response team to arrive. Task force is out on the perimeter, keeping things contained. Snoopy got them in contact
with us on the VHF emergency channel.''

"Okay, listen," Lightstone said, eyeing Paxton, "we're
fine here. Why don't you have them respond to your area
first, let the FBI deal with that guy with the cannon. Once
they do that, then you guys can come over here and spot for
us. Maas and Chareaux aren't going to get very far on foot.''

"Ten-four, watch yourselves.''

Reaching back into the rear seat, Lightstone pulled out
Mike Takahara's blue backpack, reloaded his pistol with a
full magazine, and then began stuffing loaded magazines in
the back pockets of his jeans.

"What do you think you're doing?" Paxton demanded.

"Thought I'd go for a hike. Why don't you stay here,
keep an eye out, in case that shithead with the cannon comes
back before the FBI gets here.''

"Your ass,' Paxton muttered as he reached into the backpack and pulled out the pair of binoculars, which he hung
around his neck. "Gimme some o' them things.''

Paxton stuffed three of the loaded magazines in his own
back pocket.

"You sure you're up to this?" Lightstone asked.

Larry Paxton rolled his head around, blinked his eyes
once more, and then smiled a cold, malicious smile.

"Oh, yeah," he said, "you better *believe* Ah'm up to it.''

Moving as fast as they could while still maintaining an
alert watch, they found the abandoned Jeep with the keys in
the ignition a couple of hundred yards up the road. Looking
up, the two agents could see the ancient stone Hermitage at
the top of the tallest hill in the Bahamas—an arduous climb

for the two extremely sore, tired, and furious agents.

"Bastards jes' couldn't make this easy, could they?" Paxton said, searching for some sign of the two suspects on the steep rock-and-scrub-brush-covered hillside as Lightstone retrieved the keys and put them in his pocket.

"I think Maas looks on this whole deal as some kind of medieval tournament that wouldn't be any fun if it were too easy," Lightstone replied, duplicating Paxton's visual search with his 10mm Smith & Wesson cocked and ready in a double-handed grip.

They moved up the steep trail quickly and carefully, very alert now because the surrounding hillside and the stone chapel and bell tower and adjoining buildings all offered excellent ambush points, and they knew that they couldn't afford to give men like Maas and Chareaux any more of an advantage than they already had.

Near the top of the hill, at the small, bunkerlike tomb of Father Jerome, the Catholic missionary who had built the Hermitage in the early 1940s, just below the cluster of stone buildings, they stopped and searched again . . . and saw no one at all.

"Where the hell did they go?" Paxton whispered.

"I don't know, but they've got to be around here somewhere."

Working together, they first checked the rock and concrete tomb, noting the mossy wooden gate lying loose in front of the entrance, and the words imprinted in the front of the concrete roof: Blessed are the dead who die in the Lord.

Lightstone started to turn away, caught movement in the tomb's shadowy depths out of the corner of his eye, and spun around with his finger tightening on the trigger of the double-action pistol.

Disturbed out of its slumber by the agent's aggressive movements, the little Cat Island turtle continued its slow meandering pace to the entrance of the tomb, and then paused to chew on a piece of fern, blissfully unaware of how close it had come to an early and violent death.

Shaking their heads, the two wildlife agents carefully worked their way up the narrow stone steps, and then, one by one, checked the small chapel, the bell tower, and the closet-like living quarters with the same results.

No Maas and no Chareaux.

Positioning themselves with their backs against the short, stubby, missilelike stone bell tower, so they could see any approach from either side, the two agents looked down the barren scrub-brush-covered hillside in a northwesterly direction toward Fernandez Bay.

"I think I see Woeshack and Stoner over there," Lightstone said, pointing down the mountain where a small single-engined plane was circling a small airstrip.

"Where?" Paxton asked, setting his pistol down and lifting the binoculars up to his eyes with his right hand.

"Right—uh, oh, what's that?"

From their high vantage-point the two wildlife agents could see a small twin-engined airplane taxiing out to the end of the runway. It was immediately obvious that Woeshack saw it too, because the scrappy Eskimo agent/pilot swooped down in a low pass over the runway, pulling up right in front of the twin-engined plane just as it swung around to face into the wind.

"What's Woeshack going to do, try to hit the guy with his prop?" Paxton asked.

"Wouldn't surprise me any," Lightstone said, "but he'd better watch out for that damn cannon."

"Oh, oh, there he goes," Paxton said, watching the twin-engine plane begin to accelerate down the runway before Woeshack could get the Cessna back around into a blocking position.

"Shit, the bastard's going to get away," Lightstone muttered, glaring helplessly as the twin-engined plane began to rise off the airstrip.

"Uh, maybe not," Paxton said quietly, pointing down in the direction of the coastline where three darkly painted helicopters were coming in fast in a single line approach.

"Looks to me like the cavalry just arrived."

He brought the binoculars up again. "Yep, metallic signs on the side that say 'FBI' and everything. Definitely the cavalry."

Even as Paxton spoke, the three helicopters broke ranks and swarmed down in the direction of the runway. One of the Blackhawks made a run right over the top of the slowly climbing twin-prop plane, temporarily forcing it to lower its rate of climb, and then looped around again for another pass as the smaller command helicopter and the other Blackhawk circled the airstrip.

Then Stoner came over the air, the relief evident in his voice even though they'd turned the radio speaker way down. "Hey, guys, we're getting out of here and heading back your way."

"Ten-four." Lightstone spoke softly into the radio, his eyes making yet another search of the surrounding area as he and Paxton watched the assault helicopter force the twin-engined plane to maintain an extremely low angle of climb out over the water.

"Hey, Stoner," Lightstone added after a moment, "why don't you guys take a couple loops around this hill when you get here. Maas and Chareaux disappeared on us. Can't find them anywhere up here on top."

"Ten-four, be there in one."

"Oh, oh, I think that FBI chopper pilot just ran out of patience," Paxton whispered.

As Lightstone turned his attention back to the air battle, the Blackhawk helicopter suddenly broke out of its side-by-side following pattern and looped around into a broadside position with respect to the low-flying plane. The distant rattling sound of machine-gun fire reached the agents as the vertical stabilizer portion of the small plane's tail section seemed to come apart in shreds. Responding to the assault like a suddenly stunned pelican, the twin-engined plane began a gradual descent toward the water. Moments later, as the three helicopters moved into a wide circling pattern, the plane belly-landed into the ocean with a huge splash.

"All *right.*" Lightstone grinned. Then he looked up and noticed the rapid approach of the small Cessna.

"We'd better head back down the hill, see if we can help them spot these assholes," Lightstone said.

"Right. You take the point, I'll get Woeshack and Stoner oriented," Paxton said, stuffing the 10mm semiautomatic into his sling and picking up the radio.

As Henry Lightstone began moving cautiously out across the open ground, heading toward the narrow winding steps that led down to the open tomb, Paxton followed a few yards back and brought the radio up to the side of his mouth. "Hey, Stoner," he said in a hoarse whisper, "you guys see anything up here?"

"Negative, but we're coming around to make a full loop," the deep-voiced agent replied.

As the Cessna started to bank around the small stone Hermitage buildings, Henry Lightstone went down the narrow steps, glanced to his left to confirm that the mossy wooden gate was still in place, and then started moving in the direction of the tall crucifix figure to his right.

Paxton was halfway down the steps, having to watch the placement of his large feet, when the Cessna came into sight around the bell tower. Paxton was starting to bring his right hand up to wave when Stoner screamed into the radio: "Larry, look out!"

Startled by Stoner's screamed warning, Paxton missed one of the tiny stone steps, stumbled forward, and then flung his plaster-casted left arm up in a futile effort to regain his balance, sending his pistol and the radio flying just as Gerd Maas rose to a standing position—far to Paxton's left—with a camouflage-painted bow in his hand, and sent a broadhead shaft streaking straight toward the center of the acting team leader's chest.

By the time that Paxton realized what was happening, the broadhead arrow had punched all the way through his plaster-covered forearm and lodged into his sternum at the juncture of his second right rib, effectively pinning the cast to his chest.

Paxton's agonized scream was drowned out by the roar of the circling Cessna.

Distracted and partially deafened by the circling plane, Henry Lightstone never saw or heard Alex Chareaux come running out of the tomb. But then he realized that his inner senses were screaming for attention, and he started to turn to his right in an instinctive move to protect his back.

But in spite of the subconscious warning, the primary thing that saved Henry Lightstone's life in that brief moment was the fact that Chareaux was completely focused on the spot where he intended to drive his knife blade home, and he never saw the small Cat Island turtle that was trying desperately to get out of his way.

Intending to drive off his right foot and send the knife blade plunging into Lightstone's right kidney with one savage thrust, Chareaux's foot twisted off the slippery turtle shell, and he gasped in shock as he stumbled forward off balance with the knife.

At that moment, and as Henry Lightstone was still coming around into a defensive stance, a burst of pistol rounds behind his back ripped into the nose cowling of the low-flying small plane. Lightstone continued turning to his right, blinked in disbelief when he observed Paxton thrashing around on the ground with an arrow shaft sticking out of his arm and chest. Then he saw the flashing knife blade out of the corner of his right eye.

Lightstone had only an instant to set his feet, drop his pistol, and deflect the thrusting knife hand, before rolling backward into a combined wrist-lock and leg-thrusting judo throw. Then he and Chareaux were tumbling down the hill, furiously striking and clawing and gouging at each other's vital points, completely oblivious of the shuddering Cessna overhead that was desperately trying to gain altitude before it finally surrendered to gravity and nose-dived down into the barren hillside less than fifty yards away.

Breaking loose from Chareaux and coming up to his feet—completely obvious of anything other than his determination to survive and to kill Alex Chareaux with his bare hands—Lightstone lunged forward with his right foot, slammed the heel of his right hand into the underside of Chareaux's jaw, continued his turn until he was in tight with his back to the Cajun poacher, drove his right elbow sharply into Chareaux's lower chest, breaking three of his ribs; and then twisted around sharply with a *ki-yi* scream and a back-fisted strike that smashed the Cajun's nose in a spray of blood.

Stunned but hardly incapacitated, Chareaux held on to Lightstone's shirt, and then retaliated by first slamming his forehead into the agent's face, splitting the skin over Lightstone's left eye, and then slashing down at his femoral artery—a move that Lightstone barely deflected in time with his open hand, causing the sharp blade to slice across his open palm.

As he twisted back into a crouched defensive stance, pressing the palm of his left hand into his hip to stem the bleeding, Lightstone saw—for the first time—the crumbled and burning Cessna.

Eyes widening in rage, Lightstone lunged forward again, using his slashed left hand to block Chareaux's savage attempt to gouge out his eyes. Then, moving in close, he thrust the extended fingers of his right hand deep into the Cajun's exposed stomach, clenched his right hand into a tight fist and drove it into Chareaux's already broken rib cage, then hammered the cursing Cajun to the ground with a spinning roundhouse kick that nearly dislocated his jaw.

As he scrabbled around blindly on his hands and knees, Chareaux's fingers brushed across the handle of his knife. Grasping at the weapon, he staggered to his feet with a feral snarl, his reddened eyes glaring furiously.

Meeting Chareaux's rage with an expression of cold determination, Henry Lightstone casually stepped back into a loose defensive stance, the palm of his freely bleeding left hand now pressed against his tensed thigh, as he prepared himself to block the knife thrust—from whichever direction it came—and then take Chareaux out with a killing blow to his throat.

"That is enough!" Gerd Maas yelled out from his position about halfway between the two combatants and the burning plane. "*Herr* Lightstone is mine now!"

"No, he is not! He is mine! He killed my brothers!" Chareaux screamed through his horribly split and bleeding lips, ignoring Maas as he slowly moved toward his hated adversary.

Keeping an eye on Chareaux and ignoring the bow in the German counterterrorist's hand, Lightstone yelled out: "Wait your turn, Maas! When I'm finished with him, you're next!"

Gerd Maas smiled and shook his head. "No, you are injured. I wait no longer." Then, in a quieter voice that was just barely audible to Chareaux over the crackling noises from the burning plane, he added: "And besides, *Herr* Lightstone didn't kill your brother. I did. And unlike McNulty, he truly *did* die like a terrified pig."

Chareaux never hesitated. Twisting around furiously, he started to send the deadly fighting knife spinning into Gerd Maas's exposed abdomen, and then gasped in shock when the broadhead arrow punctured his sternum with a loud thunk, and sliced through his heart.

Chareaux was still falling when Lightstone started toward his dropped pistol. But then he hesitated when Gerd Maas yelled out: "Stop, or I kill your friend!"

Looking up, Henry Lighthouse saw that Maas had the hunting bow drawn back again, only this time the broadhead arrow was aimed at Larry Paxton, who had managed to come up to a kneeling position. Lightstone glanced back once more at the 10mm semiautomatic that was only a dozen feet away, and Maas shook his head.

"No, *Herr* Lightstone," he said in his barely audible voice. "You cannot possibly get to it in time. And if you try, your friend will surely die."

Lightstone stood there and glared at the German counter-terrorist.

"Give it up, Maas. An FBI SWAT team will be here in a few minutes. And they're not going to worry about that bow, or the two of us, for that matter. They're either going to take you in or put you down."

"No, I don't think they will be here so fast." Maas smiled as he took a few steps closer, bringing the bow down but keeping the lethal shaft notched and ready. "They are very busy, I think, trying to locate *Herr* Riser and his amusing rifle."

"Herr *Riser*?"

"My new employer." Maas smiled.

"Ah. Well, I hate to burst your bubble, Maas, but the last I saw, the FBI was fishing your new employer out of the bay. And when they get back up here, I don't think they're going to be all that interested in negotiating over a couple of agent hostages."

"But why should I negotiate?" the white-haired counter-terrorist asked, his eyes gleaming with amusement. "It is you that I want, and you are here already."

Henry Lightstone cocked his head for a moment and then smiled in sudden understanding.

"Okay, Maas, if it's a little one-on-one you're after, open fields, flashing banners, the whole works, that's fine with me." Lightstone made a show of looking around. "But it looks like one of us forgot to bring the horse and lance outfits. So how are we going to do it? Knives, rocks, bare hands?"

"The knives, I think," Maas said thoughtfully, ignoring the agent's deliberately taunting words. "A more noble way for you to die, *ja*? But first, you will disassemble your pistol."

"You're going to let me pick up that gun?" Lightstone asked skeptically.

"*Ja*, but slowly, by the barrel, with your right hand. Empty and disassemble with your left."

"My left hand is cut," Lightstone reminded him.

"But not so bad, I think." Maas smiled. "Do it anyway, or I put this arrow through your friend's heart, right now, just like Chareaux. Only this time I will be sure not to hit his cast. You understand?"

Nodding in agreement and keeping his left hand pressed tight against his hip, Lightstone stepped forward and slowly picked up the 10mm Smith & Wesson semiautomatic by the slide with his bruised and swollen right hand. Working slowly and methodically with his painful and bloody—but only superficially cut—left hand, he released the magazine, racked the round out of the chamber, disassembled the slide and barrel, and then dropped the pieces to the ground.

"And now your friend's weapon too—in that exact same manner, if you please, *Herr* Lightstone."

Lightstone walked over to where Paxton was sitting, wobbly, on his heels, his eyes glassy but still glaring with rage. He'd managed to pull the broadhead out of his sternum, and his shirt was now starting to soak through with blood.

"There's a round in the chamber and nine in the magazine," Paxton said softly as he continued to keep his eyes fixed on the German counterterrorist. "Put the bastard down, Henry. That's a direct order."

Lightstone smiled as he reached down and carefully picked up Paxton's stainless steel Smith & Wesson by the barrel with his right hand.

"Sorry, buddy, but supervisors aren't allowed to give direct orders when they've sitting on their butts with arrows sticking through the middle of their arm casts," he said as he went through the same painful process of slowly emptying and disassembling Paxton's pistol, and then dropping the pieces to the ground, taking care to keep his hands in open view. "One of those new rules. Read it somewhere in my federal employee's manual."

"Don't give me that bullshit, Lightstone—you've never even opened that damned manual," Paxton muttered.

"Soon as you're done complaining, how about lending

me that handkerchief,'' Lightstone said, and then waited patiently for Paxton to remove the sweat-stained handkerchief from around his neck. Holding one end of the cloth rectangle in his teeth, Lightstone awkwardly double-looped it around the palm of his left hand, tied it as tight as he could with his right, and then tightly clenched his hand around the cloth in an effort to slow the bleeding that had already soaked the left side of his jeans.

"How the hell do you think you're gonna take him on with only one good hand?" Paxton demanded. "You saw those tapes from that training center. Surgery or not, that bastard's got reflexes like a goddamned cat."

"Not a problem." Lighthouse smiled with a calm expression in his eyes as he turned to face Maas. "I picked up a couple of new tricks from Snoopy."

"Snoopy!? What're you talking about? Takahara can't fight worth shit,'' Paxton rasped, glaring furiously at Maas as he tried to pull the arrow out of the cast, and nearly fainted from the resulting pain.

"Yeah, I know.'' Lightstone nodded. "That's why he cheats."

"And the radio, *Herr* Lightstone,'' Maas added in a cheerful, anticipatory voice, having moved closer to the two agents so that he was now less than twenty feet away, his cold blue eyes focused intently on the movements of his chosen adversary.

Lightstone picked up the radio and tossed it in the German counterterrorist's direction. Then he walked over and picked up Alex Chareaux's knife, and started toward Maas, when he spotted the movement. He turned back with a gentle and pleasant smile on his face.

"Hold it a minute, Maas,'' he said over his shoulder, "we've got a noncombatant in the way."

Reaching down, Henry Lightstone scooped up the small Cat Island turtle, walked over, and handed it to Paxton.

"My lucky turtle,'' he said. "Keep your eyes on it.'' And then, saying each word slowly and distinctly: "I mean it, *keep your eyes on it.''*

Paxton's eyes were barely focusing, but he could see enough to understand what his wild-card agent friend was up to. ''You really think it'll work?''

''We didn't exactly *run* ten miles.'' Lightstone shrugged. ''But I figure it all amounts to pretty much the same thing.''

''Hey, Maas, you asshole,'' Paxton called out in a slurred voice, keeping his eyes focused as best he could on the approaching counterterrorist, ''whadda you think about a guy wants to pay off a debt with an endangered turtle he stole from a priest's tomb? That the kind of hero you want to fight?''

''I think you Americans are much too soft when it comes to animals,'' the German said indifferently as he tossed aside the bow and arrows, quickly disassembled and discarded his pistol, and then drew a deadly sharp fighting knife from his belt sheath. He held the blade up so that the sun glittered off its sharpened edge. ''It is a failing, *Herr* Paxton. And in your case, a fatal one. After I kill *Herr* Lightstone, I will kill you and the turtle also, to prove that it is not such a good thing to be soft and weak.''

''You hear that, buddy?'' Paxton mumbled down at the struggling turtle. ''Now we're both on the endangered list.'' Then he looked up at Lightstone again.

''Okay, Henry,'' Paxton rasped, his eyes glassy, ''the turtle and I are both rooting for you. Tear the bastard's heart out.''

Henry Lightstone walked forward until he was about ten feet away from the grinning ICER assault team leader.

''You ready for this, Maas?''

''*Ja*, I am ready. I have waited for this moment for a long time.''

''Good.'' Lightstone nodded as he squatted down and casually tossed Chareaux's knife aside. ''Then I hope you enjoy it.''

Gerd Maas blinked in momentary confusion.

''Stand up and pick up the knife,'' he ordered.

"No, I don't think so." Lightstone smiled, looking up into the cold blue eyes of the now furious counterterrorist.

"What is this? Are you hurt so bad you cannot fight?"

"No, I can fight just fine."

"What is it then? You are a coward?" Maas demanded accusingly.

"No, not really."

"Then you must get up and pick up the knife, or I will kill your friend."

"No, Maas, I don't think you're going to do that either. You see, Paxton and I made us a little deal a while back. The deal is, he and I have to chase the bad guys though ten miles of swamp land, or whatever." Lightstone waved his hand to indicate that the scrub brush of Cat Island would be an acceptable substitute. "And then, after we do that, he and I get to sit down and pop a beer—only, see, we forgot to bring the beer—"

"Get up, *Herr* Lightstone, or I kill you now," Maas warned in a hoarse voice, his blue eyes deadly cold.

"—while Stoner finishes the job."

"Ah, but your big friend Stoner is no longer—" Maas started to say. But then a sudden sense of understanding flashed in his eyes, and he twisted away just in time to avoid a lunging tackle by the singed, bloodied, and barely conscious ex-Raider.

"Ha! You think . . ." Maas started to laugh, but then whirled back around with inhumanly quick reflexes, bringing the knife around into an upward thrust as he sensed Lightstone coming in fast.

The knife blade was only inches from Henry Lightstone's exposed stomach when the agent drove the open palm of his already injured left hand forward in a tightly focused defensive move.

Gerd Maas felt the jarring block all the way up his arm, and thought he'd missed. But then he saw the bloody blade sticking out the back of Lightstone's hand. Grinning widely, Maas started to jerk the blade upward in a cruel slicing motion, and then his eyes opened wide when he felt the fingers of Lightstone's impaled hand close around the hilt of the knife.

Recognizing the danger immediately, Maas tightened his grip and started to pull back when he suddenly understood that Henry Lightstone's deliberate act of discarding Chareaux's knife had caused him to pay less attention to the agent's right hand—a mental error that Henry Lightstone capitalized on by driving the heel of his right hand hard into the lower edge of the German counterterrorist's rib cage.

Had he been able to twist clear, Gerd Maas would have recovered from the punishing blow in a matter of moments. But the superbly conditioned hunter of death *couldn't* twist clear, because Lightstone still had a tight grip on the hilt of his knife *and* his hand. And by the time that Maas comprehended the magnitude of his error, it was too late. The German counterterrorist screamed and cursed in pain as the edge of Lightstone's slashing shoe tore into his surgically reconstructed left knee.

Desperately trying to recover, Gerd Maas twisted the knife handle sharply in a vicious attempt to distract or disable his unyielding opponent, drawing a wide-eyed scream out of Henry Lightstone. But it didn't stop the furiously fighting agent from driving the lethally extended fingers of his free right hand deep into Maas's throat, just missing his larynx.

Stunned, severely injured, and down on his hands and knees, Gerd Maas had no intention of quitting. He was lunging toward Lightstone once more, going for the eyes of the dazed agent—who was down on his own knees, working to pull the twisted knife blade out of the palm of his hand—when Maas suddenly found his left foot caught in the muscular grip of Dwight Stoner.

Snarling with rage, Maas whipped around and drove the heel of his right shoe square into the face of the burned, bleeding, and nearly unconscious ex-Raider . . . and then had to strike out a second time before he was able to pull his severely damaged leg loose from Stoner's clenched hand.

Coming up to his feet, Maas hobbled forward into the beginning of a savage kick that would have easily broken Stoner's neck. But then he gasped in agonized disbelief when Lightstone suddenly lunged forward, caught him by the left arm, wrenched him back around so that they were face to face, drove Chareaux's fighting knife deep into his lower abdomen, and then—in one furious motion—yanked the razor-edged knife upward.

For a brief moment the two men stared into each other's eyes. Then, just as Gerd Maas's lips began to form a bloodied smile, his blue eyes glazed over and he collapsed to the ground in a lifeless heap.

Dazed and nauseous from the pain in his horribly cut hand, Henry Lightstone had to crawl from Stoner to Woeshack on his knees and one hand to confirm that both severely injured and now unconscious agents were still alive.

It then took him almost a full minute before he could get his hand rewrapped in the handkerchief, pick up the discarded pack-set radio, call for help, and then get up on his feet and stagger over to where a barely conscious Larry Paxton was still sprawled on the ground, trying with very little success to reassemble his pistol. There were faint sounds of automatic-weapons fire in the distance, but neither agent paid it any attention.

"Thought I told you to watch that turtle," Lightstone whispered heavily as he knelt next to the fumbling and glassy-eyed Paxton.

"Too busy picking up after mah team—gawddamned people leave their shit all over the place," Paxton mumbled. Then he tried to focus his eyes on the blood-covered form of his partner. "You get him, or he get you?"

"I got him . . . thanks to Stoner."

Paxton blinked and then stared out across the sloping ground, trying unsuccessfully to focus his blurred eyes on the smoldering plane and the three unmoving figures.

"They alive?"

"Who, Stoner and Woeshack? Yeah, I think so," Lightstone said groggily, trying not to bump his agonizingly painful hand against anything solid. "Both of them are out cold, but they're breathing okay. Probably got internal injuries from the crash. Gotta get some help out here, get them to a hospital soon as we can."

Paxton smiled a glassy smile.

"Ol' Stoner ain't got none o' your fancy moves, Henry, but you gotta admire the man's style."

"Yeah, we'd be in deep shit if we didn't have—" Lightstone started to agree, when the still air was suddenly ruptured by a distant, echoing explosion.

Staggering painfully to their feet, the two agents stared out toward the distant airport and watched in silence as the pieces of a shattered Blackhawk helicopter tumbled and fluttered to the ground like bloodied and broken leaves.

Chapter Thirty-seven

SAC Hal Owens, the commander of the FBI airborne raid team, had been directing the air search of the Fernandez Bay airstrip property from the small surveillance helicopter when the firefight began.

He had sent the larger and slower Blackhawk up high, to monitor the situation with its cargo-door-mounted M-60 machine guns (while Jim Whittman and his hostage rescue team in the other assault helicopter were recovering the occupants from the downed fixed wing), when a concussive rifle shot from the airstrip office doorway blew out the armored glass right next to the Blackhawk pilot's shoulder, killing him instantly.

As the stunned and blood-splattered copilot sent the chopper skyward in a desperate effort to avoid any more of the armor-piercing slugs—and thereby causing the cursing door gunner to miss the small airstrip terminal building completely with a sustained burst of 7.65mm rounds—a second 1900-grain slug tore through the armored engine cowling and ruptured a fuel line. Seconds later, to the horror of all aboard the command chopper, the still-climbing Blackhawk disintegrated into a ball of flame and tumbling debris.

Owens got on the radio immediately.

"May-day! May-day! Air Unit Two, disengage and respond immediately! Air Three is down! Repeat, Air Three is down! Suspect is located in the Fernandez Bay airstrip building. Move it, now!"

Unarmed, and otherwise helpless against a weapon as lethal as Riser's four-bore rifle, Owens ordered the lightly armored surveillance helicopter to stay high out of range, waiting for the second Blackhawk to disengage from the rescue effort and respond.

Less than three minutes later, having left a dazed Sam Tisbury and two FBI agents floating in a quickly inflated life raft, the second of the raid team's military assault helicopters made a roaring pass across the airstrip terminal building with an M-60 machine gun and seven M-16 assault rifles blazing—punching hundreds of holes through the glass windows and thin wood and metal walls.

At Owen's direction, the Blackhawk made two more similar passes with almost identical results.

"Want me to insert the team in now?" the pilot of the Blackhawk asked Owens over the radio, and got a confirming "ten-four" from the raid commander.

The assault helicopter was starting to come around again for a final pass when a pair of explosions erupted from a small garage next to the main airport building. One of the massive slugs streaked through the open cargo doorway, causing the machine gunner and the seven agents—including Whittman—to duck reflexively. The second slug ricocheted harmlessly off the Blackhawk's body armor.

Smiling grimly to himself, the chopper pilot quickly

whipped his helicopter around in a looping half-circle, presenting its opposite side to the garage—but now a good hundred yards farther away.

"Okay, guys." The pilot spoke over the intercom system. "We should be out of his range now. Let him have it!"

At that moment a stream of 7.65mm bullets ripped across the side of the hovering aircraft, badly wounding three of the agents—including Whittman and the machine gunner—and starring the armored glass next to the copilot. Continuing to use the M-60 that he had taken from illicit arms dealer George Hoffsteadler weeks earlier, Riser sent a second stream of bullets into the assault chopper's engine, causing the churning aircraft to shudder and start billowing smoke, and then a third burst in the direction of the rapidly departing surveillance helicopter.

The second pilot was a combat veteran who immediately disengaged and shut off the engine, triggered the fire extinguisher, and then auto-rotated the crippled aircraft down into an emergency landing that looked a lot more like a barely controlled crash, about three hundred yards from the airstrip building.

As soon as the helicopter hit the ground, Riser started firing again. Using short, controlled bursts, he emptied one full disintegrating-link belt of ammo—and then half of another—at the grounded Blackhawk as Whittman and the surviving members of the air assault team pulled themselves out of the wreckage. Working desperately to put the downed helicopter at a safe distance between them and the deadly machine-gun fire, the agents dragged each other to a defensive position about seventy-five yards behind the still smoking Blackhawk, and then began to tend to their wounded comrades.

As SAC Hal Owens called for backup and then began circling helplessly above the surviving members of his raid team, Riser picked up the M-60 in one hand, the four-bore rifle in the other, and turned to the suntanned young woman who was cowering behind a large bale of recycled paper.

"We've leaving, right now," he growled, and then ran out the back door of the garage and around to the nearby sheet-metal hangar.

Once in the hangar, Riser unlocked and dropped open the door of his waiting Learjet while the young woman—who, in the period of a few short weeks, had made the amazing transition from being a bodyguard for an illicit arms dealer to the accomplice of a professional assassin—started to pull open the large hangar doors. She had one side fully open and was starting to work on the other when she saw it.

"Wait a minute, what's that?" she demanded, pointing in the direction of the office structure in the far rear corner of the hangar.

Riser looked up and then blinked in surprise as he saw the man-shaped silhouette that had been cut through the plaster-board office wall. His mind instantly flashed back to the similar cut he had made through the wall of a Westin Hotel closet back in Boston. At that moment sunlight suddenly let in through the corner window inside the office caused the silhouette to glow brightly—almost like a human-sized ghost.

"What is it?" the azure-eyed woman who no longer had to call herself Anne-Marie demanded again, but Riser simply twisted his face into an evil smile. He quickly scooped up the M-60 and then triggered the remaining hundred-or-so rounds in the chain-link ammo belt through the thin walls of the office in one long, sustained burst that sent the young woman staggering to the concrete floor with her hands clenched over her ears amid dozens of bouncing, expended casings.

Tossing the machine gun aside, Riser was starting to reach for the four-bore when a movement at the rear door of the hangar caught his eye.

"Go ahead, pick it up. See what happens," Henry Light-stone said as he stepped inside the hangar with his 10mm Smith & Wesson pistol out and ready.

Riser remained motionless, his practiced eyes making a

rapid assessment of this newcomer, noting the soaked handkerchief wrapped around the left hand that appeared to be dripping blood, the torn and dirt-encrusted clothing, the bloodied, familiar face . . . and the deadly cold expression in his eyes.

"I'm very disappointed in Maas and Chareaux," he finally said in a deep, growling voice. "They should have had no difficulty in dealing with you." Then he turned to look at the silhouette again. "However, that *was* a clever diversion on your part, Mr. Lightstone. You went to the hotel, I take it?" he went on in a conversational voice.

"It was a memorable scene."

"Crude, but obviously effective." Riser shrugged, still staring at the office wall that now had over a hundred bullet holes in it, in addition to the roughly cut figure. "What did you use?"

Reaching behind his back with his tightly wrapped and bloody left hand, Henry Lightstone pulled the fighting knife out of his belt and tossed it to the floor.

The blood-and-plaster-covered knife clattered loudly in the cavernous hangar as the young woman slowly removed her hands from her ears. She remained there on the floor, blinking and staring, uncomprehending, at the slender, jean-and shirt-clad figure who seemed not the least bit intimidated by her absolutely terrifying employer.

"I borrowed a knife from Chareaux," Lightstone replied evenly. "He wasn't going to need it anymore."

"You killed Chareaux?"

"Chareaux, *and* Maas too."

Riser nodded slowly.

"You were outside the building, of course, when you let in the light?" the huge man said matter-of-factly. He didn't seem to be interested in the fate of his most recently hired employees.

"That's right," Lightstone said, keeping the 10mm semi-automatic pistol extended in his right hand and centered on Riser's chest.

"Please help me," the young woman whispered, starting to tremble as she stared at Lightstone, trying desperately to decide . . . and knowing that she didn't dare be wrong.

"Who are you?" Lightstone asked, never taking his eyes off the huge man standing next to the open door of the Learjet.

"My name's Valerie," she replied in a tremulous voice, staring wide-eyed at the impassive face of Riser. "He—he kidnapped me. He said—he was g-going to hurt me real bad if I didn't d-do what he said."

"What did he want you to do?"

"What? I don't know . . . he didn't . . . please, let me get away from him. I'm afraid he's going to—"

"It's all right, he's not going to hurt you. Just move over there, by the office," Lightstone directed, continuing to keep the front sight of the 10mm pistol centered on Riser's broad chest.

"Please, I just want to go home," the young woman whispered as she slowly backed away from Riser toward the still-glowing silhouette.

"Where did he kidnap you, Valerie?" Lightstone asked in a quiet voice.

"Uh . . . at the marina."

"Which one?"

"Uh, uh . . . I don't . . ."

"Which side are you on, Valerie?"

"What?"

"Which side, Valerie? You need to decide, *right now*," Lightstone said in a cold, unforgiving voice.

"Uh, uh . . ." Then, in a moment of blind panic, the young bodyguard went for the pistol that had been only partially hidden against the small of her back—which caused Lightstone to shift his aim, and Riser to lunge for the four-bore and start to spin around.

The huge professional assassin was still turning, his fingers instinctively finding the grip and trigger, when he realized that the gun in his young assistant's hand was coming around at him and not at Lightstone.

Reacting instinctively, he paused in mid-turn to trigger one of the buckshot-loaded barrels, an act that created a horribly concussive boom in the partially contained hangar as the savagely torn body of the young woman was flung against the far wall like a cloth doll.

The first two 10mm hollow-point bullets caught Riser square in the center of his chest, causing his eyes to blink in shock. But his body and his hands were still in motion, continuing to bring the barrels of the devastating weapon around, when the third 10mm, semi-jacketed hollow-point ripped into his forehead just above the bridge of his nose.

Dying as he fell, the man known as Riser never heard the echoing sounds of his stainless steel four-bore rifle clattering loudly on the concrete floor.

Henry Lightstone walked slowly over to the sprawled body of the beautiful, azure-eyed young woman. He saw the blood-splattered tattoo of a Scarlet Macaw on an exposed portion of her right breast and shook his head sadly.

"You made the right decision, Valerie," he whispered, unable to hear even his own words over the shrill ringing in his ears. "You just waited too long to decide."

Then he started walking out of the hangar toward the rapidly approaching FBI surveillance helicopter and the cautiously advancing agents.

Chapter Thirty-eight

"I think you're going to enjoy this flight a little better than the last one," Henry Lightstone said to a moderately sedated Dwight Stoner as two burly Coast Guard crewmen strained to lift the stretcher up into the Sikorsky Sea Stallion helicopter's cargo bay.

"These guys know how to fly, huh?" the huge agent mumbled.

"Most likely. And even if they don't, you're not going to know about it, anyway."

"Hey, come on, Henry, ol' Woeshack did okay for himself out there," Larry Paxton said in a raspy whisper from the stretcher at Lightstone's feet.

"You're only saying that now because he's unconscious and he can't hear you," Lightstone responded, glancing over at the thoroughly sedated figure of Thomas Woeshack, who was being attended to by one of the Coast Guard medics.

Larry Paxton started to laugh and then winced.

"Yeah, he did do good," Lightstone admitted. "And if you hadn't been so chicken-shit about flying with him, you could have ended up being the hero instead of Stoner."

"Good leader always lets his raggedy-ass crew get the glory," Paxton mumbled, finally giving in to the sedative and closing his eyes.

"Amen to that, buddy," Lightstone said, patting Paxton's shoulder with the one hand that wasn't tightly bandaged and throbbing as the Coast Guard crew picked up Paxton's stretcher and set him into the waiting helicopter.

"Hey, don't forget this," Lightstone said as he handed a small wooden box with several holes drilled into the side up to an extremely young-looking air crewman sitting in the Sea Stallion's cargo bay.

"What is it?" he asked, peering cautiously in through one of the holes.

"My lucky turtle. Cat Island subspecies. One of the last of its kind."

"Yeah, so?"

"So if you guys will guard that box with your lives, and deliver it to a guy named Sidney Bordeaux, the manager at Arthur's Town airport, then he's not going to sue the United States government for destroying his airplane, and Larry and I won't have to marry his daughter," Lightstone explained.

"That so?" The young crewman grinned. "What's she

like? A real battle-ax?''

"You married?''

"Nope.''

"Got a serious girlfriend?''

"Not really.''

"Ever heard the term 'Conchy Joe'?''

"No, can't say I ever have.''

"Then I'll tell you what,'' Lightstone said. "Why don't you drop that box off in person, tell the manager you're feeling a little airsick, and see for yourself.''

The young crewman cocked his head suspiciously, then shrugged and nodded in agreement.

"And in the meantime, take good care of these guys.''

"Yes, sir, will do.''

Henry Lightstone and Mike Takahara waited until the Coast Guard pilots and their crew teams finished securing the stretchers bearing the three sedated wildlife agents to the floor of the helicopter next to the four wounded FBI agents who had already been strapped in.

"Clear!'' the pilot called out through his opened window.

Stepping back as the rotors began to turn, Lightstone and Takahara waved to the young crewman who was strapped in by the open door with a small wooden box clutched tightly in both hands.

"Justin's going to be pissed at you for that,'' Mike Takahara said.

"Yeah, I know.'' Lightstone nodded. "But she's ready to get on with her life, and he's not. Give him a couple of years and he'll be back out here looking for her younger sister.''

Then, as the powerful Sikorsky rescue helicopter rose in the air, hovered, and then banked away in the direction of the Nassau Hospital where two surgical teams were waiting for their arrival, Lightstone and Takahara walked back toward the villa.

As they did so, they noted that the bodies of the ICER Committee members, as well as those of Maas and Chareaux and Eric Tisbury, had already been placed in black body bags and laid out in a temporary morgue area in the villa's garage. They tried not to think about the bodies of the two pilots, the crew chief, and the six FBI agents who had died in the exploding Blackhawk out at the Fernandez Bay airstrip.

When they got inside, Lightstone and Takahara found Theresa Fletcher and the four supervisory wildlife and FBI agents—Halahan, Moore, Grynard, and Owens—sitting in the living room talking with a severely shaken but apparently still defiant Sam Tisbury. Tisbury had been given a bathrobe to replace his wet clothes, and was being guarded by two very solemn-looking FBI hostage recovery team agents.

One of the FBI agents processing the scene looked up.

"Agent Takahara?"

"Yes?"

"There were a couple of calls for you a few moments ago." The agent looked down at his clipboard. "A Roger Dingeman, from your forensic lab in Ashland, and a Dr. Kimberly Wildman from the National Biological Survey. Both of them said you'd been trying to get hold of them on an urgent matter, and that you'd left this number."

"Great, thank you."

As Mike Takahara disappeared into the back bedroom, Lightstone walked outside on the rear deck and stood there, staring out over the water. A few moments later Theresa Fletcher came outside.

"Mind if I join you?"

"No, not at all, have a seat," Lightstone said, gesturing toward a pair of deck chairs.

Fletcher watched as Lightstone gingerly set himself down in the chair. She shook her head.

"Hate to be the one to say it, Henry, but you look like hell."

"I've felt better," Lightstone acknowledged with a rueful smile.

"I thought you were going with the others to Nassau?"

"I was, but the guys they shipped out need medical attention a whole lot more than I do. Figured I'd just end up at the end of the line, sitting around bare-assed in one of those open-ended hospital gowns with Paxton, listening to him complain.''

''Not a sight for the fainthearted, I'm sure.'' Theresa Fletcher smiled. ''What about the hand?''

Lightstone looked down at the tightly wound tape and bandages that covered his entire left hand and about half of his forearm. ''Doc says it should be fine, long as I keep on taking the antibiotics and painkillers. No major nerve damage as best he can tell. He put a few stitches in to hold everything together until we get back to Fort Lauderdale.''

Theresa Fletcher stared silently at Lightstone's bandaged hand for a long moment.

''I understand it got pretty wild out there,'' she finally said in a conversational tone.

''Yeah, I suppose it did,'' the ex-cop turned federal agent responded. ''Craziness in all directions. You don't think much about it while it's happening. You just follow your instincts, go with the flow. It catches up with you later.''

''The deaths, you mean? The people you ended up . . . killing?''

Lightstone nodded.

''How do you feel about that?''

''You mean, were their deaths justified?''

Theresa Fletcher nodded silently.

''Is this one of those leading conversations where I should be asking for a lawyer?'' he asked, watching her eyes.

''If you need one, I'm available.''

''Thanks, I appreciate that,'' Lightstone said with a half-smile. ''But I don't think it'll be necessary. Maas and Chareaux weren't going to stop coming after us, no matter what we did. As for the other guy—Riser, whatever his name was—I don't know. I could have dumped him when he first came into the hangar.''

''But instead you played with him.''

''You mean the silhouette?''

She nodded.

"I wanted to distract him, and I wanted to be sure."

"That he killed the Crowley boy?"

"Yes."

"So, in a manner of speaking, you did set him up."

Lightstone stared into the cool eyes of the prosecuting attorney for a long moment.

"How much of a retainer fee do you usually charge?" he finally asked.

"A beer will do fine."

"You've got yourself a client." And then, after a moment: "And yes, you're right, in a manner of speaking, I probably did set him up."

"You set the stage, but then you gave him a chance to surrender, correct?"

"It was there if he wanted it."

"But he didn't?"

"Either that or he didn't think he could lose," Lightstone said, remembering the chilling expression on the huge man's face when he realized that his beautiful young assistant had changed sides at the last second.

"You said his name was Riser?"

"That's what Maas called him."

"Has anybody figured out how he got involved in all this?"

"Best guess is that he was a hired gun. The question is, for whom? And speaking of which," Lightstone said, looking to change the subject, "who's the guy in the bathrobe?"

"Some hot-shot industrialist named Samuel Tisbury, the CEO of Cyanosphere VIII."

"Cyanosphere? What's that?"

"I don't know, some kind of big international mining outfit." Fletcher shrugged.

"So where does *he* fit into all this?"

"*He* claims he doesn't," Fletcher said with an irritated shake of her head. "Or at least not directly. From what I've heard so far, he and his father and some of their wealthy industrialist friends like to meet out here at the family villa every now and then, for some fishing, card playing, and general relaxation. He admits that Alfred Bloom was a part of that group, but he claims to have no idea why anyone would want to kill his father or his son, or any of the others, for that matter.''

''So why'd he run?''

''Because at the time, he believed that whoever it was who shot and killed his son would try to kill him too. Which, I suppose, is a reasonable concern, when you stop to think about it,'' the deputy U.S. Attorney added. ''He mentioned you guys too. He has no idea why you followed him and his son back to the villa.''

''Is he blaming us for the shooting?''

''No, not really, just that he's confused and doesn't understand what's going on.''

''Well, if he was so confused, why didn't he stop running—or flying, for that matter—when he saw the FBI choppers?''

''Basically, the same answer. He claims he was trying to keep from being killed and never saw the magnetic signs on the helicopters that said FBI in eighteen-inch-high letters.''

''Do you believe that?''

''No, not really. But it's not a question of what I believe,'' Theresa Fletcher reminded, ''it's what I can get a jury to believe. Especially if we're going to try to charge a wealthy industrialist with conspiracy to murder a number of federal agents in a situation where both his father *and* his son were murdered by people intent on killing those same agents.''

''It does sound complicated,'' Lightstone admitted.

''Yes, it does.''

''What about Maas and Chareaux? And Operation Counter Wrench?''

''He claims to have no idea what we're talking about.''

''Really? Then how did he explain Walter Crane's being here?''

''He says Crane flew out here to meet with Alfred Bloom,

who never did show up. He has no idea what their meeting was going to be about, but he does admit to knowing Crane. He also indicated that he and his father have used Little, Warren, Nobles & Kole to represent them in some civil matters.''

"So what it all comes down to is that we still have to find Bloom if we're going to make any sense out of all this,'' Lightstone said glumly.

Theresa Fletcher gave Lightstone a strange look. "Oh, that's right, you don't know about Bloom, do you?''

"Know what?''

"He's dead,'' the federal prosecutor said.

Henry Lighthouse sagged in the chair.

"How?'' he asked.

"Some fisherman found him about a mile off the Hawk's Nest inlet early yesterday morning. According to the Bahamian Defense Force official who responded, it appeared as though Bloom, and a female employee from his yacht dealership named Anne-Marie Sawyers, got their prop caught up in a net, tried to cut it loose, got tangled up themselves, and drowned.''

"Hell of a coincidence,'' Henry Lightstone muttered, numbed and frustrated by the realization that their one solid link to the people who set Operation Counter Wrench into motion had just disappeared.

"Yes, it is. Especially when one of the bodies appears to have been frozen recently and not entirely thawed.''

Lightstone turned to the prosecuting attorney, his eyebrows wrinkled in confusion. "What?''

"The girl,'' Fletcher said. "The coroner's investigator got suspicious when he saw a lot of fresh bruising on Bloom's hands and arms, where it appeared he'd been struggling with the nets, but no such bruising on his companion, even though she was just as badly entangled.''

"Suggesting that someone killed her early on, put somebody else on the boat, and then switched back after they did in Bloom,'' Lightstone nodded thoughtfully.

"You think that's what happened?"

"It's not only likely, but I think I know who the substitute was."

Theresa Fletcher was quiet for a moment, then her head came up.

"You mean the young woman out at the hangar?"

"It would make sense, all the way around," Lightstone nodded.

"Be nice if *something* about this whole deal started making sense," the prosecutor said, "because it gets a whole lot more confusing when you toss in the bodies of four deputy U.S. marshalls, and Jason Bascomb . . ."

"Bascomb? What does *he* have to do with all this?"

"Boy, you really *have* been out of things, haven't you?" Theresa Fletcher said, and then began to explain.

A few minutes later Henry Lightstone found himself staring out at the ocean again.

"So this Tisbury character is pretty much our last hope of figuring this whole mess out, isn't he?" he said finally.

"It looks that way." The federal prosecutor nodded.

"Has *he* asked for a lawyer yet?"

"No, amazingly, he hasn't. As a matter of fact, he's been rather insistent in making sure we understand that he wants to cooperate in any way he can, to help us track down and prosecute the people who killed his son and father."

"Of course it's a lot easier being cooperative *and* keeping your story straight if you're the only surviving witness," Lightstone said sarcastically.

"Typical, suspicious-cop attitude."

"Yeah, I know, but I can't help thinking that phone call his son made at the courthouse *must* have had something to do with all this. It's just too much of a coincidence otherwise."

"I have no idea what you're talking about. What phone call?"

Lightstone was halfway through his description of how he'd run into Tisbury's son in the basement of the Arlington courthouse when he realized that Theresa Fletcher had a stunned look on her face.

"That was the phone call I got before you showed up late at my office," she said, blinking her eyes and shaking her head in confusion. "I remember him saying the word *Wildfire*, and also something to the effect that I shouldn't forget I heard it from him first, but what—"

At that moment Mike Takahara came out onto the deck with a big cardboard box in his arms.

"You folks want to hear an interesting story?" he asked, a satisfied expression appearing on his face.

Ten minutes later deputy U.S. Attorney Theresa Fletcher walked back into the living room with the two wildlife agents in her wake. After getting a go-ahead nod from FBI Agent Al Grynard, she approached the living room area where Sam Tisbury and the four supervisory wildlife and FBI agents were sitting.

"Mr. Tisbury," she said, "would you mind if I asked you a few more questions?"

"No, not at all," Tisbury said, gesturing with his hand to one of the empty chairs. "As I've said before, I'll be happy to cooperate with the U.S. Attorney's Office in any way I can."

"Thank you, we appreciate that," the federal prosecutor said as she settled herself down in one of the chairs and then gestured to the two agents. "Mr. Tisbury, this is Henry Lightstone and Mike Takahara. Henry and Mike are Special Agents for the U.S. Fish and Wildlife Service."

"Oh, really?" Sam Tisbury said, managing to look appropriately confused. "But I thought—"

"That he and the other two men ran a charter fishing boat? That was a cover they were using as a part of their investigation."

"I see." The industrialist nodded with a neutral expression on his face.

"There are some things we've collected here at the villa as evidence that we'd like to show you," Theresa Fletcher vent on, and then nodded to Mike Takahara, who reached nto the cardboard box.

"I found this nylon bag in the back bedroom," Takahara aid, holding up the bright, distinctively colored bag, "and I vas wondering if you knew whom it belonged to."

"No, I'm sorry, but I don't believe I've ever seen it efore," Sam Tisbury said, shaking his head.

Mike Takahara nodded as if he had expected that answer. 'Presumably it was brought to the villa by one of the men nvolved in the shootings," the tech agent said. "Some of he contents are fairly interesting." He reached into the back und brought out what appeared to be five short pieces of :hrome steel pipe wired together, with manila tags on each iece.

"As best I can tell right now," Takahara said, "these are eplacement barrels for a 10mm Model 1076 Smith & Wes-son semiautomatic pistol, which is the duty weapon issued to pecial agents of the Federal Bureau of Investigation *and* the J.S. Fish and Wildlife Service. My suspicion is that these gun barrels—all of which, by the way, appear to have gun-powder residues in the bores—were used to kill a number of people and then intended to be placed in the weapons of the agents named on the manila tags. Those names being"— Takahara held up the ring so that he could read the tags— 'Paxton, Lightstone, Takahara, Stoner . . . and Grynard," he added with a slight smile as he looked over at the seemingly startled FBI agent.

"I don't understand what this has to do with anything here," Sam Tisbury said, looking just as confused and puz-zled as Grynard, "other than the fairly obvious fact that these criminals, whoever they are, were planning on making t appear that—uh—you and your fellow agents and, I guess, agent Grynard here were involved in the killings."

"Exactly." Mike Takahara nodded. "Then I found this."

He reached into the bag again and brought out a small por-able computer.

"A computer?" Tisbury said.

"Actually a very special computer," the tech agent said. He turned the computer on its side, carefully removed a small square piece of clear plastic from one of the connecting ports, and then held it up for everyone to see.

"What's that?" Grynard asked.

"It's the end of a connecting cord for a modem," Takahara said. "And if I send it to the Boston crime lab, I think there's a pretty decent chance that they're going to be able to match it up with a broken connector cord that agent Lightstone and I found in a hotel room where a young man named William Devonshire Crowley was murdered. Which ought to make your buddy Rico pretty happy," Takahara added, looking over at Lightstone.

"Yeah, I expect it will." Lightstone nodded, watching Tisbury's face closely now.

Mike Takahara turned his attention back to the still puzzled industrialist.

"Apparently this William Devonshire Crowley and your son Eric knew each other," the tech agent said. "Or at least we can assume that, based on a twelve-hundred-and-thirteen byte E-mail message that Crowley apparently tried to send to an Eric Tisbury, but apparently hit the wrong key and saved the message in this computer's hard drive instead of sending it. I'm assuming *that* too, based upon the fact that when I checked with the network that the computer was programmed to use, the system operators informed me that a twelve-hundred-and-thirteen byte message has never been sent through that account.

"Oh, I suppose I should explain," Takahara added, "that based on the way this computer was programmed, it's pretty obvious that Crowley didn't know much about computers or computer programs."

"So one of Eric's friends was murdered too, and his computer was stolen," Tisbury said, still looking puzzled. "I'm afraid I still don't understand—"

Then the industrialist blinked as the tech agent lifted something else from the cardboard box.

"What are you doing with that?" he demanded.

"Actually, I was about to ask you the same question," the tech agent said as he carefully held up a polished and hinged wooden box that was about eight inches square and sixteen inches long.

Placing it on the coffee table, he opened the box and cautiously removed a metal cylinder approximately six inches in diameter and twelve inches long, with extended one-inch knobs at both ends. The entire cylinder was covered with a chemically etched brown-and-green camouflage pattern.

"You took that out of my room."

"Yes, that's right." Mike Takahara nodded, meeting the industrialist's accusing glare.

Tisbury turned to Al Grynard. "I'm not sure that I like—" he started to say, but the supervisory FBI agent held up a cautionary hand.

"Mr. Tisbury," he said in a professionally controlled manner, "with all due respect to your father and your son, several people were murdered in this villa, which, as far as I'm concerned, makes this entire residence a crime scene."

"Yes, I realize that, and I don't mean this the way I'm sure it sounds, but surely the FBI has no jurisdiction to investigate a homicide in the Bahamas," Tisbury said.

"No, of course not." Grynard nodded. "However, the FBI *does* have a mutual assistance agreement with the Royal Bahamas Defense Force, and as a result of that agreement, the FBI has a special task force working in the area. Special Agent Hal Owens over here"—Grynard nodded toward the supervisory agent—"is in charge of that task force. Which, as I understand the agreement, fully authorizes agent Owens and any federal agents under his command to take suspects into custody and preserve evidence until a Bahamian officer can arrive at the scene."

"I'm not trying to be argumentative," Tisbury said, "but isn't agent—uh—Takahara a wildlife officer and not an FBI agent?"

"Yes, he is," David Halahan said, staring at the industrialist with eyes that could only be described as cold and predatory, ''but Technical Agent Takahara and all of the other *remaining* members of Bravo Team have been temporarily detailed to the Special Bahamas Task Force.''

''Under whose authority?''

''Mine,'' Halahan said in a voice that made it absolutely clear what he thought about the word ''remaining.''

''And I might add that, as the commander of that task force, I have authorized Special Agent Takahara to conduct a complete crime scene investigation of this residence in co-operation with the remaining members of *my* team,'' Hal Owens said in an equally frosty voice.

''We understood that you wished to cooperate fully with our investigation, Mr. Tisbury,'' Grynard went on in a carefully casual manner. ''But if you wish to have an attorney present—''

Tisbury shook his head. ''No, no, I fully understand my rights, and I have absolutely no wish or need to have an attorney present. ''I . . . I . . . apologize, gentlemen. It's just that with the death of my father *and* my son, I hardly know what—''

''That's perfectly understandable, Mr. Tisbury.'' Grynard nodded in apparent sympathy. ''Several of us here in this room lost people we deeply cared about as a result of this case, and emotions are understandably running high. So if you'd like to continue this conversation at a later date—''

''No, please, I *do* want to help you with your investigation in any way I can,'' the industrialist said, making a point to look over at the deputy U.S. Attorney. ''I was just startled because the Crucible project is a rather sensitive piece of industrial research.''

''Crucible project?'' Mike Takahara asked.

''Yes.'' Tisbury nodded, seeming to regain his confidence now that they were off the topic of jurisdictional authorizations. ''What you're holding in your hands is a prototype—a beta model.''

"What does it do?" the tech agent asked, turning the cylinder in his hands.

"Well, that's the sensitive part, but I suppose I can trust you fellows with the information," Tisbury said with a discernible lack of enthusiasm. "Basically, what our engineering team created is a very efficient thermal device which can be used in sequence with several identical devices—one device igniting the next in a timed sequence—to, well, mine precious metals."

"You mean by *melting* them out of the veins, through *rock*?" Takahara asked, his eyebrows furrowing.

"Yes, essentially." The industrialist nodded.

"Then you must be talking about generating a tremendous amount of heat," the tech agent said, continuing to turn the device in his hands.

"Yes, actually, we are."

"I suppose that's why you have this little radioactive isotope warning label here," he said, pointing to a small symbol etched into the head of the cylinder.

"Uh—well, that's something I really can't discuss."

"So, basically, what you're doing is creating a miniature meltdown every time you ignite one of these things," the tech agent said, nodding to himself. "Boy, I'll bet the environmentalists must really love *that*. But then I don't suppose you've gotten around to mentioning your Crucible project to any of the environmental groups, such as Wildfire, have you?"

"I beg your pardon?" Tisbury said, blinking his eyes in confusion. "No, of course we haven't—" he started to say, but Mike Takahara interrupted again.

"Were you aware, Mr. Tisbury, that somebody has been bolting blank camouflaged signs to trees in the Yellowstone National Park area? Signs made out of a specific metal alloy and camouflaged with a specific chemical etching process, both of which—according to our crime lab—were patented by Cyanosphere VIII. Signs that when exposed to intense heat, such as you might get with a raging forest fire, melt away the less-heat-resistant portions of the sign to display the word *Wildfire* in big, bold letters?''

"What are you talking about?" Sam Tisbury demanded. "*Our* process? Are you—''

"According to Deputy U.S. Attorney Fletcher, Mr. Tisbury, Wildfire is the name of an extremist environmental activist group that advocates, among other things, the complete destruction—and ultimate resurrection—of the earth by fire.''

"What does that . . .''

"Were you aware, Mr. Tisbury, that your son Eric was a member of that group?''

"Eric?!" Tisbury's mouth dropped open.

"And then there were the signs in Sequoia National Park that say''—the tech agent picked up his notebook—" 'And one day soon, when the ember falls, and the sky is filled with fire, He shall rise up from out of the darkness, and none shall stand before Him.' '' Have you ever heard that quote before, Mr. Tisbury?''

"I don't understand any of this," Sam Tisbury said, turning to Grynard with a furious expression on his face. "If the FBI intends—''

"If not, Mr. Tisbury," Mike Takahara said softly, "perhaps you can explain to me why *your* son, with his last breath, whispered in my ear: 'And one day soon, when ember falls—'?''

Sam Tisbury whirled around and stared at the tech agent with widened eyes. "What did you say?" he rasped hoarsely.

"One day soon, when *ember* falls.'' Takahara repeated the words slowly. "Not 'the' ember," he emphasized. "Just ember. Like it was a name.''

"Oh, my God," the industrialist whispered, his face ashen.

"Who is Ember, Mr. Tisbury?" Mike Takahara continued on in a gentle voice that—to Sam Tisbury—had become almost hypnotic.

"My—my daughter. We called her Ember. Childhood nickname, because . . ."

His voice drifted away, his eyes first blinking and then staring off somewhere in the distance, as his face turned deathly pale.

"Mr. Tisbury, how many of these Crucible devices has Cyanosphere VIII made so far?"

Lost in the horror of his sudden realizations, Tisbury shook his head. "What?"

"How many Crucible devices have you made so far?" Mike Takahara repeated.

"Two thousand."

The room went silent.

"Do you know where all those devices are right now, Mr. Tisbury?"

"Eric, he was responsible . . . testing, storage." Tisbury spoke the words as if he could barely believe them himself.

"Mr. Tisbury," the tech agent continued, "is there anyone in your organization you could call, right now, who might be able to verify the location of those devices?"

Four minutes later Sam Tisbury looked up at seven waiting sets of eyes and rasped in utter dismay: "They're not there. They're gone."

For another fifteen seconds the room remained silent. Then Mike Takahara said softly:

"I think I know where they are."

Chapter Thirty-nine

At four-thirty that Sunday afternoon, Fish and Wildlife Special Agents David Halahan, Henry Lightstone, and Mike Takahara, and FBI Special Agent Al Grynard, buckled themselves into four of the six overstuffed captain's chairs in the cabin of an executive Learjet that Halahan had leased at the Nassau airport when the agents discovered that nothing else fast enough was available.

Mike Takahara waited until the plane was high up over the clouds and beginning to steady on course. Then he adjusted his seat around so that he was facing the other three agents, and began to describe the hour-long conversation he'd had with Sam Tisbury—the last surviving member of the ICER Committee—while all of the other FBI agents, FWS agents, and Bahamian officials were moving in and out of the villa trying to make some sense out of the Cat Island crime scenes.

"It was the Tisbury tradition that really started it all," Takahara said. "At the age of sixteen all the Tisbury males are brought into the family business. Apparently it's been that way for six generations. So when the twins, Eric and Erica—his daughter's real name—hit sixteen, Eric was brought into Cyanosphere VIII."

"And Erica was shuffled aside?" Lightstone said.

"That's right." Takahara nodded. "The only trouble was, Erica was the better engineer by a factor of ten. Her father—Sam Tisbury—recognized that and tried to make an exception to the tradition, but *his* father—Harold Tisbury, one of the DOA's in the dining room—refused to consider it, which apparently resulted in one hell of a family blowup. The mother ultimately filed for divorce over the whole deal. But Harold was the patriarch of the family, so that was that.

"Except that it wasn't"—Takahara smiled—"because with her father's help, Erica went ahead and worked at Cyanosphere VIII anyway. Changed her name, worked her way into the engineering department, and came up with the idea for Crucible."

"That was *her* idea?" Al Grynard blinked in surprise.

"That's right." Mike Takahara nodded with a smile. "Good old Erica. Probably would have turned out to be a tougher industrialist than her father and grandfather put together. Actually, what she *did* was come to the perfectly reasonable conclusion that all the accumulated nuclear waste in

Russia and the United States was just sitting there not being used. So she decided to try to find some way to use it. She couldn't get permission to work with the stuff in the United States, but that was when Russia was opening up and looking for people to help them figure out how to get back on their feet. She had a decent chunk of her own trust fund money to support the basic research, and I guess their regulatory process was a little more lax.''

"So she used *Russian* nuclear waste to design Crucible?'' Grynard said incredulously.

"Or at least a crude version of what is now Crucible.'' The tech agent nodded. "And in the process managed to absolutely fry her bone marrow.''

"Leukemia?''

"Apparently, only she didn't know it then,'' Mike Takahara said. "If she'd been careful—taken routine precautions, limited her exposure, and gotten regular checkups—then none of this might have ever happened. But she didn't, probably because she was so damned determined to show her grandfather *and* her father *and* her twin brother that she was just as good as any male Tisbury.''

"Which she was.'' Lightstone shrugged.

"No question about it.'' The tech agent nodded. "And they were duly impressed when she showed them what she'd done. So impressed, in fact, that they immediately turned the project over to their chief engineers to refine, develop, test, and market.''

"Let me guess,'' Grynard said. "They put Eric in charge of the testing and shoved Erica right out the back door.''

"Close. Actually, they held a special meeting of the board of directors, presented her with a plaque and a whole bunch of money, essentially a corporate pat on the head, and *then* put Eric in charge. Whereupon Erica found the back door on her own, put a copy of the blood work-up that she'd just received the day before in the mail to her grandmother, and then effectively disappeared.''

"Jesus!'' Grynard whispered.

"Oh, they tried to find her," Takahara said. "Sent flyers to every police and sheriff's department in the United States, hired dozens of private detectives, placed coded messages in engineering association newsletters, the works. No go. Every now and then she'd send her grandmother another blood work-up sheet with the lab and patient name and case number torn off, but they all knew it was about her."

"Christ, with all their money, couldn't they have helped her?" Lightstone asked.

"Like with first-class treatment in the best chemotherapy clinics in the world? You bet." The tech agent nodded. "Only by then, I guess, Erica decided that she didn't *want* to be helped, and there wasn't anything in the world they could do to make her change her mind. Kinda funny, in a sad sort of way, because by disappearing like that, she was basically proving her case: that she really was a true Tisbury. Which, as I understand it, means she's got a stubborn streak a mile long, and a temper to match. According to her father, that was why they gave her the nickname 'Ember' as a kid.

"Anyway," Takahara went on, "after receiving a half dozen of those lab work-up reports, the grandmother finally ended up drinking herself to death, which really hit the family hard, but I guess that wasn't enough for Ember."

"So she and her brother go right for their throats, in their own nasty little way," Grynard said. "Hire this Riser character to take out the ICER Committee, and then set it up so that you guys get blamed for the whole thing."

"She was definitely going after her grandfather and the committee in general," Mike Takahara said, "but I'm not sure about the father. I kind of got the sense that he didn't think she blamed him quite as much as she did the rest of the family."

"How does that hold if she turned that cannon-shooter loose on the committee in general?" Grynard asked.

"My theory is that her father wasn't on the hit list." The tech agent shrugged. "Way I understand it, this Riser character had plenty of opportunities to blow him away if he'd wanted to. Either that or Eric might have been trying to protect his father by taking him out fishing when the hit was scheduled to do down. With Riser and Eric both dead, I suppose we'll never know for sure. But either way, the crucial thing now is that Ember and her environmental activist friends came up with a really clever way to set this 'cleansing' fire they were always talking about, and then blame her grandfather's corporation for the whole mess. The classic two-birds-one-stone strategy. Finding that network communications program in Crowley's computer, and then having your guys hit their headquarters in Reston gave us the final link we needed. What it all came down to was four words: 'The Ember has fallen.' ''

''*Has* fallen?'' Henry Lightstone blinked.

''That's their code for the ignition of Wildfire,'' Takahara explained. ''Ember and a guy named Harris have it all plotted out. According to your agents, they even rigged up a pretty scary computer simulation. It's pretty simple, actually: They ignite the 'ember,' which is presumably one of the Crucible devices hooked up to an ignition system, and then drop it out of a small plane at the center point. In x number of seconds, they get to watch the first device ignite every other Crucible device within a ten-mile-radius circle, each of which will ignite the next set in x number of seconds, and so on and so on. Two thousand devices capable of generating enough heat to melt gold out of a mining vein, every one set ten miles from the next and going out in all directions. If we don't stop them, it's going to be one hell of a fire.''

It was six-thirty in the evening, mountain time, when the executive Learjet touched down at the Municipal Airport in Cody, Wyoming, where the FBI's local senior resident agent, two additional FBI agents, a National Park ranger, an FBI sedan, and a pair of unarmed Army Blackhawk helicopters and their crews were waiting.

Al Grynard quickly introduced Halahan, Lightstone, and Takahara.

"We've set up a command post at the airport tower," the senior resident agent said. "The Army's provided us with four Blackhawks and crews. We've got two of them up in the air right now, with assault-rifle-armed agents, sweeping the western quadrants of the park. These two will take you guys up into the eastern quadrants. We've got other resources on standby, but we figured we needed to locate the suspects first."

"Sounds good." Al Grynard nodded.

"Al and I will be at the command center," Halahan said to Lightstone and Takahara. "You guys keep us informed on what's going on out there."

"Yes, sir," Mike Takahara said.

"Absolutely." Henry Lightstone nodded.

Al Grynard gave Lightstone a long look, shook his head, and then followed Halahan and the senior resident out to the waiting sedan as the two wildlife agents and the park ranger walked over to the waiting helicopters.

"So how many of the Crucible devices have you found so far?" Mike Takahara asked as he and Lightstone and the park ranger quickly climbed into the helicopter, strapped themselves in, and put on the radio-equipped crash helmets that would allow them to listen in on the pilot's conversations, and communicate through the aircraft's intercom system.

"Two, we think."

"Two! That's all?" the tech agent said incredulously.

"And we're not even sure about those two." The ranger nodded. "Do you have that example one with you?"

"Yeah, right here." Takahara nodded, pulling the hinged box out of his duffel bag and handing to the uniformed ranger the prototype Crucible device he'd seized from the Tisbury villa.

"Hey, can that thing go off?" the warrant officer copilot demanded, looking back into the cabin as he and the pilot began their preflight routines.

"No, not a chance. There's no fuel in this one," Takahara said quickly.

The warrant officer muttered something unkind about civilians in general, and then went back to his preflight as the ranger continued to examine the device.

"Yeah, this looks like what they described," he said. "Man, look at that camouflage job. No wonder everybody's having so much trouble finding the damn things."

"Do you know how far apart the ones were that you *did* find?"

The ranger thought for a moment. "As I recall, about five or six miles."

"Shit." Mike Takahara winced.

"Why, what's the matter?" Jim Whittman asked.

"I was hoping they'd be spreading them out for maximum distance, which would have been more like ten miles," the tech agent explained. "That way, every one we find would break the pattern, because the ignition signal wouldn't reach twenty miles to the next one. But if they're putting them five miles apart, then there's going to be an overlap, which means just finding a couple isn't going to do it. We've got to find a whole bunch of them."

"Either that or their ignition device," Lightstone reminded.

"Yeah, what does that look like?" the park ranger asked.

Mike Takahara reached into the hinged wooden box and handed the ranger the ignition system with the dangling cable.

"How does it work?"

"Just snap that cap on the end of the cable over either end of the device, set the timer, press the ignite button, and then get the hell out of the way," Takahara explained.

"And they can set this whole Wildfire business off, all two thousand Crucibles, just by hooking one of these ignition systems to any one of those devices?"

"As long as each ignited device is within ten to twelve miles of the next one, that's right." The tech agent nodded.

"The only real advantage we've got right now is that it's going to take them a long time to place two thousand devices in that wide a pattern, presumably through forested areas that'll burn."

"How much time will we have once she ignites the first one?" the ranger asked.

"Zero to ten seconds for each successive ignition, depending on how she sets the delay timer on each of the devices," Mike Takahara answered. "If you figure the maximum delay, then the fire ring moves outward from Whitehorse Cabin at a rate of five to ten miles every ten seconds, unless we can break the pattern."

"Christ," the ranger whispered, "then we'd better hurry up and find this Ember gal pretty damned quick."

"Why's that?" Whittman asked.

"Because once it gets dark around here," the ranger said, as the pilot called out on the helicopter's intercom system for everyone to put their carryons into the cargo storage nets, check their seat belts, and hang on, "we're never going to find any more of those devices, no matter *how* hard we look."

They were coming in over the southeastern corner of Yellowstone National Park, the lead Blackhawk at two hundred feet and the trailing one about a mile back at six hundred feet, when the pilot in the lead helicopter spotted the lights of a small plane flying at about a hundred feet above treetop level. The pilot advised that he was going in close to take a look.

Less than a minute later he was back on the air.

"Looks like it's a Department of Interior plane," the lead pilot said, his voice audible to the four special agents and the park ranger through the Blackhawk's intercom system. "One of the occupants identified herself as Dr. Kim Wildman, from the National Biological Survey, helping to coordinate the ground crews."

"That sounds right." Mike Takahara spoke into his radio

mike. "I talked to her again this afternoon, just before we left the Bahamas, and she told me then that she was planning on taking part in the search."

The pilot relayed that information to the lead helicopter.

"Ten-four," the lead pilot acknowledged, "I'm going to start a grid search at the northeast quadrant."

As the lead helicopter angled off to the right, away from the small plane, Henry Lightstone looked over at Mike Takahara.

For almost a minute Henry Lightstone watched the helicopter lights disappear into the distance. Then he spoke into his intercom radio mike. "You know, since this Dr. Wildman's one of the few people who have actually seen that camouflage pattern on those signs, I'm kind of surprised she isn't down there on the ground with her crews, helping them with the search."

Mike Takahara blinked, a puzzled expression appearing on his face.

"Hey," the copilot yelled before the tech agent could respond, "I think I just saw something fall from the bottom of that plane!"

"What was it?" Mike Takahara demanded.

"I don't know, it's too far away and it happened too fast," the warrant officer admitted. "It was just a flicker of something. Might not have been anything."

"Pilot," Mike Takahara said, "can you ask the pilot of the lead helicopter to turn back, recontact the plane, and ask Dr. Wildman the name of the agent she talked with a few hours ago?"

"Ten-four." Then: "Echo-Tango-Two, this is Echo-Tango-One, request you recontact the Department of Interior plane and ask Dr. Wildman the name of the agent she talked with a few hours ago."

"Echo-Tango-Two, ten-four."

The pilot waited thirty seconds, and then tried again: "Echo-Tango-Two, did you get a response?"

"That's a negative. You want me to—"

"Hey! There it goes again," the copilot yelled. "I know I saw something fall that time!"

"That's got to be them!" Mike Takahara spoke into his radio mike. "And they're still dropping those damn Crucibles into the pattern!"

The nose of the Blackhawk helicopter dipped forward as the pilot immediately got back on the radio.

"Tango-One to Tango-Two," the pilot called out, immediately dropping into a combat short-hand code, "Negative on your ID! That's our bogey!"

In what appeared to be an immediate response to the helicopter pilot's warning, the small plane banked away to the left and shut off its running lights.

"Shit, they're on our frequency," the pilot cursed, and then called out: "All Tango aircraft in the Yellowstone sector, go to combat frequency four."

The two Blackhawks sweeping the western quadrants called in an acknowledgment, and the flight leader directed them to maintain their positions as a blocking force.

"Tango-Two, on four," the head helicopter pilot called out. "Call it."

"Tango-One to Tango-Two. Move in and advise the Cessna pilot to land immediately. Repeat, land immediately."

"Command Post to all Echo-Tango units." Al Grynard's voice broke in. "Be advised, if that plane does *not* land immediately, then the agents on board your aircraft are authorized to shoot it down."

"Echo-Tango-One to Command Post, requesting a confirmation." The military pilot spoke slowly and clearly. "If the plane refuses to land, the agents on board have a green light to destroy it in the air. Is that a roger?"

"Command Post to Echo-Tango-One, that *is* a roger. Do not hesitate. Shoot it down," Al Grynard repeated.

The pilot looked back into the cabin. "You guys copy that back there?" The two wildlife agents and the park ranger all gave a thumbs-up signal.

"Tango-One, ten-four," the pilot transmitted. "We copy."

The other three helicopter pilots gave a similar acknowledgment.

"Tango-Two, we're going in," the lead pilot called out as he banked his helicopter.

"Christ, that plane is really hauling," Lightstone commented as he stared over the copilot's shoulder at the little plane that was rapidly disappearing in the growing darkness, followed by the larger Blackhawk.

"Not a problem, sir." The warrant officer grinned. "Just wait until you see what we can do with these birds."

As the copilot promised, within thirty seconds, Lightstone could see the lights of the lead helicopter coming alongside the dark shadow of the small plane.

"Tango-One to Command Post, Tango-Two's ordering them down now," the pilot advised over the intercom. "We'll give them . . . shit!"

With the dark mass of trees as a backdrop, five billowing streaks of flame had suddenly appeared from the side of the plane.

Then: "Goddamn it! Tango-Two, May-Day, May-Day! We've been hit. I've got warning lights—we're losing oil pressure. I've got to put this thing down!"

As the Blackhawk pilot started repeating his lead pilot's May-Day signal, calling out the coordinates as he accelerated the assault helicopter toward the rapidly fleeing small plane, the copilot looked back into the cabin. "Okay, folks, looks like we're it until the other choppers can get here. Anybody back there who's armed, get ready."

The park ranger looked pale as he started to stand up near the open cargo doorway. The copilot spotted the hesitation and reacted immediately. "*You*, sir," the warrant office copilot said to Lightstone over the intercom, "help me get that man hooked into one of those door gunner harnesses."

The copilot and Lightstone strapped the uneasy park ranger into the left-door harness, and then, with the copilot's help, Lightstone got himself into the right-side harness. He checked the chamber load on his 10mm double-action pistol as the rumbling helicopter continued its rapid descent toward the barely visible small plane.

"Gunner, left side," the pilot called out over the intercom, "we're going to make a pass over the top, from the rear, your side. You'll have about a three second window to take him out."

"I understand," the park ranger acknowledged, bracing his feet and leaning his weight into the harness straps. The pilot looked back as the ranger was double-checking the load in his .357 revolver.

"Gunner, left side, that pistol isn't going to do much good against that plane. Don't you have a rifle?"

"Negative, this is it." the park ranger shrugged, holding up the sidearm as he spoke into the intercom mike.

"Gunner, right side," the pilot called out, "what is your armament?"

"Same situation. Ten mil, semi-auto, ten rounds." Lightstone spoke into his mike, uneasily bracing himself in the doorway.

There was a pause, then: "Either of you guys ever done this sort of thing before?"

"That's a negative," Lightstone replied.

"Same here," the park ranger added.

"Okay, folks," the pilot said with an audible sigh. "After I make the pass, I'm going to loop around to the right and get back on his tail, try to force them down. If they won't respond, and you have to shoot, give them a little lead, aim for their cockpit . . . and try *real* hard not to hit our rotor."

"You got it," Lightstone acknowledged.

"Okay, people, here we go," the pilot said, and then Lightstone had to wedge his bandaged left hand in through one of the overhead support straps, feeling his stomach start to turn as he felt the Blackhawk accelerate.

Then the copilot yelled: "Look out, gun!" and the Blackhawk suddenly swerved away in a hard right turn as a pair of bright reddish-yellow explosions erupted from the copilot's side of the small plane.

It was all that Henry Lightstone could do to remain upright as the park ranger emptied his .357 at the suddenly blurred and rapidly disappearing plane image.

"What the hell are they shooting with?" the copilot demanded over the intercom.

"It looked like a long barrel, probably some kind of autoloading hunting rifle," the park ranger said, fighting to maintain his balance and choke back his growing nausea as the powerful helicopter continued its gravity-defying sharp turn, the heavy rotors churning furiously through the thin air.

"And probably using armor-piercing rounds to boot, if they got through Tango-Two's engine cowling armor," the copilot added.

"Wonderful," the pilot muttered over the intercom. "Anybody have any idea what kind of effective range we're talking about?"

"It's gotta be a lot farther than we can shoot," Lightstone replied.

"Yeah, roger that," the pilot acknowledged.

At that moment another billowing explosion erupted from the distant plane, followed almost immediately by a loud whack! as a rifle bullet ricocheted off the Blackhawk's light armor a few inches above Henry Lightstone's head.

"And speaking of range, whatever it is, we're still in it," Lightstone commented as he triggered two rounds in the general direction of the plane, having no hope of doing anything more than causing a brief distraction.

"Shit, we need an Apache up here," the copilot said to the pilot. "Something with a little firepower."

"You want to scramble an Apache to take on a fucking Cessna?" the pilot asked incredulously.

"Either that, or get one of the other Hawks over here pretty damn quick," the copilot responded. "Just because we've got armor doesn't mean they can't punch through and hit something vital, especially if we've got to get close enough for pistol ammo to have an effect.''

"Hey, guys, we're running out of time, fast,'' Mike Takahara said into his helmet mike as he reached forward and pulled his nylon equipment bag out of the nearby cargo storage net. "They're going to try to circle around and get back over Whitehorse Cabin, and then—if I read the whole thing right—she's either going to drop the device or jump with it. And if she does that, she'll probably go without a chute. Either way we can't let her do it.''

"What do you want me to do, ram the damn thing?'' the pilot demanded.

"Do whatever you can—just give me thirty seconds,'' Mike Takahara said as he fumbled with the zipper.

"Okay, we'll give it a try,'' the pilot agreed as he brought the Blackhawk up into a steep full-throttle climb. "Left gunner, you loaded and ready?''

"Ready,'' the park ranger said with a pale but determined look on his face as he raised his .357 revolver in acknowledgment.

"Right gunner?''

"Ready as I'm ever—''

"Look out, they're going around . . . and they're starting to climb!'' the warrant officer copilot called out.

"Hang on!'' the pilot yelled, and swung the Blackhawk around in a blocking move as the park ranger sent three more .357 rounds streaking out into the blackness toward the distant plane.

"We're getting in effective range of that rifle again,'' the copilot warned. Then Mike Takahara yelled: "Pilot, swing around! Right door! Right door!''

Responding instinctively as he had done hundreds of times before in combat situations, the Blackhawk pilot banked the assault helicopter around sharply as Takahara called out to Lightstone: "Henry, grab this and aim it at the plane.''

"What?''

"Do it! Right now!''

Unwilling to release his left arm from the overhead restraining loop, in spite of the supposed security of the combat harness, Lightstone thumbed the Smith & Wesson pistol to a decocked position, tossed it into the back of the vibrating helicopter, grabbed the camouflaged Crucible device with the ignition cable attached to one end, and aimed the other end of the metal cylinder at the distant climbing plane. At the same time, Mike Takahara set the timer on the ignition system to zero, depressed the ignition button, and then said: "Okay, that's it, toss the thing out the door. It's either going to work or it isn't."

As the discarded Crucible prototype disappeared into the darkness, the small plane continued on its banking climb for nine more seconds. Then, as the two agents stood there at the open cargo door and watched in amazement, the rear of the plane seemed to glow a bright yellow . . . and then burst into flames.

Slowly and then with increasing speed, the small plane arced downward into the darkness, a glowing firebrand that suddenly exploded a hundred feet above the black treetops as the aviation fuel in the wing tanks ignited.

"All right!" Henry Lightstone screamed with glee . . . and then froze in horror as he saw Mike Takahara looking down into the darkness and mouthing the numbers silently.

Thousand-and-six.

Thousand-and-seven.

"Oh, Jesus," Lightstone whispered, "are we that close?"

"I don't know." Takahara shook his head.

Thousand-and-nine.

Thousand-and-ten.

The tech agent waited two more seconds, just to be sure. Then he visibly relaxed, looked over at Lighthouse, and grinned widely.

"Pilot," Henry Lightstone said into his helmet mike, "relay a message back to the command post. The ember has fallen, but there's no wildfire."

"Echo-Tango-One to Command Post, be advised, the

ember has fallen, but there is no wildfire. Repeat, no wild-fire.''

Then, after a moment, Al Grynard's distinctive voice came out over the air: ''Congratulations, Echo-Tango-One. What about the suspects?''

Henry Lightstone smiled sadly as he stared out into the darkness at a small glowing spot that finally disappeared, and then spoke into his helmet mike:

''Tell him, they fell too.''

About the Author

Ken Goddard is the director of the National Fish and Wildlife Forensics Laboratory. He lives in Ashland, Oregon, with his wife, Gena, and daughter Michelle. He is currently at work on the next Lightstone novel.

THE BEST OF FORGE

☐ 53441-7   CAT ON A BLUE MONDAY $4.99
                 Carole Nelson Douglas   Canada $5.99

☐ 53538-3   CITY OF WIDOWS $4.99
                 Loren Estleman   Canada $5.99

☐ 51092-5   THE CUTTING HOURS $4.99
                 Julia Grice   Canada $5.99

☐ 55043-9   FALSE PROMISES $5.99
                 Ralph Arnote   Canada $6.99

☐ 52074-2   GRASS KINGDOM $5.99
                 Jory Sherman   Canada $6.99

☐ 51703-2   IRENE'S LAST WALTZ $4.99
                 Carole Nelson Douglas   Canada $5.99

Buy them at your local bookstore or use this handy coupon:
Clip and mail this page with your order.

Publishers Book and Audio Mailing Service
P.O. Box 120159, Staten Island, NY 10312-0004

Please send me the book(s) I have checked above. I am enclosing $ _____
(Please add $1.50 for the first book, and $.50 for each additional book to cover postage and
handling. Send check or money order only — no CODs.)

Name _____
Address _____
City _____ State / Zip _____

Please allow six weeks for delivery. Prices subject to change without notice.

THE BEST OF FORGE

☐ 55052-8   LITERARY REFLECTIONS $5.99
          James Michener   Canada $6.99

☐ 52046-7   A MEMBER OF THE FAMILY $5.99
          Nick Vasile   Canada $6.99

☐ 55056-0   MY UNFORGETTABLE $4.99
          SEASON—1970
          Red Holzman   Canada $5.99

☐ 58193-8   PATH OF THE SUN $4.99
          Al Dempsey   Canada $5.99

☐ 51380-0   WHEN SHE WAS BAD $5.99
          Ron Faust   Canada $6.99

☐ 52145-5   ZERO COUPON $5.99
          Paul Erdman   Canada $6.99

Buy them at your local bookstore or use this handy coupon:
Clip and mail this page with your order.

Publishers Book and Audio Mailing Service
P.O. Box 120159, Staten Island, NY 10312-0004

Please send me the book(s) I have checked above. I am enclosing $ _____
(Please add $1.50 for the first book, and $.50 for each additional book to cover postage and
handling. Send check or money order only — no CODs.)

Name _____

Address _____

City _____ State / Zip _____

Please allow six weeks for delivery. Prices subject to change without notice.